The Channering Worm

The Channering Worm

J. P. McCONDACH

The cock doth craw, the day doth daw,
The channerin worm doth chide;
Gin we be mist out o our place,
A sair pain we maun bide.
The Wife of Usher's Well

CANONGATE

First published in
1983
by Canongate Publishing Ltd
17
Jeffrey Street
Edinburgh
Scotland

ISBN 0 86241 039 8

The Publishers acknowledge
the financial assistance of the
Scottish Arts Council
in the publication of
this volume.

Typeset by
Spectrum Printing Company,
Edinburgh

Printed in Great Britain by
Redwood Burn Limited, Trowbridge, Wiltshire

CHAPTER ONE

Macandrew into Stone

> The purpose of life is to be brought to the highest degree of disgust with life . . . Only those, who, brought to this point of disgust with life, are able by the Grace of God to hold fast to the thought that God did it for love . . . only they are ripe for eternity.
>
> *after Kierkegaard*

> Humanity's rubbish—which is a tangy way of describing the doctrine of original sin.
>
> *Dr Edward Norman*

MACANDREW WAS standing by the cairn on Ben Cromach looking at the earth beneath him with the devil at his elbow. The wind, always blowing there, lifted his greying hair, flapped his clerical suiting about him, threshed through the heather. Still he was, as the granite pillar itself that he pressed with a flat, cold palm, holy Moses cherishing his tablets of stone on the mountain, drawing the rock's sterile serenity into himself. Rock of ages, let me hide myself in thee. Open your unyielding gates of being that I may enter and be one with you. Share with me the miracle of your eternal entity, of your insentient, unseeding singularity. Surrender the secret of your hard perfection. Under my covetous fingers I feel your granular certainty, all unaware of me and heedless. Transform my surface into yours, no surface but a mere extension of the obdurate, unfeeling core, covering no animate complexity, no yearning bowels, no fluttering heart. Grant, granite, me the recipe of petrifaction. O stone philosopher, wrapt in the secret, yield me thy alchemy. Transmute my baser mutability into thy mute endurance.

The low clouds wreathed about him, spat raindrops at his blind, indifferent face. The earth below him, engendering in its woods and tillage, spawning in its waters, vanished from his empty eyes. His legs grew into the heather-grown soil. An outcrop from the tumbling moor, a reef emergent from the breaking smother of life, life, life, he upreared arduously into inertia. The wind, always blowing there, smote the heather, the granite, Macandrew, and pressed on wherever. Sheep cropped the fresh blades where found and nickered peevishly. The sky leant on the ben, twin cairns indenting it.

See him cased again in the narrow belfry of his father's church. Climbing to his airy cradle, he rocks to respite, seeking rescue, pretending escape from the father-bred, mother-borne disgust below. Child prodigal, he runs from the human family circle into the stone quadrangle in the sky. For peep in where his sweat-bedewed mother heaves, bedded anew by the good shepherd, his reverend father, who studies his flock's increase—in vain. His first-born son alone survives from all his paternal labours; one son to watch precociously the hideous gestation, milky nurture, and demise of biennial little brothers and sisters puking their way from birth to death. Oh the revulsion from that procession of doomed foetuses that haunt him, scanning with fascinated eyes his mother's contours for another. Shall not the earth be peopled? thunders paternoster from the pulpit; and the parish leers assent and gossips of the chances. You'll have seen the mistress is on the way again? queries old Cathie in the kitchen. Poor body, she maun be sore tired o't. Ay that. But himself is not so easy tired, I'm thinking. I wonder he'll not think shame. But eh, it's the Lord's work he's at, when all's said.

And all this chain of mountainous parturition for only the mouse himself. Oh, how he envies his brothers and sisters, hating their getting and birth. Never to know where they came from or went to. And head down he burrows into the wind on the bens, escaping from the peopled earth. He stands by the hanging precipice, where nothing comes but wind and water, stares at its locked and secret fastness, fingers enviously its granite face. And God said, Be ye fruitful and multiply. But this was unsown and unseeding, stood quite outside the endless sequence of mortality. No sweating sheets, no crying in the night, no sleeping visions of amorphous evil, no waking revulsion from the body's needs, no odious birth and death, no father and no mother: only the thing itself, in eternal careless being. Boyish ambition scales it to perch, an inaccessible minute granule on its front; bores into the depth of it, a hidden crystal in the dark. But his unclean human destiny recalls him inexorably down to the squalor of living, where his slattern brood-mother waits on the next and his lecherous, saintly father cons the begatitudes.

He's an orra-like loon is yon, says old Cathie in the kitchen.

Not like neighbours an' others he's not, I'll tell you. And floating in the boat, he wonders, while the lochan water trickles through his cold fingers and he peers down into its calm. Down there is the trailing weed-growth of neighbours and others, the spawning pool of life that he wrestles to eschew, but can he? This sky-bright water mirrors clean nonentity but shelters what dark-hatched, slime-bred living things within its seeming purity. Observe the water-lilies, white to the daylight, but floating in time their festering transient petals in corruption. How can he hope to elude the snare of life, that trammels every living being: birth, propagation, senescence and decay, each phase more repulsive than the others? Down there, within his entranced stare, waver Donald's pet Angoras, coupled oddly in their hutch, while Donald and the ploughboy snigger, mistaking his anguish for innocence: swims, rosy in her night-shift, Nelly the kitchen-help, late rising from her attic dreaming. Have you not got a kiss for Nelly, young Andra, she giggles, pulling him to her where her warm bed smell envelops him. Down there slaver his doitit old granny and Peter the beadle, drooling from his senile lips: moulder all the corpses in the churchyard, breeding grass and worms with his little brothers and sisters: floats his own pallid, intent face, gazing questioningly back at him from among the neighbours and others whom he isn't like but is surely? Through the dulling water his premature wit spies her meaning and he shies from its implications. His fingers, chilled and bloodless from immersion, he chafes and blows on to bring back life, bring back life.

But this ingrained antipathy persists. See him combat it, courting human contacts, swallowing down revulsion, bringing flowers to his mother's bedroom, tom-peeping on young lovers in the hedgerows, conning guiltily his own excrement, that by familiarity he may learn acceptance. In vain. In the schoolroom he sits, fending off knowledge. Terrestrial wombs swell in his history atlas, bringing forth new races that covet only further increase. Marco Polo delivers himself of Asia, Drake circles with concupiscent design the belly of creation, and Columbus incontinent begets America. Keep learning hence, that floats into his ken new populous places. His own little corner has room enough for life enough to appal him. Those infinite land masses, fantastically full of living, lie across his dreams and smother him. Think of the Ganges plain, silted with gravid mothers, hot and fruitful with grain and timber, crawling with beasts and insects, all feverish with life, life. The water in the ewer is cold and the marble washstand comforting beneath his hand. But in his dreams such sterile sane-marks are lost under the ooze of generation. And so he sits at the window, gazing at the stars until he wills himself among them. But the apple falls to the earth that bred it, airy aspirant bobbing in the light but momently, drawn back into its native mould. Here is original sin, original penance. Listen in the Sunday pew to the fall of man, from Eden to earth, from fable to fact; and read with fascination his continuing testament of fallen glory—as Abraham, as Jacob, as David, as Samson, as Job. Curse God but do not die: live on and multiply. History runs with blood and sweat and purulence. It smells to heaven, endless reiteration of identical blind travail in corruption. See him study it to point his anathema, squirm in it like a maggot in a dung-pile, track out its one increasing lack of purpose, its belly-down crawling on its mother earth. See him, too, to fill his father's pulpit, forced to rummage in the jumble of pretentious cant hoarded through the centuries by the race's witch-doctors, wise men, blind mouths, the apostles of divinity, makers of souls. The professor orates from the lectern, making accustomed facile progress through words, words, words, which are but slanders, for he is, when all is said, only a greybeard with wrinkled face, eyes purging thick amber and plum-tree gum, tottering on most weak hams. Set down his slanders neatly in your note-books, pretty students; but note him well, whose wisdom cannot keep him from the chamber-pot at night. Hearken to this decaying clot of matter rant of his immortal soul, seeking release from his loathsomeness in ethereal promise. Mr Macandrew, your essays show considerable, even exceptional, knowledge. But they reveal a deplorable spirit of antitheism which I cannot countenance. You must amend it, Mr Macandrew. You must amend it, or change your vocation. But to amend it, cynically easy on paper, was beyond him in fact. Observe him in the dentist's chair contemplating a decayed molar, mankind's epitome; in the bus, staring at the scurf flaking someone's collar; in a public convenience wrinkling his nose. Remark him envying his image in the shaving-mirror; his fingers caress the glass, soliciting entrance. In the art gallery, stand with him while he gazes jealously at statuary and, neo-Pygmalion, forgets himself to marble, inhabits bronze. But dusk ejects him. The statues stand, placid through the darkness, while he frets, caged in his lodgings, locked in his clay tenement.

His landlady considers him askance. A queer-like student body yon is. Never a laddie like him have I e'er had for a lodger.

It's no trouble he is, mind you. There's neither late nights nor drink nor loose lasses for him. Faith no! Not his ways at all are yon. He's like a ghost about the place. He frights the bairns on the stair. I'm not right sure he doesna fright me at times. There's whyles I think he's maybe touched a wee. Ay that. As sure as I stand here. He's not cannie, so he's not. There's a want somewhere, or I'm sore cheated. But a right good lodger for all that. And he eats less nor the cat. I doubt he'll not claw an auld pow, he winna, as my granny used to say.

The lamp throws his shadow to mock him from the bedroom wall. He stares at it, thing of unborn, undying transience. He puts out the light and it goes without trace. But he remains, substantial in the darkness. The blood throbs from his heart, his palms are moist with sweat, his print-weary eyes smart, and all his body's odious chemisty persists. He is alive. Feet sound on the stairs and strident voices through the wall. Outside in the street, the people come and go, intent on their identical business: millions and millions of important people coming and going through endless time and space, impelled relentlessly by body's hungers, while the mountains stand still about them and the constellations wheel above and the winds blow. He broods in his lonely agony on their complacent acceptance of their revolting destiny. He observes them, gorging and swilling and belching with relish, scratching their private places with appreciative fingers, jesting at their bodies' functions. Gross laughter rocks them, shaking paunch and breast, and furtive longing gnaws rapturously in the darkness. Enamoured of life, they embrace it avidly, and whimper when it slips from their grasp. With fascination he watches them wallowing in the dung-ball rolled by the beetle god up and down the planet. And beside him brooding reclines his mother, smelling of milk and babies.

I know what you want, young Macandrew, says a fellow student. Needless to tell him, spying waitresses in tea-shops, schoolgirls lolloping in haste for tramcars. He knows and blushes in the night with shame and chagrin. Shall not the earth be peopled? thunders paternoster at the Lord's work. His father's mantle falls on him and he cowers beneath it, hiding his nakedness. But Adam will out, and out he sallies: into the dark alleys and entries, seeking who may devour him. See him coupling in the stews, under a dark staircase, in some stale garret, yielding himself all for love like Saint Francis enfolding the leper. Note his pathetic revulsion, the closed eyes, the reluctant hand, all powerless before proud Adam, erect and importunate. Perversely he revels in the proof of the manhood he abominates, delves deeper in lechery that he may more firmly base his forlorn cynicism. Each squalid encounter vindicates further his abhorrence of life, each yawning wanton resurrects Queen Anne his mother, maturing his precocious hatred. So in his own he flagellates all flesh and cherishes more righteously his antipathy to life. The brass knob on her creaking bedstead tempts his fingers from her noisome contact; and he slinks home eyeing hopelessly the incandescence of the street lamps, scraping his hand lingeringly along a roughcast wall, pondering the metal of the tram-track.

He that lives by the sword shall perish by the sword. Pity him, contemplating with nausea his wounded body, sneaking in the night for succour and consumed with self-disgust and self-contempt. Contempt—for here the paradox that haunts him attains hyperbole. Supine in physical corruption, he should be exalted to the heaven of righteousness. Here is the excellent proof, in his own vessel, of mortal degradation; here is his justification of faith. Let him now rot by hideous degrees, savouring the logic of his argument. But the irrational vital element defeats him. Life is accursed and repulsive; but he clings to it, seeking his body's health. Drown the world, but leave him swimming—in new depths of morbidity.

And now, the old dying man his father in Ferlie hears rumours of his wayward conduct and sends remonstrance. Were it not that my informants are beyond misdoubting, I should scorn to believe that a son of my body should thus defile the temple of God and dishonour his father in the evening—nay, the deepening night—of his days. I, who have loved and cherished you with an almost immoderate zeal, who have built all my hopes upon you, am stricken dumb by your viperish ingratitude and infamy. Unnatural child, had God but granted me another son, I should banish you and send you forth like Ishmael and you should no more come near me. But since, despite my service in His cause, he has not seen fit so to bless me, I, who was wont to humble myself before God alone, do earnestly beg you to repent of your sinfulness and once more prove worthy to be called my son.

He laughs to think his proven worthiness has thus earned paternal rebuke. He laughs but he obeys; for when all modes of vital being appal, there is no occasion for preference. And so come home with him, prodigal cleric, home to Ferlie to his father's kirk and manse. Here the would-be patriarch lies alone, drained and bedridden, where his wife had lain by him so fruitlessly. Come to Abraham's bosom, my one son, Isaac. But he recoils from such contact, there in the cradle of his abhorred creation, and averts his gaze to the raindrops on the window. His father mumbles in vexation on the pillow. You were always a strange one, a strange one. An unfilial child you were always, I well remember. You are not changed; you are no way altered. Perverse and unnatural from the time you left your mother. There's an unchancie thing about you. God forgive me, sometimes I think you bewitched her and brought all her babes to naught. God forgive me for the thought. It was not my fault. There was no blame in me. And she did her best, I am sure, poor woman. And all for you—a kind of Hagar's child, a stranger. I do not know you, nor ever knew you. Who are you? no Absalom, Benjamin. But you are all there is. There is no-one else. And you have obeyed your father's command and come back to me. I see you ordained and in my place, which I coveted for you. I must be content. I will be content. For a little time longer only. God bless you, my son. He watches the words runnel haltingly down the glass leaving an unclean trail. He hurries from the room.

In the churchyard, his mother resumes her wasted seed. Blankly he contemplates the earth-plot, the headstone fouled by the birds that above in the branches carol and breed from egg to end.

CHAPTER TWO

Alec by the Lochan

Chimborazo, Cotopaxi,
They had stolen my soul away!
W. J. R. Turner

Thus have I had thee, as a dream doth flatter,
In sleep a king, but, waking, no such matter.
William Shakespeare

YOUNG ALEC was carting dung from the steading to Alison field on the brow above the lochan. Steaming it was and he with it; and its stench in the afternoon warmth that dewed and puddled the sweat in his nooks and crannies bemused him, seducing him from the actuality about him into the brothel of erotic fancy he stewed in so often. He was hot with unfocussed lust and absurdly erect though his dejected shoulders stooped with the slow gelding's that clinked on, whisking his tail uselessly. Although at home in the thoughts he harboured as the swine in the muck he carted, there was no happiness in Alec; only vexation in his untried self.

He rummaged through the rags of his inexperience, matching their hodden grey with the Joseph's coat weaving on the loom of fancy—vainly matching. Between the aspiration and the reality fell the shadow of his insufficiency—and life's. For only the failure of fact gainsaid him—surely. His houris and odalisques, his Greek anthology of chaste pulchritude, his seraglio of fair figments, all in their splendid places and he with them, they were not Meg in the byre, a-sweat and cow-smelling or Jenny furtive and eager against her mother's back-garden fence in the rain last night. The cattle snuffled, waiting with heavy udders, the cobbles reeked slippery beneath his feet, and Rab whistled passing from the stable. Rain from the trees dropped on his nose, his hands slithered clumsily over her wet mackintosh, and a light appeared, a question in the window.

Young Alec where he slouched by the gelding's drooping

withers along the lochan road was nineteen and should have been a man long since like all his grown and callous peers. There was Tam, forever mocking him for a virgin gomeril, and Angus the baker's delivery-man, who boasted every skivvy for twelve miles round, and all the rest whose stake in life was planted many times and places. But Alec bathed in waters none of them dipped toe in, entered other portals than the dank alleys they probed so ruthlessly. Young Alec looked down far vistas on his father's four hundred acres. But one barrier foreshortened them all: he wasn't a man and he knew it hurtfully. He watched the farm beasts, the casual barnyard fowls, the calendared cattle and pigs and sheep, their coupling. And in the mating of his cronies and the people of the village the similarity was with them rather than with the unsullied inamoratas of his frustrate dreams. Desire was strong in him, as many a local lass knew; but always he would shirk the consummation, and, derisive and resentful, she would leave him in a sweat of humiliation and self-abuse to slink home, dry in the mouth and moist about the middle, as he was now to his habitual dejection.

They came out of the water. You might have thought they were Latins, so olive and sleek they were, deep-breasted and rather large in the hip to be so young. They walked upright, jutting their breasts aggressively, even now as they came across the narrow pebble strip to the trees on feet more often than not unshod and hardened like their distant ancestors'. Their hair hung heavy with water to their shoulders, black as a crow. Alec had no eyes for their faces, watching the water trickling round their brown curves.

On a flat stone their clothes lay, carelessly thrown: a woollen jersey and a kilt apiece and nothing else whatever that a girl might be expected to wear for one reason or another. They had not one towel between them, and they stood, sullen and silent, palming the water from their bodies with Alec in their hands. Then the gelding jingled restlessly and one, pushing her head through her jersey, spied Alec like a novice satyr, all smouldering eyes in the coppice half-dark.

'But soft, we are observed, sister,' said she with amusement, standing momentarily quite still, fronting him wide-legged right up from the ground. But the other with a yelp scuttled into the bushes.

'Why, it's young Alec,' she said, pulling the jersey down, reluctantly it seemed. 'His eyes won't penetrate you.'

She reached for her kilt and wrapping it round came into the gloom beside him, where he stood uncertainly. 'Hello, my Alec,' she said. 'Were you looking for something? Or maybe just looking?' Young Alec found nothing to say, just glowering there, dismayed by her unabashed approach. But the other, emerging from concealment, berated him incoherently till her sister intervened.

'Be quiet, nun-thing! What the hell's the fuss? You're still intact, aren't you? Can't a man even put an eye on your bits and pieces without you screaming rape?'

'He's disgusting. Peeping and spying like some—'

'What's he expected to do? Cast his eyes down reverently till the goddesses go by? Or shut them tight so your beauty won't blast them? He's a man, isn't he? Aren't you Alec?' she added, appraising him mockingly.

'He's a beast!'

'Well, it's the same thing to you, madonna. Now, you get off home and dream about the beast. And leave me here with the man.'

'You'd better come too. And leave him to his dung-cart. He should be in it.'

And she made off through the trees as her sister called. 'He'd find more heat and promise there than he's like to find in you. As for you,' she went on, turning to Alec, 'are you dumb, you great bullock to let that frigid little bitch crop you like that? You should've taken and shaken her till her bouncers dropped off. But you couldn't do a thing like that, could you now, shy Alec?'

She drew nearer and put a hand gently on his shoulder, smiling up at him as he stood there speechless, his eyes avoiding hers.

'Did you like what you saw then, peeping Alec?' she whispered. 'The mould's not broken, you know, though it's under cover—for the moment.'

Swinging round, she leant against him and pulled his arms about her, not smiling now but with her face set grim and frightened and her teeth in her nether lip. Her wet hair was on his cheek, smelling not of the loch but of perfume exotic never snuffed by his muck-breathing nostrils. He could glimpse a green strand of weed meshed in it and the chiselled lines of every temple and cheek and neck he dreamed of and the lashes heavy on the blue smudge under the hidden eyes of Salome Sheba Cleopatra and all the regal ones and nautch girls and damsels on dulcimers in a vision often seen. Strange melodies on strings and reeds quivered about him; cymbals clashed among the pine branches wreathed in incense smoke; gold-burnished barges floated on the grey loch water under other skies; and veiled women scanned the thronging Ganges from marble-fretted balconies—and he alone with the key to the door of their locked desire, the key for turning not against the creaking garden gate or the spattered byre wall but aloft in cushioned dalliance in some rose-red city. Through the soft wool and softer flesh he felt the blood of all his fabulous succubae coursing lustily beneath his hands, and as he closed them about these apples of comfort for his thirsty self and pressed hard behind her, a spasm of revulsion twisted her waiting face and, wrenching herself free, she was off through the trees and along the road with never a word.

Young Alec made no move in pursuit. He watched her out of sight, and then stood, his hands thrust deep in his pockets, kicking the pine cones.

CHAPTER THREE

Candida in the Corrie

Splendide mendax et in omne virgo
Nobilis aevum.
Horace

CANDIDA LAY prone in a hollow she haunted on the shoulder of Ben Cromach, glowering at a bumble-bee that tongued the florets of heather an inch from her nose. Her chin was hammocked in her hands, and her back sloped down to the hummock under her kilt. Fronds of heather tickled her midriff bare between jumper and skirt, and stems of heather nudged insinuatingly between her thighs as she felt again Alec behind her. The bee blundered off, and she rolled over on to her back so that the little sun there was shone in her perplexed eyes.

She listened to the burn that trintled through the heather down to the lochan and heard in memory the monsoon water running from level to level of the bunded paddy-fields, quickening the rice to sprout. Macandrew hated the monsoon, which brought resurgence to the parched land and set the cattle and goats leaping on the rising pasture. Only when the monsoon brought inundation and death did it please him more than contemplation of the arid landscape and its two and four-legged scrawny caricatures hirpling through their annual deprivation. Everything alive or procreating was hateful to him, and that country so emphatically vindicated his detestation and provided texts for his preaching.

She saw in the clouds that ran across the sun above her the Calcutta pavements a-sprawl with sleeping derelicts or thronged with mendicants displaying their deformities for *pice*—and the girl in the doorway giving birth to the casual interest of the bystanders. To such enormities he directed their attention purposefully: to the excrement and the stench dropped over and pervading all India; to the crones with their dugs flapping on their skeletal rib-cages; to the toddlers barely toddling under their swollen empty bellies; to the girl wives dropping yearly labourers to till the soil and tend the beasts that would sustain the family that provided girl wives to drop yearly men children to get children to sustain the family ad infinitum. And he showed them, depicted on the walls of caves and temples, the gymnastic contortions that disseminated odious life, so that they might share his loathing of generation, its methods and its product.

Candida writhed where she lay, and her hands slipped inside her waistband down past her middle as she recalled how they would lie, himself in the hollow between, all three naked under the net, denying the flesh and its craving as his hands moved placidly over their pubescence, and forbidden to react they fought to repress their disgust and obscure longing. And he would take a hand of each in turn, guiding it ever so slowly down his belly, through the coarse brush, to the warm soft slug that nestled there. And when on occasion it would awake and threaten to rise, he would incontinently thrust them out of the bed to go and console themselves guiltily this way and that.

She turned on her side and hugged herself for comfort, as a cloud masked the sun and the breeze embossed goose-pimples on her exposed surfaces. A lark rose, spilling its mindless unscored music over the ben—meaningless clamour from a morsel of animate flesh that bred annually in the clods until time or some random mishap put an end to its throbbing pointless life. But how have the cascading song without the singer?

He would have none of it; nothing that emanated from living entity, animal or vegetable, found his favour. He would scythe with his walking-stick the blossoms from their stems, avert his eyes from the ripened grain that overspread and hid the parcelled plots of land, despise buffalo and tiger alike, curse the monkeys at their business on the station roof. But how often had they stood close beside him under his umbrella while he absorbed the sheet-lightning and the thunder that illuminated and shattered the night? how often gazed with him at the distant peaks briefly clear of cloud, forever void of life? But always the ants foraged over the ground, the flies pastured on the cattle, the women's thighs wide-spread to push the infant out stayed open to take in the makings of the next. Was he not right to abjure it all? Was she not wrong to pine over her non-participation?

A peewit piped urgently, and she crouched low like a hare in her form as she heard someone thrashing uphill through the heather and a tuneless voice singing incomprehensible words that ended:

'It'll be all right in the middle of the night
Putting it in together. Christ!'

And then there was silence but for the droning of the bee or another adjacent and the susurrus of laboured breathing above her. Turning her head, she saw through her lashes a triangle of grey sky outlined by two robust black-haired legs with, at their apex, a pronounced bulge that seemed to grow as she eyed it.

'Are you all right?' said the voice with comical uncertainty.

'I'm not sure. No-one's ever told me,' she said without shifting the line of her vision.

'For a moment I thought you were . . . you were dead,' stammered the voice.

'No, I'm not dead,' she said. 'At least not clinically. Why should you think so?'

'If you saw what I'm seeing, you'd agree you might be dead—from exposure,' replied the man-thing tittering sillily.

Twisting her neck, she glimpsed the plenty he saw plainly but made no move to screen it, replying, 'If what you see offends you, you needn't look. I didn't ask for company.'

'If you had done, I'd have been waiting for you—not you for me,' said he.

She ignored that, as somehow he suspected she would, and to offset his recognition of the feebleness of his flattery he added: 'But do cover up, please. All that excites me.'

'I can see that,' replied she. 'Sit down then and conceal your excitement. Or lie down and assuage it.'

'For God's sake, girl,' said he weakly and sat down, shaken by her naked insolence.

'No, for mine,' she murmured, smiling wanly at an ant that scampered under her gaze.

He sat there, staring stupidly at the symmetrical hillocks of pale umber flesh, the long thighs, and the legs weaving teasingly against the sky. A yard of heather and light years of disbelief separated him from her. It was impossible, unreal, like some weird dream conjunction. He leant forward and ran a tentative finger up from the cavity behind the knee within reach. She shivered, but whether with delight or revulsion he could not guess.

'You're freezing, lass,' he said and pulled her kilt over her bottom.

'That's not the medical term for it,' said she, adding hastily, 'And there's no hint you'll be raising my temperature.'

He took a minute to consider this: the implication of the first part and the invitation of the second. It was difficult to believe that she knew what she was saying to him, a stranger come upon her on a lonely hillside, and she as vulnerable as a baby waiting for its first clout. But she did know, he was sure, for certainly she was half of the manse twins he had heard about, the pricksy-tricksy one, who had immaculately upped and downed all the lusty lads in the parish and was recklessly trying the same with him, whom she'd never seen before. She needed to be taught a lesson, but he was oddly reluctant to teach it.

'Patience, little Salome,' he found himself mumbling. 'I have to adjust you know.'

'Is that what's going on under your shorts?' she asked rhetorically.

'You're an observant little lady, aren't you?' said he, involuntarily smiling, for he wasn't amused. 'I was referring to a psychological adjustment.'

'If you're going to intellectualise the situation, you'd best be on your way,' said she caustically. 'I've no time for that.'

'You seem to be in rather a hurry, if I may say so,' he countered.

'I dare say I can wait—a little longer,' she replied in quite a different tone, which affected him strangely, so that he slipped a hand under her chin and raised her head, gently brushing her damp hair aside.

'God,' he said, 'they didn't do you justice. You are beautiful.'

'Yes,' said she. 'And so is the Venus de Milo, they say. But she never opens her legs either, does she?'

Although by this time fortified against her audacity, he flinched at the crudity of this allusion. She discerned his reaction and continued almost impishly, because she was unaccountably enjoying herself: 'Are you still changing gear then?'

And he was, uncertain whether up or down or even into reverse, staring blankly through the tartan at what he knew was there and at the expectancy below that and between. And he sat there, vaguely appraising himself, the randy Ewart, terror and delight of the women's Union, with more hymens to his discredit than would together jacket a hard-back issue of Fanny Hill; the accomplished Ewart, schooled by professionals in various capitals. Was he afraid of her maybe? If he failed in action, she would flay him remorselessly; not because she had knowledge of what could be done, but because she had not. He wondered momentarily what she expected, poor intrepid novice, aware that it was far more than he could supply, or anyone. But she had exalted him to the pitch, and maybe toss for that matter. If he subsided, he'd do so of his own volition not hers.

And why should he renegue, he wondered, squinting round the corrie and up to the summit and down to the lochan, with nothing to see but the landscape and nothing to hear but the wind freshening through the heather. He could do it no doubt, and looking at her again he thought why the hell not. But it was not only the cold wind blowing up his shorts that staled his relish for the dish; nor was it John Knox protecting the manse and its outsprigs. Simply the girl's behaviour was unnatural. She'd toy and flaunt and taunt and provoke, and then when he moved, she'd fight him off. And that wouldn't be nice at all. Not his kind of loving was that. The prospect repelled him.

Breaking the silence that oppressed him more than her, he said, 'Is it just my compelling virility or are you always so, shall we say, approachable?'

'Always,' she said. 'Anything male's worth a try. Even an unconverted one.'

Temporising flagrantly, because he was sure she had not, he said, 'But you must have converted plenty. Playing such an aggressive game, I mean.'

'Maybe you'll be able to tell,' said she. 'If you've a mind to. Or what else it takes. You've got that, I can see. And from what I hear, you don't let it hang about idle for long.'

'Slander stalks me always—even in strange places,' he replied in affected sorrow. 'But how would you know?'

'It's Ewart you are, isn't it?' she said with no interrogative inflection. 'The n-th year medical student rusticating at Braelochy. So busy satisfying the women you can't find the energy to satisfy the examiners.'

'You're a cheeky young devil, aren't you?'

'Just candid—appropriately,' she replied.

'So that's the one you are—as I thought.'

'So well you might,' said she with never a glance at him. 'With the other one you'd never have got even this far.'

'Do you tell me that now?' he said, not unhappy at this distance. 'But they said you were like peas in a pod.'

'That's not what they said exactly, prissy gentleman. A teaparty simile,' answered she with no notable interest.

'But you are twins, aren't you?'

'By birth, yes,' she said patiently. 'We're by no means identical by disposition. My sister would never dally with the likes of you. But I see you've been reconnoitring the ground, Mr Ewart.'

'Come now, that's a bit unfair,' he protested.

'Yes, I suppose it is,' she conceded. 'After all, what would men in Ferlie talk about if not the manse women?'

'It's no affair of mine,' said he ridiculously politely, 'but you must admit yours is a family that invites tittle-tattle. Or seems so from my limited acquaintance.'

'You're slow to extend your acquaintance, Mr Ewart,' said she, patently bringing him back on course, to his annoyance.

'Maybe I am, maybe I am,' he said hesitantly. 'But there's something very far wrong about you, though I can't put my finger on it.'

'You're hardly likely to—at that distance, Mr Ewart,' she replied, mischievously literalising his commonplace. 'You'll find I have all a woman's parts.'

'I could scarcely fail to be aware of that. You don't go about to hide them,' he said a shade irritably, uncertain now whether he was being switched on or off by her unflagging provocativeness. To determine which, or for some other reason, he slipped a hand between the heather and her woollen bosom, rather maladroitly for him, and inventoried what was there.

'Yes, you have some nice pieces,' he remarked. 'Very pleasingly disposed, if you will pardon the trite compliment, Miss Macandrew.'

'With difficulty, Mr Ewart' said she suavely. 'And you're not really enhancing their arrangement, you know.'

'Do forgive me,' said he absurdly, and withdrawing his hand he employed it to tilt her head full-face to his enquiring eyes. Unabashed and serene, she held his gaze until it faltered and he said with unmistakable sincerity, 'Yes, superlative, I'm bound to say.'

'Elspeth thinks,' said she without a hint of complacence, 'that we are the most beautiful creatures this side of the Himalayas.'

'Does she now? Well, I've never been the other side, so I shall believe her.'

'But what's the use of it?' asked she, willing him to answer seriously. 'All this chaste, so-called beauty, what's the use of it here in Ferlie?'

'The use of it!' he exclaimed, feigning incredulity. 'Must it have a function? You know what the poet says about a thing of beauty?'

'That shilpit whey-face,' she retorted scornfully. 'What the hell would he know about it? "It's loveliness increases" indeed. Like my arse does. Ask Elspeth what she thinks, Mr Ewart. Besides, the thing I thought we were talking about—still talking about—is not, even kinkily regarded, a thing of beauty. But it has a function, and you're acquainted with it—familiar with it, so at least they say.'

'For a daughter of the manse,' he said defensively, 'you've a very loose tongue, Miss Macandrew.'

'I've maybe a loose tongue,' said she, 'but the rest of me's tight enough. As you'll find out, if you ever get down to it—which I doubt.'

'I doubt it too. You don't bring me on with that line of talk, you know,' he said almost ruefully, wondering what was the matter with him.

'That line of talk,' she exclaimed. 'Christ! What are we at—a cocktail party?'

'We still might be,' he replied somewhat doggedly, adding with a grimace, 'You see it's catching, the double entendre.'

'It's not catching much,' she sneered. 'Certainly not the nearly doctor. Something far wrong with me, you say. You dumb bullock, it's you there's something wrong with I begin to suspect.'

She pivoted on an elbow to front him, her eyes surveying him upwards to settle on his, which regarded her morosely for a long moment before looking beyond her over the heather and down to the lochan now like beaten pewter under a cloud. He did not react to her lewd contempt, as he knew she naïvely expected him to. He was groping through his recollection of what he had heard of the mad minister and his wayward wife and bastard twins, seeking some explanation of the girl's extravagant solicitation. He was certain she was chaste; her brazen self-exposure, physical and verbal, was comical, like a toddler tottering in her mother's lipstick and high heels. But he did not feel like laughing; nor was he inclined to pluck the flower she was ostensibly offering. He was deterred not aroused by her crude importunacy, divining its facttitiousness but unable to diagnose satisfactorily its cause.

Was she aping in her amateurish way her mother, whose ear-catching past and on-going present Niven had been at pleasure to recount? Why then her scandalous reputation for always retreating from her own prepared positions, as she certainly would retreat from this were he to engage her? Might it be simply fear, O little hunter, simply fear? he wondered, stealing a covert glance at her and catching her appraising him under the eaves of her lashes. It might be that, a failure of nerve in face of the quarry she had brought to bay. And yet anyone better equipped physically to quell what she was chasing he had seldom had to do with. There must be some powerful inhibitory factor halting her frenetic urgency. And he ransacked again the confused gossip they had fed him about her eccentric unnatural parent and his obsessive misogyny. The poor wretch might be see-sawing on the up and down impulsions of her familial elders, pushed sky-high by the impetus of one, dragged down by the negativism of the other. Assuredly, with exemplars like them, a girl could scarcely be expected to behave normally. God, Ewart, he thought, how clever you're being. And he wished he had spent more time studying the psychology of sex than he had its more gratifying elements. He might have been able to identify the source of her disorder and more important, to prescribe the appropriate therapy.

And then he said to himself, Ewart, he said to himself, Ewart, you're thinking like a smooth-talking quack. There was only one self-evident cure for this little lady; and he had it here in full measure. And he had too, for he was beginning to feel decidedly hungry, despite his avuncular solicitude. What the hell! Here they were, snug and secret in their hollow, with no-one else on the ben, not even a sheep to spy them, and not only the time and the place propitious but the loveless one yearning for service all open and offering.

She was on her back now, propped on both fore-arms, her bosom pouting and knees inelegantly up, so that her kilt-apron was down in her lap. Inviting she was, certainly; but her brows were scowling, and as he watched, tears welled from beneath her lashes to follow the curve of her cheek. She disdained to sob or sniff but she was weeping; and though it might be from mere chagrin or even petulance, the contrast it made with her previous effrontery reinforced his constrained, however diminishing, compassion, so that he found himself close beside her, his right hand tenderly engaged in damming the flow of her tears. She made no move to repulse him and none to invite him farther, as though incuriously awaiting his next manoeuvre. With her warmth against him and the silk cushion of her cheek under his fingers, he speedily felt himself coveting more, but he continued to dither inanely.

'There now, don't be upset, lass,' he said soothingly.

'Don't be upset,' repeated she with a snarl. 'I'm not likely to be—with you patting my cheek like an ayah wiping the tears away. Why don't you tell me it'll be all right in the morning?'

'Ach,' said he, 'don't fash yourself. It'll be all right before then, maybe.'

'I doubt it,' she said sombrely, and he shared her certainty, paradoxically enough. And it irked him so that he transferred his hand from her cheek to her knee and slid it down the inside of her thigh, relishing every inch but delaying its unopposed progress partly because he liked it that way and partly because he felt in her a tiny *frisson* that betrayed her reluctant misgiving or so it seemed.

'God', said he nonplussed, 'you're a strange one, aren't you?'

'Oh yes,' she replied. 'Strange I am for sure. Queer even maybe. You'd likely get on more easily with Sadie Sauchie.'

'Who's she then, when she's at home?' he asked, changing his position unobtrusively beside her.

'She's the glaikit kitchen-help at the Crown. She's had more men through her this summer than Macandrew's kirk door,' she replied, ignoring his tactical re-deployment.

'You don't aim to emulate her, I take it,' said he with sharper sarcasm than he immediately recognised was appropriate in the circumstances.

'Goodness me, no, Mr Ewart,' she whispered, affecting incredulity. 'I shall keep myself for you alone.'

'I think I'd like that,' said he, and before she could prevent him, even had she wished to, he was securely ensconced in the saddle her posture provided, his hands firmly anchoring her feet in the heather. She made no attempt to hinder him, collapsing under his weight from the support of her elbows on to her back with a little gasp. And so they remained for a time at gaze, her eyes wide and quite calm regarding him. Try as he would, he could discover no reaction behind them, or in her body beneath him, except the rise and fall of her, responsive to her breathing.

Hell, he thought, this'll be the oddest coupling since Danaë and the shower of gold.

But now he was resolved to enjoy what he could of her, co-operation or not. He planted his mouth on hers and occupied himself about her. Her lips stayed immobile, and he withdrew his.

'You are familiar with the topography, Mr Ewart,' she remarked blankly.

'I've been in such places before,' said he. 'But always made more welcome.'

'It's virgin territory, of course,' said she. 'Never yet inhabited.'

'There's always a first time, you excellent bitch,' he retorted with some vehemence for his dander was up at his failure to rouse her and his stamen up with it, too long for his comfort, long enough for hers. Fumbling with himself, he released what she needed or wanted or didn't want. Past caring he was. And then to his amazement she inserted a hand between them that palmed what he presented.

'That's an awful lot of Ewart, Mr Ewart,' said she in the same expressionless tone.

'A poor thing but mine own,' he said, moderately encouraged by this response. 'And yours for the nonce.'

But his incursion was balked by her holding on. What the hell was the tantalising oriental mystery up to now? he wondered, unaware that she was not tight and captive under him, caught in her own web of titillation, but away, nauseated, under the mosquito-net in the dark with not his but Macandrew's thing in her hand and it no longer inert or stirring but erect and insistent, and she with no place to steal to for solace with her furtive sister in shame.

He felt her fingers tighten as she panted not with lust, as he crassly fancied, but disgust, hearing not his drivel in her ear but Macandrew's repeated recitative of obloquy. Goats and monkeys scraping their flea-ridden pelts matted in excremental stench going to it like the gilded flies tonguing her moist hair; hooves and paws and spidery soft feet and hands laid on female yielding backs and breasts and buttocks in forest and farmyard in cracks in the wainscot and windowframe in ditches and under hedgerows and haystacks and laundered sheets; the diabolical event to and from which the whole creation moves; the rush of blood to toes and probing fingers, inflaming the eyes of bull and stallion and homo rapiens thrusting rude and ruthless as his cave-seeking progenitors. As she felt him tunnelling against her spastic occlusion, she opened aghast eyes to the sky. Sudden rain splashed on the parts of her he was not covering. Her stomach rumbled, and, retching, she spattered vomit over the jersey rumpled on her shoulder.

He withdrew and recoiled, face and hands and all of him. She lay as he left her, all exposed and impregnable. Clumsily he straightened her dishevelment that strangely shamed him. 'Christ girl,' he said, 'why did you tease me—?'

'It wasn't you I teased,' replied she flatly.

'But why didn't you stop me before I—?'

'But I did stop you, didn't I?' she gravely answered, adding, 'Though you got farther than anyone yet—if it's any consolation. To either of us. Ciao, lover.'

And she was up and tussocking away down the burn-side, leaping and swerving like an ibex. God, she'd make a grand three-quarter, he thought, as he watched her dwindle under his eyes as he himself dwindled under a comforting hand.

CHAPTER FOUR

Elspeth in the Bothy

Too much of water hast thou, poor Ophelia,
And therefore I forbid my tears.
William Shakespeare

Train up a child in the way he should go; and when he is old, he will not depart from it.
Proverbs

SOMEONE WAS climbing through the copse from the road. Gavin heard in the hush outside the snapping of twigs and the complaint of wakened birds. He glanced at his watch—two o'clock—and wondered. No poacher moved so noisily; who could be traipsing around at this hour? Before he could decide what to do, a footstep sounded on the threshold, a knock on the door. 'Who is it?' he called. 'Come in. Just turn the handle.' And he threw back the coverlet to rise and welcome the guest. But he snatched it back over him with boyish modesty when she entered, in a black cloak with the hood thrown back behind her improbable red hair.

'Don't be alarmed, fair sir. I've not come to attempt your virtue,' she said: and she smiled slightly, standing with her hand still on the open door, through which a little wind came from the woody darkness outside. She blinked at him with frank interest, which he returned in oafish silence, struck pardonably dumb by her sudden apparition. Even the loose cloak clasped at her throat swelled momently in the deep surge of her breathing that came and went audibly through parted lips. Her long heavy eyelids flickered in the sudden lamplight, and her colour was high as a schoolgirl's.

'You must be young Ewart, Marion was telling me about. I'd forgotten about you,' she said, more to herself than to him, and fixed him now with an appraising stare, under which his own faltered as the silence lengthened. 'Who,' he at last found voice to say superflously, 'are you? And may I ask what you want?'

'Why, you silly boy,' she replied, lifting her gaze from him to survey the room, 'I'm Mrs Macandrew, of course. From the manse. And I'm looking for my little black twinlet, Candida. She isn't, is she,' and her questing eyes returned, 'by any chance in bed with you?' He jerked up as if her question had bitten him in a soft place, but before he could find tongue, she continued: 'No, I can see she's not. She's rather a portly little baggage—in places. Not so easily pressed between sheets. But now that I've seen you, young man, if she's seen you first, it would not surprise me to find her here. You're sure you wouldn't be concealing the truant darling somewhere, Mr Ewart? To save her reputation—or your own?'

'Why, Mrs Macandrew! I don't know what you're talking about. I don't understand.' His expostulation sounded, even in his own ears, unconvincing. Leaving the door to swing back on creaking hinges, she rustled long-legged across the floor and, before he even guessed her intention, adroitly raised the lid of the long kist in the corner, to drop it with a crack. 'A pity,' she said, 'so romantic a refuge should disappoint.'

Rather wearily she sat down on the chest in silence, as if forgetting him altogether. Her face, near him now and in repose, betrayed in the white light its maturity. He saw the fine lines by her eyes and painted mouth, the unfilled skin of her throat, faded against the black cloak. Then, disconcerted by her suddenly lifting her eyes to his, he hurried into speech: 'Do you mean to say you're disappointed not to find your daughter here, in such a . . . such a compromising situation? You surely don't think much of her virtue.'

'Stop talking like a Sunday newspaper, boy,' she snapped. 'Of course I'm disappointed. Wouldn't I rather find her here in bed—even with the likes of you—than with the kelpie in the lochan? What do I care for her virtue—whatever that is? It's herself I'm wanting. The bitch has me worried now. Where can she be? I've looked everywhere I can think of.'

'But what made you think of the bothy here?'

'A man used to bide here, Mister Ewart. That's what. Where a man is a maid's not loth to be. I'd forgotten you'd taken over, or I might have spared myself the trouble. From the depth of your voice and what I can see of you—prim there with the sheets to your chin, like a sick old maid when the minister calls—you seem to have the parts of man. But heavens, I'm like to misdoubt it. Another night, I might take time off to make sure. But I must find that lassie of mine. God only knows where she's wandered to. I must think. Go back to sleep, poor lad.' And she turned from him, a frown of perplexity chasing the mockery from her brows.

'I'd never take you for a minister's wife, Mrs Macandrew,' said Gavin angrily, ruffled in his proudest feathers. 'You've no call to be talking that way to me. How the devil am I to know what the manse gets up to in these heathenish parts? I'm only an innocent tenth-year medical.' He glowered at her heedless profile, expecting something. But nothing came and he continued: 'If it's the girl I met on the hill today you're looking for, it wouldn't surprise me to find her in any man's bed. But by God, I did think it might surprise her mother!'

She was up from the chest and standing over him, a hand on his shoulder. 'Then she has met you?' she said eagerly. 'Where? Was it by the water, tell me?' And in her anxiety she shook him impatiently.

'What would a girl like yon be drowning herself for?' he asked, ignoring her questions for the one that worried him stealthily.

'Who knows what a girl like her will be doing? I wouldn't be knowing, her own mother. And you certainly wouldn't. Where did you come on her?'

'I found her up there on the brae-side, in the heather. In tears she was.'

'In tears was she? She wouldn't be telling you why, though?'

'No. No,' he said hesitantly, remembering. 'She wouldn't do that. We talked for a wee while. And then away she thrashed down the brae and into the loch.'

'Into the loch! Christ! and you came home to bed?' She recoiled from him and sank once more on to the chest, gaping at him incredulously. Her mouth hung foolishly open and one hand fumbled with the clasp at her throat. 'In the name of God, man,' she said with a rising inflection quite unlike her natural, controlled tones, 'are you mocking me? You're not telling me you watched that poor demented lassie drown herself, without lifting a hand—and then came home to bed? What kind of a man are you at all?'

The transformation in her was startling; her colour was gone, and her lips were drawn back grotesquely from her teeth; her eyes glowed out of blue shadows daubed in, it seemed while he looked on her withering face. She frightened him so that his voice rose to meet and defeat hers.

'For heaven's sake, woman, get a hold on yourself! You and

your damned suicidal daughter! Of course I didn't watch her drowning. What do you take me for? She didn't go in and under. She just splashed into the shallows and waded away out of sight behind the firs. Going home I thought she was, of course. I'd never met the brat before. How was I to know she needed watching?'

He ended on a peevish note that betrayed to himself the perplexed anxiety he was trying to repress. Was she down in the lochan, then—the water lapping in and out of her, her lank hair streaming like the grasses, and the trout nuzzling round her? Her mother was right. She'd have been better here with his mouth searching her than the fishes'. The mad little devil! It couldn't be true. It wasn't death she was after, the precocious hot twitching little bitch. He knew that all right. But he'd done nothing, although she had provoked him shamelessly. They couldn't blame him, if she lay swelling and stained in corruption. Not guilty, my lord. She was virtuous for me—by virtue of a stomach turning beneath me, emptying itself in my face, my lord, in nervous reaction, not filling in muscular action as charged. Neat medical jurisprudent alibi in the case of the rape of the Ferlie Ophelia, found drowned in the loch and dishonour. Ewart in the heather witness loch: The woman attempted me but I resisted who resisted she resisted why? She was a minister's wife's daughter or she'd been eating onions or the moon was wrong or something. I don't remember why. Who knows what a girl like her will do?

She was sitting in the corner still, and he left his shadow falling kindly across her face, relaxed and pensive. Her hands lay quiet in her lap. Her eyes were veiled from him, looking elsewhere, looking far beyond his brief afternoon's acquaintanceship.

Born in water, the child should fairly die in water, going prematurely out of season as she came, unnaturally born and dead, foredoomed like the little black bastard her sister from the outcome—one, two, black as my shoe, pushing their impatient heads into Bengal, that night of terror when life came twice unwanted and death stayed sulking. She trailed clumsily along the dirt-road banked above the flooding paddy-fields, her sandalled feet deep in mud. The rain pasted the tussore over her ponderous body, curtained her eyes that strained to glimpse in the lightning some place of refuge, some floor to lie on to ease the agony wrenching her apart, as those inside her, untimely shocked awake, battled for the gate. Ridiculous in his soiled and sweating khaki, fever in his gaunt cheeks and shining eyes, he posed with pointing finger on the verandah, like some inexorable husband in melodrama ejecting the never again to door darken adulteress. Into the outer darkness with her, scarlet woman, shame-bringer. Off with her and her burden of sin, into the night and the pit, go, go, go. No clemency from the righteous wronged.

Outcast, the watery grave of night received her, labouring blindly along the embankment, going nowhere, until a thunder-blast directly overhead beat her to her knees, screaming uncontrollably. Little brown men carried her over the brawling ditch and through the bamboo thicket that rustled in the rain. Their women tended her, Mary in the stable with the oxen drooping, dropping in their miry corner of the dung-reeky hovel, whose thatched roof dripped water on the earth floor, to hiss in the brazier like the rain this morning showering the lochan. Their bracelets tinkled about her intimately as they did their immemorial office, ancient hag and suckling adolescent matron, bringing double deliverance that sent death packing away over the flooding rice-plots, empty-handed. Two more joined the seeding millions, carelessly sown and now transplanted under water; and now one again transplanted under water, northern hill-dark water never monsoon-borne. Sooty-rimmed eyes stared then from the puckered brown face, up from her cradling arm, black eyes now filmed and swimming with what guilt, real or fancied, staring through the lochan at the stars.

Such a mongrel litter is doomed to an evil end, he had said when he received them. But surviving their perilous birth, they had flourished in body and beauty to mock him, she had thought, laughing too soon. Unnatural children he'd made them, warped and bewildered by his perverse influence, which she could not combat. Better they'd be with their own father yonder in some shuttered zenana than free as the eagle here, but jessed by the fascination he exercised over them, bemused converts to his lunatic faith. Happier they'd be with silk and sweetmeats and gold brocade, unbroken siesta in the sunless rooms, leisurely wandering in the painted gardens by the lotus pools and the fountain splashing, babbling indolence day in day out and nights for his lordship's delight or whose? Young Ewart in bed here seemed likely enough, with the parts of a man under the close-drawn coverlet. Between stealthy lids she eyed him where he crouched at her elbow, arms folded on his updrawn knees and a frown misshaping his brows, looking inside and not liking the survey whatever the reason. What kind of a man are you, who didn't watch her drown in the shallows going home? For she wasn't home, nor on the brae, nor in the wood, nor here where she might have been—to her mother's relief, disgust, chagrin, what?

Leave that, and think where the girl could be—anywhere but the lochan, surely. Lying alone in the heather she'd be watching the night sky, in some tinker's tent, standing at a city corner, guddling trout in the river over by Crowdie. Your damned suicidal daughter! That was nonsense. The other one, maybe, madonna emulating alabaster, but not Candy, lusty as she'd been herself in girlhood under a haystack with the grieve's son or climbing the ben with her brother's friend home for the holidays but colder than the snow on the summit with his sahibly inhibitions gentlemanly shunning a breach of hospitality in the lee of the cairn and she warm in desire and an offering sweater but he at distance unwilling to close. No cause for suicide there—mere passing unappeasement. That wench would never up and drown herself whatever. Yet who knows what a girl like her will do, frustrated by his doctrine, all her urgency dammed and stagnating? He was to blame if she lay foundered and waterlogged, like her mother when she bore her in the rain, sun-burnt bastard doomed to an untoward end like her shameful beginning. Enough. The cuckold called too often, and forebodingly. Let her be going home now and find the lass secure in bed, unaware of all this uncharacteristic maternal anxiety. There was nothing else to do.

Her movement from the chest roused Gavin from nightmare, spiralling contemplation of his ruined career. Convicted of rape and maidslaughter, accused maintained it was all a nauseous mistake, he training to cure sickness not cause it and no such thing had ever happened before in his urban practice and why had his friends never told him. The girl must have been of unsound mind in unsounded body and any evidence of violence was the kelpie's doing not his whose promising future was past before ever present.

'I'm going now, Mr Ewart,' she said. 'I'm afraid I've compromised you.'

'You don't think she's drowned herself, do you?' he asked, but she would not reassure him.

'I don't know what to think—and that's a change.'

'And what will you do now?'

'Go home and see if she's got back in my absence.'

'And if she hasn't?'

'She must have!' she said with remarkable vehemence. 'And

I'll make the little horror wish she hadn't. Good night.'

For a moment he looked at the door, slammed shut behind her, and then he rose and dressed hurriedly. He overtook her on the road and walked beside her.

'And where would you be going?' she asked, without stopping.

'I'll come along with you, if you don't mind, to the manse. I'd like to know if the girl's all right.'

'Why? What's it to you?' she asked, and although she did not stop or even turn her head, he sensed her renewed interest in him, of an ambivalent character, partly unwholesome it seemed. 'What's it to you, Mr Ewart—to stir you from your monastic retreat? Was there something happened between you on the brae then? Eh? Tell me now.'

'Of course there wasn't! What could happen between us, for God's sake?'

'What branch of medicine are you studying, Mr Ewart? You seem childishly ignorant of elementary sexology.'

'Less ignorant than you are of elementary psychology!' he said with some heat, not at all at ease. 'Do I look like the kind of man to go playing round with schoolgirls like your daughter?'

'What does that sort of man look like, Mr Ewart? Has he two heads, or goat feet and little horns? Yet I'm not so suspicious of your playing round—as you charmingly put it—with my daughter. It's my daughter going to work on you that strikes me as a possibility. But we'll let it go, since the possibility seems to disconcert you. We'll assume you're concerned about her merely from kindness of heart.'

'After all, Mrs Macandrew,' said Gavin, willing to make good this escape, 'I seem to be the last person who saw her alive—I mean, before her disappearance. Naturally I'm interested. But I'm sure you'll find she's at home.'

'Of course,' she said, with no conviction or even interest, dismissing him.

'And if you don't?'

But she made no response, and they continued in silence, till Gavin cursing himself for an ingénu, was forced to break it. 'Do I understand, Mrs Macandrew, that you asked nobody to help you search for her?'

'Young man,' she answered, 'if I sent out search parties every time that fly-by-night didn't come home for supper, the manse would be even less highly thought of than it is. This is no new thing, Mr Ewart. But,' she added, mending her pace, 'I've never felt this way before.'

They were approaching the steading, white walls dimly seen on each side of the road, curtained by shadowy trees. From the gateway on the right came someone—old Niven himself, seen in the light of the storm-lantern he carried. He halted, making encounter inevitable, and scrutinised them, his eyes even in the half-light quizzical for Gavin.

'You'll not have seen one of my brats tonight, Donald—around the place?' said she, cool as you like. 'Candida hasn't been home all day, and devil the glimpse of her anywhere, though I've tramped myself an inch shorter to come at her. She's not been about here at all, has she?'

'That she hasn't, Mrs Macandrew,' said he easily enough, with lamplight or something making his eyes twinkle. 'Neither the one nor the other nor both nor the same one have I seen all day. And that's a wonder. A fine time of night for a lassie like yon stravaiging the countryside. Or her mother either, for the matter of that,' he added, coughing to disguise too suggestive a chuckle. 'But I see you're well squired, though.'

'Mr Ewart's walking as far as the manse with me. Fell worried he is about the bairn. And to tell the truth, I'm worried myself—this time.'

'Ach, I'd not be worrying, Mrs Macandrew. You'll find the lass snug in bed by the time you win home. Yon one'll not be losing herself—whatever else—I'm thinking.'

'You're late on the go, yourself, Donald,' said she, unwilling to seem to hurry away in the embarrassment he was wishing upon the two of them. 'What would be wrong, then?'

'Ach, d'you see,' said Niven, 'old Meg dropped her foal today. And it's the last she'll drop. The knackers' men carted her off the night, poor lass. Ay, and the foal's gey poorly forbye. I'm just away in to see to him now. So good night to you. You'll surely find the hizzie right enough, Mrs Macandrew, never doubt it. And you, young Ewart,' he added, 'you'll be minding the day starts early here at Braelochy.'

'I'm not forgetting that, Mr Niven,' answered Gavin over his shoulder, hurrying after her as she made away already.

'That man has a farmyard mind, Mr Ewart,' she said without bitterness. 'I'm afraid your Ferlie reputation's gone. He thinks I was lying about the brat to make an alibi. The old fool! He ought to know me better, one would think.'

Gavin was still pondering this when they were arrested by a low whistle from behind. Niven stood in the middle of the road, waving his lantern.

'I never thought of that, stupid that I am,' she murmured, with relief and vexation at once.

When they rejoined him, 'Your lost lamb's safe enough,' said Niven. 'In the wrong fold maybe, but none the worse for that. Come away in.'

In the lantern's circle of light they saw her, sprawled among the hay in the loose-box, embracing the foal, whose long face lay wistfully across her blue bosom. Disturbed by their entrance, he raised his head, but her arm round his neck pulled him down again and she nestled more closely against him, still asleep. They looked, all three in silence, at this embrace that wove itself so variously into their different contexts of the night and the past, each of them teasing it through and through to fit or mar the pattern; till Elspeth with a peevish frown bent forward and shook the girl roughly.

'Mind the foal, now, Mrs Macandrew,' exclaimed Niven.

She woke reluctantly, spilling her treasure of misty imagery into the loose-box full of theirs, and looked at them sulkily, trespassers prying her suspiciously, probing her alert. What was she doing here, sleeping with this little man of a different colour that whimpered for his dead dam's teats, useless and unyielding like her own that those others groped for—Alec in the pinewood, Ewart in the heather, rapacious for the lure she joggled only to recoil breathlessly from the strike that sought ingoing for outcome like the wet baby colt's this morning from his sweating old mother labouring her life out and in among the straw? What was she doing here out of her chaste bed?

Who knows what a girl like her will be doing? Beyond her mother's ken she was, who had never in a wide experience slept in a stable with a horse below the age of consent. Was she better here in the straw than in the bothy bed with Ewart or in the loch with the leaping kelpie? Elspeth, recalling her own brief innocence, wondered what the girl was coming to, seeing whence she had come, reluctant to con too carefully her own maternal feelings at her daughter's thwarted foraying.

I didn't have her, he thought. No-one had her playing here with a toy horse at her breast like a little maid after all with her dolls, as he had first fancied her till she began playing fathers and mothers with him in the heather. But no, she cried, I'm not for jockeying with you. You make me sick. I'd rather have a little harmless horse to ride. What was wrong with him then? This other her mother would stay the course, he'd bet, if the chance offered, as it might with time off to find out under the coverlet and he not sweating for his ruined already blighted career for nothing, curse her and her baby whore's flesh.

She's at least kept the little piner warmer than straw would, with enough under that kilt to warm old David himself into action. But she couldn't feed him yet though it wouldn't be long, she shaping like her mother still game as a girl up in the bothy all night with young Ewart and then fell worried about the brat on the way home to the old death's-head Macandrew, who had never laid hand on her 'twas common knowledge since the day he'd married her God knows why. Long ago that was and he himself in the running for mad Elspeth Cameron and not so far behind neither that night after the County Show. But too drunk he'd been, and she mocking him like the coarse mare she was for all her French finishing-school. Finished with him she was after that—never the same one twice then and still taking it if she fancied someone, like this young Ewart her own son he might be and better matched with yon black jade glunching in the straw, and she'd not be satisfied much longer with a sick foal in her arms though an orra lass she was if pub clavers spoke true. Better watch Marion with this Ewart devil on the loose about the place—though it would do her no harm maybe a night in that bothy whatever her lady mother might say. Ach, it was time he won back to bed, and be damned to it.

He moved towards the foal, but Elspeth forestalled him. Pulling the girl to her feet, she said, 'Have you no bed to go to? You thoughtless, night-raking little trollop—snoring away here and me tramping miles in the dark to find you. In the lochan we thought you were.'

'A right good skelping's what she needs, Mrs Macandrew,' said Niven with some relish, his eyes on her.

'You're right there, Donald. But I'm so relieved to know she's safe. You had me frightened this time, child,' she murmured, drawing the girl closer. But she made no response to that, rubbing one instep up and down the other calf, her eyes betraying no emotion as she looked at them in the lamplight.

'I'm cold,' she said. 'I want to go home.'

Through mocking laughter Elspeth exclaimed, 'Do you tell me that now! You want to go home. Can't you think of something else to do? Donald's old boar's through the wall there. Maybe he's lonely tonight. What would a lass like you be going home for at two in the morning?'

'I want to go home,' the girl repeated wearily. 'If you've seen enough of Mr Ewart for tonight, let's be away now.'

Elspeth smacked her hard across the cheek, and a little smile came to crease the mask of her face, as Elspeth upbraided her in a voice scarcely audible but vibrant with anger: 'You ill-tongued, ungrateful little slut! I'll warm you right enough when I get you home. Come!' She dragged her unresisting into the darkness, calling behind her as she went: 'Good night, Donald. And thanks. Good night, Mr Ewart. I'm vexed to have bothered you. Come to the manse soon and I'll have this lady apologise properly. Good night.'

Niven was already on his knees in the straw, feeding the foal with a nursing-bottle, and Gavin lingered, at a loss for parting. 'That's a strange kind of wench, surely, Mr Niven?' said he.

'Which one would you be meaning?' said Niven, without turning.

'Why, the daughter, I mean.'

'Ach, there's little to choose between them for that,' replied the farmer, and he bent an appraising, half humorous, half reproachful gaze on Gavin. 'I was thinking maybe you'd found Mrs Macandrew herself unco strange for a minister's wife,' he said.

'Well now, and I did, when I think of it,' said Gavin, and he thought of it. And then, half willing to be misunderstood, he ventured to add: 'You're not suggesting, Mr Niven—?'

'Ach, man, let it be,' said he, rising stiffly and lifting the lantern. 'It's no time this to be blethering about kittle cattle the like of yon. Away you up to your bed now, and get some sleep. The day begins early at Braelochy, mind. Good night to you then.'

The day begins early, thought Gavin, as he loped back up the road. By God it would need to, to hold all that one had held.

CHAPTER FIVE

Macandrew in the Bothy

Yet further, you never enjoy the world aright till you so love the beauty of enjoying it, that you are covetous and earnest to persuade others to enjoy it. And so perfectly hate the abominable corruption of men in despising it, that you had rather suffer the flames of Hell than willingly be guilty of their error.

Thomas Traherne

They that deny a God destroy man's nobility: for certainly man is of kin to the beasts by his body; and if he be not of kin to God by his spirit, he is a base and ignoble creature

Francis Bacon

MACANDREW SAT on the edge of the kist staring at the lamp like a moth ignorant of its destiny, unfascinated, merely staring, his gaze fastened there by chance instead of on the fireplace, the bedclothes, the door. Seduced he was hypnotically as ever from his material milieu away into the invisible, asensual, a stickit yogi transcending the local, balked by the temporal; yet not balked but rather fenced within its concentric ever-widening ever-narrowing circuits that careered like cinematic illusions about him central, Macandrew on the edge of the kist staring at the lamp; outside the window watching his virtuous wife seated sedately, twined in bed with the young man, glowing with whisky at the County Ball, gravid with chi-chi twins in the rains, coveting his caresses in the Red Sea, posing her bold silhouette against the grey manse window—Elspeth, wife of Macandrew staring at the lamp.

By this time halfway along the road to the steading, she was still there for him. He had spied her striking over the brae and followed her to the bothy to witness new peccadillo peeped at through the uncurtained window, bright new nails for his bed forged in another's. But she had deceived him for she had sat, contained and pensive, in this corner that held her still—not only the warmth and smell of her, felt beneath him on the wood, teasing his nostrils from the air, but the other intangible being of her assaulting as always his wincing self.

He had heard from without their conversation about Candida and observed her quiet communion with the past; and the memories wreathing through her still hung like smoke in the corner for his inhalation, at once exciting and narcotic. He shared them all: her anxiety for her seeming second self, whom she loved not maternally but rather as her second coming in his despite, a woman creature to taunt him, now drowned unhanselled and virginal, fulfilling his birthday prophecy of doom; her recollection of that monstrous birth in circumstances primitive as the process itself; her derision of his rejection of her, the betrayer not of his honour but his creed, as she thrust her mocking tumescence before him, who was newly back from a lengthy sojourn up-country, anguished with fever and revulsion from all he had seen; and most keenly of all, her implacable hatred of him, deepened immeasurably by his influence on the children. Her long, searching thoughts, potent and lingering as perfume, distilled themselves about him, losing their identity in his.

Better if Candida were under water, potential lightning conductor of life, filled out for in-filling like her mother for it, despite his teaching. Who knows what a girl like yon will be doing? She knew and he knew and had striven to forestall her, more nearly successful with Nigretta, her counterpart, who cowered in her shell of self-disgust and denial, crept small in the stony cloister-garth of his nihilism, trailing the veil of renunciation, confirmed convert to his gospel.

There is no god, but there is no god, nor Jehovah nor Allah nor Zeus nor Brahma nor any manifestation of any, as thunderer or sun, rainmaker or chaste moon, avenger or destroyer, protecting all-father or fertile earth-mother, as Gaea or Sakti or Venus, peopling the planet avidly for generation after generation for generation: the seed the shoot the off-shoot timely drowned, the blade the stalk the corn in the ear the gem in the nose of the bazaar harlots who disseminated decay more noisome even than that of the withering bracken on the hillside above the graveyard where his parents festered from their bones with their misbegotten brood under the mouldering clods under the decomposing leaves, dust to dust consigned, a host for worms in death as in life. If any god anonymous or multinominal, if any fiendish agency had contrived this putrescent animate creation, grass and flower and fruit, winged and finned crawling and upright genera, and the ultimate human culmination, each and every organic manifestation lingering towards death and corruption from the instant of conception, nourished on death and corruption throughout their varying spans of life, if any quasi-divinity had malignantly or idly or experimentally set in motion this preposterous funeral procession interminably stalking down the ages littering the visible scene with its rotting remains, he must long since have swept the whole clamjamphrie into limbo.

No god, there was no god, there could not be. Only some hideous random mating of circumstances, some blind chemistry unluckily operating on the insensate planet had sullied it with the seeds of animate being that aeon after aeon with equal lack of purpose strove to propagate itself, knowing nor caring why: like the cataract-scaling salmon millions spawning in suicidal instinct; or the leaping rats in the barn; or the breeding sow that devoured her litter; or the acorn not content to end as mast but darkly germinating putting forth its root and phallic shoot to stand for centuries of phyllomorphous proliferation, yellow leaves seasonally falling through the forest in Assam, where the cow elephant shambled foraging for sustenance to round the biennial unborn womb-fruit of her mountainous labour of love in some hot hole in the jungle, wearing the while on her melancholy countenance grief for such futile destiny. Futile and febrile all of it was, in inception and evolving cycles, from amoeba pulsating in grotesque effort at self-generation through fish reptile and fowl, cold-blooded piscine relics still hot to persist in their frigid deeps, ophidian sloughing creepers sluggish in all but one coil, and the winged flying things aspirant to nothing but feathers ruffled in mounting. In the Taj gardens swam ornamental fish in stone pools imprisoned in their own open-mouthed vacuity but egged on inexorably to prolong it to infinity. And once in a dry well he had seen a painted viper absurdly extruding baby slivers in maternal providence. The vulture beautiful and effortless on the bleached sky telescoped to glut on carrion its oviparous fertility and the farmyard dames momently topped by Chanticleer squawked pretended fright and clucked their triumph over a tenanted eggshell.

Let there be life, more life. Ask not its purpose, its meaning; ignore its witless urge to offset its own dissolution by self-reiteration; dispute not its value in whatever revolting shape, as swine mandrill hyaena squid maggot tarantula rhinoceros hedgehog bulldog leech louse dung-beetle alligator gorilla human woman; accept and glory in the prolificity of creation with wondering eyes and emulous loins; praise laud and bless, increase and multiply. And thy seed shall be as the sands of the sea for number. For number only; for the sands of the sea were sublimely divorced from all this seminiferous mating, part only of the insentient stage for its performance, mere intrinsic being moved but by wind and water in time as in an hour-glass pouring its eternal fragments heedless of the generating generations. Rased from the rock the sea-sand raised no offsprung rock in turn but endured hard and imperishable in unvexed detachment.

Here was the icon for his devotion, the godhead he aspired to and revered: insensate material essence, devoid of any psychic constituent, untrammelled by instinct appetite or any such physical urge, never eating excreting sleeping lusting, unborn unpropagating immortal, contained in its inviolate selfhood, immune from the contamination that defiled life in all its evolved variations and incurably cancered the ultimate paragon that he reluctantly personified: mankind born of womankind, apple fruit of her body's hunger, Eden-exiled from the garden bestiary aviary fishpond snakepit where the life stream surged in innocent sunlight into the leaf-covert of guilt and self-disgust. Knowledge of good and evil only evil, as the subtle serpent knew curling his lip over un-aproned Eve, impatient matrix womb of woe, whose vulval mouth yawned for irruption. Such knowledge was the source of misery: better the lowest form of animate creation, throbbing unaware through its odious destiny, than mankind, observing it with anguished fascination. But better far the grain of sand, the rock-face in the corrie, the slate on the roof, the watch-spring finger-ring window-pane, the cairn on the ben, the cobble in the yard; better the Buddhic stupa than Gautama himself, dead of a surfeit of rotten mushrooms, or his fatuous devotees doomed to repeated incarnation; better the painted effigy than Mary far from immaculate since mortal, the marble than its sculptor or fleshly prototype, the granite headstone than the deliquescent pulp or carious bone it commemorated; better, far better, the inorganic entity free of metabolism, the thing itself in utter singleness without heredity or progeny urge or regression, the purity of mere existence unborn unliving undying. Here was the ideal, in the material, unattainable alas; for even death would not bring it, or long since he would have attained it. But death appalled him even more than life, and he remained alive studying petrifaction, coveting the atrophy of all his senses, pores for the ingress of the sewage of life.

But he fell far short, too prone to point his revulsion by contemplation of its origin, faithless to the ideal he cherished, betraying it: leaning over Niven's pound, visiting the sick, burying the dead, stealing furtive glimpses of the twins' cleft bosoms openly swelling or long thighs meeting in moist secrecy; every day and night he backslid, but never recanted or acknowledged lapse, rather reaffirmed his denial of the animality he abhorred. As tonight, although his Elspeth, superb promiscuous Elspeth, vital as Vesuvius in heat for all but him, for whom like Everest the abode of snow, although she had lured him anew to alien sowing to watch through the window like some vicarious Onan, he would have retired to vilify with strengthened venom the lust that drove her bedward, the insatiable loin-deep hunger.

But tonight she had given no such occasion, sitting here decently composed in reflection on her cross-bred cross-grained thrawn daughter, who had sunk in the lochan all her rich inheritance, hitherto held in chancery by his austere guardianship. Had she then fled at once his regimen and the mother-bred licence it constrained? Who knows what a girl like yon will be doing? Bound to come to a bad end with such a beginning, he had said, when he received them all three carried on a charpoy that should have been their bier through the rain to the mission bungalow, she defiant and suckling them brazenly before him, from no mother's solicitude but only to torment him, for she cherished them only as spears against him, thorns in his flesh, and especially this one, who but for him had threatened to out-Jezebel her mother. That threat at least would never see fulfilment now, with all the zest going out of her into the cold-blooded fishes. But what fresh stimulus was here for their antipathy!

Whatever her considered response to the girl's death might be, relief at a rival eclipsed or anger at his prophecy come true or grief over a bloom of her sap come early to nothing, all feelings would be submerged under hatred for him, the cause. Her hatred remained implacable though time had all but exhausted its source, his ingrained detestation of her excellent sexuality from that night of her belated bridal through a score of offering years. In the hotel bedroom she undressed professionally, a little here a little there, Messalina feigning modesty, while he observed her, disgust fighting with desire. And when she came and kissed him, not passionately but with promise, pressing privately against him, despite himself he grew hard against her before he thrust her away and left her. Like Satan put behind him she hated him, Elspeth rejected by a man, a poor shilpit minister body at that, whom she deigned to favour. From then on he was a perpetual challenge to her, a keep untaken, whose impregnability mocked her and reduced her in her own esteem. And so they continued, their preposterous marriage binding them in a mutual aversion that had proved more enduring than love, taking her eastward with him when nothing else would have done so. The more adamant he was, the more pertinacious she became in enticement, and with frustration her loathing for him deepened, with his reciprocal, and sought fresh justification until its original cause receded, supplanted by a less exclusively selfish antipathy. Her mind always open to his sounding as her body never, he easily perceived when her silly compulsion to vindicate beneath him her scorned carnal allurement became the conscious determination to seduce him from the way he followed, compel him to deny his creed and acknowledge the mastery of his physical being. Even her utter revulsion from him, as from some mutant, some Martian visitant, failed to blunt her purpose, pursued through the years with varying intensity and means, countered by him with effortless success and sometimes with malignant irony.

In the humid darkness, sweating on the verandah, staring hour-long through his net at the stars as often here in the cool north he stared, in envy of their remote objectivity, willing himself among them chaste impersonal denuded of all life and all life's furniture of yearning flesh and spirit, he felt himself succumbing, enfeebled and tormented as he was by days and nights of heat that enveloped him like some fecund womb nourishing importunate life more life more flourishing life flushed with rising sap and coursing blood bent on fertility. Against the sky he saw in silhouette the twitching foliage of the wistaria that twined up the pillars and along the roof, seeming astir with irrepressible growth, microcosmic pattern of universal propagation. And the night was clamant with the hallelujah of frogs and the laughter of scavenging jackals and through all throbbing the village drums in time to the pounding of his blood, calling irresistibly towards sordid immersion and solace. Not for the first time he felt temptation, and now he knew himself impotent against it as he stood up in hardihood for his downfall, Macandrew, not staring at the lamp but at her naked and sprawling under her net like Aphrodite meshed by

Hephaestus for his skilful puddling and hammering, at her awake and panting in heat in the lower berth sailing past Socotra, expectant for his maleness merely, all animosity and feud of wills forgotten. But not by him, hard as the granite in the quarry, even with intolerable urgency quivering between them. He had left her fretting in abandoned solitude and crept for relief into clinking bangled arms in the bazaar. He would not share his self-betrayal with her or gratify at once her flesh and her determination that he should.

For he was stronger than she; and she was strong as life, exuding potency like sweat from her exuberance, astride under the mosquito-net, dancing a reel with Niven at the County Ball, flirting with young Gupta in the vestry after service; opulent she was as a field of young corn, a farrowing sow, the rain-clouds swollen with promise. But he was stronger; and he would punish her, the epitome of odious creation and procreation, and triumph even in defeat, skulking in shame to her musky brown sister in some dungy brothel: he, whose strength to hate revived Antaeus-like from contact with his mother, abhorrent life: he would punish her, the personification of everything he reviled, the more so bearing to spite him her half-bred illicit twins, doomed to an evil end he had rightly predicted and half contrived, with one already, water-born water-harvested, laid barren in the lochan. What fuel was here for the long smouldering furnace of their contention.

Upright in the corner, his hands immobile on his knees, his face betraying nothing of the cauldron simmering within him, with blind gaze on the lamp before him, like some ancient Pharaoh everlasting in obsidian he sat, outside the world he rejected, locked in the purgatory that supplanted it. He heard nothing of Gavin's crackling approach through the wood and not with a glance did he acknowledge the young man's entrance. Gavin remained arrested on the threshold by the sight of the figure occupying the place so lately filled by the woman his no less unexpected guest. Although they had never met, he knew this was Macandrew the doitit minister and viewed his presence with less than favour. He had had enough of this eccentric manse ménage for one day and night, had Gavin: first, the perverse nymph of a daughter; then the incomprehensible mother; and now, in the small hours with Niven's threatened early day just ahead of him, this wanchancie unholy-Willie installed there like some heathen idol awaiting libation. That was an idea, anyway. He could use a drink himself. He deserved one, by God.

Heeling the door shut, he crossed between Macandrew and the lamp. Macandrew awoke from his dwaum but said never a word or shifted his gaze, which rested now perforce on his host where he stooped to draw from under the bed a half-bottle of Haig half empty. The bottle uncapped in his hand,

'You'll have a dram then, Mr Macandrew?' said Gavin. 'It's a snell air rising outside.'

Macandrew's eyes moved from Gavin's to the bottle and back with little apparent interest. He spoke then, his words falling flat between them like cards on a table. 'If you examine your bottle, young man, you will perceive, I jalouse, that I have already had a dram. In your absence, I fear. A liberty, maybe, but pardonable—with the snell air rising outside.'

Gavin stared at him for a moment before raising the bottle to sight its level. He grinned ruefully. 'Ay,' he said, 'you have that. The air must be colder than I thought. But how did you know the bottle was there?'

'Where else would it be? Where else would a poor scholar keep his bottle if not by his bookis black and red at his bed's-head? Within arm's reach but under the bed, surely, where he wouldn't be knocking it over carelessly. I wasn't born a middle-aged clergyman, young sir.'

Divinity students are always the worst, drinking and gambling and whoring on borrowed time before the loan's foreclosed by some girning Kirk-session. He was face down over the bed in gawkit Annie's garret up the close spewing his guts up all over her patchwork and she long-suffering trollop in a rage no wonder rolling him downstairs to lie derelict on the landing till he came to, hearing his host addressing him: 'You'll have one for the road anyway?'

And high time he was on the road, too, thought Gavin, the supping old dotard, swigging a man's bottle unasked at two in the morning. But Macandrew was in no hurry to go, savouring the dram Gavin gave him in the chipped enamel mug. Gavin lipped the bottle-neck, replaced the cap, and stowed the remnant definitively under the bed. He regarded his guest interrogatively.

'It's a powerful solace for a man, the whisky,' said Macandrew placidly.

'Makes me sleepy at this time of the morning,' replied Gavin, yawning demonstratively.

'Indeed it is a creature of infinite capacity,' continued the other unheeding. 'There is nothing it cannot do. It warms the blood against the chittering wind and refreshes you exhausted in the heat. It can make you ill and yet it is a sovereign medicine in sickness. It can exalt, so that a man sits with the so-called immortals, careless of his kind, master for a time of his servile destiny. It can depress and humble him to crawl in the excrement of his own miserable bowels of self-compassion. It can sharpen a man's awareness of the world outside him and of the specious prospects within him; and it can dull his senses and his wits, equating him with the wormy clod he is in fact. Without doubt it is an unpredictable, multi-consequential intoxicant, imbuing its partakers with manifold desires and proclivities: some to sleep and some to bestir themselves; some to preach and some to blaspheme their imagined creator; some to meditate and some to fornicate. Much abused, by its addicts and its traducers alike, it is a complicated simple, the whisky, pure in essence but diverse in effects; and against it none can prevail.'

'It makes me sleepy,' repeated Gavin. 'And I could chance a guess at what it does to you, Mr Macandrew.'

'I am fortified against it, young man. The toothful I've supped tonight will scarce affect me one way or the other. But I regard it as one of the few clean alimentary items a man can put in his belly. It is an Olympian liquor, a Caledonian nectar, a Platonic distillation transcending other potions as the ideal does the real, surmounting its earthly origin as electric radiance or the rain-shower on the ben. Adulterate in origin as all things organic must needs be, it is yet less so than most.

'Consider first the corn, the masculine bearded barley, hard and granular, swinging in the northern caller air, balancing slenderly above its outgrown mother earth as a thought hovers over its clay conceiver. Contrast with this aspiration from the unclean womb the humility of the hop, restrained on stilts from crawling back to root in the corruption it crept from, or the cloying gravidity of the grape, succulent with syrup as a woman with milk.

'Think next of its mode of harvesting, cut clean by the bright sickle scythe or the combine's flashing knives. Shall we not prefer this clean-garnered crop to the hop, plucked by the filth-lingering fingers of seasonal slum labourers, or the vine fruit, scissored from the stem by purpled hands and trodden under sweaty calloused feet?

'Reflect too, if you dare, on the processing, the chemical

commingling in noxious bubbling stew that decomposes naturally putrescent ingredients to produce the barbarous beers and simpering wines beloved by lesser breeds. Consider in contrast the confection of the cratur, nay, the disinfection one might more truly say, whereby all that is gross and earthly in the raw material is purged in the fire, and the ultimate product, all but vanishing in vapour into pure non-being, condenses and distils itself, the excellent elemental quintessence of refinement, into this glass bottle. But man, I see you have removed it now.'

In silence Gavin retrieved the bottle and passed it over. Whisky splashed into the mug.

'Observe too,' resumed Macandrew, 'the colour—incomparably superior to the muddied sedimentary dun of ales, the artificial clarity of lagers, the anaemic or sanguinary hues of white and red wines—as though a man should drink stagnant peat water or the liquids in his own gross body. And then, nose the pungent antiseptic aroma, sterilising as flame. And finally, savour the austere bite on the palate and all down the gullet, like molten igneous lava or a draught of solar fire purging its passage. Who bloats himself in puddles of mild or bitter, ponderous hop-sludge or pressurised horse-water, who pours down sweet or dry, still or effervescent, sugar or vinegar southern juices knows no such shriving relish.

'Think further how those brewed and fermented liquors continue their vile chemistry in a man's locked and silted canals, simmering like a witch's cauldron, to seek gaseous eruption in bi-terminal belching or watery profitless emission in bladder-flushing piss against a wall. How infinitely blessed compared with such blind swilling mouths is he who sparingly and decorously imbibes this ardent amber medicinal tincture, this breath and finer spirit of the barley, this disembodied irreducible extract. Could a man but sustain himself upon it, he would go far to escape the pestilential dungeon of his bodily habitat that so imprisons and degrades him. Verily, it is an unearthly dram, the whisky. Slainthe.'

And he trickled back the last vestige and with sober caution placed bottle and mug on the floor.

CHAPTER SIX

Nigretta in Bed

Unsullied, chaste, and fair,
  A lily-flower thou art;
As I gaze sadness wells
  Strangely about my heart.

An impulse comes to lay
  Hands on thy shining hair,
And pray God keep thee ever
  Unsullied, chaste, and fair.
    after Heine

Vivamus, mea Lesbia, atque amemus,,
  Rumoresque senum severiorum
  Omnes unius aestimemus assis.
    Catullus

NIGRETTA WAS lying in bed, her down-lidded eyes squinting along the shallow col of her night-gowned bosom at the gold locket that lay there. Her sleeved arms lay maidenly along her sides on the coverlet and her hair clouded the pillowcase. The lamp burned beside her, feeble ally against the alluring repellent phantasms that peopled her sleep and night-waking, frightening her and defeating her daytime resolution. She lay like some sepulchral effigy in marble, some calm sculptured church-laid lady, and sought internal repose like her outward semblance, refuge from the vital stirrings he had taught her to hate and deny.

The locket, the nugget of gold, the unbreathing bloodless metallic thing, the thing, look at the thing, gaze rapt and concentrated at it solely, be one with it, become it, get inside it with him whom it contained in miniature, inside it with him. And the locket, warm in its fold of amber sun-stained father-stained flesh, bobbed in the swell of her distressed breathing, a failing talisman; although she earnestly envisaged his cold blank gaze, his level utterance, his remoteness from the hectic coil of Elspeth and Candida and the cattle and the poultry and the labourers and the village girls. Always impassive he was, always present here in her sinful breast to strengthen her, flat and frigidly encased in perdurable gold, unfeeling, not warm and caressing on her sinful breast. Look, look at the locket, ignoring its rocking cradle. Forget the man creature enshrined in replica within; reject his maleness as he did himself, who emulated the picture in its frame. Be like him as he was like the picture the frame the locket, immune from the world the flesh the devil, Elspeth, Candida, the cloven furrow, the rooting swine, the swollen bird-fouled plums in the orchard, the steaming midden behind the barn, the byre cobbles running with waste and splashed with filth, and the warm-flanked beasts dangling their udders. The locket, look at the locket, only the gold thing, never its fleshly setting mounting double mountain twin paps twin hillocks curved and cairned; if only they were but that, like the cold eroded bens, her loins some corrie among them, her limbs their stony ridges, and her face above them some ice-riven creviced precipice, forbidding in its granite austerity. To be free of this pulsating pulp, this virgin meadowland prime for the plough and the seed; to be free of it was impossible. Not even he could escape the body. But live cold within it, revile it as animate and therefore evil, yield not to its temptations.

All this he counselled, and she struggled to obey; walking the flags of renunciation, loathing her body's motions, deriding what those others called her beauty. This oozing of refuse from within, hourly daily monthly dredging of excrement from ever-filling sewers—could beauty reside in such a noisome suppuration? What they named beauty was only a bait to tempt to further refinements of carnal pollution. She knew, for he had told her of coupling more odious than that of the farmyard, themselves the twin product of such. Elspeth gloried in it; Candida courted it, parading her nakedness for that dung-beetle Alec in the coppice. How could they do it, Elspeth Candida Mrs Niven all of them women, how could they covet such contact, more than covet—achieve and revel in it? Their own corruption sullied by others', the heaving of hungry bodies battening on each other's living carrion to generate fresh decay—how could they, how? How could she, asleep alone an hour gone dreaming, with him on her breast unlocked unlocketed, between her here no flat simulacrum cased in metal but hot and vital, probing obeliscal inside her here? How could she in open surrender, how she they all of them women? And worse than all the rest was she, Nigretta, who cried rape by a pair of eyes peeping from young Alec by the lochan and lay all night with the minister between her breasts and beyond. A ghost walked over Nigretta's grave.

But that was a dream, only a dream. Light the lamp and escape to wakefulness. Look, look at the locket, secure and static, fast and fastened tight, shutting out everything everything but sheer inanition. Contemplate, emulate, become it. Waking dispel what night-crawling steals its way into her defenceless, out of the locket issuing deliciously—no, odiously shamelessly like Candida stride-legged on the shore, cows streaming on the cobbled floor or splashing dung for Alec's furrows warrened by worms and slugs and ants and earthbound creatures guttering through corruption; like all that he had taught her to hate; like all she did hate in her steadfast conscious self; hated now, again alone, supine in the lamplight under the chaste sheet. Cruel that darkness and solitude should so often seduce her into self-betrayal and betrayal of him with him under him over him—him or another: Alec no longer simply staring, or Gupta at the mission, lean and brown and yearning from his black eyes, or some virile nameless stranger seen by chance and forgotten to come alive by stealth to pleasure plague her, or Candy so wickedly delightsome even in fancy.

He had no control over her alone and dreaming asleep or awake. Then her erring self acknowledged no tabus he erected for her. No granular crystal mineral forms of being occupied her reveries; no solar fire lunar light stellar radiance lit their secrecy; no sterile landscapes topographed them. Without compass, she wandered blissfully, took hands and danced in orgy with their denizens till some belated cock crew thrice and the locket in its muddied trough gleamed reproach in her eyes that were closing again to imprison her in her private places. She raised herself on her pillows in an effort to capture consciousness. Tears seeped through her lashes to dim her vision of the amulet, which nestled now snug in its cleft for whom? In its gold sheath him under the banyan tree Gupta by the lochan Alec fondling and mocking Candida whom? Lay me down to sleep and pray someone my all to take.

She was swimming in the forbidden tank behind the mission-house, Macandrew finger shaking from the bank among a round-eyed crowd of villagers; floating she was serenely in the polluted water, past the shit-buffaloes sloughing their mire and ordure. A group of girls waist-deep bathed their glistening brown torsos, scooping the water over them to trickle between their breasts and down their rounded backs. And when they hitched their sari skirts to micturate, their laughing white teeth lipping the surface, she hunkered with them gleefully. Little fishes whiffled tickling exquisitely between and through to swell her concave stomach up to rival that of Niven's old mare trailing her belly in the pasture. But when she waded from the lochan into the pines, the golden chain pendent from her hips dangled between slender loins the locket over her virginal triangle modestly, for he shook reprovingly a long forefinger from the cairn on Ben Cromach. Native boys with swine snouts and maggots worming from their eyes joined hands and danced a riotous circle round her where she postured among the pine-cones, which all at once took root between her splaying toes and sprouted up and up while Elspeth and Candida watered them and Alec spread his waste with careful fingers. Arboured in their tall close trunks in the reeking darkness once more alone she trembled for the locket's leaves parted to shoot out his stiff member swaying to and fro and again he was all about her encompassing insinuating solace and she opened to take him arching in abandon until Candida's voice shrilled in her ear:

'What the hell do you think you're up to, you sodomitish little she?'

Nigretta struggled awake in terror and reaching in the unexpected darkness for the lamp overturned it to crash on the floor. 'What is it? Who's there?' she cried.

'Who in the devil's name were you expecting in your bed?' sneered Candida. 'Young Alec? Or the gardener's gomeril boy? Or him next door more likely? Somebody more fully furnished than I am, for sure.'

'I don't know what you're talking about,' whimpered Nigretta. 'I was asleep. What are you doing in my bed?'

'Who's been eating my porridge?' echoed Candida. 'Who's been clipping my wings, fingering my things? I came in beside you because I was so cold and you were so cosy and warm. But heavens, it's not warm you are. You're in heat. I'll feel the benefit over in my own bed.'

She slid out before her sister could restrain her, and Nigretta was left to plead childishly: 'Don't leave me, Candy. I'm scared. It's those awful dreams. Stay here with me, Candy. Please.'

'Go to sleep, you silly tawpie,' said Candida not unkindly. 'I'm not in the mood. I've had a trying day.'

She smiled ruefully at the ambiguity of the word, which Nigretta was not slow to interpret as her rejection prompted her: 'You never stop trying to get what you want, do you? It's a wonder you bother with me at all.'

'It's no great wonder—just the unnatural product of our early conditioning by our reverend mentor,' replied Candida. 'It's time it stopped, though. You're a big girl now. It's time you swallowed the oyster, instead of turning your platter of baby saps upside down in a tantrum.'

'What are you talking about?' asked Nigretta crossly. 'Swallowed the oyster—what oyster, for heavens' sake?'

'I guess it is a pretty cryptic expression,' said Candida, mischievously obscuring it further. 'Yes, too worldly for a novice like you—all tight shut and clammed up as you are.'

'You must always be showing off—one way or another,' said Nigretta querulously. 'Baby food and shellfish—what kind of a diet's that?'

'Alternative diets, stupid,' said Candida, reluctantly amused by her sister's annoyance. 'But you're getting warmer, for I'm not referring to the oyster's shell, or its improbable pearl. I'm talking of its flesh—its flesh.'

'God, yes, you're a glutton for that,' said Nigretta scornfully, unaware of her sister's grimacing in the dark as her regurgitation in the heather came back to her sickeningly.

'But can't you see,' persisted Candida patiently against her judgment, 'don't you understand that to an appetising tit-bit like you the world's your oyster? It's out there, wide open and succulent, to be savoured and sucked in, while you shrivel here in the manse on hunger strike.'

'You've a ridiculous way of putting things,' complained Nigretta, 'but the drift's always the same. And your time's always wasted. You're forever on about it. But you know I loathe the very thought of it—all that sweaty handling and coupling, and the abomination of its outcome—and the futility of it all.'

'These are only words, little sister,' said Candida. 'And they're not yours. Will you never put away the devilish alphabet of lies our guru taught us? He sat us down under the barren fig-tree as soon as we could listen. And we've been rooted there ever since.'

'And a good thing too,' retorted Nigretta. 'Who wants a part in all that beastliness?'

'But you have a part in it, like it or not, simpleton,' replied Candida. 'You were on stage minutes ago, weren't you?'

'I was dreaming, for God's sake,' expostulated Nigretta. 'I can't help dreaming, can I?'

'Perhaps you could—if you were living,' said Candida. 'Instead of lying embalmed behind the stone he's rolled to entomb you—a stone scrawled and sprayed with obscene graffiti he's conceived in his lunatic mind. Can I never convince you how wicked and destructive his counsel is? Only look what it's done to him—a frightened whisky-steeped monster, stalking the parish like some bizarre cartoon figure animated despite himself. Yes, despite his preposterous aspiration. He covets petrifaction no less. He's nearer putrefaction—and the sooner he achieves it the better for all of us.'

Candida was mildly pleased with that, but only mildly. And she paused, recognising that her vehemence, pointless as she knew it to be, proceeded from her humiliations of the day; she was assailing Nigretta, vilifying Macandrew, to relieve her own frustration. Better have done with it. But Nigretta would not.

'But he's right,' she insisted defiantly. 'And you know he is, within yourself. To covet petrifaction, I mean. So do I. I'd rather be marble than me.'

Candida was compelled to laugh at the nonsense of it, but not mirthfully. What a Jesuitical triumph the old corrupter had won. They were for life his, their course predetermined and immutable, jib or balk or peck as they would—or as she would, for surely Nigretta was nobbled beyond treatment. And yet, she could not help suspecting, Nigretta was more likely to escape than she—by virtue of her very stupidity.

'Can't you see, my bovine beauty,' she argued however vainly, 'you can't be marble? You're the wrong colour to start with. Your head's maybe stone, but the rest of you's not and can't be. You really are exasperatingly obstinate.'

'I am not,' protested Nigretta. 'I'm loyal and consistent—unlike you. You believed what he taught us, didn't you?'

'Christ, booby,' exclaimed Candida angrily, 'we were innocent children then, ignorant and powerless against his mumbo-jumbo. As the twig's bent, they say, the tree will grow. And so we did, the pair of us—all askew and warped. But the tree's growth can be re-aligned if it's caught in time. And surely you and I could see, years ago, the vicious falsity of his teaching?'

'Yes,' said Nigretta sombrely, 'we could see it maybe. But what could we do about it—crooked saplings that we are? What can we do about it?'

Reluctantly moved by her sister's pitiful resignation and in her different fashion sharing it, Candida was momentarily halted. Nigretta proceeded wistfully:

'I know—you don't have to convince me time and again—I know I can't be a glacial boulder in the glen, or a star-beam, or a frost-fern on the windowpane. I know that well enough. But what can I be? Tell me that, sister.'

Candida, aware of her sister's mournful Magdalen eyes bent on her through the half-dark between them, found herself at once irritated and sympathetic. With an effort she answered evenly: 'Can't you be what you are—a beautiful woman being?'

Under the sheet Nigretta ran her hands down her body from breasts to loins, where they stopped. She shivered and answered waspishly: 'Beautiful, always beautiful. I can never understand how you can call it beautiful. My body, your body, every body—how can this hot moist palpitating lump of squelching stuff, gorging and voiding through its obscene vents—how can it be beautiful I wonder. God, I'd rather be a porcelain figurine. Think what's inside this for a moment—mind you, only for a moment. Think of the blood-streaming arteries veins capillaries snaking all about—and those revolting coiling entrails channelling sewage. Ay, and the other sludge that finds vent monthly. Beautiful! Like a cow-pat or a bull's ball-bag, maybe.'

Candida gagged at Nigretta's gloating imagery and found it hard to counter, so graphically in line as it was with her recent experience. But controlling her disgust and anger, she replied trenchantly: 'You crazy bitch! can't you see you're merely tormenting yourself as he's taught you to? Can't you understand I'm trying to help you? God, can't you see I've tried for years back to break the spell he's cast on you—cast on us both?'

'Are you still under it then?' asked Nigretta with mock incredulity. 'Despite your filthy adventures?'

'Yes, yes, I am,' exclaimed Candida almost hysterically. 'And you know it, you spayed tabby-cat.'

'Oh yes, I know it,' said Nigretta composedly. 'We're not twins for nothing.'

'No, but we're women for nothing, God damn it!' shouted Candida.

'Not for nothing, little sister,' murmured Nigretta insinuatingly. 'Why can't we be content? Between us we've more than enough to pleasure each other.'

Candida was out of bed in an instant to stand menacingly over her sister.

'You unnatural slut,' she almost whispered. 'You she-pussy-catamite, you'd better be chaste than that. God, I could strangle you.'

'Hush, Sugar Candy, what a fuss you're making,' said Nigretta soothingly as she sat up, opening welcoming arms.

The now pendent locket glinted in what light there was. Candida clutched it and wrenched it from her sister's neck. She made for the window, threw up the sash, and flung the bauble into the mirk of the garden.

'There, empty bosom,' she said furiously, turning to her sister, who was speechless with dismay at this response. 'There's an end at least to your sinister fetish. Maybe you'd like now to cross the landing and entertain him in fact—I think not.'

She slammed down the window and returned to her bed. Nigretta sank back on her pillows, momentarily dumbfounded, chafing her neck where the delicate chain had scored it. Presently she said conciliatorily, 'I don't see the need for that, Candy. I can see that you're vexed by something that's happened today—or hasn't happened. I was simply trying to make up for it, that's all.'

Candida said nothing, in no way mollified by Nigretta's justness of perception. The silence grew pregnant between them, heavy with their brooding contemplation of their common bafflement. And suddenly Candida found, in place of the hard masculinity she had that day invited and declined, her sister's warm lushness snuggled beside her.

'There now, Treacle-toffee, don't sulk,' whispered Nigretta. 'Don't be fretting about him, whoever he is. We have each other.'

Candida made no move to expel or acknowledge her bedmate, and they lay together as close and immobile as earlier in Elspeth's womb, until presently Nigretta fell asleep.

But Candida did not sleep, watching the wall whiten in the dawning light, hearing the birds talking in the garden below and cockcrow from the farms all round. She was reluctantly reviewing the ineffectual embraces of her day and night, with two men and a little black horse in the straw in the heather by the lochan and now here in her maiden bed with her amorous misdirected pitiful counterpart, who never played away from home or mixed doubles or dreamed of opening her treasure outside the family triangle but ached obtusely within it, poor maladjusted wretch. And all this woe fallen from Beelzebub the foster-father, who nourished nullity, promoting deprivation, mis-shaping his bastards in his own emaciated image, entrancing them like sleeping beauties in their dungeon of suspense. I've tried for years to break the spell he's cast on us. And after all, it should be easy enough. The fairy prince, smartly out of his rugger shorts, will kiss you awake all hot and hungry with the heather fronds tickling your back and the bees pollinating all about to encourage you. And if you shouldn't fancy him, it's no trouble. You simply puke in his startled face, and his arms release you to run and wash off contamination in the shallows.

Less easy, however, to cleanse the contagion caught from that other, the leprosy of revulsion that condemns you to quarantine forever. Surely not forever? Candida stirred involuntarily, as if shrinking physically from such an imposition, and Nigretta, disturbed, drew even closer as a baby to her mother and did not awake. Against her inclination Candida caressed her sister's warm smoothness. Yes, forever it might well be. Escape was more arduous with each effort, each effort more feverish in its urgency, more humiliating in its inevitable failure. Come out from behind the stone he's rolled to entomb you. Laboriously thrust it back and reveal yourself recklessly open and accessible—but always scrambling to shelter, shuttered and impotent on impact. Why didn't you stop me? protested that one in the corrie nearly there but not for she had stopped him and not he her. What a blushing skirmish that had been. Better be like Nigretta, physically untouchable in her amulet or appeased in her sister's arms, than forage forlornly here and there to her own frustration.

It was not, she easily persuaded herself, that she was ambitious to follow her mother. In fact, she had never cared to analyse her attitude towards Elspeth and her filthy adventures, as Nigretta called them. She knew there were areas of activity much more fulfilling for a woman. But first she had to ascertain that she was a woman—no longer a mermaid unforked and frigid as the water that enveloped her, no longer a siren singing to her own shipwreck again and again the same song with the same anticlimax scored long ago under the net and since by the felt pen of the foster-father, the gelder of stallions, the suturer of females, the abortion-bringer, the reviler of living and about to live, the forestaller, the path-blocker like Apollyon straddling the way to realisation.

Are you always so approachable? the luckless possibility had asked, astonished by her invitation. And she was—approachable but impenetrable like a rock-face on the ben. He had done his best, poor devil, and just failed to score a bloody fine try, as he would doubtless have put it—and how right he would have been. But never mind, he must have had an easier game with Elspeth in the bothy bed. And for a moment she was Elspeth, twined expertly with the young man, rewarding him in kind for his valorous ineffectual effort to apply the kiss of life to one of her moribund vestals. But she could not for long personate Elspeth. Such a being was beyond her power of self-projection, little embryonic enclosed self that hers was. But perhaps it might be different another day or another night. She who fights and runs away lives to yield another day. All might yet be well.

Candida, exhausted by the non-events of the day and night and harassed by her premonitions of more to come, closed at last her eyes and joined her sister in bondage in sleep.

CHAPTER SEVEN

Gavin in the Back Parlour

Let brotherly love continue.
Be not forgetful to entertain strangers: for
thereby some have entertained angels
unawares.

Epistle to the Hebrews

Hear how he clears the points o' Faith
Wi' rattlin' and wi' thumpin'!
Now meekly calm, now wild in wrath
He's stampin' an' he's jumpin'.

Robert Burns

WHEN GAVIN entered Hector Fraser's back parlour, there was no-one there but Hector himself, glowering in the half light over a large whisky and water.

'Good evening, Mr Fraser,' said Gavin courteously, with marked respect even in the voice. 'A grand day it's been.'

Hector peered a moment in an effort at recognition, and then, with no affability at all, 'Ach, it's you is it?' he said. 'And who was it invited you in here, will you tell me?'

'Why, Mr Fraser,' Gavin answered, confidently enough, 'I was in here the other night, remember? With Mr Niven, and the rest of them?'

'Ay, you were so, maybe. But don't be thinking that makes you free of the place. There's a bar next door for the likes of you, my mannie. Faith now, is a man to have no place of his own to drink his own whisky in private, or maybe with two-three of his friends?'

Fraser's scowl darkened, but Gavin noticed it was directed not at him but at the tumbler turning round and round in his fingers; and well primed beforehand by Niven, he stood his ground, though somewhat uncertainly. 'Well Mr Fraser,' he said, through rather tightly smiling lips, 'maybe I was hoping I might come under the head of friends.'

'Hech!' grunted Fraser. 'On the strength of a night's acquaintance! Man, is that the way they make friends nowadays? Stand me a drink and forge a friendship! That'll be right enough for picking up women for a night in some low howff in the town, maybe, where you come from. But don't think to be bringing your lightsome ways here, young man. You'll find Ferlie folks are not so easy won over. They'll take your drink right enough, and thank you kindly. Ay, they'll do that. But you'll not get much on the strength of it. Deed, you'll get little enough anywhere for that—a trollop for a night, maybe. But never a friend. Eh, but you fair amaze me. Friend, says you, as bold as brass. Would you in one chance-lucky night be thinking to come under that head, as you so glibly put it, along with those old good-for-nothing devils I've known since we were laddies plunking school together every other day the sun shone? Friends! God's sake, boy, but you've an unco mannerless, forward way with you to talk that way to Hector Fraser in his own back parlour.'

By God! thought Gavin, bridling despite all Niven's warnings of Hector's queer ongoings, I'll not stomach this. Let the old tosspot sit drooling to himself in his damned back parlour, if that was what he wanted. There were other pubs in the village. 'Well,' said he, feeling for the door-knob, 'if that's how it is, good night to you, Mr Fraser. If the parlour's too good for the likes of me, the bar's not good enough. I can drink elsewhere, in better company.'

'That you can not, my wee mannie!' bawled Fraser. 'And fine you ken it. So don't be letting anger twist the truth in your mouth. There's not a house in the place worth wetting your whistle in, bar Hector Fraser's.'

'Hell, then,' said Gavin, between amusement and irritation, 'what would you have me do? Trail back to Braelochy, my dry tongue licking the dust?'

'You might do worse, laddie. But och, sit you down where you are, and stop girning. Since here you are, here you can bide. For I'll not send you away to mix with all yon godless clamjamphrie of drunken, maundering, whoring, witless blellums across in McNish's bawdy-house—and that's where you'd be going, I've no doubt at all.'

How right you are, thought Gavin. That's where I am going, just as soon as I'm good and ready. But it was early yet and nothing doing, and so he sat demurely down on the end of Hector's horse-hair sofa and glanced across at what he could see of his ungenial host, head and shoulders outcropping from the darkening window and his face in shadow, giving nothing away but dour silence.

'Do you think,' ventured Gavin, 'do you think I might ask you to get me a pint?'

The glass crashed down on the table, spattering its contents. 'Do I what?' thundered Fraser, his side-whiskers bristling in silhouette. 'God preserve me! Are you for treating me like some twopenny-ha'penny tapster—and me sitting private in my own back parlour? Where were you bred, boy? Get you a pint, says you! Am I to rise from my table of an evening in my own house and run at the arse of every milk-mouthed loon that ettles for a pint his belly's hardly big enough to carry? Fetch you a pint, says you! I'm in the mind to fetch the tawse and skelp you into some respect for your elders.' He paused for a moment, want of breath staying his vehemence, and then grumbled on: 'Still and all, since you're here, thrusting in like the lustiest in a sty, belike you'd look less out of place with a drink before you. Ay, so you would likely. Well then, you know where it's kept, fine enough, don't you? Away through and draw a pint for yourself. The third barrel from the door. And don't be forgetting to put your siller in the drawer, mind. Fetch you a pint, by God,' he muttered to Gavin's retreating back. 'In my own back parlour, the impudent hafflin!'

Gavin found himself in the tap-room, the bar on his left and on his right a row of barrels mounted on gantries. Little of the evening light came through the windows placarded with brewers' notices, and the inhospitable howff, stone-flagged and gloomy and fetid, held little promise of symposial elegance. A place of purvey it was merely, forbidding even for him, who still affected a partiality for the sordid. He came to the third barrel, the spigot dripping into a flaked enamelled pitcher. The cat, hunched on the barrel regarding him dispassionately, suddenly came to life, arching its spine and snarling over his stooping shoulders. Gavin straightened himself and looked behind. A sheep-dog entered, nose to ground, through the loose leaves of the swing-door. It sniffed in small circles round the doorway, paused, and raised a questioning head towards Gavin and the spitting cat behind the bar, holding them a long moment at wondering gaze, all three together in the gloom, hearts beating, blood pulsing, eyes shining, and behind their looking eyes what unknown, incomprehensible what? Then, dismissing them, it scratched a little in a leisurely, uninterested fashion, cocked a leg against the doorpost, and thrust its way out. Gavin eyed the puddle forming in the hollowed flagstone scooped out by Ferlie topers down the years.

'What the hell's keeping you in there?' came Fraser's voice from the parlour. 'Are you having a fly one, you young chancer?'

'No, Mr Fraser, of course I'm not. I'll be with you right away.'

'Hech! I can wait for that, right enough,' Gavin heard him mutter through a smothered chuckle. 'But you're not to be meddling with yon spigots. Faith, I could have drawn off a barrel in that time. Ay, and drunk it too, maybe. And mind, if you drink two pints, pay for two. There's no drinks on the house in Hector Fraser's. Not even for his trusty cronies of a week-end's standing.'

Gavin could hear him rumbling with derision, and he grinned ruefully as he bent to the tap. Ridiculous to resent the queer old fellow's leg-pulling—for that was all it was, and the expected reaction only provoked him to further malice. Niven had warned him of Fraser's unconventional style of hostelling and his special penchant for ragging young townies like himself. It was a challenge he could scarcely refuse, with Niven's quizzing blue eyes on him. Besides, he had liked the talk of the men he had met in the parlour, friable and fertile as the soil they nursed, and full of reminiscence of the rural past in which he had found so unsought an interest. There was an ingenuous earthy reality in all this Ferlie ambience that charmed him by its contrast with the book-buttressed, daedalian culture that imprisoned him.

The beer was frothing over the rim, down his inexpert arm, up his sleeve, into the pitcher. Turn off the tap, for Christ's sake! He'll charge you for two. He wiped his hands on a sodden napkin draped over the barrel, winked at the cat, and moved through into the parlour, leaving a spatter of beer in his wake.

'Sorry I took so long, Mr Fraser,' he said, resuming his seat. 'Beer's a bit brisk, isn't it?'

'Ach man, I didn't miss you that much,' said Fraser across the darkness. 'And brisk, is it now? It's for brisk men, laddie. Would you be having beer come seeping out flat as a dead cow's milk, then?'

'I don't think I've ever seen a dead cow's milk, Mr Fraser,' replied Gavin meekly, and dipped his nose into the beer's top.

'No, like enough, like enough. You'll be nearer acquainted with your own mother's, I'm thinking.'

'Oh, come now, Mr Fraser,' Gavin remonstrated mildly, looking along the waiting beds in the maternity ward. 'I'm not quite so young and inexperienced as all that, you know.'

Fraser clucked through his moustache. 'Young is it you're not then?' said he. 'Ay, you're no doubt old enough to have mouthed other nipples than your mother's. Fine I know you randy young stots. But don't be thinking you've a weight of years on you yet. Nor a wealth of worldly experience. There's a lot you'll not have seen, my bonnie young man. Ay. You'll not have seen the wee drawer, maybe, ben there in the bar. Have you then?' and his voice came like a bomb blast out of the darkness, so that Gavin started in his seat, spilling beer all down his trouser leg.

'God almighty Mr Fraser!' he exclaimed with vexation. 'There's no need to tell the whole village, is there? I'm not deaf.'

'Maybe not. But you don't see any too well, do you?'

'Come now, you're not thinking I meant to drink without paying? As for seeing—that place in there's as black as the devil's insides. Don't you ever light a lamp?'

'Don't be telling me how to run my house! I'll light a lamp when the time comes. There's aye light enough for a man to see to pay his score—if he's a mind to.'

'Nonsense, man,' said Gavin, uncertain whether he wanted to laugh or lose his temper. 'I clean forgot about the money, and that's the truth. But here it is now.' And he rose, fumbling with the change in his pocket. But Fraser's voice came at him again, arresting him.

'And will you stand there and fish for pennies to pass across my own table to me in my own parlour, you brazen young gomeril? Have you no sense of the thing at all? D'you pay your lass at the door, when she takes you ben for supper—and whatever else she's fool enough to give you? In the name of God, boy, have you no respect for anything? Will you fling your host a sweaty shilling for a drink, and he entertaining you—like a friend—in his own back parlour? What sort of men are they rearing nowadays, for God's sake?'

Gavin struggled in vain against his anger. 'To hell with you and your back parlour!' he shouted. 'I was a fool to set foot in it, you crabbed old devil! But I'll not leave till I've sunk this pint, say what you will, and be damned to you, parlour and all!' And he tossed a coin on the table.

'Och now, the laddie has a temper,' said Fraser with grotesque irony. 'Well, well now. I was thinking the smeddum had been all bred out of you pavement-piddling sheep from the towns. Eh, but I am surprised right enough. I am so. It's very gratifying, now, to find the makings of a man, where a body never expected to. But just to please a crabbit old devil, take up your siller again, and get you away ben with it to the wee drawer, or as God's my judge'—and his voice bellowed out again—'you'll drink no pint in here!'

Gavin hesitated in the middle of the room, searching for Fraser's face, which he knew would belie his wrathful accents; but his host spoke from the invisible almost, like some angry god uttering from a cloud to overawe his erring votary. The clock in the corner ticked ponderously and footsteps clumped across the floor upstairs. Inclined he was to defy the old sore-head and leave him to it; but there was nothing to gain from petulant obstinacy and nothing to lose in surrender. Give the old dotard his little victory. *Jeunesse oblige.*

He set down his beaker on the table and fingered for the coin. 'I'm sorry, Mr Fraser,' he said humbly. 'I'm sure I didn't mean to be insulting. I hope you'll not hold it against me.' And he veered uncertainly towards the door.

'No lad, I'll not be holding anything against you. Devil the bit,' said Fraser, complacent in triumph. 'And when you're there, fetch back the bottle of Special from the shelf in below the drawer. You'll never mistake it. There's only it there by itself, more's the pity.'

The cat's eyes shone dimly from the barrel as Gavin palmed his way along the bar. The woodwork was sticky with unmopped overflow, and the drawer-handle came away in his fingers. But he managed and, finding the bottle underneath, made his way back to set it down carefully by Fraser's hand.

'Why don't you keep this beside you in here, Mr Fraser?' he asked, to break the silence which, in the deepening darkness, began to unnerve him. He almost heard Fraser's brows come down.

'What's that?' said he irritably. 'You're not telling me it vexes you to do a bit service like that for me, are you now?'

'Heavens no, Mr Fraser! Of course not. I was just thinking it would be handier, that's all.'

'Handier, is it? Man, you're right. It would be that. It's a deal too handy where it is though.'

He found an empty glass on the window-ledge behind him, and Gavin heard the liquor leap from the bottle. The glass was pushed along the table towards him. 'There now,' said Fraser, with grudging geniality, 'get that down your craw and content you. Hector Fraser's not such a crabbit old devil after all.'

He sat without speaking for some time, while Gavin listened to his breathing and his fingers tapping the table-top and a whisky belch stifled in his throat. And presently he continued musingly, as though forgetful of Gavin's presence: 'But eh, he's a worried man. Fell perplexed in mind. Ay that. It's small wonder you had no great welcome tonight, laddie, rushing in here foolish-like where angels wait to tread.'

'Angels! In your back parlour, Mr Fraser?' exclaimed Gavin with an involuntary smile which, even in the darkness, he banished for a traitor, thinking the while that there were no angels here the last time or he'd had more to drink than he thought. What was the old fellow raving about? He repeated, with an attempt at gravity: 'Angels did you say, sir?'

'Ay, that's what I said right enough,' answered Fraser, adding with a resurgence of his old ferocity: 'And don't be letting mockery rise up in your empty young heart!'

'Nothing of the kind, Mr Fraser, believe me. A man's bound to be astonished to find he's forestalled an angel into Hector Fraser's house.'

'Forestalled, d'you say! The angel I'm expecting nobody forestalls. Deed no, he bides his own good time, and comes when he's ready. And I'm thinking he's near hand now. Three publicans he's come at this month and I see no reason why he should pass by me—a sinner if ever publican was. Three struck down in a month. There's old Macfarlane at the Crown—a fortnight come tomorrow. Young Robertson, over to Carsie, last week—and he with a wife and three bairns. And only yesterday, that rascal McNish at the Thrawn Wife—and I hope the devil's boiling him in hell in a barrel of his own watered whisky, the slandering, swindling, womanising reprobate!'

Gavin began to understand. He took a pull at his glass to steady himself, and spoke into the darkness: 'This angel you're speaking of, Mr Fraser—do I understand you mean the angel of...?'

'Of death, laddie,' said Fraser valiantly. 'Don't be blate to say it outright. There's no sense in being feart of him. He'll come just the same, if come he will. And I'm bound to think,' he continued, his voice drooping at the corners, 'he'll not be long. And me no ways ready for him—what with six cases of Special due in next week. Eh, but it's hard to thole.'

'But Mr Fraser,' said Gavin, constrained to attempt reassurance, 'what reason can you possibly have for fearing death?'

'Who said I was fearing death?' roared Fraser, thumping the table. 'Mind your tongue, boy! I said nothing of fearing, did I?'

'I didn't mean it that way. Expecting death, I should have said. Why on earth should you be?'

'Why, you ask? Am I not telling you? Have you no gumption at all? no understanding? Am I wasting my time—the wee bit time that's maybe left to me—confiding in a fusionless loon with no more sense in him than Bella's glaikit skivvy? Why, says you! Three licensees in the district snuffed out in as many weeks, and you ask why I'm expecting a call! What for would I not be? Tell me that, will you? Who am I to escape the scourge of the avenger? the wrath of a jealous God? The Almighty's plainly making a set at the trade—who's to blame Him?—and I can't let on He's like to make an exception of Hector Fraser.'

He spoke with such patent sincerity, such a penitent resignation to a just but grievous condemnation that Gavin found himself seriously concerned to disabuse him. He was too precipitate, however. 'Come Mr Fraser,' said he, 'you're not telling me you actually believe there's anything in these deaths but sheer coincidence?'

There was a brief, almost frightening hiatus between them. And then Fraser uttered a strange growl, like a lion, thought Gavin, mouthing its kill. 'Coincidence, is it!' said he, with majestic contempt. 'I believe in no such heathenish, scientific invention, I'll have you know, my clever young man. There is no such mechanical contraption in Hector Fraser's creed. And don't you be preaching damnable heresy in my back parlour with a glass of Special in front of you—and it not paid for. Coincidence, says you! I never heard such irreligious, godless paganism since Macandrew got in here one night, while I was out at the back for a minute. But I'll have none of it! I know when the hand of the Lord is over me, and I sit in its shadow now, and wait. And don't you be lighting any of your penny candles of rationalism to drive the shadow away, for I'll snuff them out as easily as He'll snuff me out—and you out—when the time comes. Hallelujah!'

And Gavin heard him swallow a mighty dram from his glass and smack it down on the table. Gavin had no answer to this. At first mildly amused by the old man's morbid apprehensions, and then generously engaged to dispel them, he was beginning to find them envelop him, and himself with little power of opposition. Fraser's breathing quivered through the room and the clock ticked like a deathwatch beetle in the corner and through the door the unsleeping cat's eyes glimmered now and then in the dying light, as if signalling some baleful oracle that transcribed itself in his reeling fancy. The hand of the Lord is over the house, recoiled from the rake McNish, the good man Robertson, the senile Macfarlane, hovering to smite again and spare not the acolytes of the trade, ministrants at the alien shrine. The Lord thy God is a jealous God before Whom thou shalt have no other. Too long have I suffered in silence your effluent libations to the heathen. But now My wrath is kindled against you, traders in wine of mockery, raging liquor of blasphemy and iniquitous turning away from the straight and narrow. And I will send Azrael, Angel of Death, to destroy you, one after one, and overturn your vats and tuns of sacrificial offering, until all is utterly destroyed and vanished from the face of the earth. Once, twice, not twice but three times, have his pinions shadowed Ferlie and the death-mark brands your brow, Hector Fraser, ancient and stubborn in conscious sinfulness. Vengeance is Mine, said the Lord. I will repay. Azrael is coming, with death on the lintel.

Gavin's thoughts, merging in tipsy sympathy with the fuddled death expectancy of Fraser brooding in the dark, were interrupted by a sudden rapping on the outer door. He leapt off the sofa, to stand trembling, poised for escape from death knocking at the gate. 'In God's name,' he whispered, 'what's that?'

'What ails you, man?' said Fraser testily, moving in his chair. 'Lowping there like a flushed hare. I can hear your chappers chattering from here. Are you feart in the dark, then? Here, have another nip.' And he slid the bottle across.

'But who is it?' asked Gavin, handling bottle and glass unsteadily.

'Ca' cannie there now, laddie,' cautioned Fraser anxiously. 'A shaky hand's fell hard on a bottle of whisky. Who is it, says you? Ach, it's just the lads clamouring for drink, what else? Bella's late down the night, whatever's keeping her. But let them cool their heels a bittie longer. It'll not harm them at all.'

'But the bar door's open,' said Gavin, puzzled.

'Ay, it is that. Always open at the statutory hours. I know the law, young man, and uphold it.'

'But . . . but why don't they come in, then?'

'Just let them try,' said Fraser, grimly jocular. 'The sodden bar-propping wastrels! I'll have none of them ben there till I'm good and ready for them. And that's not till Bella's down to serve them. She's late a wee. But she'll be down directly, and in they'll troop, breinging and jostling like pigs to a filled trough, to load their bellies with swill and away home ranting to their wives. Eh, but it's small wonder the Lord's hand's risen at last against the trade, for it's a Godless, back-turning business when all's said. Ay, it is that. Still and all, I'll be sorry to go. Faith, but I will so.' And he gave vent to a mournful, hiccoughing sigh and purled another measure from the bottle.

And now, Gavin, determined to merit the old man's hospitality and vindicate his long nights of tipsy eloquence in undergraduate rooms, collected himself and gave voice: 'Now look, Mr Fraser, I'll just not listen to that kind of talk from a man like you. It's clear to me you're hale and hearty as a youngster, and all Ferlie knows it. Why, you're good for another twenty years at least—and be damned to the curse on publicans!'

The onslaught of retaliation he expected for this daring sacrilege was not forthcoming, and so, draining his glass, he swept on with the spirit burning through him: 'Admittedly, the fact that three men in so small an area as Ferlie, all engaged in the identical profession, vocation, or trade, to wit, the sale of spirituous and malted liquors—the fact, I say, that three such men have, in so brief a period of time, been summarily summoned to account, may to the unenquiring mind present a curious, even ominous, aspect—especially if the mind in question is predisposed to accept such sudden summons as a just and proper judgment on the parties involved, by reason of the allegedly sinful, God-provoking character of their calling. Now, these two hypotheses I mention most certainly are valid in your case, Mr Fraser, who are a publican in Ferlie, like the dear departed, and one, moreover, admittedly much vexed in mind and grievously perturbed by consciousness—unwarranted, I may remark in passing—of the graceless and maleficent influence exerted by your purveyance. And though I would never presume to suggest you have an unenquiring or superstitious mind, yet I would hazard that long and lonely contemplation of the aforementioned circumstances, allied with a naturally humble and God-fearing spirit, has blunted your perception of the real nature of the situation and persuaded you to a quite erroneous interpretation in line with your conviction of persistent sin, meriting death. Do I make myself clear, Mr Fraser?'

'Faith, laddie,' replied Fraser at once—to Gavin's astonishment, who had begun to think him asleep from his negative response to this harangue—'Faith, laddie, but it's the whisky speaking, and what could be clearer than my Special? Ay, you've the gift of the gab, all right, and a good heart with it forbye. Here, have another drappie. You'll never bend me, but I like your trying. It argues a friendly spirit.'

'Thanks, Mr Fraser. You honour me indeed,' replied Gavin, rising with a dignified bow to his invisible opposite. 'But if you'll listen, I shall prove on grounds of logic, doctrine, and common sense, that your meek submission to the rod of chastisement is undemanded and untimely, indeed unchristian.' And he took advantage of his inclined posture to secure the proffered bottle.

'Hech! do you tell me that now?' exclaimed Fraser condescendingly. Gavin ignored this, hotly pursuing his argument.

'Consider, first, your belief that the Lord has risen to sickle down the publicans of Ferlie for evil doing. This conviction you base on the close series of three deaths among the neighbouring licensees. But when three ploughmen die in near succession, do all glebe-treaders trudge in the shadow, keeking back at the gulls for doom-ravens? If three pedestrians dying monthly in the city streets presaged divine revenge on jay-walkers, who would not order his coffin forthwith?'

'Bide a wee, young Daniel,' interposed Fraser. 'I'll not have that. Damn that for a false analogy, if ever I heard one. Three out of tens of thousands is a different proscription from three out of a miserable death-marked half-dozen that was. And forbye that, pedestrians, if all I hear is true, are courting death each time they cross a street. Theirs is a fell perilous existence.'

'And what of yours, Mr Fraser?' Gavin rejoined. 'What of yours? I'd scarcely call yours a sheltered occupation—or if sheltered, the danger shelters with you. Tell me, now, how did McNish come to his end?'

'McNish! Why, it's well kent for twelve miles round the rakehell rascal drank and whored himself to death.'

'Did he now? Did he now' said Gavin with portentous significance. 'And Robertson, that good young man, so cruelly torn from wife and orphaned bairns, what carried him off?'

'I'm not right sure, to tell the truth. But I do hear tell he fell arse over tip down his cellar stairs and broke his neck, poor devil.'

'Well now, and would you credit that?' said Gavin. 'Both of them, you see, Mr Fraser, killed in the line of duty, as you might say. It's evident enough yours is a dangerous calling, sir. There's no denying it. And old Macfarlane was it? What of him?'

'Ach man, he's been dead for years, the dribbling, gin-soaked old dotard. The Lord was only collecting an outstanding debt when he took Macfarlane.'

'Reflect now, Mr Fraser,' Gavin adjured him gravely, wagging a finger in comical but unseen admonition. 'Let us recapitulate and examine what you base your grisly expectation on. Three publicans dead in a month, you say. But of the three, one died long ago; another by a most untimely accident; and the third by his own hand, or other member appertaining. If Macfarlane had gone when he should have, Robertson put more water in it that night, and so postponed his departure a while, you would have not three publicans carried off in a month but one—and that one a shame to an honourable profession and a damned good riddance all round. How can you claim to see the hand of punitive Jehovah over all in the belated death of one profligate publican?'

Gavin took a deep breath, a sip of his glass, and a long, blind look across at the dormant but rumbling Fraser, who spoke up for the honour of the house but with some of the froth gone off him: 'Ay, ay, young man, very clever, very clever, no doubt. If "ifs" and "ans" were pots and pans, the tinkers would go hungry. All your fine learned disquisition and argument have in no way altered the stubborn fact that Macfarlane and McNish and Roberston did not die when your untimely accidents and so forth might have taken them. They died, all three, in quick succession, this very month. Ay, did they—all three of them.'

Gavin dismissed this feeble counter with a large gesture. 'A purely fortuitous circumstance, Mr Fraser,' he remarked lightly.

'Fortuitous, my foot!' roared Fraser, erupting again to Gavin's dismay. 'A circumstance foreordained and brought to pass by divine decree. Predestined from immemorial time, you infant heathen, and irresistible as the crack of doom!'

A thunderous assault on the outer door drowned his further speaking and brought Gavin again to his feet despite himself. 'Whisht, will you then, you impudent whelps!' Fraser shouted at the window behind him. 'You'll knock more cannie at the gates of hell, when your time comes, I'm thinking. But faith, I'll have to see what's come over Bella,' he added irritably to himself. 'She's fell behind her time the night. Bide you here, young man, while I come back.'

Gavin heard him creaking out of his chair. 'I'll away and draw myself another pint, Mr Fraser, if I may,' said he.

'In you go then, laddie. But I canna see at all for why you

want to mix that horse water—and pay for it, forbye, mind—with my Special that I'm pouring down your thrapple for nothing. God help me, but it's droll men they're rearing now, right enough. Ay, orra kind of men.'

As he groped his way none too steadily along the bar, Gavin hear him calling angrily: 'Bella! Bella, what ails you, lass? It'll be closing time before you open. Where have you got to, woman?'

When Gavin returned, carrying his spilling pint with extravagant precision, and resettled himself on the sofa, he still heard the old man moving and mumbling on the stairs. Gavin perceived that he was becoming pleasantly tight. He knew by his unwonted loquacity, his sedate and studied movements, by the drumming of the blood in his ears. He smiled a funny little smile to himself in the darkness, and, keenly catching himself at it, he knew too by that. So he smiled another little smile to prove it. Hector's Special certainly was special. He took a long pull at his mug, for he was thirsty. Drinking always made him thirsty—as if increase of appetite had grown by . . . something or another. Hamlet it was said that, he recalled. But not about drink. Hamlet took a poor view of the late sessions at Elsinore. He'd not feel at home in Ferlie at all, at all. But then Hamlet wouldn't feel much at home anywhere. Took a poor view of the whole mortal coil, he did. Pessimistic type he was—full of gall and bitterness. Like that daft minister Macandrew he was—though not in the matter of liquor certainly. For Macandrew liked his whisky, your whisky, anybody's whisky. A powerful liking for the stuff he had. Reasoned the business out too. Purest thing a man can put in his belly. Hardly scientific reasoning that, though. Metaphysical flight rather—religious, poetic, you might say. The same kind of extravagant fancy as had conjured up this illusion of a monstrous presence here in the darkness with him. From the moment he had sat down, he had sensed the thing beside him, at the other end of the sofa, and fled from its mere possibility into rambling contemplation of his own alcoholic confusion of mind, which might be made to account for it. Which must be made to account for it. No such divine or diabolic visitant found bed and board in Gavin Ewart's philosophy. Nothing incapable of clinical dissection walked the earth for him. No ghosts, goblins, or things that went bump in the night dismayed him, waking or sleeping, drunk, sober, or half and between. But why didn't old Fraser return to help in disputation push further back this usurping conviction of Azrael's intrusion, which his premonitions had surely summoned?

Gavin felt his skin prickle and the chill oozing from his armpits. There was something beside him, something uncanny, something hostile, at odds with life, at home here in the menacing darkness. The beaker in his sweaty hand slopped beer over to splash on the floor, but he held on to it tightly, dreading to stir and put it down lest movement should excite the thing to action. Stay silent, feigning ignorance, and without provocation or excuse it might vanish, discouraged, whence it came. Push down the upwelling clamour in his throat, the panic urge to rush screaming from the room, the alien triumphant at his heels. Match its own relentless patience, refuse acknowledgement, and it was powerless to harm him, fenced, as it must remain, outside the charmed circle of his disdain. Maintain this immunity only a little longer, till Fraser returned with the lamps and some salvo of abuse on the fretting topers outside to exorcise the angelic fiend. But Fraser lay dead at the foot of the stairs, fallen arse over tip to his expected doom, his blood puddling round his grey whiskers, fourth vessel of wrath shattered beneath the just Lord's decree on his kind and old Bella the belated cowered petrified in some faraway cupboard, hiding from the shadow of death that was over the house, and the waiting carousers had fallen silent and skulked home one by one, overawed by the presence, and the presence was here in the parlour with him—Azrael, Angel of Death, herald of irate Jehovah, exhaling the odour of perdition from folded wings on the sofa's end. Grimalkin on the beer barrel hunched, basilisk unwinking, in midst of mad Walpurgis reeling while swinging gibbet corpses beckoned him to join the dance careering in the kirkyard, and dissolute McNish, cleeking a Cutty Sark on each arm, leered promise from a new-dug grave, and Robertson, sprawled in drunken remorse down the infernal escalade, bewailed his orphan bairns. Old grizzled, blood-bedabbled Hector, upturning an empty whisky bottle, grinned mocking vindication of his death-divining. And the shadow of death was over all, smelling of the mould. It spread to overcloud him. The gruesome circle widened to include him. Grimalkin arched and spat in fury. Azrael the doom-bringer stirred to action on the sofa's end. Dry-mouthed and gasping with terror, Gavin shrank where he sat, completely spent and dismayed. The glass left his fingers and crashed on the stone flags.

Fraser came in carrying a lamp, which he set on the table. 'You clumsy young fool!' he exclaimed, turning on Gavin. 'Yon's one of my best beer-mugs. Why, you're white as whey, man.

What's come over you, in God's name?'

Gavin sat speechless, staring at the sofa's end. Fraser bent and shook him by the shoulder. 'Ach, laddie,' he chuckled, 'I doubt your stomach's not weaned for my Special yet awhile. You're looking gey poorly. You'd best have a wee dram to pull you round, I'm thinking.'

He turned away to find the bottle and recoiled in astonishment. On the edge of the perimeter of new lamplight sat Macandrew, bland as a degenerate Buddha, Gavin's whisky-glass in his hand, the bottle at his feet.

'Where the hell,' asked Fraser with disgust, 'did you come from? Under the stones?'

'Good evening, Hector,' said Macandrew equably. 'Your good health.' And he tossed over his drink. 'Our young friend here appears somewhat distressed. Your discourse has maybe proved too much for him.'

'And what would you be knowing about our discourse? Tell me that, now.'

'You know well enough, Hector now, I have always an ear for intelligent argument.'

'A nose for whisky, you mean,' muttered Hector.

'Especially conducted in the forthright manner you employ, Hector. And the savour I caught from without prompted me to join you. In the hope, too, that I might bring some comfort to a sore perplexed member of my flock.'

'I'd sooner seek comfort from the Pope in Rome—or Auld Nick himself! And fine you ken it,' said Hector scornfully. 'There's no welcome for you in my house, Mr Macandrew.' Retrieving the bottle, he turned his back on Macandrew and glowered at Gavin, as if reproaching him for conjuring up the minister to discomfit him.

'Ah, Hector,' said Macandrew, 'it's stubborn in Godliness you are. And your heart is shut tight against aught but your own bigotry. It's a graceless thing in a man of your years is sinful pride, Hector. It is that, now.'

Rejoinder to this inverted accusation was prevented by the irruption of Bella, carrying in each hand a lamp for the tap room. 'God save us, the minister!' she exclaimed, arrested momentarily in her hurrying passage. But, glimpsing Hector's louring brow, she speedily continued into the bar. Whereupon a minor bedlam arose, which swept into the parlour and reduced them, all three, to temporary silence.

Through the swing-doors came a clatter of boots and a babel of voices raised in angry or jesting complaint against Bella's tardiness, clamour for drink, and exhortation to make good the wasted minutes of waiting.

'Jesus, woman,' said one. 'A fine end to a Saturday this—with scarce time for a dram before the bus goes.'

'There's other pubs to drink in,' retorted Bella. 'If drink's all you're wanting.'

'Ay maybe,' shouted another. 'But it's not just the drink brings Geordie here. And it's you kens that, my bonnie woman.'

'Shame on you, Charlie Simpson,' came Bella's voice above the laughter. 'What kind of a way is that to be talking, then?'

Came another voice, slurred with liquor: 'Ay, there's other places, right enough,Bella—'

'I can see plain enough you know where they are, Archie Murdoch.'

'Ach, he's not particular whose bottle it comes from, is Archie. Just as long as it keeps coming—steady-like.'

'Ay, but still,' persisted Archie, 'there's none of you'll deny there's only the one Hector Fraser's. There's none of you'll deny that, now. And you're fell late, Bella, in opening up the night.'

'Your wife'll thank me for that, Archie. For the world kens her cleckin' o' bairns was aye fathered on Saturday nights.'

There was a crescendo of acclaim for this sally: 'Good for you, Bella!' 'God, you've touched him there, Bella!' 'Archie, man what d'you say to that?'

Murdoch's voice came with a rising inflection of anger in it: 'That's a gey doubtful-like thing for a decent single woman to be saying, Bella Fraser. Think shame on you, then.'

'Havers, man. Single indeed! What's the odds between married and single? Your wife was a decent single woman till you married her.'

'I'll thank you to keep your clippit tongue off my wife, then. There's not a finer lass for twelve miles round. And fine you ken it, Bella Fraser, that went to school with her.' Murdoch was furious, in fuddled righteousness, and his voice rose loud and lonely in the hush that stilled the company.

'Whisht, Archie man,' said Bella quietly. 'Dinna mind my daffing tongue. It's no secret for twelve miles round she's too good for the man she's got. Here's your nip. Drink it up, lad, and away home tell her I said so. Eh now, and it's you, young Alec, is it?' she went on. 'And what's your pleasure, my bonnie young man?

Whisky, is it, then? Faith, it's lucky old Niven's not ben the parlour and me selling his Benjamin whisky. I'm loth to do it, at that. Still, if you don't get it here, you'll likely get it otherwhere. But if your da catches you fou the night, don't be letting on I helped you.'

'Oh, you needn't worry, Miss Fraser. I'm not so easy made drunk. He'll never know a thing about it anyway.'

'That he'll not, by God!' someone interposed, laughing. 'Old Niven's too fou himself the night to bother himself about Alec. I saw him in the Crown an hour syne, drinking whisky in a half-pint tumbler, and boasting of the black mare he's bought from Murray up at Gralloch.'

'And a braw beast she is, too. Seventeen hands and a chest like Mary Taggart's.'

'Ach now, there's a lass for you, Alec. God, she's got enough to make up for all the chances you've missed.'

'You're right there, Jock,' said another through the mocking laughter. 'Man, I saw her posing at the Cross this afternoon. Dressed up to the ninety-nines she was—in her wee sister's yellow jumper and a skimpy bit black skirt, that tight across her hurdies you could near see the furrow between them. Jesus, if I wasn't so far ben with my Ellen, I'd have a go at yon myself. Ay, would I!'

'Ach Wull, there's not much wrong with Ellen, is there? I'd not mind being as far ben with Ellen. She's got a right bonny twin-set—as they call it—herself, has Ellen.'

'You're telling me, now, are you, randy Tam? Ellen Macdonald's my lass. And if I catch you as much as squinting the road she's on, I'll break your bloody neck, so I will.'

'You might try, at that,' came the answer, matching in truculence. 'But I'd not be so bloody sure of the outcome.'

'That'll do, then,' came Meg's voice, sharply. 'We'll have none of that here or out you go—every last one of you.'

'Come, Bella, don't be daft,' intervened another, conciliatorily. 'You know fine there's never any fighting among us. They're just joking, these two. Always at it—especially when there's lasses in it. Put them up again, Bella, please. Four pints—and one for young Alec.'

And then in a loud undertone, heard because of the group's position by the door, he added fiercely: 'For Christ's sake, shut up, you two. Fine you ken how strict Bella is about argy-bargying in here.'

'Well, let him keep his filthy tongue off Ellen Macdonald, then.'

'Heavens man, Tam was meaning no harm. Don't be so damned touchy. What did you say just a minute syne—about Mary Taggart?'

'Ach, that's not the same at all! Ellen's my lass. None of you has any claim on Mary, or I'd never laid tongue on her. Mary's on the loose. She's asking to be talked about.'

'Ay, you're not far out there, Wull. She's asking for more than talk about her, is Mary. She's itching for a man about her. That's plain to a half-blind tinker.'

'Ay, and I'm thinking she'll not have long to wait.'

'Like enough, with lowping rams like you about the place, Tam. Old Bella back there's not safe herself from the likes of you. Thanks Bella. Ay, that's right. Five pints. If they want nips, they can buy them. Here, lads, drink up. Time's wearing on.'

'Ach,' said Wull's voice, disparagingly, 'Mary Taggart's not for Tam. A cut above a tractor-driver yon mare is. Young Alec here's the lad for Mary, no two ways about it. Eh Alec, what do you say?'

'Who? Me and Mary Taggart? Lord, Wull, I doubt I'd never have the nerve for Mary. She'd laugh at me, likely.'

'Laugh at you? And why that?'

'Well,' came Alec's voice diffidently, 'I'm not much of a hand with the lasses, Wull. And it's fine they know it.'

'Ay, you're maybe a wee bit slow. But God, I'll bet a pickle of them are keen enough to quicken you—old Niven of Braelochy's son!'

'Man, Alec, you don't make the most of your chances.'

'He does not, then! Half the cattle in Ferlie would drop them the night for a chance at a share of what's coming to you, Alec.'

'And the other half have dropped them already for a share of what comes to me,' said Tam, complacently. 'Eh, lads, you're bound to admit it. It's not what a man's father has the lasses care about. It's what he has himself.'

'Did you ever hear the like of that!' exclaimed Wull's voice, between laughter and resentment. 'You don't half fancy your chance, you wee kail-runt you. You'd think all the lasses in Ferlie were in heat for you.'

'Ach well, now, there's more than a few of them have been, one time or another. And I doubt the rest will be, sooner or later. Good gear comes out of small book, you ken, lads.'

'There's one lass that'll not be—and don't you forget it!'

'Where ignorance is bliss, Wull—we'd maybe best leave it there, eh?'

'Why, you bloody wee—! I'll knock the—!'

'For God's sake, shut up, you damned loud-mouthed fools,' intervened again the peacemaker, but too late. For Bella's voice from the far end spoke decisively: 'That's enough, then, you drunken young devils. Out you get! Come now. Drink up your drinks and get out.'

'But it's all right, Bella. I'll keep them quiet. There'll be no rough house. Don't worry.'

'There will not, then. It's not the Thrawn Wife you're in, mind that. Swearing and blaspheming and dragging decent lasses' names through the muck, you dirty young messans! That'll maybe do across the street, where there's none that's not stoven in drink and debauchery. But it'll not do in here. And you, Alec Niven, think shame—consorting with such-like wastrel company. If your mother or Marion hears tell of it, you'll not have your troubles to seek. Now away with the whole scummy boiling of you—don't be showing your faces in here till you think you can behave yourselves.'

'But what harm are we doing? Can a man not be having a friendly bit argument in a pub?' expostulated Wull. And Tam's less moderate tones came disparagingly: 'Pub? Who'd be calling this a pub? More like Macandrew's kirk this is. A good pub wasted—with the likes of you and yon Holy-Willie Hector in it.'

'That's enough of your lip, Tam Macleod. I'll wrap this dish-clout about your lugs, if I come across to you. Out you get now, or I'll have himself from ben the parlour to you.'

With much thudding of empty glasses on the bar and angry muttering, they finally clattered out, and the tap-room was left in comparative silence with Bella recriminating to such as remained in douce confabulation at the other end.

During all this half-drunken clavering in the bar, the parlour had remained in silence, at first because the noise next door had prevented conversation, and when the initial uproar had subsided, for reasons personal to the three inmates. Macandrew, more at home in utter quietude than anywhere, would willingly have maintained it all night except to ask for drink, and such request he judged inadvisable just then. Fraser sat, dour in his chair by the window, refusing to acknowledge his enemy's presence yet hesitant to eject him. And Gavin slouched in the sofa corner, fighting his way up from the pit down which Macandrew's apparition had thrust him, befogged with whisky; and having reached a comparatively normal state of consciousness, he found himself engrossed in the conversation from beyond the door, the more completely because he was by now attuned to the key it was played in.

This Mary Taggart, now, seemed a more promising companion than glum old Hector moriturus or moribund Macandrew. From Wull's appreciative outline she seemed a likely lass enough and only one of many game to wanton a little more or less when occasion offered. A little squalid dalliance would refresh him after this session of liquor and arid disputation. He knew what he wanted—not necessarily much, but something. He wanted something else, too; and with a muttered apology, he rose to go in search of it.

The night air hit him like a buffet on the mouth and sent him reeling. Shaking his head like a wet spaniel, he leant his brow against the wall above the stinking gutter. You look gey poorly, Hector had said: and he didn't feel so good, recalling white sheets and his mother's cool hand on his forehead. Go to sleep now, Gavin. You'll be all better again in the morning. It must be something you ate. Something you ate. He smiled wryly and found difficulty in getting his mouth back into repose, so dry it was and stiff. If she saw him now, fumbling to make water against a wall, his legs buckling under him, their flannel sopping with spilled beer! From the middle down you look well enough, with the parts of a man under the chin-drawn sheets perhaps. Who said that? mother and daughter? both or neither? Mush of a mushness—like his parts of a man from the middle down, not much use to either of them now, or Mary Taggart arched at the Cross in her wee sister's jumper with the vomit spattering all down her beauty. But retching painfully, he yet perceived that was not Mary but the daft minister's daft daughter, who had teased him in the heather with her afternoon sickness jetting suddenly all down the wall all down her blue wool rucked to her oxters by his twin-set hands now palming the masonry. Ach, what a come-down for Gavin rampant, straddled once there now here against the wall, a lad of parts like him, his parts all come to nothing and dangling dejectedly before him like a pot-bellied cupid's.

He sniggered foolishly. The absurd little noise, seeming to splash down the wall in its turn, recalled his maundering wits. Let him get his brain, his expensively educated brain, functioning soberly. He couldn't be drunk on a few glasses of Scotch, surely? He straightened himself, one steadying hand against the wall, and blinked energetically in the darkness. There was the wall, the angle of the wall, with the rain-butt bellying into the cobbled fairway. Approach with circumspect, unhurried step. Drink, toper, drink, and bathe your fevered brow. You'll be all better in the morning, Gavin. Go to sleep now, my little one, pretty one, your curly pow on the cool pillowcase, and mother will kiss you goodnight, her dual fragrance drooping over you into the rain-barrel.

His head, thrust hard from behind, was submerged in the water, and came up sneezing and gasping for breath, with rude laughter in his ears and a voice exclaiming: 'Did I not tell you 'twas young Ewart? I'd ken that hinder-end from any in Ferlie, I would!'

The voice was Niven's, thickened with drink and raised in unwonted joviality. Through streaming eyes Gavin could just discern him and a second figure swaying in the dim close.

'Small respect you're paying Hector's liquor, man—out drinking from the water-butt, by God! Wait till I tell him. Eh, Lachie, what say you!'

'Ach, had he been in our company, he'd not be thirsty for water. But maybe it's some new-fangled, city-like way of drinking the like of you and me'll not be up to, Donald.'

'Deed now, you're maybe right. But ach, the old way's good enough for me. Has Hector not been gleg enough with the bottle, laddie? He can be gey slow to fill up at times with strangers. But you come inby with Lachie and me, and we'll see you're not sent home dry, eh Lachie?'

'Ay, we'll do that. And if you are, lad, there's enough in Donald's pocket there to warm your belly for the night.'

'Whisht, man! That's for the morn. The wise man aye puts by a bittie for the lean time to come. We'll not crack that the night. Dinna forget now.'

'I'll be minding, Donald. Never you fear.'

'And now, bide here a minute, laddie, while we have a bit draigle to ourselves, Lachie and me, and we'll away in, the three of us together and have a dram with Hector.'

They clattered off, steadily enough, their heels striking sparks from the cobbles, and presently he heard them about their business, rumbling with laughter that made him grin ruefully to himself. And then Niven's voice came, serious, out of the splashing darkness:

'Man, Lachie, whyles I think Himself up yonder must have

been fell cannie with the drink, to make us such a muckle hole to pour it into, and such a wee bit spout for it to go out by.'

'Eh Donald, it's not just the most convenient arrangement, I'll agree. But I dinna doubt He had good reason for it.'

'Like enough, like enough, Lachie. I must mind and quiz old Macandrew on the subject. He's a fair mine of knowledge on all matters appertaining to the drink, is Macandrew.'

'Ay. But I'm thinking he's not so well acquaintit with his Master up yonder.'

'No Lachie, I'll allow you're right there. Ay, you're not far wrong when I think of it. Ach, well, let's be getting inby, or Hector'll not be so glad to see us, the thrawn old devil.'

Gavin, meanwhile, pondering escape from the imminent renewal of his session in the parlour, had reluctantly decided against it, fearing Niven's sober censure even more than his drunken approval, and loth to run out on him in so unusually amiable a mood. His unintentional cold douche had fairly cleared his head, and he foresaw that he could, with discretion, make a show and slip out unremarked before long. When they rejoined him, with much back-slapping and jocularity, they all three steered course for the parlour. But before they reached it, Hector's voice came forth, thundering like Knox haranguing the runaway Mary from the pulpit in Saint Giles.

'A generation of vipers, you'll not can deny it. But they'll not sting the flinty heart in your bosom that's helped to nurse them in their ill-doing. You were hearing them ben there, the loose-mouthed, tippling young blellums. Nothing but drink and blasphemy and womanflesh. A shame they are to the fathers that begat them and the Church that's supposed to direct them. What's to come of a people whose young men are wholly surrendered to flesh and the Devil?'

'In God's name, who's he got in there with him, the old Jeremiah?' asked Niven with a chuckle. 'He's not missing him and hitting the wall, I'll tell you.'

'It's the minister, Mr Macandrew,' replied Gavin.

'God sakes, do you tell me that, now? How did he get in? But whisht, till we hear.'

Macandrew's flat tones fell on the silence: 'Such a people, Hector my friend, will go on, begetting itself on itself, generation after corrupt generation, as it was in the beginning, is now, and shall be evermore, until some similar random concatenation as called it into being recurs to remove it utterly from the material plane.'

'In the name of God,' exclaimed Hector, 'what damnable heretical doctrine is this? Am I to be plagued all night in my own back parlour by heathens brazenly denying their Creator and His eternal ordinance? It's past tholing, so it is. But half an hour syne, here's a bit student body sits on that very sofa, drinking my Special and havering of coincidence and fortuitous circumstance. And now here's yourself, an ordained minister of the Gospel, miscalling your Maker for a . . . for a random concatenation. Never, in a long life spent among wicked men, did I hear sacrilege the like of that. But tak' tent, Mr Macandrew. Beware, minister. God is not mocked, nor His dominion set at naught. You're a woeful backslider, Mr Macandrew—a crying shame to the Kirk. Have you forgotten your divinity, your theology? Have you recanted your confession of faith? Renounced your apostolic duty as the servant of God? Tell me that, will you?'

'All this I remember, Hector,' intoned Macandrew. 'To my own undoing—and God's.'

'Yours is the sin of apostasy, the Judas crime,' said Hector solemnly. 'I'm but a simple man. I'll not can comprehend the hellish heresy, the heathenish creed you've preached in here before the night. But sat here in the shadow of death, waiting hourly on the Angel's coming, I'm no ways blate to tell you you're irrevocably damned to reprobation, minister. Ay. And for why God should have permitted you to wolf it here in Ferlie for so long in shepherd's clothing is hid from me.'

'His ways, Hector, as you well know, are past finding out,' said Macandrew, no shade of mockery in his dispassionate voice. But Hector was roused to fury, thumping the table.

'I'll not have the Devil at my own board, quoting Scripture! And if it was not for the cloth you're wearing there, to the shame of the Kirk and its Creator, I'd kick your arse out of the door and down the close or my name's not Hector Fraser!'

'Crivens!' chuckled Niven, fairly hopping with delight. 'Did you hear that Lachie? This is better nor the night Macandrew won the drinking bout.'

'Violence, Hector, violence,' came Macandrew's voice again. 'Do you think it becomes a man with the death-mark on his brow to offer chastisement to fellow mortals, be they clergy or laity?'

'No, no, indeed you're right. I'm too gleg with my tongue, and quick to anger,' said Hector, his voice falling remorsefully. 'I'll not deny it. I'm fell hardened in sin. My face has been hid from the Lord these many years, and now His is turned from me.

I ken it fine, I ken it fine. I doubt I'm deep sunk in reprobation, and the pit of perdition yawns for me.'

'God sakes!' chittered Lachie, hunching his shoulders nervously. 'What ails the old warlock? He's groaning away there like the whole Kirk-session in one.'

'But mind you,' continued Hector with revived spirit,'I'm not lacking company in Ferlie. From the minister right down to Jock Graham in the county gaol for wife murder, they're all far gone in sin. A right Godless community is this, a city of the plain, ripe for destruction. The Day of Judgment will find few sheep in Ferlie, I'll be bound. Where are the Elect, will you tell me? Cast about and find them if you can, for I cannot. Even the bairns come early out of sin into sin.'

'So do they everywhere, Hector, not only Ferlie. Even your own religion you're so glib to threaten with affirms that. Sin is original, inescapable, imposed inexorably by your crabbit, relentless Creator on all Adam's mortal progeny, incapable of virtue.'

'I ken my dogma, Mr Macandrew,' said Hector accusingly. 'Better nor you, I ken it. For you've forgotten something, have you not? Incapable of good they may be, by their feckless selves. Ay, but by the grace of God the Father and the merciful intercession of Christ the Son, they can yet be redeemed to sit in glory.'

'Hallelujah!' uttered Lachie, with mock fervour, while Niven thumped Gavin on the back in an ecstasy of ribald appreciation: 'Faith, is he not a right dab at the doctrine, the old rascal? They should change coats, yon two. Hector could fill the kirk and Macandrew empty the pub, and all Ferlie would be happy. Whisht now!'

'Maybe so, maybe so, Hector,' Macandrew replied mildly. 'On whom, may one ask, does this divine grace, this intercession, fall?'

'It falls on the Elect, as you know very well.'

'And who then are my brothers, the Elect? Speak their names, that we may emulate them and attain immortal saintliness.'

Hector answered gravely, his anger manifestly assuaged by unction: 'Must I, a sinful publican, be teaching you your doctrine you're supposed to uphold and propagate? Fine you know, Mr Macandrew—unless God has punished you, as well He might, by taking away the Light from you—fine you know that salvation is won or lost not by works of sinful men, but only by the grace of

God through the atonement of the Saviour.'

'We do not know the Elect, then, Hector?'

'God alone knows the Elect—chosen and foreordained by divine decree, made in the beginning and unchangeable forever to eternity.'

'You take too much upon yourself then, do you not, my friend? Searing the brand of reprobation on the general brow of Ferlie, yourself included. Has God revealed His saintly roll to you, Hector Fraser, that you vindictively deny Election to your friends and neighbours? Jock Graham himself, condemned by man to hang, may find his seat in glory. Mounting the scaffold, he may find the ladder reaches to the throne of light. And all this generation of vipers, twined in depravity, may wear a halo underneath their goats' horns—if I may confuse a bestial image. If salvation comes not from good works and holy living, but by act of grace predestined and irrevocable from the origins of created life, how then can you, stubborn and self-righteous, dare to condemn yourself and Ferlie to perdition? Have a care, Hector, have a care.'

'By heaven!' muttered Niven, 'Macandrew's gripped him there. This'll not do at all, at all. We must away in, I doubt. I'll not have the old devil worsted by Macandrew even to save my immortal soul.'

'It's high time we went ben, anyway,' said Lachie, shivering. 'It's fell drouthy work, this theology. I'm sore in need of a dram, Donald.'

Niven's hand was on the door-knob, when Hector's voice was heard again, controlled and passionately patient: 'You're a wicked man, Macandrew. Your tongue's as forked and subtle as the serpent's, your mind tortuous as its belly worming in the dust. But I can bruise the serpent's head. Ay, that I can, sinner though I am. Would you think to fob me off with such-like wastrels and gallivanting midden-waders for God's elected saints? You're wilfully twisting the doctrine to your own godless, pagan ends. But I am patient to confute you. Have you forgotten the call to salvation that the Chosen hear and obey? Would you be telling me yon Ferlie evil-doers have been granted enlightenment and understanding of God's will? Have their hearts of stone been softened—any more than yours, or mine? Have they acknowledged the divine grace, recognised the atonement of Christ, and given thanks in their hearts for it? Can you see the spirit working in them, or their swine's ears cocked to hear the Word of the

Good Book? See you in them, do you think, the virtue of repentance and their faces turned towards the Light? Shame on you, Macandrew, shame on you! to go about to knock down your own Kirk steeple and paint haloes on such hell-bent brows!'

Niven spoke over his shoulder: 'Eh man, Lachie, did ever you hear the like of that?'

'Ay, many a time. And so did you. But not from this side the door. Get in, for God's sake. My tongue's fair hanging out.'

Macandrew spoke: 'Verily, Hector, a Calvin come to judgment—'

'And a Niven come to drink!' exclaimed Donald heartily, pushing a way for all three into the parlour. 'Ay, Hector man. Evening, minister, you're there then, I see. It's a grand night outby, but snell-like. Lachie and me looked in for a warmer. But what's this, Hector? Naught but an empty bottle on the table! Have you gone over to the enemy at last—at your time of life? Faith Lachie, we'd have done better to bide in the Crown. A cold welcome here the night I'm thinking.'

'Ach, devil the bit, man!' said Lachie. 'An empty bottle's better than no bottle at all. It shows we're in the proper place, right enough. I don't doubt Hector has the means to replace it. Eh, Hector?'

'Man, I'd not remarked it was empty,' said Hector, tilting the bottle incuriously. 'The minister and me were that deep in disputation. And one of the two of us out of his depth, had you not come in when you did,' he added, sneering at Macandrew, who paid no heed at all, so that Hector continued: 'But to tell the truth, you find me in a sore troubled frame of mind. Ay, sore cast down in spirit I am the night, and that's a fact.'

'God sakes, Hector!' put in Niven. 'Is it any wonder—and the bottle empty on you? Bella! Are you there, lass?' he shouted through the doorway.

Through came Bella from the bar, with little welcome in her face, to stand silently eyeing the company. Fraser addressed her: 'Bella, here's Donald and Lachie looked in for a bit dram. You'd better away up and fetch down the bottle from under the bed.'

She went with never a word.

'It's the last of the Special, d'you see,' explained Hector. 'I was thinking to keep it for the night hours. I'm sore vexed with sleeplessness.'

'The whisky's good for sending you to sleep,' said Gavin, with unstudied gravity.

'Ach laddie,' laughed Niven, 'it's not so much that. But it does make lying awake easier to thole.'

'You're there, then, young man?' said Fraser, noticing Gavin. 'Faith, I thought the minister had frightened you away for good. Though why he should is hard to seek, for you're both much of the like heathenish mind, I'm thinking.'

He said this like an angler casting a fly on dark water, but none rose to it; and Lachie, who took little pleasure in theological argument, made haste to steer talk other ways: 'You'll not have seen the bonnie mare Donald's been and bought the day? Eh, but she's a strapping beast, yon!'

'No, but we've heard of her,' said Hector, without interest.

'And how that?' queried Niven.

'Some young rapscallions through the wall there were talking of her,' Hector replied; and Bella, entering then, interposed with disapproval: 'Like Mary Taggart they would have her, Donald. The dirty-mouthed young devils!'

'Like Mary Taggart, eh?' said Donald, musingly. 'I'll not say I can just see the likeness. But if Mary Taggart's had the stallion half as often as my Queenie, she's not the lass her mother thinks her.'

In the general laughter, Bella banged the bottle on the table and went billowing out in a huff.

'Eh man,' said Lachie, 'she doesn't like such daffing, Bella doesn't, about the young bit queans. Think you she maybe counts herself among them still? Though I doubt she's near past it.'

'Ay, and without e'er coming to it, at that,' reflected Niven. 'An unco strange thing for a comely lass like she was. What for did she never marry think you, Hector?'

'Who? Bella?' said Hector, rousing himself from renewed self-communion. 'Ach, I never speir at her for that. But she's aye been too independent. She's aye gone her own gate, has Bella. I doubt she'd never share her bed with any man—or her thoughts for that matter.'

'And yet,' said Lachie, 'there's been them would have jumped at the chance. More than one there's been gey gleg to try Bella, or I'm cheated.'

'I doubt,' continued Hector, 'she's seen too much of men, ben the bar-room there, to offer them a chance at her. They're not so couthie in their clavers, Ferlie men, when they've drink taken. I doubt there's many a lass would be less ready to lie down, could she but hearken to the bestial ranting ben there.'

'Havers, man!' retorted Lachie, with a grin. 'You're blethering like a virgin bachelor. Think you they dinna ken what men are after from the time their maiden paps are big as seed-tatties? Fine they ken it, and hanker for it—like you for the bottle. Put another dram in here, Donald man,' he added, tendering his empty glass. 'Ach, they're not sweart to lie down, the lasses—God be thanked!'

'Well, well, maybe so,' said Hector. 'I'll not argue, being less well acquainted with the matter than some. But I'll not believe the bonnie bit birds are all made that way.'

'Faith, they're all made the same way that I've had aught to do with. And I've no great complaint about the pattern. Though I have heard tell in eastern parts there's minor variations. Maybe the minister here, who's been to India and such-like places could tell us. And maybe not, of course, him being a minister—and married forbye.'

Lachie keeked maliciously at Macandrew in the corner, and the others regarded him with different kinds of expectancy: Hector forbidding, Niven faintly apprehensive, and Gavin frankly curious.

Macandrew, since the irruption of Niven's company had broken off his wordy bout with Hector, had resumed his wonted detachment. But he was aware of their conversation; and Lachie's apologia for the feminine chimed assonantly with his own anathema: that crooked, caliper-like frame, hinged to encircle fumbling man through three hundred and sixty degrees of creative corruption, from Greenwich through the date meridian, straddling the universe like some colossal Gaea, the earth-mother, supine or erect receptive always, everywhere, in occident or orient, from fabled Eden to Ferlie now, hankering for it insatiably, impelled to vindicate under the male yoke its veritable dominance, *femina almissima victorem ferocem capiens:* lie down, lie down, and share my bed of adulterate essence, mouth the breasts that nourished you, hide in the loins that thrust you forth, creep back to the womb that spawned you: return, return to your carnal cradle; come down, Icarus, from your asensual sublimation; come back, Odysseus, from your male venturing: I am the heat that melts your wings, the lodestone that retracts you to your port of origin: renounce aspiring, surrender chastity, acknowledge the pit from whence you're hewn, root in the filed mould whence you grew, confess corruption, be thou me—omniparous, gynaecian, fertile fleshhood, chested like the black mare with a ruby in her nose and a yellow sweater revealing her beauties, heaving in the hot dusk, repulsed on the verandah, conquering in the bazaar.

'Woman,' said Macandrew, addressing the room but looking nowhere, 'is the vilest manifestation of vile animate being, admitting no variation, east or west, in her corporal pattern or in the evil principle it incarnates, the principle of obdurate fertility, persistent, triumphant, earth-bound pollution. She is the epitome and prototype of organic existence, the alpha and omega of growth and decay, the vicious, excellent perfection of the biological cycle, the origin and ultimate of the metabolic continuum. And even as these are odious and accursed, so is she, their zenith, their supreme culmination, odious and accursed. She is the fecund earth waiting for the seed-harbinging ploughshare, fecund in her hot depths, bland and benignant in her outer semblance. She is the generous host, cherishing parasites to augment and multiply her careless omnipotence. She is the eternal maternal womb of generation, gross and abundant, copious and effluent with progeny, ever asprout with thriving life, life, life. The symbol of life she is, and therefore the symbol of evil; the root and branch, the blossom and the fruit of evil.'

He ceased and, with the last words, casually presented his glass to Donald, who poured out without a word.

'Mercy on us, minister,' gasped Lachie, 'you're fell hard on the lasses! I'll bet a pound you don't speak to your wife in that strain.'

But Niven cut in swiftly, through a warning cough: 'I would be loth to go with you in all that you say, Mr Macandrew. But, whyles, I think you're maybe not that far out. Women! Faith, they can be a gey sore trial to a man, in more ways than one. But, God save us all, where would we be without them?'

'We would not be, Donald,' replied Macandrew. 'We would not be. And what more desirable consummation could we aspire to than that? An end of living, an infinite suspension of animation—and of the mortification succeeding it—the planet purged of organic creation, whirling in the cosmic space, a blank, beautiful spheroid of petrous sterility. I drink to it.'

And now Hector, whom Gavin had remarked chafing by the window, sprang to his feet, overturning his chair, and crashed his glass with an oath against the wall. 'No more!' he shouted. 'I'll hear no more of this damnable blasphemy. I've sat and suffered—here in my own back parlour—I've sat and suffered, like the man Job, patiently. But it's past all enduring, it is. Get you out of my house, Macandrew! Out with you this minute! Or, minister though you be, I'll do you an injury. I swear it—by the God you've set at naught!'

Startled by Hector's fury, they were all on their feet now, except Macandrew, who maintained his inhuman composure, not even glancing at his intending assailant. Niven took stance between them and spoke to Macandrew, leaning towards him confidentially: 'It might be best Mr Macandrew, if you said good-night now. You've fairly riled the old rascal this time. And there's no need to tell you he's gey hard to handle, when his hackles are up. I'll not be long behind you. If you wait in the car, down by the Crown, I'll run you back to the manse. You'll maybe find a bit nip in the right-hand pocket, if you're lucky.'

Macandrew rose, put his glass on the table, and bent his expressionless gaze on Hector: 'Violence, Hector, violence. A deplorable sin in one of your years and faith,' said he, and then: 'A kind goodnight to you.' And he stepped sedately out, closing the door carefully behind him.

'God almighty!' sighed Lachie, subsiding into his chair. 'He's an orra cratur, yon. I doubt he's more nor one slate loose up top.'

'Ay,' said Niven, 'he's not like neighbours and others, the minister. But what for do you not draw in your horns, Hector? You ken his ways fine enough by this time, surely.'

'Ken his ways! It's just because I ken them so well I can never thole him near me, the black-hearted reprobate! He's an agent of the Devil. There's whyles I think he's Auld Nick himself, and that's the truth. Under his clerical coat, there beats a more sin-hardened heart than any in Ferlie. Did you not hear him there—preaching destruction? Sitting there callously denouncing all of creation?'

'Ach man,' said Lachie, 'I wasn't understanding the half of his clavers. I thought he was just having a bit skelp at the lasses. And with a wife and two queans like he's got, I'd not blame him too much.'

'Eh Lachie, my friend, you don't rightly comprehend the upshot of it all. You see in a glass, darkly. But I—I see him face to face, for the evil, wanchancie thing he is.'

Niven stood, swilling the spirits in his glass round and round, frowning the while. He said: 'He was aye by-ord'nar' strange, was Macandrew. And since he came back home, he's been more agley than ever. Sometimes I jalouse some black foreign warlock's put a spell on him.'

'The Devil himself's put a spell on him. The evil spirit's

inside of him,' said Hector harshly. 'He's an emissary of Satan. Ay, is he. And I did right to cast him out.'

'Well, maybe so,' said Lachie. 'I'll not can answer for that. But he's gey sore on the womenfolk, whatever else. I'd thought you'd maybe find to agree with him in that—an old crusted bachelor like you, eh?'

And Niven, keen enough to leave Macandrew, seconded Lachie. 'Man, Hector,' he said, 'Lachie's right there, now. Here we're talking of Bella biding single, but what of yourself? Have you ne'er thought to take a wife?'

'And what would I be doing with a wife?' said Hector, moving uneasily in his chair.

'Well now,' said Lachie, leering sideways at Niven, 'there's maybe not much good you'd be doing her now. We're none of us so gleg as beforetime, eh Donald? But why were you not thinking of it earlier—when the spigot poured steadier?'

'Ay, Hector,' added Niven. 'Do you never wish you'd not been so blate with the lasses—now you've the time to feel lonely? Even the Special's not the same thing as a wife beside you.'

Old Fraser, his self-restraint enfeebled by whisky and emotional storm, sat downcast, his hands stirring nervously on the table-top. At length, he found voice: 'Time to feel lonely, you're saying, Donald? Lonely, is it? Eh, I'll not deny there's whyles I feel sorry I never took a wife. No time I was having for the gimmers—ay, and there's more nor one would fain have had Hector Fraser. Scorned them I did for light-minded fleering hizzies, well enough maybe to tumble with of a night, when the need was on, but not for a serious man to plague himself with all the days of his life. But, man, I've had my doubts. I'll not deny it. A man gets lonely by himself, when all his cronies put back their last dram and steer away their ways to bed with their wives, and he's left but his own self and the bottle and the dreich night stretching in front of him, like the moor below Ben Cromach. It's a dour kind of a life, an old grey bachelor's, with neither wife nor bairn beside him in the ingle.'

His voice had lost its strident tenor and drooled pathetically, quavering with self-pity. Lachie blew his nose diligently and Niven, reaching for the bottle, sighed: 'Ay Hector, maybe you have the right way of it there. There's a power of comfort in a woman-body, give the Devil his due. A very present help in trouble.'

'Eh Donald, old friend, that's just what I'm missing—now that affliction's sore upon me.'

'What ails you, then, Hector?' asked Lachie. 'Is it the rheumatism's got at you again?'

'No, Lachie, no. It's something a sight more tormenting nor the rheumatism even. Heard you not about McNish's sudden taking-off?'

'God sakes, man!' exclaimed Donald, spluttering in mid-swallow. 'You'll not tell us that disturbs you. McNish! It's time he was out of the way.'

'It is so, then!' replied Hector, with a spark of his former lightning. 'A sore thorn in the flesh he was to me, the lecherous, drunken devil. And a shame to the trade, forbye. It's not his dying that's upsetting me. It's what's behind it, Donald. Man, reach me across what's left in the bottle there, till I tell you.'

Gavin, since Macandrew's sudden ejection, had found himself less and less vividly aware of the colloquy proceeding about him. He had set his glass unlipped on the floor at his feet and for some time now had contemplated it with no relish at all. His eyelids drooped stubbornly and, despite repeated efforts to call back his sliding wits by sundry head-shakings and changes of position, he found it increasingly difficult to attend to the conversation. His eyes remained closed for longer and longer spells, his head lolled unregarded on his shoulder and he slipped into brief, untroubled sleep.

He awoke to Niven's voice, distorted with laughter: 'Man, Hector, I never did hear the like of that—not even in this back parlour! A judgment on the publicans of Ferlie! Not but what some of them deserve it, what with watered liquor and short measure at that. But I scarce think Him up yonder is any judge of liquor. Take my advice, Hector. If this black wing-flapping Angel of Death you're blethering about steps across the threshold here, sit him down and pour him two-three nips of Special, and he'll soon forget what he came for.'

And Lachie added: 'Ach Hector, you're daft. Shadow of death be damned! You'll see us all out, you cannie old devil. But I doubt, Donald, I'll have to be taking the road. Are you for off?'

'Ay that,' said Donald, looking appraisingly at Gavin. 'You'll be coming, young Ewart? You're fell quiet the night, laddie. You're not fou, are you? Well now, Hector, goodnight. And don't be fashing yourself with such auld wives' notions. I'll look in the morn, maybe, if I'm near hand. Goodnight.'

They trooped out together, leaving Hector silent and dejected, alone with his forebodings.

CHAPTER EIGHT

Alec at the Thrawn Wife

. . . one that slept in the contriving of lust, and
waked to do it.
Wine loved I deeply, dice dearly, and in woman
out-paramoured the Turk.
William Shakespeare

For my enemy is dead, a man as divine as
myself is dead,
I look where he lies white-faced and still in the
coffin—I draw near,
Bend down and touch lightly with my lips the
white face in the coffin.
Walt Whitman

ALEC, MUSING on the settle by the fire, marooned on the fertile island of himself by the sea of drunken bawdry breaking round him, was temporarily left in peace by the cronies.

Queen, the bonnie black mare with a chest like Mary, Queen should be home by now, safely stabled at Braelochy, clinking new cobbles, pricking restless ears, nodding her strong neck up and down, up and down, rolling white eyes in the unfamiliar dark where unseen, unknown companions snuffled and pawed and champed; Queen, the young mare, chafing and flighty in glossy arrogance, battering her steel-shod, disdainful feet in old Bess's quiet stall. And old Bess, O faithful female servant for the last time untimely served, and dead in childbed, get thee to the knackery, go, thy bleeding birth-torn carcase still for man's ingenious, curious purposes, thy patient, gentle spirit—whither? Aloft in the equine Valhalla, unharnessed, chewing no bit of servitude, straining no sweating flanks in pressed labour, did she browse now in Elysian flyless shade, cropping serenely, tail and mane still, asphodel, trefoil and lucky clover, dreaming an eternity of pastoral quiet, roused by no mirk-morning yoking, never driven beneath tormenting sun or sleet-storm on alien, human ventures?

See her, not wither-wrung and harness-sore, but Queen-like and sleek and arched of neck and haunch and barrel, tempting the stallion pride of immortal peers, Pegasus, Bucephalus, capering and curveting like Mary Taggart at the Cross for Jock and Wull and Tam and who might look but never him, the wilful gelding nibbling his lonely portion of frustration. Forget, forget.

The black mare was fractious, corn-fed and full of unbridled mettle. Bess in her youth had been the same. But see her, shoulders sloping, shanks faltering, bellows wheezing, straining up to the ridge, her feathers squalid with loam, her nostrils flaring; or see her plodding home her gloaming way to stall. Queen was high-spirited like Mary. But the yoke was heavy. Soon wed, her maiden prowess all forgotten or regretted, she'd hirple on, an often pregnant drudge, chore-sore and bairn-trauchled, her panoply of girlhood pendulous about her, her expectant eyes dimmed and looking backward. Mary at the Cross, hungry for her destiny. Close your eyes and open your legs and see how life will use you. Here is the ultimate of bliss, under the hedge in the darkness. Refuse, and ape Tantalus forever. Mary would never refuse, powerless as Queen to resist the mastery, bondslave to her appetite as the mare to her foreign overlord. This was the fate in every human horoscope, the universal pilot-star, magnet for never-wandering barks, the fruit for watering mouths however sour its taste was proved for others. Mary could see on every hand her future, the broken spirit and the beauty all fordone. But Mary would press on regardless, for life was stronger than chastity. For all except for him, who fled it, virtual eunuch though equipped for other office, as that one knew in the coppice teasing him effectively and all for nothing when at last he seemed well lost and swooning into life about her semi-oriental bizarre offering, the ivory satin under the tartan, jasmine in her hair, cardamom breathing from her pale lips. Here was the girl thing of his waking, sleeping longing, the apple of knowledge long ignored for its coarse rind in the cowshed, at the garden gate, Meg or Mary, here it was at his mouth for tasting, the manse houri, redolent of the erotic east, Scheherazade, Salome, sugar and spice, jade and jacinth, silk and brocade, here was fruition ripe but not rotten, communion not smelling of the farmyard and the beasts' leaping. But she slipped from under his hand—no hand with the lasses—and ran away laughing. Mary Taggart would laugh at him, Niven of Braelochy's son, Mary, the flighty mare, chesty and strong in the haunch, prime for man's yoking but not his, the fastidious

Adonis whom even Venus' sweating pits would disenchant.

Preposterous refinement, fending off life, pushing to arm's length Mary and Meg and Jean and all Tam's willing cattle, while others less endowed, less nice in choice, wantoned their fill and boasted their virility. What perverse fortune was his, acutely conscious of his easy-rising manhood—white lonely sheets or the sodden raincoat against the fence, an odalisque cushioned in the fantastic dreaming night or Elspeth provoking at his elbow on the road from church—easy rising to no purpose, empty falling. What half-man, what fairy changeling was he? What satyr of timorous delicacy, docking himself with the knife of unnatural revulsion, dread of the crude vitality that coursed impatient through him, fear of the touch, the coil, the intimate conjunction that would lose him his sheer integrity, his inviolate identity, and make him another toiling copulant, a sweating link in the endless chain of generation? But no! That was not himself, Alec. That was Macandrew insidiously crawling into him, to rationalise, to justify his innate, unnatural, craven aversion from life, his scalp prickling at the stealthy approach to the unknown, known to all but him, his fingers hesitant to grope their way to the mystery unfolded to all others, himself recoiling from the fascinating waiting flesh, evading the astonished question in her eyes, slinking ashamed from the other mocking in the byre, refastening her blouse, from her by the lochan carelessly naked, fearing no evil from young Niven of Braelochy, no hand with the lasses. Forget, forget! Ramp through reverie and dream, always triumphant; or consort with these drinking, womanising mother-outlawed cronies, and in their cocksure company share manhood, hope that their contact, their precept and example, might one night procure him, primed or bemused with drink, release in woman.

He had come here tonight for this only purpose, resented but irresistible, overcoming even his father's stern injunction to hie off home direct with the new-bought mare. A boy could lead her home, he had protested. But his father had insisted that he took Queen himself, skittish as she was and apt to jib on the road, too valuable a charge for any hafflin. But a boy had led Queen home, young Peter Logie with a shilling in his pocket, pledged to secrecy; and the mare would be securely stabled now while he sat here, pretending enjoyment, preparing fresh chagrin. Far better he'd be now in his own room under the roof, monastic with a book or watching the lochan shivering in the starlight or listening to old Angus improvising on his chanter; better even restless under his mother's prattle. Her hands fluttered like moths in the lamplight about her needlework, long-term, ladylike, silk embroidery, heraldic lions and fleurs-de-lis or lotus flowers and gold pagodas, while her gentle accents minced through clichés, and he and Marion feigned attention just enough not to hurt her. Marion—bitter-sweet stay-at-home in discontent, flickering through magazines, sprawled in the armchair swinging over the arm one long leg dangling a slipper, most unladylike, thinking of her Ranald gone to Canada or Fraser breeding sheep and bairns the other side of the ben or the second ploughman's arms round some skivvy at the dance; Marion, ripe for rebellion against her mother, release from the lace afternoon-apron-strings that tethered her still. There in the drawing-room, monosyllabic and bored to peevish tears, Marion would rather be here at the Thrawn Wife, swilling beer and telling smutty stories, and here he sat, yearning inanely for the family half-circle. What a queer hatching they were, he and she: maladjusted, mother-bred children of refinement, stork-borne, cabbage-found, black-bag babies, weaned on maternal tea-party culture, Medici prints and literary journals in opposition to the dung-midden fronting the back door and the crude behaviour of byre and stable, the bawdy influence of ploughman and cattlemaid. Keep to yourselves, Marion, you and Alec. I won't have you playing with the grieve's children. And here, even among the companions he courted, he kept to himself in his self-centred Coventry, walled in by home-made, maidenly prudery that isolated him from them more completely than Marion chafing out at Braelochy.

Well, Queen should be home by now. If anything had happened on the road, he'd have heard before this. But nothing could happen, anyway. The mare wasn't that fractious, and young Logie was a strong lad and knowing. His father had only wanted him out of the way while he went on his customary batter round about, the drunken, bragging old devil. If anything had happened to that mare on the road home and the old man found out he'd disobeyed him, there'd be one hell of a tirrivee. But nothing had happened or he'd have known by now. Queen was safely bedded down in old Bess's stall out at Braelochy, where Marion, escaped from her mother, smoked cigarettes at the kitchen door and sulked over her dreich existence: and his mother, pausing in her needlework every now and then, cocked an ear for the noise of the car and wondered just how drunk her boorish Donald would be this Saturday and where he was, her misguided renegade son, who was slipping farther and farther from her care and ken. Her pale, foolish eyes swam under ready tears; her shoulders drooped pathetically. *Mater dolorosa,* acquainted with grief, bitten by the serpent's tooth, the bosom-sheltered thankless child, him, Alec, here on the settle, his sleeve in the beer slops, eating the swine husks, potato crisps and bar-room bawdry, shunned by his evil companions, who regarded him more as a butt for jest than a fellow roisterer.

Tam was singing from the Ball o' Kirriemuir, inevitably rendered sooner or later when the drink was in and adapted *ad libitum bibitum.* Having dealt with the minister's wife and twin daughters, Tam, leering acknowledgement round the room, spied Alec glooming by the fire. He winked largely, clapped him on the shoulder, and gave voice:

'Now, young Braelochy, he was there—
  Fie, fie for shame!
He caught a glimpse o' Mary's . . . knees
  And ran back shiverin' hame.'

The roar of laughter following this sally set the lamps shaking and the cronies competing:

'Poor young Eck! He should've been a lassie himself.'

'God, and maybe he is. There's little o' the man about him for all his muckle brawn.'

'Ay, the lasses'll get nothing out o' Alec. Man, I'd let him sleep the other side o' my Aggie and think nothing o't.'

'Ach, somebody was careless with the shears the night Alec popped out.'

'Ay, that must be the way o't. Eh, Alec, what do you say?'

Her pale weeping eyes and unfounded reproaches: I'm losing you, Alec. You're not my son any more. But he was, her retarded ineffectual prodigal, wasting his mother-bred substance on wine and women with long tawny legs right up to the source—Were you looking for me, your shyness, or something? It's here all right, all tight, but not for you in the coppice at the Cross in an easy-shed jumper and skirt for young randy Niven his mother's wastrel son whoring in the town while she waited at home weaving pathos in her silken tapestry grieving for her son like father.

He sprang to his feet with a roar that sent them back. Seizing his untouched glass, he splashed the beer in an amber arc that ended in Tam's startled face and sent him stooped and spluttering hors de combat. Two more, shaping laughter at Tam's plight, he grasped by the collars and, knocking their heads hard together, flung them sprawling in a corner. The rest recoiled in dismay out of arm's reach and he made no move in pursuit, but, arms akimbo, surveyed them fiercely.

'You mangy pack o' yapping messan-dogs! You'd make a sumph o' me, would you? Because I'm not for cocking a leg about every lass like a collie at every gate-post. Braw men you think you are, gleg to jump every bitch that's handy. Christ! any tinker's whelp can do the like when the bitch is hot, and the bitches you take on are aye in season. Bonnie men you are, right enough—cowering away there like sheep in a blatter o' snaw when I turn on you. It's not slow you are to cowp some glaikit besom that's fair itching to let you. But you're not so spry to tangle with a man, eh? Ay, a man, I said, that's not got all his strength dandling between his legs like you have. For a card o' pins I'd take on the lot o' you and send you shiverin' hame—instead o' the gormless hizzies you're aiming to serve the night.'

He ceased, and the silence of sheer astonishment was broken by old John from behind the bar: 'Now then, Alec, dinna be starting anything in here. Especially with himself lying upstairs not right cold in his coffin yet. What's gotten into you anyway? You're not like yourself, the night, fleering and flyting there like a drunk piper. The lads were only having their bit joke as usual. What, think you, would your mother say if she heard you?'

What would his mother say, grieving at the recreant's fancied viciousness—only fancied. With an oath he overturned the table into the fireplace; glass crashed on the hearthstones and the beer hissed and spat on the live coals.

'God save us all!' gasped old John; 'the devil's in the laddie—like old Donald himself he is, in his heyday. There'll be mischief done in here the night, or I'm cheated.'

'Keep my mother's name out o' your slobbering mouth, you old pimp. And as for him upstairs—do you think I care a straw for him, the rotten sotted old ram? Not right cold in his coffin, you say. The heat in him'll never cool this side o' the grave. They'd best bury him fell deep, or keep the women wide o' the kirkyard in the dark. Ay, he was the daddy o' you all, he was. You'd need to show him reverence. But he's a filthy stink in my nose—even more than you are.'

'That's an ill way to speak o' the dead, Alec Niven,' said Wull, finding courage in righteousness.

'Ay, is it,' another put in. 'And it's a daft-like way you're carrying on—like the Mains prize bull at the Sunday School picnic.'

'There's none here wants to fight with you. We're friends here, having a dram and bit crack. What's needled you, man?'

'No need to get your birse up for a wee joke, Alec man,' said Wull. 'Come to yourself now, and have a nip on me—and we'll see you get a lass the night. Eh, lads?'

But the lads' ready approval was choked in their throats.

'By God!' roared Alec, 'if I'm for a lass, I'll have her—without a muck-mouthed go-between the like o' you to help me. Ay, and if it wasn't that I'm loth to stall where you've been draiglin', your easy-jumped mare, Ellen, might have Alec up the night.'

'Eh, you dirty young devil, I'll smash your bloody face in!'

'Come away then. You're sweart-like to start, are you not?' sneered Alec, wide-legged among the sawdust, brows down and dander up, crowing defiance. If he couldn't ruffle the hens, he'd claw the cocks that did. Fearsome enough young giant he looked too, towering up out of the lamplight, his bunched fists on his thighs. But Wull was fairly nettled by this second threat in an evening to his claim on Ellen; and, though he had no wish to measure up on his own to this new run-amuck softy, he was bent on halting his career. He surveyed the others scornfully.

'D'you hear this gelded lambkin ranting away here with a couple o' nips in his belly? Would you listen to him? He'll take any lass he fancies. Him! God, I've seen him look the other way when a bairn bent to tie her shoe-lace. He's not got the guts o' a louse, so he's not. But he's for mashing us up, two at a time. Christ, are you for standing there like straw stooks in the rain and let yon mother's milksop craw so crouse above you? Come in about, will you? We'll take some o' the whisky mettle out o' him. Turn him up and take his breeks off and see the right way o' him. Come on then.'

The cronies, irresolute against the bar, were far from keen on the assault; but they were many to his one and, whipped up by Wull's harangue, they girt themselves and shambled uncertainly into the challenge.

Alec laughed aloud and made no move to retreat to a more tactical position by the door. Like a lamb he might lie down or not in love, but they'd find him rampage like a bull in a tussle of this kind. Gawkit and ill at ease with the women, he was spry enough to manhandle the men; and what Ellen and Mary might look for in vain, Tam and Wull would not have to seek. The mould's not broken, said she in the coppice offering, round and soft like a pouter's crop. Unbroken by him, but he'd smash its counterpart, Wull's breastbone, with his horny-hooved fist not cast for caresses, and Tam's loose crutch with an upthrust knee, and Peter's drawn mouth with the brown stumps showing, hers in the gloom smiling for a kiss. They'd lie down for him if the lasses didn't. Let them come on and try his virgin mettle.

'Come in about, you birkie men. You're not so keen to meddle with me!' And he laughed wildly, fronting them like Goliath the host in Judah, waiting full of vaunt and confidence while they approached cautiously, scuffling over the sawdust, each one attendant on the others but drawing gradually nearer. Never a word they uttered, even Wull silent now, watching him uneasily, uncertain of his next move and with no stomach for the business at all. And old John gawked from behind the bar, nervously wringing a dish-cloth.

'Have you no respect for himself upstairs? You thrawn young devil, I'll let Braelochy ken o' this. I'll get the polis ben to you if you dinna quit. Eh, if it wasn't that I'm old and done, I'd knock some o' the spunk out o' the lot o' you.'

He faltered into fascinated silence as their creeping arc contracted to envelop Alec.

'You would not then, granpa,' cried Alec. 'For the lasses have done it already. There's devil a dribble o' spunk left in them. Come away, my braw lads. Come away, you byre-muckin's, you sheep's driblets, you spent rams. Here's another kind o' tumble in the hay for you. Dinna hang back like feckless young Alec. Get in there and prove your hardihood. I'll mangle the pack o' you, all on my own.'

'Not so, young Alec. Here's one will keep the bridge with you, and fend off the Etruscans.'

And through the swing-doors blundered Gavin, more drunk than sober, dangling in each hand a black bottle and blinking foolishly in the new light.

'Stand ho!' he bellowed, 'you rabble of low degree. What, will you brawl in an ale-house?'

Dumbfounded by his sudden appearance, his unfamiliar face and strange address, the cronies paused, gaping oafishly. Alec squinted annoyance at him.

'You'd best get back where you came from, Ewart. Else you'll maybe get hurt. I'll manage this trash without any help.'

'Brave words, and bravely spoken, great Alexander. And yet

it argues a selfish spirit to claim all the glory of so notable a joust for one's only self. Here hang honourable laurels enough for two noble brows. And Ewart, being in so far, demands his share. Lay hold of my trusty McEwan here, and I armed with his no less lethal Younger brother, we shall do such mayhem as the chronicles of feats of arms have never recorded since Odysseus slew the suitors in the great hall or Samson swung his jawbone among the Philistines.'

He thrust a bottle into Alec's unwilling hand and stood swaying gently, focussing the laggard enemy. 'Hah!' he exclaimed; 'as goodly a gathering of swede-bashers as any in Ferlie, I'll wager. But slow to come on, surely. Lay on, caitiffs. Come and be slaughtered.'

Now these two large and buirdly chiels, both of wild and unholy mien, and armed with one of the most barbarous weapons an ingenious civilisation has devised, presented a far from tempting prospect to the half-hearted enemy, who remained at gaze. Even Wull, bent on revenge though he was, stumbled into words rather than action. 'Who the hell are you, bursting into a private argument?' he managed but with little assurance.

'Who am I?' answered Gavin, with preposterous gravity. 'Alec, gentle cousin, what manner of men are these, who know not the great ones even when they stoop to honour them? Barbarian bumpkin, O rustic clown, stem of a witless, clay-rooted stock, know that I am Gavin Ewan Stewart Ewart, failed Baccalaureate of Medicine and Chirurgery, cousin distant to this noble sprig of youth and terror to his enemies. Know me and tremble, base clodhopper.'

'I don't ken the half o' what you're saying. You're drunk, if you ask me,' said Wull and glanced around for corroboration. Some nodded assent, but none ventured to repeat the charge.

'Drunk am I?' said Gavin, his brows rising in unfeigned interest as he considered the accusation. 'Drunk is it I am? God now, and if I'm drunk, it's not with what I'm knocking back in here. Is this your Ferlie hospitality? Who's on the bell, for Christ's sake? Get 'em in Alec, get 'em in, before I blush for you, neglecting your sweet cousin and he on his holidays too, for shame. It's thristy work, this jousting in the sawdust. Let's call a barley, a truce, a brief recess, and seek refreshment.'

Here was the honourable retreat the cronies were sweating for, and though they had lacked the wit to contrive it, they were not slow to effect it offered to them. They fell back gladly to the bar, where old John, bent on peace, was already spreading olive branches as fast as he could pull them. Alec stubbornly held the middle of the floor, denied the exit his frustration and self-loathing clamoured for, nonplussed but adamant against reconciliation. A fool he looked, and he knew it, standing there by himself, his brows masking his troubled eyes, staring at the craven group by the bar. They all ignored him, the cronies because they avoided the conflict, Gavin because he had forgotten all about him.

Willing to seduce the henchman farther from his cousinly alliance and draw his thoughts from blood and rough house, one ventured into question: 'You are a stranger then in these parts, Mister . . .?'

'Ewart, sir, Ewart. Stewart Ewart, to be euphonious and precise,' replied Gavin, contemplating his beer with a vacant eye. 'But stranger I am not,' he added, tossing his head like a restive horse and surveying the company with little interest. 'Ewart is no stranger anywhere. Ewart, friends, is a man and where he finds himself the world revolves about him. *Nil humani a se alienum putat. Nil,* in fact, *humani aut inhumani.* And thereby he out-Terences the worthy Terence, who was after all but an upstart Punic some two thousand years ago, and *ipso facto* somewhat limited comparatively in his contacts. Poor good old sage, how ignorant, how virtuously unaware, how innocent. Ah me, the mad days I have seen.'

He shook his head solemnly and inclined it till his chin rested on his breast. His downcast eye lighted on the bottle still dangling from his hand. Raising it he kissed it reverently and stowed it carefully in a side pocket.

'The wise man lays in a store for the lean years: thus spoke the prophet Braelochy, and thus have I done, sitting at the feet of the masters to learn wisdom. Yet surely you were twins when I got you? Smooth and round and black-a-vised like the minister's beautiful brats, man-comforting and comely, but hiding devilish woe and disenchantment in your curves. Where is your little sister, beautiful black bottle? I've walked myself to my knees looking for her. And there she was all the time, snug round the foal in old Bess's stall.'

Gavin's soliloquising faded into silence while the cronies winked slyly at his drunken maundering and Alec looked morosely at Queen Candy Taggart arched on the corner for his collie's leg, trampling proudly on old Bess's cobbles, flayed and boiled in a vat at the knacker's, all her humplocks levelled unexplored. Three strides he took and clapped the bottle down by

Gavin's hand.

'Here, take your damned screw-top, Ewart. And I wish you'd mind your own bloody business and not come interfering. If you'd not butted in, there'd be a few of them here lipping the sawdust—and hell mend them!'

'Ach, whisht, Alec man,' said Tam, 'and drink your glass. God knows what's gotten into you the night, for I dinna.'

Alec glowered at him, but saying no more, laid hold of a glass. Gavin, roused from confused self-communion, threw back his head and fixed a tired eye on his cousin.

'There you are then, Alec. What'll you have, eh? But you've got something I see. You're bonnie tipplers, you Nivens, and no mistake.'

'By the looks of things you're one of the family, right enough,' said Alec with never a smile.

'God, you're not far out there, Alec,' said Wull, laughing. 'This lad's not been wasting the night chewing the rag like us in here. Your cousin is he now? I'm right glad to meet him.'

'Ay,' cried Alec belligerently, 'I've no doubt you are. He came in gey conveniently for you.'

'Man, but you're not easy put down, I'll say that for you. What chance do you think you'd've had against the squad o' us? You're daft.'

'Daft, am I?' sneered Alec. 'I'll not say the same for you. You've not got the guts for that kind o' daftness.'

'Now, now Eck,' put in old John hastily, 'dinna be starting again, like a good lad now.'

'For Christ's sake, Alec man,' said Tam, 'pull your horns in and let's forget it. What the hell's eating you at all?'

'Can you not speak to your young cousin there, and pacify him?' said Wull to Gavin. 'Else he's like to set all Ferlie by the ears before the night's out.'

Gavin regarded the disputants benignly: 'Young blood, young blood, strutting and fretting and looking for trouble. Still, a bit blood-letting's not unhealthy for lusty young cocks like you. Myself, I have some prickings of mere violence itching me tonight, sere and yellow though I am. But yet, *in loco parentis* as I stand to you, my springing cousin, noble Alexander, I must counsel sweet reason and the buried hatchet. Let not drink spur you into action you'll maybe regret. You know the hard man, your father, will not brook competition from under his own roof.'

'That he'll not,' said old John approvingly. 'Faith, if

Braelochy knew you were here, Eck, making all this camsteerie, I'd catch the rough side o' his tongue, I would—and not for the first time either. So, if you'll just drink up and go your ways out o't, I'll be muckle obliged to you.'

And head bent to avoid Alec's scowl, the old man set himself diligently to mop the counter.

'I'll go when I'm good and ready,' said Alec. 'And not before.'

'Ach, there's no hurry at all,' said Wull. 'The night's a bairn yet. And there'll be no trouble, John. So dinna you fret.'

'Well, maybe so. But I'll not be happy till I see the back of you all and the door shut on you. It's not Christian, so it's not: drinking and swearing and brawling the like o' this, and himself lying in his box up the stairs yonder. It's fair sacri-leeg-ious. Ay, is it then.'

'Ach, whisht, will you!' exclaimed Tam. 'Old fool that you are. It never vexed him alive, that I kent o'. What way would it be worrying him now that he's dead?'

'If a tulzie the like o' this annoys McNish, it'll only be because he's not helping to make it,' said another, laughing.

'Ay,' said Tam, 'he was an ill man to keep out o' a ploy with drink or lasses in it. God! if he hears us at all, he'll be up out o' his coffin and down here among us in his death-sark for a glass and a pint.'

'You godless young devil!' said John, scandalised. 'What a way's yon to speak o' the dead?'

'You old humbugger, fine you ken I'm right—if anybody does in Ferlie. Many's the lass you've helped him to, drunk and sober. What for will you be whitewashing him now, just because he's been taken? You're a shameless old hypocrite, that's what you are.'

'Nothing o' the kind, Tam Gourlay. It's sinful to slander a dead man, bad and all as he was maybe. He'll not can defend himself now.'

'Maybe not,' said Tam. 'But we'll give him the chance anyway.' And he raised his voice and shouted at the ceiling: 'Hey McNish! are you there, you old ram? Come away down and have a last dram before they screw you in.'

Silence, incredulous but expectant, possessed them all. Beer plopped from the spigot into the basin below, and each man stayed arrested where Tam's adjuration found him. Old John paused in mid-sweep, his other hand poising a tumbler raised from its puddle. One left the drink at his lips untasted. Wull's lighted match flamed up unheeded. And all eyes, even Alec's and Gavin's, were upturned, whites gleaming blindly, to the ceiling as to heaven for a sign. But the silence persisted until with a nervous laugh Wull shook the match to the floor.

'He'll not have heard you, Tam. I doubt he's too busy trying Maggie to heed.'

Their sketchy laughter was interrupted by the tinkle of a bell from above the inner door. 'God save us!' whispered John, rolling an eye that way, but paralysed where he stood. The others could not but see which room the summons came from. Said Tam swiftly, with a general wink:

'Would you credit that now? The old sot's fell uppity grown and proud-like since Auld Nick's asked him ben. He'll have a dram right enough, but he'll not have it in the public bar. You're to fetch the bottle upstairs, John. Away with you, man.'

Old John's voice quavered: 'You'll not tell me that was the upstairs bell, Tam Gourlay. For I'll not believe it.'

The bell jangled again, this time transmitting impatience. 'Bide a wee, McNish!' cried Tam. 'You're not going under till Monday morn. There's no hurry in it. Eh John, what ails you man? You're whiter than a coffin sheet. Get away up there with the bottle. You'll not have the dead wait on the living, will you? Content you, McNish!' he roared again. 'The old man's coming with your last sup. Keep your shirt on.'

Old John turned slowly round, shaking like a scarecrow in the breeze, and raised his frightened eyes to the board, where the bell still jigged on its spring. The company exploded into salvoes of mocking laughter, even the intransigent Alec perforce joining in, as the ancient, leaping from terror into rage, fairly hopped behind the bar, cursing unheard and swiping at them all with his dish-cloth. Someone pushed open the inner door. A frowsy female head poked enquiringly round and withdrew when Tam flicked a cigarette butt to settle in its hair. Gavin raised his hands at length, and gradually they subsided into exhausted, choking sobriety.

'Gentlemen,' said Gavin, 'the jest was full. I haven't laughed so much since Professor Waister stitched up the wrong slit in old Meg Wauchope of the Wynd. But, John, it seems some damsel behind the door would have service. Dead men have no thirst to slake, but there's some here have empty glasses. Set 'em up, John.'

'By God, you'll get no more drink in here if you bide all night! Damned, graceless young devils that you are, there's nothing sacred to you. Dead or living, the Lord above or Auld Clootie below yonder, all's one to you, ranting there in lust and hardihood. Black burning shame you should think on yourselves, making a cod o' McNish, and him laid by and canna answer you. Ay, and me an old done man, one foot in the grave, near as helpless as himself. I've seen the day you'd've been slow to meddle with me—as you were with young Braelochy there not many minutes gone. Fell quick you are with the fork when the bull's fast tied.'

The old fellow lapsed into muttered curses and a senile tear glittered in his pouched eye. 'Come, sir,' said Gavin, a little abashed to see old age so openly put down, 'don't take on so. We meant no harm to you.'

'Ach, John,' added Wull, shuffling in the sawdust and looking anywhere but at the discomfited old man, 'what's like wrong with you? Only a bit joke we were having, when all's said.'

'Our jokes,' said Tam ruefully, 'dinna seem to plough very straight the night. But hell, man, there was no harm in it. You'd never think 'twas old randy McNish up the stairs, the song you're making about it. Who'd go for to give any respect to yon sinful old bastard, in his coffin or out o't?'

The bell jangled again, long and peremptorily, the wire pulled by someone losing patience so that the spring creaked above the clapper's sound. 'Man, John, you'd better get ben to yon old cows in the parlour,' said one, 'or they'll have the bell dinged off the wall.'

'Phemie and Jean it'll be,' said Wull. 'A couple o' cast-offs o' old cold Solomon up the stairs.'

'Christ, he had more women than I've ploughed furrows,' said Tam. 'And me with four shares ahint me to his one in front. Eh, but he never spared himself.'

Old John, disposing of bottles and glasses, was grumbling to himself. Gavin, toying with his tumbler on the bar, regarded him silently for a time and then, 'Perhaps,' he said, 'you'll take a dram yourself, John,' And he slid a coin before him.

'Thank you kindly. I'll not say no, and my head birling like Murdoch's mill-wheel in a spate. I'll split a glass with you, young man. But not one drop o' liquor more goes across this bar to the rest o' you the night. And that's flat.'

The cronies grinned and held their tongues. 'I gather,' said Gavin, turning to them, 'from what I hear that the deceased McNish upstairs lived in no chaste celibate cell, was not chary of his masculine favours—was something of a dog, in fact.'

'I'm not right sure what you're saying,' said Tam. 'You've a queer-like tongue for a Scotsman. But if I get your drift, you're right enough about McNish. He was the drunkenest, jumpingest ram in all Ferlie and twelve miles round. Ay, he was that.'

'Ach, Tam, dinna be modest. I'll back you to beat him, come another two hairsts—if you can stay the pace.'

'No, Wull, that's not on. I'd never compete with the like o' yon. McNish was by-ord'nar', so he was. Man, he wasn't human.'

'Well, by God!' exclaimed another, 'if he was divine, there's a right flock o' angels without wings here and there about the place.'

Here Alec broke his long silence: 'Is there never a thing to talk about but whoring?' exclaimed he fiercely, banging his tumbler on the bar. 'You'd scunner Rabbie Burns himself, forever boasting and slavering o' womanising and grunting in dark corners. You're not like men at all. You're like stud-beasts with the gift o' speech.'

'Ach, Alec, what else would we crack about, if not the lasses? I'll bet their tongues are seldom still about us, if you but heard them. It's only human nature after all, as the saying goes.'

'Human nature!' cried Alec. 'It's not human. It's bestial. Would you call that hulk up the stairs human? Was there aught about him my father's bull hasn't got? By God, if that's human nature, let me have the dumb cattle that ken no better.'

'How now, sweet cousin, what youthful heresy is this? No lovers' meetings in the corn-rigs bonnie, O? Must we sit in the Dutch kirk always then, man and perennial maid on opposite sides forever? No love, no nothing at all?'

'Alec's got a bee in his bunnet about the lasses,' said Wull. 'He takes them all for plaster saints a man should gawk at but never cowp for fear they break.'

'They're not so easy broken, Alec,' said Tam.

'That swine, McNish, broke a few in his time, did he not then?

'Ach, he maybe cracked a pickle. But they soon came together again. And if he hadn't, some other would've done it. What else are they for, tell me?'

'Do you think they dinna ken what's what, and itch for it?'

'Man, there's no use talking. There's only the one way to find out. And till you try it, you canna argufy. And when you've tried it, you'll not want to argufy.'

'Hell, no. He'll want to try it again.'

'I don't doubt McNish himself thought the same as Alec till the first time,' said Tam, visibly savouring this fantastic possibility.

'Ay, like enough,' said Wull. 'The first step's aye the best.'

Alec quivered anew, lusting impotently, his hands cupping the unbroken mould, his eyes glinting in the light from the rain-splashed window, his mouth dry for Meg and Mary, willing to wound but always afraid to strike. McNish he was, rampant, insatiable, McNish in urgency and need; but cold and lifeless as McNish in fact in coffin, shrouded in channering self-denial. And always they nettled him to itch and burn with it, taunting him, curse them, far more effectively than they knew. Curse them! Damn them to hell, with McNish, their prime exemplar!

'To hell with you and your human nature! If you hadn't barged in, Ewart, they might've seen another side o't.'

'Gently now, cousin,' said Gavin. 'I own the lads are a wee bit coarse in speech and thought maybe. But pay no heed to it. It's all but talk—or nearly all. *Cum grano salis*, Alexander, take their piping hot and lusty braggadocio. Remember, heroic deeds are seldom chronicled by heroes.'

'Heroic deeds, by God! Looks yon wee runt like a hero?' And Alec crooked a thumb at Tam. 'Or the maggot-eaten dog upstairs?'

Before Tam could find words to dispute this summary dismissal of himself, Gavin resumed: 'Well, maybe I have seen more worthy claimants than our friends here. But this McNish, this fabulous libertine, this legendary fornicator, what of him? Such renown as he has garnered in his own country, this something smacks of the heroic, the grand manner, the huge hyperbole of demi-gods.'

'If you saw the blotchy wee bastard, you'd change your mind.'

'Our friend, Tam, here supports me, all the same. By-ord'nar' human, he says.'

'Subhuman, he means. And for once he's right.'

'Maybe so, cousin,' mused Gavin aloud. 'But I'd dearly like to look on this McNish. Greatness commands homage from us lesser mortals, no matter what the guise it walks about in. I hate to think of such remarkable excellence under the roof with me, and I not opportunely paying my respects. It irks me sorely.'

'Damn it to hell, Ewart, you're as bad as the rest of them! Respects! To yon puddle o' dung and disease. He stank when he was living. God knows what he smells like now.'

'Whisht, you young heathen,' interposed old John. 'Yon's a foul-mouthed gate to be speaking o' the dead.'

'Indeed, Alexander, your manner is most improper. I don't

mind ill-speaking of the dead, but disrespect for the eminent—dead or alive—is unbecoming in a gentle youth.'

'Eminent, God help us! McNish was the lowest of the low. Even his claque of toadying, arse-crawling bar-flies admit it, now he's away.'

'The lowest of the low. But is not that excellence, superlative achievement? Even eminence in baseness is still eminence; and as such must command acknowledgement and due homage. Truly, young cousin, you lack the inclination to reverence—a fault of youth perhaps, but deplorable.'

'Ach, put a bung in it, Ewart. You're talking through drink. Reverence for yon leaping hot wee baboon! Even these lads here, who try to ape McNish's antics one way and another—even they'd think twice o' speaking to his credit. Even Tam boggled at McNish.'

Alec was constrained to enlist support even from his enemies, against this mad-brained, drunken pseudo-academic tilting with new weapons at his self-mined ego, acclaiming the loathsome epitome of the prowess he coveted in vain and so denounced.

Tam said: 'Ay, he was a devil was McNish, no doubt o't. He went too far in everything. Man, I've seen him soak in here till it ran out o' him at both ends. And then away up the stairs with some bit bairn new in from Lochan school for her first yoking in service.'

'Nothing female was safe from him,' said another. 'Nothing at all.'

'Ay, but he was a celebrated character in these parts,' said Wull. 'Man, folks from far out would come in here, market days, just to have bit keek at him, and maybe a dram. Not because they liked him at all, mind you. But just to say they'd done it.'

'Why,' added Tam, 'that kenspeckle was McNish that Anderson the bus-hirer used to run trips into Ferlie from the town for folks curious for a glimpse at him. Eh man, a famous figure was McNish o' the Thrawn Wife.'

'Say no more, gentlemen,' intervened Gavin. 'You have convinced me. Shall I visit London and not see Saint Paul's? Promenade the Louvre and not gaze on La Gioconda? Shall I carouse in Ferlie, tipple here even in these unhallowed precincts of his heyday orgies, and not look upon this yet unburied Caesar of debauchery, this mortal satyr, this grave-bound rural Haroun? Never let it be said that Ewart so carelessly let slip the chance that fortune offered. Tomorrow is too late. Tonight's the night. I'll cross it though it blast me. Where lies this paragon of profligacy? Where sleeps the great one? Speak!'

'Why, he's in his coffin in the upstairs parlour,' said Alec. 'But you can't go up there, for God's sake. You're daft, man.'

'Can't, Alec? I know not can't. Would you withhold the pilgrim from the shrine? Or Turk-like block the Crusade? I'll see McNish before the worms do, or my name's not Gavin Ewan Stewart Ewart.'

'But old John'll never let you by.'

'Old John, that good old man,' said Gavin. 'If he were Charon himself, I'd circumvent him. An obolus will do it—in a glass.'

Alec looked on, happily sceptical, as Gavin leant across the bar. Reassured by the comparatively calm behaviour of his patrons, old John was busied at the sink, paying little attention to them.

'Will you have a dram then, John, before I go?' said Gavin, not so very drunk. 'And put some beer up for the boys when you're at it.'

Having thus surreptitiously breached the defence, when all were once more drinking, Gavin whispered in John's ear. The old fellow at first demurred, but with the petitioner's whisky in his hand, soon gave in. Gavin beckoned Alec to him, and raising the counter-flap pushed him through and followed before John could prevent.

'Is that young devil for upstairs too? I'm not sure o' him.'

'I'll stand surety for his behaviour,' said Gavin.

'But I'm not going,' protested Alec. 'What the hell would I be wanting with McNish's rotten corpse?'

'Hold your tongue and get through the door,' said Gavin. 'Farewell, gentlemen. We ascend to behold the mighty dead and ponder on his greatness.'

'God!' said Tam, 'you'll not see muckle, bar you lift his coffin sark.'

To the noise of laughter they passed through the door.

'Go up the stairs and take the second on the right,' whispered John. 'Not the first, mind. His sister's sleeping there. She's come for the burying. And for God's sake dinna make a noise and waken her—or himself either.'

They went carefully up the dark staircase, which creaked at every tread.

'What kind o' a ploy's this you're on, you daft devil?'

whispered Alec, groping reluctantly behind his cousin, fain enough to retreat yet following despite himself, as once he had trailed after Marion up the ladder to the attic, dreading the gruesome things he would find there, after Wull to the Thrawn Wife the first night, after Meg, teasing him down the cleft in her bosom to the dark end of the byre, after Mary Taggart to the dance tonight, doomed again to dusty answers. The bannister rail was smooth under his hand, like Queen's flanks or her in the coppice. Queen would be home by now, maybe twitching the straw in the rack, quiet at last in her unfamiliar stall and content like him never in his unquiet bed, like McNish in his hell-bent coffin sleeping alone for once the dirty bastard, his eminence laid down at last under his shroud. What was Ewart after, skulking up the stairs to see nothing much bar you lift his coffin sark? He was drunk, drunk, Gavin McNish Niven, creaking on Queen's smooth rump up the dark stairs to the stance of the lord of generation, his other frustrate self. Beer-logged and bladder-straining, he tiptoed mazily wondering after Gavin, who mounted full of inebriate purpose, intent on the moment, reckless and unaware of its precedent, consequent, coincident absurdity, climbing lamp-posts to put the light out, serenading ladies' lavatory attendants in the bowels of their subterrene chambers, conversing sagely with the skull on Duncan Murray's writing-table. So he mounted, sniffing the quarry. How now, old mole, doth rot into earth so fast? A corpse, a corpse unburied, prime like a high-hung haunch, high now, higher once and erect like a busy-loined stud bull swishing his tail like Niven's new Queen but not. Now lies he there, fordone with human nature after all, martyr to rural venery and barleycorn, second on the right on the mortuary slab Jenny the drab fished last night from the river mud with the lochan weeds green-filleting her hair and the kelpie's teethmarks printing her breasts that pillowed his head wistful in old Bess's orphan's stall. I want to go home, I'm cold—cold my corpse, cold as thy lechery that once was hot as Venus in the copse, the tusk-killed corpse McNish, the future legendary love-lorn horn-torn ploughing publican of Ferlie, dead by his own horn hand in poetic justice not by old Hector's divine visitant on the sofa's end Azrael Macandrew in the dark wings folded waiting with the mug slopping on to the stone floor and old Hector blood-slopping at the stair's foot at the stair's head supine in his coffin third of the reprobate trinity second on the right under the Angel of Death over all in the darkness breathing down his neck close behind him treading clutching at his coat-tails Christ! But no, that was Alec, breathing beer and terror. His hand on the newel-post, he ventured into the unknown, groping along the wall for the second on the right, not the first, where the mourning sister slept. Alec followed, reluctant but jostling Gavin in his anxiety not to lose him.

'Careful, you young fool,' whispered Gavin. 'You'll waken the old woman.'

'What for are we up here at all, tell me that? Come away back down to the bar, man.'

Gavin gently swung open the door, and darkness met on the threshold darkness. And the sweet fog of death was in their nostrils: Gavin in the mortuary, callous among the derelicts, Alec swooning in the unknown.

'God!' said Gavin, sniffing suggestively, 'we've come none too soon to see him before he festers from the bone. He smells, true enough, as you remarked.' And he nudged Alec, who leant on the doorpost, stupefied alike by the new majesty of death's near presence and the odour of incipient corruption. An ill way to speak o' the dead—the dead dead: old Bess, unmindful in Valhalla of her weary carrion processed at the knacker's; the fiend McNish, filling the room with his mystery more than his stench, the question of his absence stronger than the assertion of his presence. McNish, McNish, where are you, smelling to heaven, sweltering in hell, sloughed from your rotten rind, whither? The ribaldry oozing from the leering mouth, the unslaked thirst, the lust darting from eyes and loins, all that made the thing McNish, where was it? Creature compact so close of flesh, even more than the gentle heavy mare, was all still here, polluting the air, all of it here and nothing vanished into eternity, no divine spark, immortal enduring essence of vitality? Out of the invisble coffin the question rose, luminous in the darkness, noosing his curiosity. O eloquent death, posing rhetorical questions. McNish, where are you? Potent in new impotence as once in virility, contemptible and dissolute in life, how strangely august in dissolution, still, abiding no question, giving pause to the willing reviler, stemming contumely. An ill way to speak o' the dead, the maggot-eaten dog, the puddle o' dung and disease, a stink in the nostrils, yes, all this and more but more also. What? And the empty coffin, full of McNish flesh what echoed, whispering through the malodorous darkness into Alec's respectful ear, stilling his downstairs tongue, halting him perplexed and awestruck in the doorway. McNish, where are you? Downstairs in your grave sark for a glass and a pint, scuffling in the kitchen with Bella the help, astride the Ram in stellar space, capping yarns with the Devil in hell? Where? Not here in the waiting coffin: only the muckings here, the beer-soaked sawdust, the rank residue, not McNish the Mona Lisa, kenspeckle worthy, charabanc goal. Gone away he, bourne-bound or fiend-wracked or transmigrated into what gilded fly or virgin heifer, or flame-quenched and quite annihilated. McNish, where are you? In what new unseen realm or state of being? Or quite spent, quite quite dissipated, reft into nothingness, are you nowhere, not at all, gone to earth? Tell, tell, tell, you crummy little bastard, reverend in your novel mystery, under false colours, shroud-white sepulchre concealing what? Open Sesame, *nil nisi bonum;* lift his coffin sark for the *malum phallum.*

The scraped match flared and Gavin picked a way in his nimbus of light across to the box on the trestles: 'Let's have a keek at this notorious cadaver.'

White linen and the wan death's-head swam into the light like a drowned man floating to the surface in moonlight. Alec glimpsed the undertaker's mask, waxed and moulded into serenity. Under those placid lids what lecherous glances lurked? The salacious mouth was closed, the veined, debauched face and hanging jowl smoothed and powdered into comeliness. O majesty, benefaction, cancellation of death! McNish, my enemy, where are you, heaping coals of fire in hell or on my head? The match went out, taking the dead with it: 'As pretty a stiff as ever I saw—male or female,' commented Gavin, scratching for another one. 'Though I wager he's not so prettified under the cloth. Would you like a peep, young Alec?'

'Christ, no!' said Alec. 'Come away out o't now.' And he tugged the other's sleeve. But before either might make a move, there came from the landing the slither of naked feet, and Lady Macbeth in her nightgown, ghostly under the light of her candle, Maggie, come for the funeral, come to protect the dead.

'Who's there?' said she, uncertain in the doorway. The two of them aped the third, breathless in silence. Unsatisfied, she ventured in, peering from the halo of light.

'Who is it, then? Is it you, John?'

And Gavin in sepulchral accents answered: 'Who would it be then but myself, wife? Can you not leave me dead to rest in peace?'

'God save us!' she whispered, recoiling. 'It's himself come to life again.' And uttering a shriek as if rehearsed, she collapsed into the darkness, dropping the candle.

'Eh!' exclaimed Alec, 'you've fairly done it now. What'll we do?'

'Wait and see the fun, of course,' replied Gavin through his laughter. 'What else? Bide a wee.'

Up the stairs they clattered, cursing as they stumbled in the dark. The first man, jostled from behind, came hurtling through to trip over the prostrate Maggie and come to rest under the coffin.

'Mind out!' he yelled. 'There's something in the way.'

'Let's have some light, for Christ's sake,' came Wull's voice. 'It's like the grave in here.'

Matches rasped, dredging from the darkness the white-gowned figure on the floor.

'Holy Jesus! It's himself out o' his coffin, right enough.'

They ebbed on to the landing, muttering; and he under the coffin, that side of death, fairly gibbered in terror.

'Here's old John with a lamp,' said someone.

'What is it? What is it?' came the ancient's quavering voice. 'What have these young devils been up to?'

'I'll not can tell you that,' said Tam. 'But here's McNish been up to some pliskie on his own. I told you he'd not bide in his coffin and us boozin' in the bar below. But I'll own,' he added in a hushed strange voice, 'I didn't right believe what I told you.'

'It's not decent,' said one in querulous, drunken tones. 'What way can he not bide where he belongs. They should've screwed him in ere this. It's not decent, so it's not.'

'Decent or not,' said Wull, 'we'd best hoist him back where he came from. Move your old bones there, John. I'm not sure I like it up here.'

'What's like wrong then?' queried old John as he hirpled in, bringing light that chased error. 'God save us, it's Mistress Maggie! Is she gone too?'

The cronies erupted in mingled relief and vexation:

'Why, the old bitch! Scaring the piss out o' us.'

'What for's she gallivanting about in her night-shift? We took her for McNish himself—up and down for the last time.'

'What the hell's going on anyway?'

The lamp, placed on the sideboard, revealed McNish undisturbed in his place supported by Gavin rocking with laughter and Alec swaying bemusedly. Out from between the trestles crawled Tam:

'I dinna care to lie long under McNish, dead or not. And what have you two been up to with the old cow there?'

Maggie had by now regained her senses and John helped her to her feet.

'He spoke to me. He spoke to me from out o' his coffin, McNish did. He did so, then. I heard him, sure as death.'

'There now, mistress,' said John, 'you'd best get back to bed. Eh now, see how you're trembling. Dinna fash yourself, wife. You're all right.'

'But I heard him, John. I did so. Plain as I hear you. He spoke to me.'

'Just so , Mistress Maggie, just so. Get you away ben, now, and I'll see to things here. Wull, see the wife to bed while I fetch a dram up. The poor thing'll catch her death—and we'll have two corps to bury come Monday.'

'Had you not best see her ben yourself and let Wull fetch up a dram?' said Tam suggestively. 'She'll maybe catch something else if Wull there beds her down. She's a fine sonsie-like woman to tuck in by herself.'

'Steek your gab, you foul-minded devil!' said Wull fiercely. 'Come away, mistress. You're best out o' here.'

'Old John'd sooner risk the wifie than the bottle out o' his hands,' laughed Tam incorrigibly.

'It's not decent, so it's not,' came in scandalised tones again. 'Dead or alive, McNish must aye have a woman in beside him.'

'Who are these men in here, John?' said Maggie stupidly. 'Can you not let me rest in peace, he said. I heard him.'

She allowed Wull to lead her away.

'Christ, it fair hums in here!' exclaimed Tam, lighting a cigarette stump he drew from behind an ear. 'It's time McNish was under. Still, let's have a keek at him since we're here.'

They all drew nearer the coffin, staring down in silence.

'Humph,' said one at length, 'he's a brawer sight dead than he ever was living. Ay, is he.'

'Are you satisfied now you've seen him?' asked Tam of Gavin. 'There's little enough to see, as I was telling you down the stairs. And what there is, not like himself at all. Man, you'd never think yon come-to-Jesus-looking Holy-Willie was the drunkenest, randiest devil for miles.'

'He's fell changed-like, and that's a fact.'

'Ach well,' concluded Tam, 'we must all come to it, I suppose.'

Which sobering recognition set heads nodding assent and Tam gloomily contemplating its implications.

'All that lives must die,' declaimed Gavin. 'None can elude death; all must succumb. But only those that haven't lived are loth to die, the poor, bloodless, shilpit creatures, moribund from birth, cumbering the place with "ifs" and "buts" and saws of caution and restraint and prohibition. Those that have savoured life spit in death's eye and yield him but a hollow triumph. The artist and the lecher are of this company pre-eminent—the only true heroes, I aver; for they alone, each in his fashion, exploit mortality to the full. The miserable others are but prisoners of death, out on parole and daily expecting reclaim. Hence is death fictioned always as a dark, satanic tyrant, which he is not. Rather is he, to the truly living, a gentle robot geared to the tempo of life and gathering them within his smiling maw when they are tired and ready. For death after *life,* as the poet says, doth greatly please. But millions now ostensibly living are already dead or hostages to death; and therefore they abhor death as their task-master. Learn from my homily, friends, and from our departed brother, McNish, worthy exponent of the gospel it propounds. Bow we now in homage and self-dedication to him, its prime exemplar. On your knees with me and make obeisance and petition: O Lord McNish, O master of living now opportunely dead, we that are about to live salute you. Grant us some portion, be it niggard, of your unflagging zeal in hardihood, some glint of the light of lust from your eyes now dimmed and curtained, some of your pristine zest for the assay of arms and other members, your vigour in the tussle, your upspringing ardour that drooped not with the passing of the years. Bring us, by contemplation of your superb example, alive! And chiefly for this, our young brother Alexander, stubborn to evade his man's part in life, do we solicit—'

'By Christ, Ewart!' burst out Alec, who alone remained erect during this solemn address, 'I'll knock your bloody head off if you don't quit this blasphemous carry-on. I will, I tell you!'

'Hush, boy! Can I make effective intercession for you if you flaunt your obduracy openly during our very devotions? Shame on you!'

'It's no decent. It is not then,' came the drunken one again, weary in speech but manfully refusing extinction.

'But wait,' said Gavin, his eyes on the doorway. 'Here come new ministrants to the shrine. Approach, ladies, with reverent step and join our adoration.'

In came Phemie and Jean, up from their tipple in the back parlour, curious about the clamour above them. Hesitant they were before the coffin surrounded by the kneeling figures, with the stranger Gavin at its head hailing them in outlandish speech. Their eyes blinked doubt and suspicion round the room. But Tam called reassurance:

'Come away ben, wifies. God knows you two, if anybody, should be in on this, for who knows better what life was in McNish?'

'What godless cantraip is this you're up to, Tam McFarlane?' said Jean. 'Is't praying for the dead you are?'

'For the semi-dead, good woman,' replied Gavin.

'I dinna ken what you mean, young man. But I dinna like the looks o' yon caper at all, at all. Kneeling round about a coffin—like papists at a Black Mass or something. A queer-like, foreign way o' doing yon is, I'm thinking.'

'Ay, is it,' Phemie seconded. 'I doubt this is no place for the likes o' us Jean.'

'It is not then, Phemie. But for all that, I'll have a last keek at McNish since I'm this far ben.'

She approached boldly enough, followed by her companion, who ogled Gavin across the coffin from gin-dewy eyes.

'Eh, Phemie, but is he not a bonnie corp?'

'He is that, Jean. Asleep and peaceful like a tired bairn. Ach well, he had his day, had McNish, and that's a fact.'

'Ay, and a gey time it was forbye,' said Jean.

'You were then,' said Gavin, 'acquainted with the deceased valiant?'

'Acquainted!' exclaimed Tam. 'Now there's a nice-like way o' putting it, wifies, eh?'

'Whisht you!' said Jean, 'you dirty wee bastard. Or I'll split the coffin-lid here on your skull. Ay, we kent McNish fine enough, the two o' us, lang syne. To our shame and grief we kent him'—and a maudlin tear glittered down her blotchy cheek, channelling the powder. 'That's many a year gone now, when the pair o' us were tight an' waulie queans, ettlin' and game for anything.'

'Eh, but it's changed days now,' put in Phemie, looking along the years. 'He'd have nothing to do with us this long time. But he couldn't get enough o' us then.'

'Aye the young bit kittlin's he was linking, McNish. He'd aye to be first with everybody, he had. And then, flung on the midden when he'd squeezed you dry.'

'Ach well, he's dry enough himself now. An end to groping

and grunting in the dark for him.'

'Eh Phemie, I mind as though 'twere last night—the first time. After the choir practice it was—and me setting my cap at him right through the anthem. Time and time again yon old fool, Melvin, had us sing it, and the oftener we sang it the bolder I was fetching him. Eh, I blush to think o't now. But I was fair itching to get out and along the road with young McNish cleeking me close.'

'No need to tell me,' said Phemie drily. 'It was well kent you fair threw yourself at him. But who could blame you then? A fine catch was young McNish—or so it seemed. His father at the Thrawn Wife here—'

'Ach, I never gave thought to that. Not that I was after.'

'God!' exclaimed Tam. 'I bet you got what you were after, wifie.'

'Ay,' said Jean, ignoring the jest and the jester, 'I got that and a pickle more forbye. A bold hizzie I was then, and able I thought myself to keep a man in his place—and out o' mine. But once McNish was making his way, I found I wasn't so able. I clawed and screamed like a she-cat for a bit, but ach, I'd never have thanked him for letting me go. I would not then.'

'Faith, lass,' said Phemie, 'you needn't've worried for that. McNish was never like to let go, once he'd laid hold. A masterful man, he was. Ay, and hard to put down, once he was up.'

'My mother fleered and flyted and wept when she heard o't. Said McNish had spoilt me for a man. But ach, she had it tapsalteerie. He'd spoilt all other men for me. For I've never met another could hold a candle to McNish.'

'And that's no lie you're telling, Jean. He'd more smeddum than a dozen ordinary men—ricketty-backed, dainty-like gentles, a minute there then snoring fit to deave a body. God, there was little enough sleep when McNish was ben.'

And she tittered suddenly, vividly remembering, and Jean, catching her leering eye, shook with tipsy laughter. Tam slapped his thigh and roared an accompaniment, and soon the room echoed with mirth and exclamation. McNish slept on regardless, but Alec, trembling with inarticulate fury, gestured remonstrance all unheeded until in came Wull with old John hot-foot behind him.

'What the hell are you up to, now?' roared Wull, looking round in amazement, while John stared speechless, his mouth trembling uncontrollably, the bottle in his hand like a baby's plaything. Gradually the uproar abated and Wull found peevish tongue:

'This is a fine carry-on round a man dead in his coffin. Make less noise, will you. You'll have yon wifie waken again. A fine state she's in, I'll tell you. Near half a bottle o' whisky it's taken to get her to sleep.'

'Eh now,' said Jean, 'if you ask me nicely, I'll lie awake for the other half, and keep you awake beside me.'

At this invitation, Phemie and Tam were prone to break out again. But Wull swore and spat at Jean's feet:

'You! You pox-riddled old whore you! I wouldn't touch you with what McNish has no further use for.'

'Faith, and you would not, then. For it would ill fit you.'

'Peace, now, friends,' said Gavin, intervening. 'Let's have no lovers' quarrels in the dead presence of the master of love. And Wull, it would be seemly to show more respect to one who has known his favours.'

'What! That disjaskit, gin-dribbling doxy! Respect to that!'

'What are you two wanting up here, anyway?' said old John, at last finding voice. 'Get you away down where you belong, or I'll have the polis into you. I never kent the like o't. I never did.'

'For shame, John,' said Gavin, restraining the two, who made to leave, seeing nothing to remain for. 'These two poor one-time paramours have come dutifully, modestly, to bid farewell to your master, whom they loved and who loved them. Would McNish have you spurn them, do you think, like dogs from his door?'

'Ay, that he would. He's done it himself ere now,' said the old fellow chuckling triumphantly. 'Their day's past lang syne.'

'Not so. Death changes all. And mourners, regardless of station, are all equal in the fellowship and communion of death. Pass me the bottle.'

From John's unresisting hand he took the whisky bottle and continued:

'In the absence, friends, of individual glasses, we shall be obliged to share the common vessel—a custom which has, however, some weighty sanction in our country. Let us bid goodbye to our departed brother superior: We salute you, McNish of Ferlie and creation, doyen of the dark encounterers, high-pricking knight of venery, untiring winder of the corporal coil, by-ord'nar' exemplar and vindicator of the life-force. McNish, farewell!'

He raised the bottle ceremoniously to his lips and passed it to Phemie, who took a swig and handed it to Jean. So each in turn drank in silence, even John incapable of expostulation and Alec fretting in impotent disgust at the grotesque solemnity. He was last to receive the bottle and stood uncertainly. But his hesitation went unremarked, for Jean, pushed beyond herself by this final dram and the extravagance of the situation, fell into maudlin protestations of love and grief, in which Phemie inevitably joined. And so these two, wound close for consolation, bent over the coffin raining tears and snot upon the shroud, proclaiming their undying loyalty, their memories of his caresses, and much inaudible else.

'In the name of God!' exclaimed Wull. 'Did ever you see the like o' that?'

'An affecting spectacle, Wull,' said Gavin soberly. 'A heart-rending testimony of woman's love.' And he wiped an eye with his sleeve and relieved the stupefied Alec of the bottle.

'But Christ almighty, the whole o' Ferlie kens McNish debauched the two o' them and cast them aside like a pair o' tattered moth-eaten drawers past mending.'

'Even so, Wull. Heaven hath no fidelity like a woman wronged.'

But now, Tam, through paroxysms of coughing laughter, with an arm about each trollop, asked: 'Ach wifies, since you're so sweart to part with him, why dinna you bed in beside him and keep him warm?'

They drew apart unsteadily, eyeing each other.

'If there was room,' said Phemie, hiccoughing, 'I'd do it—and gladly. There's little worth biding for above with McNish under the clay.'

'And so would I too,' said Jean. 'McNish there in his grave-sark, cold and spent as he is, has more spunk in him still than most o' you hereabouts.'

'Well, now,' said Tam, 'there's little enough room for the two o' you. But one o' you might just manage. A gey tight squeeze it would be, but you'll not be minding that. Which'll it be? Will you toss each other for it?'

'It's not decent, so it's not. Two folks in the one coffin. Not married neither. It's not decent, I would say.'

'There'll be no need for tossing coins,' said Phemie with spirit. 'The place is mine by right. I was first with him, so I should be last with him.'

'Nothing o' the kind, Phemie Slater. You were maybe afore me—young slut that you were. It never stopped itching from the minute you first kent what it was for. But I lasted far longer than you. He could never thole you about him after the first two-three times.'

'You lying, filthy-mouthed bitch! Fine you ken that's not true. McNish aye lo'ed me best o' any. You were aye jealous o' me, you were.'

Thereupon they eyed each other malevolently, only their determination to keep each her position of vantage against the coffin withholding them from blows; and Tam, grasping a hand of each of his neighbours, went capering round the trestles, chanting:

'Who'll come into my wee box, who'll come into my wee box,
Who'll come into my wee box, to heat my auld, cauld banes?'

When at length this babel had exhausted itself, Gavin once more addressed the rivals: 'Your fealty exalts you, ladies. It should be recorded in the book of fame, with the chronicle of fair Isolde or melancholy Juliet or the nameless legions of Hindu dames who embraced their lords on the pyre. Such deeds are worth remembrance and emulation. But since even one of you, buxom for love as you both are, would somewhat crowd McNish there in his unaccustomed single bed, and since we can't be certain which of you he'd choose, happy with either, to clip him close under the heaving sod till the dead awaken, you must be brave, and reconciled to part from him, to part from him.'

Phemie and Jean, but dimly aware of the drift of this, yet much moved by its solemn intonation and the sadness of its final phrase, broke anew into lamentation, knuckling their bleared eyes, fingering their drooping lips, dissolving into so ludicrous a caricature of widowed grief that even old John was drawn into the general laughter.

'Do not weep, ladies,' continued Gavin. 'Take heart, I beseech you. Some seeming trifle we may find yet to reward you: some hallowed relic you may treasure in your cruelly empty bosoms, some cherished memento of the vanished hours of love to keep his memory green.'

'Ach, dinna fash yourself,' jeered Tam. 'They've got that already. Phemie's got two—one o' them a hafflin lad out at Braelochy.'

'Ay,' said Wull, 'he aye left something ahint him, did McNish—careless-like.'

'True, maybe, true. But such are only accidental fruits of mating. Something more significant they need, more reminiscent of the tender dual time. A lip now, pressed in rapture—there's two of these. An ear, fondled in dainty titillation—one for each there too. A lock of hair, perhaps, where fingers have twined in ecstasy.'

'Faith, there's barely two o' them—on his head anyway.'

'If I had my little scalpel here, my trusty, tempered blade, my knife, sure I'd cut him up in little twin stars to sparkle in their backward-looking eyes.'

'If you'll just take my knife here,' said Tam, smirking lubriciously and presenting a gully, 'he's got two o' something else might more console them. But maybe you've been at that before we came up—to fit out young Braelochy there, your cousin, eh?'

'Whisht, Tam,' whispered Wull. 'Dinna be starting that again.'

But he was too late. Poor Alec, foundered in drink and the mystery of McNish, chafing in revulsion from this grisly burlesque but lacking resource to stop it or initiative to quit it, found the release he sought in Tam's taunt. Before they could stay him, he leapt forward, reached across the coffin, and, seizing Tam by the scruff, shook him like a raicoat. The women screamed. The trestles creaked and rocked on the floor. Old John cowered away beyond the lamp-light. On each side the cronies and Gavin struggled to separate them. Up and down, from head to foot of the untroubled McNish, they careered, cursing and grunting. At length Alec let go, and both sides taken off balance reeled against the trestles. The coffin swayed and toppled over. Out came McNish in a flurry of winding sheet to smother Alec, prostrate beneath him. Alec screamed, surrendered utterly to terror.

CHAPTER NINE

Macandrew in the Gutter

O mind, mind has mountains; cliffs of fall
Frightful, sheer, no man-fathomed. Hold them cheap
May who ne'er hung there.

Gerald Manley Hopkins

Had they deceived us
Or deceived themselves, the quiet-voiced elders,
Bequeathing us merely a receipt for deceit?
The serenity only a deliberate hebetude,
The wisdom only the knowledge of dead secrets
Useless in the darkness into which they peered
Or from which they turned their eyes.

T. S. Eliot

MACANDREW, RECUMBENT against the rear wall of the Thrawn Wife, was watching the Great Bear sliding up and down the distillery chimney, up and down, it seemed to him, the climbing, tapering mast with an assuaging, soporific motion. But, simpering in the dark, he preened his recognition that not the spheres wandered from their courses, but the mast it was that slanted back and forward on the cradling swell, gently up and down in lullaby as he had watched it often in the night, sea-borne east and westward, seeking the peace that crowneth understanding. To find it here, then, in a whisky dwaum in a Ferlie gutter? The smile lost itself as he retched, puking mildly from his dribbling mouth. The stench of vomit rose from his clerical grey, and he swivelled his head round in disgust, laying his face along the granite, whose being he coveted, caressing its impassive, in- and out-swaying surface that glinted in the starlight its crystals in his squinting eye. Oh, cruel sequence of reflected light, from star to sterile stone to flesh-held eye that rolled in revulsion from its master, man. Stark antithesis of aspiration and reality struck him anew where he lay, rasping his sprouting cheek along the masonry, tweaking the mire from his garments, smelling his own foulness. O holy hope! O base, base humility! The clean stone, the cold, grained, glittering rock, which even his vile proximity could no way tarnish, whose close integrity the quarrier's blast, the mason's chisel could not reduce, the stone all unaware rebuked him, man, the fictioned corner-stone of the temple. Perception once more of his animate corruption, besmirching like fungus the austere existence of the stone, set him squirming.

He closed his eyes as though to hide in darkness from his despair and, losing visual reference to the external world, the chimney and the wall, the cobbles and the slanting roofs, he floated in swooning circles away from gravitational pull up into the vacancy of space, Macandrew no more, the flesh forgotten, its leaky hulk, and the spirit so-called, its fruitless yearnings. With the whisky-pure waters of Lethe engulfing him, he drowned for a moment in detachment, swept from himself and the shore he rotted on. His Nirvana was all but attained as so often before, his heaven of oblivion. But as always the flesh reclaimed him. His transport turned to giddiness he could not sustain, so that he had to open his eyes and anchor himself again in the gutter. Nausea rose within him and he hawked painfully from his windy, empty stomach, his shoulders heaving out from the wall behind, his head jerking up and down as the spasms shook him. And the consciousness of his abasement, lost for a moment in his flight, again enveloped him. Tears ran down to join the saliva oozing from his mouth. Abject, supine with self-pity, he surrendered.

Futile it was to evade perception of his own frustration, vain to forget, ignore the relentless introversion that transfixed him anguished to the life he abjured. How often had he fled this hag astride him, seeking to lose her in trivial business, study, hatred of Elspeth, drink? How often, conversely, had he courted her, striving in Yogic meditation to placate, assimilate her, make her one with him and him with her, and so disarm her? In argument how often had he, cynical and fearless, expounded her virtues till he convinced himself by his own bravura? All was vanity and illusion. He was the most tormented soul alive or ever. Not Ixion on his wheel, not Prometheus spreadeagled on his crag, not Job all scabbed and derelict in Uz, had known his suffering. Others before him had borne tribulation; but always with this or that extenuation: the knowledge of guilt, the assurance of innocence, faith in God, hope of redemption, expectation of the release of death, some or another sustaining conviction. He alone had claimed new territories for human anguish—Donald Macandrew of this parish of Ferlie, a martyr in the void, pretender to no legendary fame, revered by no worshippers, enrolled in no saintly calendar. Nothing relieved his torment, here or hereafter. No salvation would reward him, and death would come, bringing no gift of long awaited release but only the ultimate phase of corruption. His creed was Draconian, offering no balm of tolerance, no unction of tenderness; only the harsh gospel of doomed aspiration, the unyielding endeavour towards the unattainable perfection of objectivity.

He shivered as the cold struck through him from the stone, blew on him sweating in sickness from out of the night spaces. He drew a cuff miserably down his face, mopping the tears and snot that bedewed it, pale and hopeless against McNish's wall, man of sorrows, lonely familiar of a new despair, Ishmaelite from odious life and yet its chafing captive. Who voyages in strange seas enlarges only the scope of suffering. Why had he pressed on to the logical ultimate of his apprehension of the basic fallacy? Why he, Macandrew of Ferlie, son of the manse ingloriously born and reared in commonplace? His shoulders were weak to bear the brunt. Better for him had he averted his eyes and passed by on the popular side, the side of acceptance and careless happiness, enamoured of copulation, giving thanks for birth, resigned at length to death and decay. There was the highway for his heedless travel in fitting company—Elspeth, the hot, insatiate bitch of a she-thing. Better Neaera's web than all his desolate, mateless misery, and he dissecting the gangrenous corpse of life, smitten himself incurably with its contagion. Better laughing with Elspeth, drinking with Elspeth, bedding with Elspeth, getting twins on her instead of fostering twins ill-gotten. Better her loosened auburn hair, her beckoning harlot's eyes, the smothered ardour of her kindling under him. He shivered again in revulsion, nostrils flaring in the smell of her. The spirituous heat in his blood sent out yearning tongues of flame that quenched themselves on emergence. He shrank into his wretched self, cowering against the wall away from the contact, like a leaf shrivelling in fire, a corpse reflexing on the pyre. O deceitful benison of whisky, promising surcease of agony, oblivion of being, but yielding instead only sharper awareness of obnoxious selfhood. Curses fell clumsily from his lips, lolloping like toads down the wall, blasphemous, vapid drooling of sheer resourcelessness.

The eastern beggars, smiling, fly-crawling in the sun; smiling, chittering in the snell early morning; those little pinnacles on the climax of creation's jest, archetypes of human misery; them he had once pretended immunised from suffering by the extremity of their affliction. Paralysed he had thought them, insensitive from custom, for he would not believe such fabulous anguish could be borne. He had since learned no agony was too severe for human passion, had come to envy those unfortunate castaways, resigned to their festering flesh and crooked bone, not forever stretched like him on the rack of rebellion. How long he had tried to compass their closed circle of patience, concentric almost with that perfect O of inanimate being that quite shut him out—the stars and the moon, the mineral and the stone, the meaningless vibrant light and space, impregnable modes of existence beyond emulation but challenging it always. In despair, he had coveted the wretched beggars' resignation, poor second-best to the ideal. But he was ill-equipped compared with them, lacking their long inherited, negative power of compliance. His northern legacy of aggressive participation in life, like some wooden horse willed from his ancestry, betrayed him. He had no inbred apathy to assimilate his suffering. Always he reacted, as here in McNish's gutter, whimpered recriminations that faltered, having no direction, writhed in fruitless efforts to escape when no escape was possible.

Back against the wall, he felt himself pushed to the limit, grovelling under a weight of misery that threatened extinction and an end. But never fulfilled it. An end—here in the night? To trickle, the organic essence of him along the gutter, down through the iron grating into the drain below, and mingle with the piddled urine of generations of Ferlie tosspots. To lie, spent and sloughed the carnal shard of him, his blood heat flowing into the cobbles through his stiffening buttocks till he was clay-cold and sallow in the half dark and they found him, mired and stinking with his own excretions, and shovelled him underground to host the worms—while she prevailed above him, arching her triumph of limbs and torso, flashing her wanton eyes in her disdain, deploying all that vitality he had rejected. His dual refusal of death again assailed him, marching its double column through his sobering wits.

His bones ached and he was numb with cold but he made no move, gyved to the wall, inert in his wretchedness, while the eagle disembowelled him again, laying bare his entrails of cowardice and self-deceit. Elspeth, Elspeth, the breadth and concave depths of her, her white, slumbering, lazy lust, he ached for her, cold and forlorn in the gutter; for Elspeth, Nigretta, Candida, whom? For the bee in the pollen, the rats in the barn, for old martyred Bess the mare, for all the lusty youth and age of Ferlie lechering behind dykes and in the darkness of recess-beds. But even in the feverish contemplation, his craven flesh cried out against it No, No, No! and he recoiled again from the seedbed, cesspool, from the unacceptable paradox. Hideous and loathsome life was, rank and repulsive. No frustrate love of that could ever hold him lingering on the fringes, always hoping timidly for sometime entry somewhere never; never that could keep him still in being when his entire self in every tortured fibre cried out for escape. Only the horror, the proleptic apprehension of corruption worse even than the living caries that he carried daily in him, only that, the graceless mouldering circumstance of death, was strong enough to entomb him here above ground. Through grating teeth he heard his mumbled words of expostulation uttering. That, that, that it was! And with cunning born of practice, that and his resolve to best the bitch Elspeth, to see her age and stale and come to chafing impotence. Hatred of her, not any perverse unimplemented lust for her prolonged his living; hatred of her, and the envy of prevailing on her superbity. But perceiving his too much protesting, and feeling despite it the lust for her stirring between him, he took refuge as always in contemplation of the monstrous deformity of life that she epitomised.

But suddenly the door along the wall opened, spilling two into the close, who clattered towards him unsteadily on the cobbles.

'Hold up now, Alec lad,' said Gavin through laughter. 'The fresh air'll soon bring you round. My God, my God, what a cantraip that was! Come on now, brace up, man. You're a right softy for a farmer's son. Here, hang on to the wall then, and try and throw up something. You'll feel better then. See if you don't.'

A foot stumbled on Macandrew's unstirring body and Gavin swore. 'Hold off a minute, Alec lad. There's someone lying in the drain here. Who's there then? Is it you, Tam? Or Wull, is that you? Christ! He must be out completely, whoever it is. Steady now, Alec. That's the boy. While I have a keek at our friend down there. By heaven, but it's a thrang wee town, this Ferlie, I'll tell you.'

He propped Alec face against the wall. Stooping towards the prostrate Macandrew, he fumbled for a match. 'Now,' said he, 'let's examine the *corpus relictum.* Ewart m'lad, you're a very present help to the afflicted. A good Samaritan you are, man, and Bacchus'll reward you bringing succour to the fallen votaries, yourself not too steady on your legs either, if the truth were told, and anyone to hear it. Where the hell—? Ay, here they are. Now then, declare yourself, my drunken brother.'

In the match flame, he peered at Macandrew's face, wan and death-like as McNish's own, eyes closed to escape the light, floating disembodied in the little hollow the match scooped out of the gloom. 'God almighty, it's the minister!' he exclaimed and stared, speechless, till the match burned out. Then, straightening himself, he leant against the wall and laughed all by himself. 'By the beard of John Knox.' he stammered, 'what a pocket of godliness you've landed in, Ewart! If your father saw you now. Down on the farm—safe and out of mischief! Hey Alec! Alec, lad, d'you see who's here? It's the minister, Alec. It's Macandrew snoring in the gutter—out like a light he is. Take heart, Alec. You're in good company the night. Good company you're in, lad. Ay, the very best of company you're in tonight.'

But Alec, swaying in time with the wall, answered never a word, and Gavin returned to the other. 'Man, Macandrew, what a fallen angel you are. They'll not say you're out of touch with your congregation anyway. Will they now? A shitten shepherd, by God, and a shitten sheep! Eh, Alec?' He nudged Alec with an elbow, asking appreciation of his scholarly wit, and nearly cowped him. 'Hold up, man. Hold up till I see to the church here.'

Steadying Alec against the wall, he groped below in the darkness and hauled Macandrew's limpness up to lean like a heavy shadow beside his cousin. 'Are you there, Mr Macandrew? Are you there, minister?' he shouted, laughing in his ear. 'Come, sober up, man. It's nearly Sunday.' He shook him unresisting from side to side; but, insecure as he was himself on the cobbles, he jostled Alec, who lost balance and toppled to the ground. Whereupon Gavin released his grasp on Macandrew to aid his first charge, and Macandrew subsided into his former position.

'Hell mend you,' roared Gavin, 'for a pair of spineless bastards! I'll prop you up no more. You can lie and stink where you are.' He stood unsteadily, railing down at them, and then once more gave way to laughter. 'But by heaven, Ewart, maybe they have the laugh on you, when I think on't. They look, what I can see of them, fair at their ease there. And you, heavy on your two tired feet, stamping round to no end. Curse me if I don't join them a while. There's no hurry in it, when all's said. Hey there!

make room for Ewart below.'

And lowering himself carefully, he composed his bulk between them in the gutter, suddenly tired, the spirit of ribaldry gone out of him. He stared up from the deep trench the vennel made in the darkness at the unfamiliar roof outline silhouetted on the sky. Along the wall, water plopped into the horse-trough. But there was little other sound than that, except for Alec, stertorous on his shoulder, and the gentle sibilance of Macandrew on his other side. The air was cool on his face; and the freshness of the night, its silence and unvexed serenity, flooding down the fetid ditch he huddled in, awoke him to his own degradation, like a homily from Ewart Senior reproving in his study.

Your last chance this time, Gavin. I'm a reasonable man, I think. You can't say I've been hard on you—or unfair. Can you, now? Can you? God knows, I've made allowances. I've tried to see it your side. You've something—I'll confess it—of my own youthful waywardness. Though it's not every father would admit as much. But there comes a time when a man's got to pull himself together or let go for good. It's come to you. If you don't graduate this year, you're finished, you're a waster—a confirmed good-for-nothing. I often wonder what your mother would think of you now. But there—the less said of that. . . . Now look here. I make no threats. But if you shirk it this time, you can expect little more from me.

And so away to Braelochy to practise pre-examination virtue in rustic seclusion. He stirred uneasily, glowering morosely at the dimly seen opposite wall. Had he found his level again then? like the piss a-stench beneath him? Had he run away round the circle of self-evasion taking the same self with him to puddle in beer elsewhere, rollick in bawdry, mock the living and abuse the dead? Where was the flaw in him? All his gentle nurture, his high-minded adolescence, his zealous ambition, the felt spur of fame pricking him on—was all that hopeful past forgotten, come adrift for good and all? If you shirk it this time, you deserve nothing, for you're worth nothing. Hell, but that was wrong, all wrong. Where had he lost his way, then? What had produced this abortive Ewart paragon, fingering and clasping anonymous women in dark places, ranting drunken nonsense in rooms fouled with beer slops and old smoke, playing the wit with admiring emulous half-wits in mock-Mermaid taverns. The firth laughed in the sun with sea-birds planing down the wind. Up yonder above the lochan, the heather shook in the breeze and the sky was unsmirched as a laundered surplice. Remember all the babies in the park, like flowers for beauty, evoking tenderness; the green lawns, and the toy yachts fluttering over the pond. Look at all the young maidens, budding with still innocent promise; and the rugby fifteen cutting up the turf for fun, like the Khan's hordes scouring the steppes. Think of the wide bleak heavens over Russia, the deep Siberian snows that stretch forever, the coolies straining up Mount Everest, the drifters outward bound across the bar; and the whales snoring on the Antarctic swell, the tiger bright in the jungle, and the Brahmaputra lost in Tibet. Remember Magellan beating about the oceans of the world, looking here and there, and Cortes on his silent peak, and Livingstone walking with his Christ through Africa; and Einstein, Pasteur, Lister, Schweitzer, and all the mighty minds of old we forget about every day, hectic Shakespeare, blind Milton, and that other and that and that. Yes, think of the library loud with whispers of immortality exhorting you forward; the lying-in ward, wailing lustily to the future hopefully; the operating-theatre, where hand and brain deny death dominion—your sober hand and brain, perhaps. There's your heritage, Ewart, spent by the prodigal supine in the gutter.

Gavin stirred irritably and lipped a cigarette. In the light of the match he found Macandrew's eye on him and, taking the offered escape, he said with sarcasm intended to savage the other for himself, 'Well met by matchlight, little minister.'

Macandrew made no answer, but Gavin, sensing his attention, continued: 'You and I seem to fish the same muddy waters. Man, I've encountered strange folk in strange places, but I never thought to share the same sewer with one of your cloth.'

Macandrew still kept mum as if to provoke him, and Gavin, stung by his non-collaboration, upbraided him: 'You're quiet then, minister, eh? Maybe you're vexed I came on you lying here in your own filth. Maybe you'd rather I'd played the Levite. You're not to worry. I'll not tell tales out of the vestry.'

'Your tale would cock few ears in Ferlie, young man,' said Macandrew.

'Are you telling me the whole parish knows how you carry on?'

The other disdained reply once more. Ordinarily the situation would have amused Gavin mightily. But incensed by his own humiliation, he found himself hot with anger against Macandrew, eager to cry shame on him that they might share remorse. 'What,' he expostulated, 'can you expect from loose-living young tearaways like them in the pub here, if you go careering in your cups through the village?'

'Expect?' said Macandrew mildly. 'What should I expect? I expect nothing.'

'You mean,' said Gavin, 'you don't care a damn how your flock behaves—or misbehaves?'

'Should I care then? And if I cared—what then? Would they change their ways, think you?'

'Of course they wouldn't,' said Gavin. 'But you ought to care. It's your business to care, damn it!'

'I fear I'm ill adapted to such business, Mr Ewart,' replied Macandrew, and Gavin could fancy his wintry, thin half-smile in the dark. 'I'm no sponsor for an aimless enterprise, a lost cause of another's making.'

'By God,' said Gavin, nettled by his failure to find a companion to share his abasement, 'old Hector was right, crazy as he is. You're a disgrace to the ministry, you are. Why the hell they don't unfrock you is beyond me.'

'They will, doubtless,' said Macandrew. 'When they get round to it. But Ferlie here's a faraway bit place. And you'll recall what they say about the mills of God. And my ministry's not just so unpopular maybe with some that they'd run to evils that they'd less prefer—some clear-eyed young cleric likely, smelling of carbolic and jovial holiness. Ferlie folks are used to me. They don't meddle much with me, nor I with them. Have you a dram about you, maybe?'

Gavin was silent. Here was no whip for self-flagellation, no remedial hand towards higher things. He should have known better than to expect it from this cynical bastard of a recusant priest. No cheers for the unseen came from this monstrous churchman, who denied not his saviour only but the vitue of salvation, whose ideal was not amelioration but extinction. And like a snail crawling along the wall came from the withered thing beside him an influence, effluence clouding his new-risen star for his wagon. He spat out his champed cigarette end, quenching its red tip under a heel. His chin sank on to his breast again. And perversely he set himself to relish the sordid abjectness of his plight. Why fret and repine? This was the burden of being, which couldn't be slipped or exchanged for any gossamer of dreams or glamorous fictions. Life was no adventure, big with beauty, ripe with promise. It was a squalid drab in a wynd, big with some random repetition of her graceless self. It was a mess, a thing done in a corner, leaving a bad smell; and all their vaunted culture and religion was mere deodorant. If you shirk it this time, you're a ne'er-do-well. The canting old fool! Of course he was a ne'er-do-well. What else, when there was nothing else but ill to do, in the nature of things? What difference would a diploma make to that? More waste-paper to blow along the grey gutters of life, mere litter—like the Gospels of the faithful, the folios of Shakespeare, the scores of all the music-makers, thick strewn to hide the invincible muck oozing underneath. He was what he was, so let him be.

But this conclusion, half petulant half ironic, gave him no satisfaction at all, no relief from his morbidity. His shoes scraped along the cobbles and he swore like a schoolgirl in a fit of temper. Macandrew, perceptive in the gloom, spoke, his words cold and detached as the drops dripping into the horse-trough.

'Man is born to paradox as the sparks fly upwards. Only the unborn, the dead, and the living dead escape its impact. If there is, if there were, if there could be any value in being alive and human, it would reside solely in revolt from one's state of being. Take comfort then, young man, from your discomfort. Nourish the viper fanging your bosom. There's much virtue in the worm.'

'What the hell are you raving about, you drunken old devil?' roared Gavin, vexed by the other's uncanny plucking out of his grand mystery, his deep-down secret cynicism. But Macandrew ignored his interruption.

'Virtue is knowledge, said Socrates. And he was right. It is the sole virtue. Knowledge of the non-existence of any virtue save the knowledge of the non-existence of any virtue.'

'You're blethering in drink, man,' said Gavin with an uncertain chuckle. 'For Socrates' philosophy surely presupposed virtue as a positive value. And you deny the possiblity of the existence of any positive value. How can there be any virtue in denying the possibility of any virtue except the impossibility of any virtue except—? Christ! can't you see how daft that is?' And he broke into laughter, and almost nudged Macandrew in the ribs.

But Macandrew was not arguing. He resumed: 'Socrates knew. All the great ones have known. But they have hidden their knowledge—most of them—under one guise or another, or compromised with it, cravenly. Had Socrates but disclosed it boldly, the harbour at Piraeus would not have held the hemlock the ancients would have drunk to end it all. But Socrates slipped out alone, like the old hen-pecked coward he was. Had Xantippe been my Elspeth, would he have gone so readily, I wonder?' And he muttered into a silent tangent of reverie.

But Gavin was roused to call him back. 'Would you have had all that Mediterranean grandeur destroy itself? Does not that very civilisation prove how absurd you are? All that sun-bleached stone? all that intellectual clarity and limpid language? That visionary excellence, distilled like . . . like whisky into poetry, or cut from the rock, is there no positive value in that? And in the effort that went to its making?'

'Mere febrile escapism, like all intellectual activity,' replied Macandrew flatly. 'A refuge simply from the apprehension of futility which so few are able or willing to accept in all its implications. Look, my young friend, the mass of humanity—which comprises most men and all women—persists inexorably in its fusionless state of ignorant pseudo-bliss. The majority merely exist and procreate themselves, like vegetation. Some of them pretend to appreciation of so-called higher things, religious beliefs aesthetic and moral values, and so sustain themselves on a weak diet of delusion seeping down from the percipient ones. These last are the only true apostates, who see truth at the bottom of the well, but avert their eyes and erect fictitious counterparts on elaborate pedestals of sand. They are the treacherous intelligent ones, who pervert their powers, put out their own eyes. They perceive the only true absolute is negation, sterility, an end. But in panic they go about to water the wasteland with lies and dreams and fantasies, and hide in the jungle that sprouts to cover it—like their fabled originators in Eden. They are the recreants, who betray themselves and all mankind, and truth itself.'

'And why have my teachers hidden them from me?' enquired Gavin, leaning on facetiousness. 'Who may these villains be?'

'Your great ones,' answered Macandrew in his unwearied monotone. 'Your immortals. The men of religion, the philosophers, poets, educators, who mask the gentle Gorgon's head with cloth of gold and tinsel finery and hide it from men's eyes; who maintain the basic fallacies, devise the values, invent the legends, and divert into the life stream the race, which else might long ago have rushed hopefully into the subterrene caverns of non-being it emerged from. They are the grand upholders and preservers, the fabricators of ambition, the pretenders to millennia, the sweeteners and lighteners of irreparable squalor and degradation and frustration. Forsworn in fear, their panic eloquence and artistry persuade even themselves, and truth is buried ever deeper, so that fewer and fewer can find it. And none but one,' he added bitterly, 'has courage to acknowledge it. Could they—or any one of them—have preached the truth as fervently as they denied it, then might this torment I groan under have vanished with mankind forever, and I never have been to endure it. But they recoiled from truth and hurried into fiction, an endless reiterative serial story, feeding on its own previous chapters from nausea through nausea ad nauseam. Will it never end, never, never end? Confucius, Moses, Plato, He of Nazareth and all His western following, all the haloed host of saintly ones, gentle men who could not look on life for what it was, but set themselves to change it, Caliban to Ariel, knowing the attempt foredoomed to failure. See the ensnaring paradox their revulsion made. In blind flight from the life they dared not face, they pretended it was thus through error only and might be transformed by this code of ethics, that regimen of conduct, by love of man, or faith in God—all mere palliatives for the incurable disease of life, encouraging persistence and futile aspiration. For when all is said, a dog walking on its hind-legs is still a dog, and returns to its vomit.'

Macandrew paused, while Gavin laboured after him along the arid levels of his discourse. 'Hold on!' he exclaimed, 'for God's sake. Are you, a Presbyterian minister, preaching the futility of human endeavour? Are you denying that there's any point, any purpose in life? Is man only a fumbling, sniffing, fleshly thing without a soul? How can a man with your background desert all the evidence to reach such a preposterous conclusion? You must be mad—mad, to ignore wilfully the prevalence of virtue, the eternal upward struggle of humanity. By heaven, I'm no saintly one myself, but I can acknowledge nobility in others. Are you sitting there asserting that life is simply one great dry privy?'

'That is so, young sir,' replied Macandrew, unmoved by Gavin's vehemence. 'And you, sitting by me in the gutter, are a singularly apt symbol of mankind, which has always lain in its own shit gaping at the stars. But you are fortunate beyond your fellows, having me to disabuse you of mankind's ridiculous aspiration.'

'But that's what keeps life going!' expostulated Gavin.

'Precisely. Hence its absurdity. Have I not told you?'

'You deny all progress then through the ages?' asked Gavin.

'Recorded history denies it.'

'Havers, man! History and anthropology and sociology are all chronicles of the irresistible progress of humanity.'

'To what end?' asked the other, mildly rhetorical.

'Why,' said Gavin oddly diffident, 'to race perfection. Think how far we have come from primeval man.'

'How far then have we come? To a different gutter and the same stars. As an argument for racial progress, you are something lacking—propped here against a bladder-washed wall in a half-drunken dwaum, recuperating for a sally among your expectant sisters. Pray don't be vexed with me,' he added as Gavin stirred beside him. 'I am not blaming you. I commiserate. It's your human destiny—inescapable. But don't plume yourself upon it. Don't crow over your despised, shambling ancestors, whose vital consummation was just as satisfying as yours, and no more bestial.'

Gavin almost spluttered in a kind of triumph: 'You disgusting old puritan! That's the Calvin cloth speaking. I see where you are now. You're simply equating life with sexual appetite and sexual appetite with sin. And from this specious exercise in moral algebra, you conclude that all life is merely sin and depravity.'

'Sin?' said Macandrew mildly affronted. 'I take no stock in sin. Sin is a fetish invented by salvationists. What have I to do with sin?'

'Well then,' continued Gavin impatiently, 'call it what you will—evil, vice, immorality. Your equations are still false. There's nothing evil in what the newspapers engagingly call sex. It's a natural instinct, a bodily function like any other. How can it be evil?'

'How can it be other?' said Macandrew. 'Spare me, Mr Ewart, your adolescent ethics, your puerile apologia for living. They are unworthy of one whom I bother to converse with. Sexual activity is odious not because of the shame and revulsion it provokes in its practitioners. It is odious in the animal and vegetable creation also, in which there is little or no evidence of such reactions. It is odious because it is the source of life, and life is the supreme odium.'

'And do you expect me to accept such a monstrous categorical as that?' Gavin asked, trying to remain the calm debater.

'What is there so monstrous about it? Is it as monstrous as the condition it defines? This so rare and admirable life of yours, this infinite racial progress you prattle of—tell me of it, pray. Convert me. Help me, happy one, to soar beside you. Acquaint me with the miraculous beauty of created life.'

To his dismay, Gavin found no more to say.

CHAPTER TEN

Elspeth in the Crown Lounge

If I have freedom in my love,
And in my soul am free;
Angels alone, that soar above,
Enjoy such liberty.
Richard Lovelace

Nondum amabam, et amare amabam . . .
quaerebam quid amarem, amans amare.
Saint Augustine

ELSPETH WAS roosting on a bar-stool, her silken fullness behind overlapping its scarlet leather seat, one heel hooked in its cross-spar, one heavy thigh hoydenishly crossed over the other, though there was none there to see except Nigel the barman, who couldn't and had seen everything before in any case. Picking his teeth with a cocktail-stick under the bottles mirrored behind,

A right game-fowl she is for a small puddle like Ferlie, thought Nigel, metropolite and confidant intended and not of many similar curving on bar-stools. A London one she might be, up north for the shooting, instead of the vicar's wife. Though she never made a pass at anyone that he'd seen. And there were plenty game-cocks here who'd take the pass readily enough. And make for goal too and chance it. Wouldn't say no himself if she asked him, as others had on an off night. But she hadn't and wouldn't, though ready enough to chat him up invitingly at times, the cock-teasing bitch. Quiet she was tonight though, just drinking her whisky and water, not turning a hair of her red head. Some dish she was, for her age. And he squinted along at her, trying not to.

She was gazing into the mirror panelled above the cash-register, but she wasn't appraising herself, Elspeth, as she might have been, admiringly. Almost she was but not quite unaware of herself on the stool and the polished bar with its glass and chromium and the white coat covering Nigel at the other end and the familiar current between them. She was never quite unaware. But she was searching the mirror like the fountain-basin in the court-yard at Lallapur, looking through and beyond her reflection not for vanishing goldfish but for the more elusive why and wherefore. Her beckoning pose at the bar was only half-conscious, product of habit not design, and her thoughts were elsewhere.

Last night in the bothy, why had she cowishly mooned over misguided Candida—she, who mocked maternal tenderness, refusing to admit the function carelessness had imposed on her—carelessness or hatred of her eunuch Macandrew, who reaped where he'd scorned to sow? I thought I had lost you, and you were sleeping with the foal instead of young Ewart as I suspected feared hoped what? No cause for tears in one blooming slut the less to point with her youth her mother's maturity, her spreading sonsiness, her fading radiance. Her eyes found her eyes in the mirror and her whole self found Nigel's upon her reassuringly. There was room enough for her still, room and to spare if she cared; if she took time off to find out and why not since old Niven thought she had done so and maybe Candy too on one leg gibing in the straw of the loose-box. Tear yourself away from Mr Ewart and come home—after hours up there in the bothy, you under the covers not I. But they were wrong. And why? Why did she lose the time wading in the lochan weeds for her perverse daughter, keening inaudibly in the corner by the big bed? Here was a golden fish that hid from her searching, skulking in deep water.

Did she love the child then, the dour little mongrel, whose brown face nuzzled her breast, and she smiling fondly? Was it love? Ease, only ease, like the appeasement of their seeding among the cushions in the afternoon. Flaunting tenderness, she suckled them before Macandrew to mock him, who loathed her fertility. It was not love but merely nurture of thorns transplanted from her flesh to his. And she smiled in the mirror, remembering his revulsion, a triumph worth the ugly burden that produced it. But for themselves she cared nothing, mere accidents to be recovered from with all haste and forgotten. Their tucker-strings would never hamper her, Mrs Macandrew the missioner's wife, the toast of Shillong Calcutta all India, imperial infamy dwarfing her girlish frolicking here in Ferlie and twelve miles round.

But while she thus neglected them, he made them his own, innocent disciples of his gospel. When she discovered that, she had returned to fight him. Why? And she sought in the mirror in the fishpond in the lochan the goldfish in the depths. Was it mother loving and defending her young from harm? Or was it simply Elspeth hating him, resenting his intrusion? Certainly her hatred of him, the scorner, and of all he misrepresented was a chain that shackled her to him absurdly, stronger even than her love of living, inevitably pulling her back into his tether despite herself. That it was surely which had compelled her to return to wrestle with him in his hollow corner, not any trite solicitude for her children shrivelling under his blight.

But the fish slithered away again as she looked at Candida struggling out of his slough of negation, Nigretta sinking deeper, shrinking from the solid footing of reality. What misfits wilfully contrived by him! Their appeal to her gained strength from their obdurate refusal to make it. Their tutored antipathy to her and the life-impulse she embodied drew her closer to them, but not them to her. She pitied them. Elspeth, Elspeth, feed your hungry lambs. Her maternal bowels yearned over them: Candida coveting the grapes beyond her reach; Nigretta sticky-fingered from her private fumblings. For she knew them as she knew herself, the round completion of their fragmentary arcs, at all points consummate; and she felt bound to attempt their rescue. Was it mother love or common pity moved her? Or the cruel joy of conflict with him, that grey impervious man of stone? Whatever urged her, she had fought for them, struggling to release his early strangle-hold. But his influence was insidious, more potent than the blood she had given them or the milk they had sucked from her or the instinctive urges of their nature. Their legacy from her and from life he had nullified, and she had failed to make them recognise its worth and spend it joyously. Nigretta was irretrievably lost to him, a travesty of womanhood locked in virginity as if in stone, yet a-throb with contradictory desires and repulsions she could never understand. Compassion clouded Elspeth's eyes in the mirror as she contemplated such perplexity beyond her power to resolve. Yet why weep for the sullen tormented little bastard, who forsook her natural mother for yon priest of perversity? Let her dree her own weird, doomed to a lifetime of thwarted longing and self-abuse. What was Nigretta to her, when all was said? Only a careless misconception, an unwanted by-product. Could such a casualty defile her sanctuary of selfhood? Had she, Elspeth the mother, breached her own defences and let in exacting love to make demands on her? Was the fish she sought this self-devouring mother love? She sat on the kist in the bothy, forgetting self, remembering only Candida, mourning the child of her bosom like any daughter's mother. Little goldfish safe in my net and I in yours, man-eating shark of maternity, you have caught proud Elspeth, who loves her daughter, selfish Elspeth aloof and unattached through a hundred attachments, your maw has swallowed her all unaware. Her trawling in the mirror in the fountain in the lochan had netted no wimpling goldfish but the cannibal fish of love she had through the years so adroitly evaded.

She dropped her eyes from the mirror, searching no further, and lipped her glass. It was useless to go on pretending she regarded the twins as the stake in the game between Macandrew and herself. Themselves it was she fought for, not triumph over him. He had stolen and corrupted her children, alienated their innocence from her and from healthy normality, and imbued them with his own baneful insanity. Elspeth, you are embroiled, your womb has undone you, twin navel cords unsevered though you thought far otherwise. Mother, mother, pull your skirts down, attend the sewing bee, walk sedately, cherish your new-found babes. Nigel, bring a stiff one for a new-delivered mother, delivered into bondage after painful labour.

She smiled in self-derision, raising her eyes to her image in the mirror, while Nigel sighted along his toothpick, puzzled by her silence and uncertain of his aim. The rogue, she thought, he's seeing no perplexed mother of two, spying other twins than I am. And she squinted down her cleavage, adjusting its quotients more conspicuously, assessing her merits in his undressing eyes, comparing herself with her daughters with no satisfaction at all. For Macandrew's baleful influence could not affect their physical beauty; in them her own was enhanced by their father's eastern delicacy of feature and colouring so that they dimmed even her lustre as the years had not. And yet she loved them? Yon presently dressed Candida, dressed or undressed, could, if she chose, with a glisk of her eye or a lift of her pumpkins pull a man out of her mother's arms. So the other could also, unknowing. Passée, Elspeth, you're passée, even here in Ferlie, if once your twain get in among the men. All her mature allure, her home and colonial experience, her exciting artifice and all the rest would not weigh one tittle against their overplus. Young Ewart was basketed already, ignoring her at the bedside for visions of her lunatic daughter met in the heather to what end? Only Macandrew kept Candida on leash. Was she to slip the bitch to her own supplanting? Conceiving novel roles to play, she lifted her eyes again to the mirror, quizzing autumnal mother aggrieved by her offspring's upspring time.

But she was still a male-tempting dish was Elspeth in the mirror, her red hair aureoling her face like flame from the unsmoored heat within her. An age of loving was left to her, let the twins do what they would. And they wouldn't, frail virgin sports of a vigorous stock; yet not so by nature but by nurture rather, warped as they had been by their crippling fostering father. Not their potential competition dismayed her, but their pitiable refusal to take part in the game. Far better if she had found Candy happed with young Ewart in the bothy bed. She could have rejoiced in the discovery that the child had broken Macandrew's spell. And yet, and yet, she had felt relief when she saw the chest yawning empty. Was that mother Elspeth clinging possessively to her babe, shielding her from predatory males? Or was it rather peerless Elspeth glad to know her duchy still intact not Candida? relieved that her child was still a child and not a rival? Could she deny this contradictory reluctance to admit them to womanhood? She would have them join her outside Macandrew's charnel house; and yet she recoiled from their doing so.

Elspeth frowned into her whisky, resentful of the web of perplexity weaving within her, whose happiness had always derived from her aloof indifference to the claims of others, her serene isolation. In this self-contained house of hers her misbegotten twins had for long squatted haplessly. She had taken them in vainly to aid them, but now they threatened to dispossess her quite, damn them. She grew cold at the implications.

Nigel furtively remarked her sullen, her gaze no longer searching the mirror as he had thought complacently but invisible under lids bent on the bar-top. How could he know, seen slily through her lashes, little worldly-wise in women lecherously appraising his chances with diffident ambition, how guess, guessing only heads or tails, will you won't you lusty lady, her abstruse problems? Her former simplicity of Elspeth he might have angled in successfully with his practised flies; but not these drumlie pools of vexation, opaque and laced with snags. Out of his depth, he would drown in her, feebly clutching his cocktail-stick. She would engulf him in his natty white jacket and borrowed continental smile. Why not? A way of temporary escape he might offer from all this uncharacteristic introspection. He was a man. She had need of a man, had Elspeth. She had need of a drink.

Without raising her eyes, 'Nigel,' she said barely audibly. He started into activity, roused from erotic speculation, and pouring a drink stepped along inside the bar. Opposite her he slid the glass across, avoiding her eyes raised to his face with an equivocal smile in them. The cloth in his left hand polished the wood needlessly. What a manikin he was after all, bright on the surface as glass among his shining bottles, flat as stale beer; less spirit he had than the tipple he served her, seeping along through life like spill on the counter, stealing in here stealing in there—in where? 'Have one yourself, Nigel,' she said and her fingers touched his as she took the glass.

'Why, thank you, ma'am,' he replied with a practised smile of acknowledgement, and his glance fenced hers for a moment trying her guard and finding none. His eyes widened incredulously before wit shuttered them from her mocking. Steady, little Nigel, you're in again. What did I tell you? Caught on the rebound or something in Nigel's safe capable hands. When ripe they fall into your mouth if you're there at the time, and Nigel's always there like a good boy am I with a thumb or a finger in for the plum what a plum. But Christ, who would have thought it? Steady, Nigel, the night's young yet. The bottle gurgled his controlled exulting for he meant to have this drink now not later, wishing it later and more than a drink on Mrs Macandrew if all went well for Nigel repressing his delight behind the bar. And the bottles winked down on his meekness bent over towards her as she swung her leg now from its pivot just under her skirt, prolonging her promising half-smile.

'To a pleasant evening, ma'am,' simpered he, venturing nothing.

'To our better acquaintance, Nigel,' said she and dropped her eyes demurely to her drink as his mask slipped for an instant and his man's look asked diffidently for assurance. His adam's-apple twitched under the razored skin as he whipped off the drink. 'First tonight,' he said with the mildest of implications.

'There'll be more to come, Nigel, I'm thinking,' said she with gentle suggestiveness, her teeth clinking daintily on the rim. You're telling Nigel, he thought, emboldened by the whisky hot in his gullet. There's you to come, my beauty—but not too soon, or you're not the lady I take you for.

'It's a quiet bar you keep tonight, is it not?' she remarked, shrugging her cloak off her evening shoulders. He looked.

'I like it better this way—sometimes,' he said with gentle

emphasis. 'But we'll liven up soon enough. Dinner's late tonight, you know. Being Saturday. And they're still next door stoking up, the residents and casuals, you know. Reckon you're just passing time till the dance gets going?'

'Passing time, Nigel. You're right. That's all it seems good for nowadays. Something tells me I'll not be seeing any dance tonight though. The mood's not on me for playing the minister's wife.'

'Well now,' said he, 'I don't suppose there's much fun in it for you?'

'That there isn't. But they like to see me there whyles.'

'Who's to blame them for that?' he ventured. 'I like to see you in here, ma'am. If I may take the liberty.'

'God, Nigel,' she said with a laugh, 'you'll bring me on, taking such liberties.' And her voice drawled on the words in mock dismay.

'No offence, ma'am,' said he coolly enough, looking at the glass in her hand. 'You know that. You're a lady that can take a man's compliment and no harm done.'

'But surely, Nigel. You're right there. I can take a man's compliment—and maybe what else he has to offer. If the notion's on me.'

Their eyes met, and this time he answered the challenge in hers with open recognition and swept his stare deliberately over all he could see of her. She sat unabashed, enjoying his scrutiny, as conscious almost as he of his reaction to it. She could not help, too, admiring his ready response, grown used to Alec and new cold from Ewart. Not so meek and shilpit he was after all then, Nigel the barman, ready and willing for a free drink or fifty pence or what have you don't ask me twice. The insolent little chancer, what did he take her for? He'd be leaving a fiver in her shoe at this rate. Ach, let it be.

'Would I be right in thinking life's pretty dull for you up here, Nigel?' she asked, finding a cigarette. He leant over at once to light it. The flame flickered in his whisky breath felt in her nostrils.

'Not any longer it's not, Mrs Macandrew,' he answered in a half-whisper, his face still close to hers. She blew the smoke into his eyes, and he drew back. Not so fast, little man. I'll make the running.

'You've found a little friend then, have you, to amuse you?'

'Not much in that line for me, you know, ma'am. Not in this dump. Ferlie's not really my scene, you know. And I'm not a man that's easily suited that way, as you can judge yourself, I'd say.'

But, enjoying the preamble, she side-stepped again and, 'Come, come, man,' she said, 'surely you're not all that pernickety? Is there never a woman about the place to please your Southron taste?'

'There's one maybe, Mrs Macandrew,' said he with weighty, faintly ridiculous significance. But she refused to meet him.

'One, says you? Are all the rest of us, then, so ill made and countrified?' she asked teasingly and reached for the ash-tray so that her breast nudged the bar-top. He slid the ash-tray towards her, looking directly.

'She's not ill made, the one we're talking about, Mrs Macandrew. And as for countrified, I guess she's been around plenty and knows what she wants.'

'Well now, that's fine, Nigel,' said she. 'For she's well matched with you if she knows what she wants. And will she get what she wants, Nigel, think you?'

'She will too, Mrs Macandrew,' he answered in level tones. 'If she wants it as much as I think she does.'

'Good for you, Nigel,' said she. 'Faith, you're a bonnier man than I took you for.' And he was too, cocktail-stick and all, with the devil's own cheek and wit to match it. She'd got him going all right, to make him un-zip like that, forgetting the knuckle to his forelock. It was no bar-tender his white jacket covered now, sneaking glances at the minister's wife out of his reach. Just a man now wanting her like hell, like so many others before him. She was still the same Elspeth, despite her shackling belt of maternity, unbuckled when the fancy took her. Open up, Elspeth, too long without it. If she wants it as much as I think she does—the insolent little beast. God grant he had enough of it to make the escape worth while. Doubtless he'd be as good as another.

'And where, Nigel,' she asked, 'were you thinking to enjoy this flower of Ferlie—if it's a fair question I'm asking?'

'After the dance tonight, I'm hoping, Mrs Macandrew. And it's a very fair question,' said he, and a little smile wavered in his half-closed eyes. 'If she's kind,' he continued, 'we'll take a turn there, and then . . .'

'The rest is silence, Nigel,' she whispered, a finger to her lip, and raising her glass, she added with unmistakable promise, 'Here's hoping she's kind, Nigel.'

'Here's hoping,' repeated he and, leaning over, drew deeply on her neglected cigarette. 'That's to seal the hope,' said he, his head still poised in the shelter of her arm, his face inclined to hers with the smoke from his nostrils jetting down her bosom and the scent of her coming up to fill them.

'So fair a hope,' said she, 'needs sweeter hansel.' And smiling open-mouthed, she kissed him lavishly on the lips. His hand slid up inside her arm as she pressed further over the bar to meet him so that the stool tilted forward on two legs. One eye in the mirror observed them thus comically grappled but the absurdity failed to impress her with her nipples rising under his teasing fingers and the rest of her in heat for him despite her disdain of him.

The empty room stretched beyond to the door, the waiting tables and chairs all indifferent; and here, at the meeting-point of space and mirrored reflection, she shuddered into escape.

'Such liberties, Nigel,' she murmured hoarsely against his busy mouth.

In the mirror the door swung inwards. She pushed him away and, loud and ladylike, 'Freshen up my glass, please, Nigel,' she said. He moved at her bidding, aware of the intrusion. Retrieving her cloak and her composure, she watched the newcomer thread his way hesitantly among the tables and chairs.

Young Turnbull it was, the new schoolmaster come to assist old failing dominie Deuchar at Ferlie school. Like him to sneak in here for his evening beaker, for he was odd man out in any other howff in the village. He took unkindly to the roistering Ferlie louts, slight myopic and mousy with aye the book in his arm never the lassie. Unless he'd come in with his eyes on the ground as they usually were, he'd have something to dream of in bed tonight, the poor creeping wee man. He passed out of the mirror to perch awkwardly on the stool farthest from her, avoiding recognition.

'Good evening, sir,' said Nigel, briskly the barman tendering service. 'And what will it be, sir?'

'A lager and lime, please,' he replied as if asking where the place was at a Women's Guild meeting, and setting his book on the bar he fussed the pages busily, neglecting the bookmark that offered his place precisely. He coughed a little artificial cough and daintily smothered it with a handkerchief drawn from his cuff. His hand strayed uncertainly up to adjust his scholarly spectacles and stayed there, finding no way back, easing them up pulling them down, while his eyes stared through the lenses seeing only black on white that yielded no message, till Nigel pushed his drink before him and he escaped into his pocket for payment. All the time Jezebel sat regarding him like an unusual specimen set on a slide.

The wicked flourish in triumph over the godly, and proud flesh vaunts itself in the downcast countenance of intellect. Quite put down he was and mocked in his church-bred book-read orthodoxy, his academic achievement and his selfless endeavour by this scandalous light woman flaunting herself in a public bar-room. The meek inherit nothing but the derision of arrogance, grovelling in small circles looking for a hole to hide in. Not all his learning or his conscious moral excellence could lift his gaze up confidently to out-stare this brazen assurance.

Grasping the glass, he took a reckless draught he could not cope with and spluttered, showering it over the counter. She laughed aloud and Nigel came to mop up with a flourish. Why in God's name had he come here? Why did he stay to endure this exquisite humiliation? Far better to retire, however disgracefully, slink off leaving the field to the Philistines. But that creeping paralysis of initiative engendered by his constraint and diffidence and itself fostering them, kept him there lame and ashamed, fingering his tie and searching diligently in his book with no purpose whatever. He raised his glass and then, as if his attention were caught by some point in the text, held it a moment, smiled a sketchy smile of cynical amusement, and replaced it unlipped on the bar. But, hypersensitive, he knew she was not deceived, feeling her probing eye upon him. He abandoned his affectation of ease and sat, utterly abashed, with the blood mounting from his collar while she, caught in flagrancy with the barman, savoured his discomfiture.

'You're quiet-like tonight, Mr Turnbull,' came her mocking voice presently. 'Have the bairns taken so much spunk out of you already?'

Raising his head like a shy schoolboy at a loss for an answer, 'Why, Mrs Macandrew, good evening,' he faltered. 'I didn't see you there.'

His glasses, white and opaque in the light, beamed and went out as his head hung down again. She laughed.

'Heavens, did you not then?' she said. 'You're an ill man to catch the eye of now. There'll be grand fiddling goes on in the back seats of your classroom, I'm thinking. What do you say, Nigel?'

And Nigel, in fancy still fiddling, replied composedly, 'Perhaps Mr Turnbull sees more than he tells, ma'am.'

'Maybe he does at that. Do you, Mr Turnbull?'

Avoiding the challenge, he bent to his beer, mumbling, 'I

don't think I quite understand, Mrs Macandrew.' And how could he understand such shameless allusion? He marvelled at the effrontery that could make a butt of him, as though he were the one caught in such adulterous conjunction. *Splendide audax,* she wore guilt like the jewels on her bosom, drawing attention not deterring it. Old Deuchar was chuckling slander in his ear, dribbling out his spicy gossip like some old grown impotent satyr recollecting nymphomaniac excess, while he rustled his papers and looked here and there, discounting it all as the old man's chair-bound salaciousness. But was it?

'You're not going to sit there on your lee-lane, Mr Turnbull?' she began again. 'Come away and give us your crack, now.'

'But I'm not staying, Mrs Macandrew,' he replied. 'I've work waiting for me.'

'Man, nobody works on Saturday night in Ferlie. Not at book-work anyway. Come now, you're not to be shy of me—the lady of the manse. The learned professions must hold together in a sinful earthbound place the like of this. Come and tell us what you think of us in Ferlie. Nigel, put up another drink for Mr Turnbull. That one's flat with him looking at it.'

To the glass placed ostentatiously at her elbow he found his reluctant way and lingered on her outskirts. 'Faith, lad,' she jeered, 'you're not very oncoming, are you? For a man whose business is words you've little to say for yourself.'

He could answer that one from practice. 'Why, Mrs Macandrew,' he murmured a shade sententiously, 'the more one values words the less one tends to bandy them about.'

'Do you tell me that now?' said she, her brows arched in exaggerated astonishment. 'You may be right. For they tell me you're an uncommonly well read man. But you'd best give your books the go-by a while, else you'll be losing your tongue altogether. And yet, when I think of it, a man can come at what he wants in this world fairly, with few enough words to help him. But I doubt if you'll be knowing the few in question, Mr Turnbull. What do you think, Nigel?'

'It's not for me to say, ma'am,' said Nigel with a complacent smirk he could not disguise. 'I'm no way an intellectual like Mr Turnbull. But I usually get what I'm after, you know. Words or no words.'

She looked through him coldly from a great distance, and he dropped his eyes and retired, cursing himself for a loose-lipped chicken-counter.

Turning to Turnbull, 'For heaven's sake, man,' she said, 'sit you down and talk decent-like to a lady. You're standing there like a bad boy who hasn't done his home-exercise.'

She patted the adjacent stool. Turnbull mounted awkwardly. His legs dangled, toes stubbing the counter. She regarded him not unkindly as one might consider an amusing mongrel dog or a stranger's baby. He sat still, his embarrassment supplanted by a compelling hatred of her that amazed him. He fought down an urge to rise against her, to hurt her, to destroy her. He longed to lay hands on her. What did he want to do? He did not know. But she knew, seeing in the mirror his eyes flicker malevolently up and down her. Here was fun.

CHAPTER ELEVEN

Marion on the Fence

Here error is all in the not done,
all in the diffidence that faltered.
Ezra Pound

Between the idea
And the reality
Between the motion
And the act
Falls the Shadow.
T. S. Eliot

MARION WAS cycling along the road to Ferlie, mirage oasis green with mispromise. Stay at home Saturday night; there's nothing there for you. Stay with mother and the Book Club Choice, missing nothing you haven't missed before. You know there's nothing there on Saturday night for you cycling all the same along to Ferlie, where Macandrew descanted in the gutter and Elspeth mocked young Turnbull at the bar; where old Hector still maundered in his back parlour and the girls and the respectable young men were already dancing in the church hall. Discontent on a bicycle pedalling to Ferlie, ignoring vainly why.

Through the manse gates came free-wheeling Nigretta or Candida—which?

'Hullo, Maid Marion, hunting by night again?' And that was Candida, black Sugar Candy, bitter as aloes, on the same errand as she, the audacious little tar-brushed besom. Marion was silent, stiffening against her impact and yet welcoming it like a cold shower in season. At that first meeting in the manse drawing-room, with exaggerated disbelief Candida had said, Twenty-four and still a virgin? What's the matter? Can't you find the place?

Marion had blushed, and her mother's tea-cup had shattered on the carpet. Elspeth had set the twins to mop up and carried on regardless of the unorthodox afternoon muffin and crumpet conversational gambit. That was Candida, frank as a finger-post pointing the highway, but rooted, never following it. Never? Marion wondered, guessing a quandary not unlike her own, but lacking discernment or experience that might enable her to read this slip of oriental precocity.

You're too young to know men, she had once said, enquiringly.

And Candida had answered: Not too young—too chaste. What is there to know, except the one thing? If it were a question of youth, then you'd be too young too. And in fact you'll soon be too old to know. And she had laughed at Marion's retreating back. And once she had remarked: In India you might be a grandmamma by now, instead of what you are. To Marion's question: And what am I then? she had replied: You're nothing at all—like me.

Marion, perceiving that most of Candy's shots boomeranged ruefully on their maker, divined a state of maladjustment even more disturbing than her own. The impudent little maid was whimpering in secret, her uninhibited chatter drowning the insistent whisper of frustration. Marion's antagonism had turned to sympathy, but incomplete from imperfect understanding. Daughter of her parents, she knew little and shrank from revealing ignorance to this premature expert.

They pedalled on slowly. The tyres whirred along the macadam. The night breeze stirred their hair and the wayside foliage. Gentleness came from ditch and hedgerow, from beasts stamping at the gates, from the night scents of soil and growth, from the sky and the silence, gentleness welling up and round them, the entrancing, deluding, treacherous peace of the earth and its serene offspring, lapping their vexed bosoms, laving their troubled minds. Look at all this velvet beauty, hear its lullaby, smell its fragrance, feel its caressing like—But no, don't! Resist it, for it's false and all at odds with truth.

'Hell,' said Candida, 'I'm fagged out pushing this damned bike.' They dismounted, breaking the calm that frightened by its contrast with their own discontent, and perched inelegantly on the roadside fence. 'Why in heaven's name,' exclaimed Candida crossly, 'did they not build the manse in Ferlie instead of way out here?'

'Well,' said Marion laughing, 'if they'd built the manse in Ferlie, Ferlie would have moved out here, most likely. God may see a sparrow fall, but the minister needn't. So it wouldn't have made much difference.'

'At least I'd have been sailing down this brae, instead of trudging up it,' said Candy.

'And why aren't you?' said Marion, mocking.

'For the same reason you're not, modest Mirren. Here runs the broad highway, straight to mirth and the dance, perchance romance, and great hairy masculine men, in whose sight we may find favour or something.'

Marion laughed. 'We'll do that, not a doubt. But they won't find much favour in ours.'

'Oh indeed, hoity-toity! And why then the foray? Why not quiet at home with Mother Niven and the parish magazine?'

'Ach well,' said Marion weakly, 'it's Saturday night. It gives you something to do for a change.'

'It gives you something to do, all right. But you won't do it. Even for a change.'

'What do you mean by that, Candida?' asked Marion, dutifully feigning ignorance. But Candida merely grunted ironically so that Marion was forced to resume. 'And you? Will you?' She heard the girl's breath indrawn sharply but no answer came. She continued: 'You won't get the chance anyway, my child. They'll gawk and leer and paw you in the dance and let their fancy wander. But they won't dare any more. For you're the minister's daughter—whatever the song says. So bide quiet and content you demurely.'

Candida laughed unpleasantly. 'I'd soon make them forget the minister,' she said. 'If only I could.'

'Yes,' said Marion reflectively. 'Maybe you would too. But heavens, Candy, these Ferlie lads are not for you. You know them well enough. Coarse as heather. Dumb as a gate-post. What would you be doing with the likes of yon?'

'Marion Niven,' replied Candida, 'for a woman of mature years you say the funniest things. What would I be doing with them? Is it information you're asking for? I wouldn't be hearing their catechism—or playing twenty questions. Dumb are they? There's little enough to be said when the thing's to do.' And she fell suddenly silent, feeling again the heather chafing her back and the Ewart man mumbling incoherently against her withdrawn cheek and the thing still to do.

'You're well enough informed for a maiden just seventeen,' sneered Marion, unable to hide her pique.

'Och now,' mocked Candida, 'there's little in it I'm not knowing this long time gone. It's easily learned enough.'

'And are you telling me, then, you could let those farmyard animals . . . take you?' She brought the word out like a daring obscenity.

'Mirren, Mirren, my God, Mirren, you've been reading the wrong novels. How can you, visibly hungry for a man, talk such rot? God help the man who finally takes you. He'll find he's giving a hell of a lot more than he's taking.'

'Candida, you little horror!' exclaimed Marion. 'What a thing to say! What do you mean, anyway?' she added, almost coyly.

'Oh for heaven's sake, stop teasing yourself. You poor belated virgin, I should pity you. If I could spare it. What do I mean, indeed! Who knows better than you what I mean?'

'And if I do know,' Marion exclaimed almost petulantly, 'what am I supposed to do about it, eh? Is it so easy, then? Do I accost the most virile labourer I can spy and haul him into the barn? Or do I get me to the city and solicit in the side-streets? Evening, dearie, looking for me?' She laughed but it didn't sound right.

'Of course,' said Candida coldly, 'there's no use discussing the thing at all if you're going to make it offensive and nasty under nasty terms. Accost! Solicit! The words are dirtier than the deeds they name—like so many in English. You're just looking for an excuse for evading the point by smearing it with filth. That's merely silly.'

'All right, Candy, don't scold me. I was only joking. But what is the answer? What's a girl like me supposed to do? You can't just take a man like . . . like a dose of salts.' And Marion shivered at her own simile.

'I don't see why not,' said Candida simply. 'Every ailment has its remedy. Even if you must hold your nose to take it,' she added almost inaudibly.

'No, no, Candida! That just won't do. That's just wild talk. What do you take me for? You turn the thing into a mere question of hygiene.'

'What else is it—at your age?'

'You insulting little devil! You surely don't think I'm past . . . well, love and all that?'

'Of course,' sneered Candida, 'if you have to fall in love with the man first—! You're certainly old enough to know better than that. That's only making a simple thing needlessly complex. It's only relieving one strain by imposing another. And the new one's not so easy to handle as the old—or so observation suggests. Is life not difficult enough without that?'

'But Candida,' remonstrated Marion, 'that *is* life, isn't it?'

'What?'

'Why, love and marriage . . . and children and so on. Surely life isn't just work and appetite?'

'And what else are your love and marriage and children but work and appetite—and the fruits thereof? All respectably organised and nicely labelled. Why submit to the pigeon-holing, the strings attached?'

'Oh Candida,' Marion almost wailed, 'you're wrong, you're wrong altogether. I'm not bold and unconventional like you but I know it's not like that. You miss out so much. You miss out tenderness . . . and self-sacrifice . . . and sharing. You miss out all that's decent and beautiful in human relationship.'

'Yes, my dear romantic elderly sister,' said Candida. 'And I also miss out what you miss out of your pretty picture. Selfishness and jealousy and deceitfulness. Spitefulness and possessiveness. And sheer boredom and fed-upness. All that's tawdry and ugly and humbugly in your human relationships. Does a lover's tender kiss or a husband stroking your hair make up for that?'

Her voice had risen in scorn, beating Marion into fretting silence. Candida continued: 'But if you're so enamoured of romance, what the hell have you been doing all those years? Does your breath smell or something? Surely there must have been stray fish even in this backwater nibbling around you. You're no ugly duckling—even under a weight of chaste summers. A bit flat maybe, in places. But you have a pretty pale face. And look at all that yellow hair. What gold for a man's fingers!' She twined a loose curl round Marion's ear. Marion involuntarily caught her hand and pressed it gently, but she snatched it away.

'Surely,' she said, 'there have been plenty willing enough to give you all you wanted—with love, marriage and children thrown in for social makeweight.'

'Yes, Candy,' said Marion musingly. 'Oh yes, there have been. Plenty.'

'Then why on earth are you still here, tormenting me with your sex problems? Why aren't you married long ago and breeding?'

'Married?' said Marion. 'Yes, I've been asked—several times. Oh I could have been married all right. But marriage is so . . . so permanent.'

'Huh!' cried Candida. 'So is that old-maidenhood you're cultivating. Permanent as death. And just as lifeless.'

'I know! I know!'

'And besides,' went on Candida relentlessly, 'if you shy away from marriage because it's so permanent—though I don't follow you there—there are plenty of temporary posts available.'

'I know! I know that,' said Marion, fidgeting miserably on the rail.

'Christ then, woman!' exclaimed Candida exasperated, 'what are we wasting all this time for? If you know all there is to know, let's be getting on where you can implement some part of your knowledge.' And she hopped off the fence. But Marion made no move to follow her.

'It's all right for you, Candy,' she said mournfully. 'Everything seems so black and white for you.'

The darkness hid Candida's ambiguous smile. 'A result of my parentage maybe,' she said softly.

'But for me,' Marion continued, 'there's no black and white, no certainty, no assurance. I don't know what I want, or how to get it, or whether I'd want it if I had it. I'm afraid to move any one way for fear I find a better when it's too late. Other people seem to carry on serenely enough, just doing the thing that presents itself. They never seem to bother about consequences. For them there don't seem to be any consequences—only a kind of unbroken circle of living. Why can't I be that way? Why can't I?'

'You're afraid of life, my poor Mirren,' said Candida, impatiently revolving the pedal with her toe.

'No, no, Candy!' Marion exclaimed eagerly. 'I'm not afraid of life. I'm afraid life may not yield me all I want unless I play my cards right.'

'And so you're sitting on them, eh? You can't bluff life, stupid. Better play them and collect. There's plenty in the bank.'

'But if I only wait a little longer—just a little longer—there may be so much more.'

'Like hell there will, greediguts! You won't get happiness by waiting for it. Or anything else. The only thing that comes to him who waits is death. So I'm waiting no longer. Goodnight.' And she was off like a ghost, floating above the road.

'But Candida,' said Marion, aware but oblivious of her going, 'I know that. You don't understand. It's not happiness I'm waiting for. It's the moment—the precise moment—the right tide to take, Candida. That's what it is. There's only one life. I can't take any chances. It's so easy to make a mistake and get bogged down in weary, workaday dullness and squalor. Like mother, for instance, or any of the women hereabouts. Surely there's more than that, Candy. That's not life, is it? Is it? Is it?'

A bat squeaked and she ducked her head instinctively without for a second losing her place in her ardent self-persuasion.

'I could have had that kind of life, easily enough. Young Murray of Drumsheugh offered that over and over again. So did John Fraser—poor honest John Fraser, who never knew how attractive he was. He just took my refusal for granted and up and married yon wee bauchle from Chapelhaugh. Two sons they have now and hopes of a daughter for Christmas. They might have been mine, Candy, and he with them, instead of a single bed and dreams to comfort me. I'd like if you'd marry me, Mirren, said he, not looking at me at all. This can't be it, I thought. Not this, surely. So gawkit he was—so farmer's-boyish. And still is, too, still is. I could never be thirled to him and his clutch of bairns. No, John, no, I'm sorry, John, but no. Always I was saying no, no, no. Ranald nearly made me whisper yes. In his final year it was. Fine I remember. On a night just like this, Candy, and me throbbing like a bird in his hands. I liked Ranald. He was wild and throughother, mother said and warned me against him—more's the pity. For yes was halfway up my throat and certainly all through the rest of me. But it was No, no, Ranald, please no. And he didn't. And why did he have to take no for an answer, Candy? Why did I have to deny him—always shivering on the edge of action? Always wondering, wondering. Should I? Should I? What is it in me then, Candy—this fatal urge to withdraw? this saving clause always? What is it, Candy? But Candy's gone. Everyone goes from you, Marion. Everyone leaves you. Because you won't play. Not even with your own toys, Marion, you won't play. Why, little flitting bat, why won't Marion play? Why gentle spider, spinning on my lashes, why? why? why? It's grown very dark. I'm afraid of the dark. For it's hard to say no in the dark, when assent is urgent and hands and desire insistent and tempting. But Marion can say it. The word speaks itself from the little voice-box inside her. No, no, please no. Juliet on the balcony, precocious little Juliet, she can't say it. No, never no. Bathsheba on the rooftop yonder all naked in the sunshine says yes, if asked at all. Guinevere the queen and saintly Heloise, Helen and the lady passing by, Creseide, Francesca, bonnie Mary of Argyll, yes they say, yes please, thank you, thank you. Mrs Niven and Elspeth and all the dairymaids never know no. But Marion does—by day or night, for better or worse, to proposals of marriage or frolic, no says Marion, no, please no. This is not the moment. It's not for this I'm waiting. For what then? Oh for what!'

A bird in the hedge twittered deprecatingly at her unnatural clamour. Marion smiled inanely and grew smaller on the fence. This was foolishness, talking to herself like a daft woman of the roads. She should get off the fence and ride to Ferlie to the dance, ride home to bed. But it was easier to stay where she was, though the wooden rail was scoring her flesh. The darkness sat on her as she on the fence, but she made no impression at all on it. What was Ranald doing in this darkness? What was Drumsheugh or John Fraser doing or any one of them all who had wanted her, whom she had wanted unavailingly? They weren't wanting her any more, quite forgotten, slid into their limbo, gone. They had achieved what they sought, recognising it when come upon. But she had achieved nothing but an awkward seat on the fence. She had nothing but her own wants and needs, the foolish virgin's portion.

What then was she looking for that she never found? Ask the bat, the spider, the bird in the hedgerow. Only Marion knows; and she won't tell—can't tell—must tell! Escape no longer into reverie. She coveted loving without love, marriage without ties, motherhood without children, a home without furnishings, event without consequence. She longed for freedom in attachment, adventure in security. If one could mould life to one's own pattern. If one could but make it a perfect engine, geared to one's own control, never demurring or going its own way. If only it might be a broken series of bright particles each in isolation, a galaxy of discrete, high-pointed stars of happiness, serene and self-existent, radiating ecstasy. But it was not. It was a warren of corridors, each new one entered echoing with voices, memories from its forerunner, whispering ghostly with hopes and fears and wonderings of the next. It withheld the present, yielding only the past and future. If one might enjoy completely a moment, a person, an encounter; drain from it all it held of rapture with no misgivings, no after recollections—there was happiness! But nothing existed in mere solitariness. Every thing, every place, every person sent out waves of feeling, lapping at one's heart, pushed sly fingers clutching, not to be eluded. Even a moonlit night, the pinewood's scent, a silly sentimental song, were clogged and cloyed with teasing associations. All this she had tried to escape, struggling hard to deny it, to pretend it was not so. Could the sun not shine without shadow, the flower bloom with no trailing root? Marion, Marion, live on the high places. Come not down, for love is of the valley, and love will snare your feet, mesh you in a thousand little threads and hold you fast forever. Give but the tiniest atom of yourself into another's keeping and it never returns to you. No, Ranald, no, please no. Close on the action's heels tread the implications, inescapable. Each deed, each attachment formed, each love allowed trails strings to coil about your heart, to trammel your feet free-stepping no more. Free-stepping where, Marion, where Marion sitting on the fence, wandering in the desert, stranded high and dry, face against the impasse? There was the dilemma that she never fronted squarely. Evade life's groping fingers and life in return disdained you. Maintain jealously your freedom of choice and no choice was granted you. You sat, cold and aloof like the snow in the high corrie, trapped fast in your own remoteness, out of life's reckoning. Marion, Marion, what have you done with all your bright talents, lover of men, mother of children, soft of breast and tender of heart?

Marion was crying softly, trying not to cry, and one hand plucked at a splinter on the fence-rail. Through her tears she gazed at the darkness, in and out at the darkness: and the night wind came and blew right through her so that her heart turned over like a little hard cold pebble in the burn.

CHAPTER TWELVE

Turnbull Agonistes in the Crown Lounge

> Let no man deceive you with vain words: for because of these things cometh the wrath of God upon the children of disobedience.
>
> *Epistle to the Ephesians*

WHEN CANDIDA entered the lounge, she did not immediately see her mother, nor was she herself seen by Elspeth, who was hemmed in by a hemisphere of hotel guests at the bar. The place was busy with after-dinner tipplers. Candida, concealing her uncertainty under a specious assurance, advanced over the carpet, disdainfully glancing here and there without seeing very clearly what her eyes rested on, wondering obscurely what she would do when the carpet gave out. She could not hide from herself the relief she felt when her mock-duchess arrogant eyes lit on Gavin, alone in a corner; and with never a thought of their last encounter, she followed the line of her glance to stand at his elbow. Unaware of her coming, he continued to stare from beneath scowling brows at the group by the bar with such concentrated distaste that she looked for the reason.

In the mirror above the cash-register, Elspeth's Saturday-night, artificial-light personality was holding court, embosomed high among the dinner-jackets. With casual poise she sat on her absurd high stool, coping charmingly with this one and that, mischievously making most of young Turnbull, who sat beside her with a large whisky in his hand and his glasses bent unwinkingly on Elspeth. Candida, who had seen the like and more many times before, could not restrain admiration and envy. What a superb creature Elspeth was—lazily unperplexed as Juno or some great cat-thing in the sun. What a mother for such a daughter!

In pique she turned from the reflection and, placing herself directly in front of Gavin, 'And you, Mr Ewart,' said she with a sneer, 'why do you hang back? Is the quarry too fast for you?'

Gavin looked up blankly and she watched recognition

focussing his drink-smudged, glittering eyes. He smiled rather uncertainly, chasing his memory of her through his fuddled brain. 'Hullo,' he said. 'Where's your little horse?'

'I'm sitting on it,' said she, looking at the chairs.

He rose at once, more quickly than was prudent, and swayed towards her across the table. 'I'm sorry, Miss Macandrew. Sorry. Forgive me. I've had a most exhausting evening. Do sit down, won't you?'

As she moved to comply, he put a hand on her sleeve. 'No, not there please. That's your father's chair.'

She stiffened. 'Macandrew? Is he here then?' she asked, her brows drawing together. But she took her place beside him, shrugging away his touch, which lingered on her sleeve.

'Yes,' he replied, without interest, regarding her with evident satisfaction. 'He's out with Alec at the moment.'

'Alec Niven! Why, this is a party!' she exclaimed affectedly to cover the discomfiture she could not evade under his tipsy stare.

'Yes,' he said with never a change of inflection, his eyes still on her.

'No need to ask where they've gone,' she said. 'Will they be back soon?' and she broke his trance by kicking him sharply on the ankle. 'Will they be back soon? I said Mr Ewart,' she repeated while he massaged the place silently, grimacing at her.

'From their appearance when they left, Miss Macandrew,' he said gravely, 'I don't think they'll be back at all.'

'And from your appearance, Mr Ewart,' she replied, looking him full in the face, 'I think you won't be long behind them.'

'But for your arrival, Black Eyes,' he said gallantly, 'I can't deny your guess might have proved correct. But,' he went on, picking his way carefully through the compliment, 'your being here to make it makes it wrong.' And he ended with such an engaging smile at his own cleverness that she had to smile in reply.

'And yet, when I came in, you didn't seem on the point of leaving,' she remarked with a swinging glance at Elspeth in the mirror. 'Deep, deep in reflection you were.'

'I own it, I admit it,' said he, finding wit to match her challenge with a visible effort. 'But what is Venus when the moon doth rise? And anyhow, who wouldn't change a two-dimensional image for a three-dimensional reality?'

'I should have thought you might,' said she against her

intention, looking at the table-top. And they were away, both of them, struggling in the heather, she clearly as though in bitter fact again, but he only dimly apprehending the memory, as if a part of another's experience, retreating from it, so at odds with present promise.

'Oh that!' he said deprecatingly, pushing a hand through his hair, glowering here and there.

'Yes,' she said tonelessly.

'Ach well,' said he, and stopped. 'Ach well, let's have a drink, eh?'

She pouted slightly, looking at Macandrew's empty chair. 'I'll have . . . coffee,' she said reluctantly.

'Coffee!' exclaimed Gavin. 'Oh, coffee. Yes of course.'

'And you'll have coffee too, Mr Ewart,' she added decisively. 'I don't like half-tipsy men.'

'Well now,' said he, 'if it's half-tipsy men you don't like, there's a shorter cure for that than coffee.'

'Black coffee, Mr Ewart,' she insisted mildly, and looked at him.

'As you say, Miss Macandrew,' he assented, smiling into her eyes.

She felt happy, quite embarrassingly happy. Under his smile, she changed colour, dropping her gaze shyly to hide the glow of pleasure in her eyes. Quite novel the sensation trembling through her; she did not understand it but she liked it. Tilting her head back, she let her delight come out, through her eyes, between her parted lips, in silent laughter. His smile vanished for a moment as he looked down at her, to flicker back again diffidently, like a boy's before a gracious headmaster.

'Very black coffee, Mr Ewart,' she almost giggled.

He bowed slightly. 'There's almost no service here. I'll order next door,' he said and moved off. But it wasn't needed any longer, for he felt quite sober from astonishment. A unique piece she was. What was she up to now? But he could not help feeling pleased with himself.

Candida sat on at the table, the laughter dying on her face, lingering inside her. This was different, surely, this open-eyed delight, from that other blind crying in the night for what she could not reach. He was a nice person. Surely this was different. She felt no desperate urge to vindicate herself. She felt warm and deliciously expectant. She fingered with no trace of revulsion the sleeve where his hand had rested. If only this tranquil promise might remain—like the warmth of the foal in her arms in the straw, quiescent and oddly appeasing. She sighed, seeing in the water carafe herself in his normal embrace, no more fluttering like a wasp in the jam pot. Perhaps it might be so.

She looked up to see not Gavin but Macandrew before her, like a wraith of Indian dust. He regarded her from lustreless eyes, holes in the clay shape of his face, into which she stared with fascination, all the new buoyancy drowned inside her, already as if it had never been. In silence he sat down, his back to the mirror, while she set herself to fend him off, concentrating on the gaiety round Elspeth. But Elspeth was far away, quite unaware of her at all. When Gavin returned with Alec, she did not lift her eyes to him. She was there, like a mirror in a darkened room, all the light he had unwittingly kindled gone out of her. He cursed Macandrew quietly, relapsing into that morbidity she had momentarily dispelled. And so they sat, all four of them in their corner, like displaced persons waiting onward dispatch.

A waiter brought coffee. Macandrew retched painfully. 'Fetch me a large whisky, waiter,' he said, closing his eyes against the black liquid streaming from the pot in Candida's hand. Alec raised his cup warily and put it down again unlipped. Gavin squinted at Candida, who ignored him. 'Is this black enough, Miss Macandrew?' he asked. She shrugged but made no other response. 'Would you like a cigarette?' he ventured. She shook her head. 'Would you, Alec?'

'I think I'm going to be sick,' said Alec, a foolish smile licking his wan face.

'Hell no!' exclaimed Gavin. 'Not again! Here, have some coffee and you'll feel better.' He prevailed on the other to drink, Alec sat back and looked at Candida, twisting his handkerchief between his hands. Gavin lit a cigarette and blew the smoke across at Macandrew, who belched again and paid no heed. 'Well,' said Gavin, 'here's your party, Miss Macandrew. What devilish, merry sport shall we begin with?'

His mood was beginning to change again. Saturday night, by God, in Ferlie! Annoyance crept in, ousting dejection. He was weary of dejection. It had overplayed its hand. Better far the bawdy by-play in the Thrawn Wife than Byronic melancholy in the lane outside. To hell with this death's-head, Macandrew, rationalising his drunken remorse. Saturday night was no time for penitent hangovers. Let them bide till Sunday. Think of him, Ewart, Gavin Ewart, lowing like a moon-calf all over the village, repenting his sins, shaking a sorrowing head over his wayward, mis-spent youth, when youth still remained to spend. O father, father, I grow more like you far too soon. No more the late nights, the ribaldry with wench and waster. Only regret for the past, ascetic study to do better. Begone light youth, you have outstayed your time. Make way for the sere and sapient spirit of renunciation. See where he comes, treading sedately on soberly trousered legs, white-collared and restrained of tie, with his little black bag in his hand and the mystic symbols after his name, with a kindly smile for the children and a cool impersonal hand for the women —Doctor Ewart, Galen come to diagnose, bile on the stomach, cold in the head; here is all the art of healing diluted in water, purveyed by the esteemed Doctor Ewart, so aloof and unapproachable and irreproachable, though they say he was a wild devil in his youth. Christ! there was time enough for such a penitentiary to close about him: the regimen of living, the rules for professional and private conduct, the responsibilities to this and that but never to oneself. Away with it! Up McNish and all the hairy ones! Thaw this untimely frost hardening the blood in his veins, killing the oats unsown. Give the primrose leave to sprout, let the chimes ring out on other midnights, chase the black hag Melancholy over the chimney-pots. Ewart is himself again, Horo! And he bellowed aloud, 'Horo!' and thumped the table so that the crockery danced in sudden silence. Heads turned, mildly reproving. Candida eyed him, wondering. Alec grinned stupidly, twisting his handkerchief the opposite way. Macandrew, with a sour look, hastily drained what was left in his glass and brooded on the spilt remnant wistfully.

'I tell you,' roared Gavin, pointing a finger at Macandrew, 'I tell you, leprous apostate from life, you are a pestilence plaguing the lieges. Brief contact with your infectious breath has all but withered the summer bloom on Ewart's brow, stilled the rising marrow in his bones. Away! you more than Satan. You renegade, petrified priest! Cancer, canker, chancre! Neurotic, nihilistic, atheistic sorcerer, you all but Jack o'Lanterned Ewart into your desperate slough. Ha, did you not? Proselytising in the piss-hole, you stinking stank damming life and laughter. You all but had me in your poisonous craw. Weak I was with liquor and licence, an easy prey for melancholia. But that was only a shadow of Ewart you joined with—a feeble, pliable creature, a veering weathervane for the first wind blowing through the lane. But now I'll cross you—blast you!—counter and confound you. I'll Sinbad you, old man of the Sargasso. You slimy crawling thing, I cast you off!' And he rose menacingly over Macandrew, who sat licking a whisky finger. 'Out, monster! Bile-blown, spleen-spewing, pox-porous vennel-vomit, out, I say!'

'Bravo, bravo, young man! Bonnie flytin', yon!' cried Elspeth, unsteadily erect on a spar of her stool, one hand on Turnbull's shoulder.

'That's an awful way to talk to the minister,' said Turnbull, goggling. 'I must remonstrate with that young waster, whoever he is.' Turnbull would have risen, but Elspeth's weight anchored him, to gaze up at her nearness like a hungry but obedient spaniel puppy.

The residents murmured. 'What's to do then?' 'Must be drunk, the fellow.' 'Somebody from the street.' 'Management should do something.' 'Who let him in?' 'Chuck 'im out.'

'I saw you yesterday,' said Alec to Candida. 'Do you mind o't? By the lochan? You hadn't a stitch to your back. Or front,' he added and dropping his gaze, he sniggered like a schoolboy reading a lavatory wall.

'Hold your tongue, Alec,' snapped Candida.

'Now then, sir,' said Nigel placatingly, crossing from the bar. 'You mustn't make so much noise, sir. Good evening, minister. Is this young gent annoying you, sir?'

'Annoying him, says you?' shouted Gavin. 'Destroying him I am. Exorcising the foul fiend I am. Chastising the serpent with scorpions. Lashing his hulk with the broth-wrath of life.'

'Ah, Nigel, you're there then,' said Macandrew. 'Bring me a large whisky, will you now. You'll not heed my young friend here. I'll calm him.'

'Damn him, you mean! If he lets you,' roared Gavin, shaking a fist.

'Lay on, Ewart!' screamed Elspeth, tottering on her perch, her gown slipping heedlessly off one shoulder to Turnbull's delighted discomfiture, red tendrils of hair webbing her tipsy-bright eyes, all her coquettish veneer overlaid by natural fervour. 'Tramp him in the dust,' she called, 'and I'm yours forever! Or nearly,' she added, propping a steadying forearm on a tall bald head in front of her. 'Faith, laddie, but I love the long venomous tongue of you.'

Interrogative, deprecating looks were bent on her by her southern courtiers, an eyebrow raised, a smile exchanged, and they drifted off to join their womenfolk bridling at the tables. All along they'd known. Only had to look at her.

Nigel didn't at all like this turn that events were taking. He could see his windfallen Elspeth being gathered into somone else's basket. But he'd just have to tag on and see. Nothing rash, Nigel boy. He addressed Gavin again: 'You really must be quiet, sir, if you please. You're causing a disturbance.'

Candida poured coffee, pulled Gavin's sleeve. 'Try this, Mr Ewart. It's blacker,' she murmured demurely, wondering why she troubled to rescue him from so delightfully scandalous a public exhibition, which ordinarily would have made her journey into Ferlie unexpectedly rewarding. Gavin looked down, open-mouthed for another tirade, and subsided reluctantly into his chair.

'D'you mind it?' said Alec, slipping into the silence. 'I saw you yesterday. You and the other one—mother-naked.'

'Be quiet, Alec! You're drunk!' she said fiercely, frowning across at him.

'Eh, but you were bonnie,' he sighed gustily, ending with an ominous hiccough.

'What the devil's he raving about?' said Gavin vaguely, irritably, unsure of himself.

'He's talking through drink, poor boy,' she replied and relapsed into silence, feeling Macandrew's impassive gaze upon her.

'And so, young sir,' he began, 'you cast me off, then? You deny me, eh? Not only me but the rational honesty within yourself. You're back in the squalor, down in the beast-pit fighting for your life, your poor gnawed bone, thrown in by chance. And all our dialectic, our research at the roots of things, our subtle riddling of the sands of being and non-being all forgotten and abjured. And all our self-denying ordinance rescinded by a female gesture. The swish of a woman's hem-line blows all your conviction away, eh? Poor woman-born, womb-lorn, uxorious Ewart, your hour-long glory is departed. Grovel again.'

'Who grovels for love is face down to some purpose,' sneered Elspeth, who had crossed on Turnbull's arm from her deserted throne and stood beside him. 'But how would you know that, you scraggy old bell-wether, tolling lambs to their doom? You've no lamb here, though, I'm thinking,' she went on, regarding Gavin with unconcealed interest. 'A ram, I'd say. And an ill-mannered young beast at that. Is there never a chair for a lady, then? I've a back-ache, jockeying all night on that damned penny-round high seat.'

She drew a chair up between Gavin and Alec while Turnbull settled doggedly behind. 'Man,' she said to Gavin, 'you wag a fine tongue in your head, Mr Ewart. I'd never have thought it, the last time we met. Of course, I've known many a fine fellow who'd little to say in bed, though he'd rant fine enough on his legs.'

Severally her listeners considered this remark and its implications—all except Alec, who was undressing Candida, trying to recapture sensually what he remembered. Macandrew, gazing again through the bothy window, saw merely Elspeth recalling the many not Ewart and cared not either way. Candida, back in the loose-box, smarted again under Elspeth's fingers applied in response to her gibe, and was in fancy her mother negligently swallowing the long tongue Gavin had proffered in the heather in vain. Gavin, more closely in memory engaged with the daughter almost unravelled in the corrie than the mother close-knit in the bothy, was not inclined to respond to Elspeth's bawdry. It was left to Turnbull, fluttering his new-sprouting wings, to punctuate the lengthening silence.

'Does not Scripture say, The tongue is an unruly member?' asked he smirking. 'Surely fine fellows the like of them in bed would merely be exercising one such appendage instead of the other, would they not?'

Quizzical eyes were turned on him, and he squirmed in his chair. 'Really, Mr Turnbull,' said Elspeth, astonished less by the wit than the temerity of her new plaything, 'I'd no idea your knowledge extended so far.'

While Turnbull was searching for a reply, Macandrew intervened. 'His knowledge, so to call it, does not extend far enough in apostolic homiletics,' he remarked drily. 'For James writes: The tongue is a *little* member and boasteth great things. Behold how great a matter a little fire kindleth.'

'For a holy man James seems to have studied his anatomy closely enough,' said Elspeth, while Candida clenched her hands deep in her lap, feeling within them two little members boasting great and greater things.

Macandrew continued: 'And the apostle goes on to say, if I do not misremember: For every kind of beast is tamed and hath been tamed of mankind. But the tongue can no man tame; it is an unruly evil full of deadly poison.'

He paused before concluding, more rhetorically than was his practice, 'Verily, James wrote wisely. For what deadlier poison can there be than the baneful secretion that breeds life?'

Before Elspeth could retaliate, Turnbull, nettled by

Macandrew's dismissive correction of his Biblical allusion, said coldly, 'Mr Macandrew, I was making a joke—'

'A dirty little joke,' said Gavin placidly.

'—and my misquotation, though reprehensible as all misquotation is, was pardonable. What is unpardonable is your accurately citing Scripture and grossly misinterpreting it for your own nefarious ends.'

'Well now,' exclaimed Elspeth, 'would you listen to that, then? Am I not in dauntless company tonight?'

'Ay, and the wee man's right,' said Gavin. 'For this perverse pervert of a husband of yours abuses everything, spoken written or materially extant, to buttress his jerry-built whited mausoleum of pseudo-philosophy. What a ridiculous gloss on the Epistle!'

'I'd not call it a gloss,' remonstrated Turnbull. 'It's a wilful obfuscation of the text, however translated. Obviously James refers to the member in the mouth, which wags mendaciously, slanderously, wickedly, and will not be restrained. Not, as you would suggest, Mr Macandrew, to the member lower down, the peniculus in its bush, pendent or upright.'

'Not the *membrum virile*, you mean, but the *membrum linguale*, if I may for the occasion tongue a phrase,' said Gavin, who was beginning to like this unexpected ally against Macandrew.

'*Membrum linguale* I cavil at,' said Turnbull primly, 'though I take your meaning. *Membrum muliebre* might more precisely identify the tongue, since proverbially women's wag more diligently than men's.'

'God, Mr Turnbull,' exclaimed Elspeth, 'have a care. You've made another joke. Here's me—ay, and Candy forbye—sitting dumb with never a word, while you gab away there as if you'd just learnt what your tongue was for—the tongue in your head, I mean. For I doubt if you've a notion what the other one's for.'

'There is no other one, Mrs Macandrew,' said Turnbull patiently. 'Except in your husband's crazy philology—and my misconceived jocularity.'

'Ach,' said she, 'I'm not so sure of that. We do talk, when you think o't, of a loose tongue and a straight tongue. That could well apply. Ay, and tongue-tied we say—like young Alec there. Or you maybe, Mr Turnbull. Though I doubt if you've enough to make a knot in it.'

And Elspeth, who had drink taken, laughed like a tinker's trull and stopped, feeling Gavin's eyes on her when she might have expected, if she had expected anything, Candida's. But Candida was looking for the knot in Alec's and not finding it, as she knew she wouldn't, impressed afresh by the pine trunk behind her in the coppice.

Although Macandrew had lost interest, he was not disposed to leave the field to such young skipjacks as those presuming to contend with him. And so he gave bland utterance once more.

'Truly, young gentlemen, all wisdom will die with you, profoundly steeped as you are in Holy Writ and percipient in the interpretation thereof.'

'I'd never claim that,' interrupted Gavin. 'And well you know it.'

'There's no question of that, minister,' added Turnbull with a modicum of respect. 'Your familiarity with Scripture far exceeds ours. But you must admit that, for reasons hidden from me, you're misconstruing James's text shamelessly. A schoolboy would see that.'

'It's a schoolboy who sees it now. And schoolboys see in a class darkly,' said Macandrew with never a hint of awareness of the enormity of his jest. 'As do their masters. I wonder at your daring, Mr Turnbull, to pretend to teach children the use of language, when clearly you assume it must intend what it superficially conveys.'

'I make no such assumption, sir,' said Turnbull tartly. 'But it does not necessarily intend what you choose to extract from it.'

'I hear you, I hear you,' replied Macandrew. 'But I hear also my ribald riggish crotch-anchored Elspeth, whose obsession illumines her insight into James whereas your lofty detachment clouds yours. I marvel that you should find it difficult to credit the justness of my perception. Have you forgotten that James was a disciple of the master parabolist? Is it unlikely that he should copy the tutorial style of his mentor, whereby the tenor of discourse is sustained by metaphor and apologue, and by indirection, so to speak, direction is indicated? Does the buried talent refer to a unit of coinage? the sower of seed to a peasant farmer?'

Gavin stirred in his chair, but before he could protest, Turnbull, unhooking his glasses and blinking with controlled exasperation, said deliberately: 'We know all about the method and purpose of the fabulist—and you know we do. But you also know that it's a paralogical exercise to argue that because a message may be, and in the Gospels often is, communicated allegorically, every message must be and inevitably is so communicated; and then, on the unstable basis of such a fallacy to fabricate a conviction that James is warning the brethren not, as he clearly is, against improper use of the tongue, the organ of speech, but against any use whatever—except presumably for urination—of the penial organ of copulation. That is patently nonsense, cynically contrived for purposes that elude any rational attempt to detect them.'

'Now then, twisted mouth, that puts your noxious gas in a peep,' exclaimed Elspeth, who had been perceptibly subdued since Gavin's unspoken disapproval of her last lewd contribution—though why the hell she should have been she wondered. She now regarded Turnbull with open admiration, quite heedless that she had shifted her position from the midden she had previously squatted in, so delighted was she to see Macandrew confuted by this winking owl of a schoolmaster.

Macandrew, however, was not finished with, she suspected. He sat, betraying no reaction to Turnbull's rejoinder but doubtless deploying new arguments, while Candida appraised the three men, discounting Macandrew. Two of them she had fruitlessly tangled with so recently: young Alec, an empty hulk now beached in sleep and ever so quietly snoring; Ewart, whom she had even more odiously deceived but who seemed not disinclined to risk the same again; and Turnbull, this incalculable little man, so gauche, so reserved, but so suddenly fluent of tongue. And with a grimace she wondered, recalling the point of the dispute. Surely not, she thought, as she contrasted him with the two massive males *manqués* beside him. Surely not, she thought. That was too impossible to contemplate. But contemplate it she did until Macandrew was back in play.

'It may be conceded,' said he, 'though I do not concede it, that there is some validity in your contention. But you present, or re-present, my argument—'

'If such it can be called,' interposed Gavin.

'You dismiss my proposition,' resumed Macandrew, ostensibly ignoring but implicitly acknowledging the interruption, 'with culpable haste and arrogance, disregarding not only the immediate context of James's advice and the dominant tone and intention of all such religiose preceptors but also the linguistic or philological provenance and possible connotations of the word in question. Imprimis, the Epistle is a homily exhorting the dearly beloved to eschew pride, avarice, lust, and other such so-called sins so exclusively preoccupying the attention of Christian moralists. In the next chapter, I am virtually certain, James inveighs against adulterers and their abhorrent partners.'

'Ay, minister,' said Turnbull sarcastically, 'and he also says, I am no less certain: Speak not evil one of another, brethren. Eh, does he not then?'

'He does, I verily believe, young sir,' replied Macandrew with more grace than might have been expected. 'But too much weight should not be placed on that—a stereotyped concomitant of all such tedious sententiousness.'

'Maybe, maybe. But relevant enough to the content of the preceding chapter anent the tongue's being an unruly evil, would you not agree?' said Turnbull, a shade smugly perhaps in the assurance that he had his adversary on the ropes.

But Macandrew, well aware from the outset that he hadn't a sound leg to stand on and enjoying the more his capering on the crutch of his sophistry, was spry enough to cut a fresh figure. 'I don't deny its relevance,' said he. 'On the contrary, I would submit that James's adjuration to the brethren to speak no evil one of another may be regarded as a mere corollary of his preceding indictment of the tongue, not as oral instrument but as *membrum virile,* in our learned medical friend's terminology.'

'How in heaven's name do you make that out?' asked Gavin, laughing despite his increasing revulsion from Macandrew and his scabrous logomachy. 'That member, however described, has notable power of utterance of one kind and another. But not the gift of speech, either with good intent or evil.'

'And that's maybe just as well,' said Elspeth. 'For it could tell a few tales if it had.'

'Really,' expostulated Turnbull, 'this becomes progressively more ridiculous. Ay, and unseemly in addition,' he added prissily, resuming his glasses and fiddling with their position on his button nose before concluding peevishly: 'Be good enough, minister, to justify your inference—if you can—and let me be quitting this sterile colloquy for more productive pursuits.'

'You have something more interesting in mind then, Mr Turnbull?' said Elspeth suggestively. 'At the dance, perhaps?'

'What dance, for God's sake?' exclaimed Turnbull, who was wishing he was out of this alien milieu that seemed to change its character by the hour.

'I'll be showing you in good time—but not for God's sake,' replied Elspeth, who was herself growing weary of the current state of play. But before she could draw stumps on the unplayable pitch, Macandrew had taken guard again.

'Make good my inference, you say, Mr Turnbull. It seems scarcely necessary. But you are perhaps too young—or secure in your innocence—to know what primarily occasions evil speaking one of another. There is envy, yes. And there is anger, pride—even sloth. But none, as a source or begetter of calumny, rivals lust—lust, the deadliest sin of all not merely in our Calvinist canon but in that of all Christian and pre-Christian pseudo-meliorists, who, intent on multiplying the harvest of souls, paradoxically encourage generation and at the same time deplore it and the corporal conjunction hitherto inseparable from it. And so it comes about that, when evil is spoken by one of another, publicly or in gossiping corners, it most often is spoken of fornication, adultery, sexual congress of this kind or that. Who knows this better than I, pilloried and mocked for that reason all the days of my life?'

Macandrew, whose voice had abandoned its habitual mildness during this excursus and was attracting notice from all quarters of the lounge, turned so demonic a glower on Elspeth and Candida that not only they but Gavin and Turnbull flinched from its malignance, and the men found nothing to say in response to his specious prevarication and its sinister climax.

'And so you see,' he proceeded, 'the connection is obvious. Evil utterance by the tongue in its persona of *lingua,* the vocal organ, is inseparable from, motivated by, even, one may justly say, identified with, lethal emission by the tongue in its nether role as *membrum privatum.* And there can be small doubt in any impartial mind what James has in mind when he admonishes the brethren against giving rein to the little member, the unruly evil. Would that they and all mankind had hearkened to his words. For if only that intractable rampant insatiable beast had been tamed and bitted and tethered, then might the urge towards procreation have dwindled, at least among humans, and the race withered into nothingness like a spent and fruitless shoot.'

His confidence fortified by the apparently impotent silence of his interlocutors, who in fact could find no words of sense to counter his nonsense and had ceased trying, sunk in a torpor of incredulity, Macandrew beckoned Nigel, who had been, as far as his duties permitted, observing from the bar the arid symposium on their oasis in the lounge. Nigel brought libation for the triumphant god and nothing for his dejected dissentients.

'Secundo,' announced Macandrew, after partaking, 'having rebutted the *argumentum ad contextum,* let us advert to the probable derivation and lexical significance of the word that so excites our interest, videlicet, tongue, in Latin, *lingua.* Has it escaped your erudite attention, or does your scholarship not extend so far, that the transliterated rendering of the Sanskrit word for the phallic or masculine principle is *lingam*? Is that merely fortuitously so—an etymological coincidence? Or does it not rather corroborate my interpretation of the worthy apostle's intended significance for the word—an interpretation further supported by consideration of many of its associative usages?'

Having drawn superfluous assurance from his glass, he continued: 'Let me but mention, for example, tongue of flame, which, apart from its recalling James's allusion to the great matter a little fire kindleth, is synonymous with a jet of fire, *jet* designating, as you know, an irrepressible ejaculation from a small nozzle or spout. Note, also the carpenter's mortising device, known as tongue and groove, gentlemen. And his use of the word *tongue* for the tapering end of a post or pole designed to fit snugly into a receptive hole or socket, specifically adapted to that end.'

Gavin, who was looking at Macandrew with undisguised repugnance, was impelled to say flatly, 'This is semantic scatology, Macandrew. I suppose someone like you—if there is anyone—must take his pleasure vicariously. But if these ladies are not recoiling from you as from any other dirty old man less plausibly articulate, let me tell you I am.'

But they weren't—agog at the increasingly scurrilous character of his illustrations, Elspeth from predisposition and experience, Candida from preoccupation and the lack of that. Little Turnbull leaned forward and declaimed with comical gravity:

'Although I find your prostitution of language intolerable, Mr Macandrew, and unworthy of attention, a sense of decency compels me to refute you, even if it's to no purpose. Philology may be said to mean by derivation love of language, but your relationship with it is illicit and meretricious—meretricious in its original sense. You treat language as a harlot, to be used basely for your unnatural delectation.'

'That could well be,' said Elspeth spitefully. 'He's been closely acquainted with that kind in his time, has Macandrew—though you'd never think it to see him sitting there like a gelded shadow.'

'Every schoolboy knows,' proceeded Turnbull with never a glance at his interrupter, 'that innumerable words have their etymological significance extended by reason of some likeness discernible between that which they originally denoted and some other object or process or concept to name which they were not on their invention intended. Language is so replete with such decayed, dead, or moribund metaphors that exemplification is supererogatory. But because your quasi-thesis is exclusively and disgustingly prompted by and dependent on your senile fixation on corporality, it may be apposite, though tedious, to cite some few usages of the kind indicated that pertain to the body and its parts.'

No-one presumed or deigned or bothered to intervene while he polished his lenses before continuing: 'Even pupils at the foot of the class can recognise the head-master, or a headland on the map for that matter. They refer glibly and unfiguratively to the face of a cliff, the brow of a hill, the mouth of a river. Ay, and their mothers likewise to the lip of a saucepan, the neck of a bottle, the heel of a loaf, the eye of a needle, the arms of a chair, a hand of bananas, a finger of toast. And their semi-literate fathers talk readily of being fed up to the back teeth with their hand-to-mouth, down-at-heel struggle to keep body and soul together. And unable to stomach it, they nightly desert the bosom of the family for a skinful in the pub, bellying home at closing time like vessels full of wind and piston-proud.'

He paused for breath not for applause, which was not accorded. Candida did not find his virtuosity nearly so stimulating as Macandrew's. Elspeth sat brooding, betraying no interest. Gavin was pondering the pertinence of it all, which Macandrew was not slow to deny, though not with marked conviction.

'I cannot for the life of me see, Mr Turnbull,' said he, 'what this pedagogic, tropological rigmarole has to do with James's Epistle and my veridical interpretation of it.'

'I did get a bit extravagant towards the end,' mumbled Turnbull reverting to diffidence.

'Towards the end, Mr Turnbull?' said Macandrew, almost sneering. 'From the beginning and throughout, I suggest.'

'Shit, Macandrew,' exclaimed Gavin. 'The wee fellow's right at the heart of the matter. And your arse is out the window—if you'll forgive the crudity, ladies.'

'Oh,' said Elspeth, 'it's appropriate enough, Mr Ewart. I think we can forgive you. Though my bowels of compassion are scarcely capacious enough to contain Macandrew, who abuses language as viciously as he aborts life.'

Elspeth was faintly astonished—as were the two young men—by the concentrated bitterness of her tone; and her eyes, beaming with hatred and contempt at Macandrew, became dim with compassion when bent on Candida, who sat snugly in her own thoughts, oblivious of her mother's concern.

'I hope, well got daughter,' continued Elspeth soberly, 'you are taking note of these two archangelic stalwarts, who wrestle so successfully with your satanic sannyasi of a guardian so-called. Maybe, God willing, they'll between them contrive to dismember him and hurtle him to hell, into the womb of nonentity he should never have been heaved from by his wretched labouring mother.'

'Yes, mamma, I do hope so, if that's what you'd like,' simpered Candida affectedly, suddenly a-brim with mischief that spilled over so copiously that not only Gavin but Macandrew cast an interrogative glance at her where she sat demurely, struggling to hide her expectancy of what the night might hold—treacly sweet Candy, with an easily peeled wrapper and a centre hard as granite to date but perhaps not tonight. And she caught Gavin's eyes and smiled uncertainly.

'There's no occasion for flippancy, clever cat,' retorted Elspeth, angered by her daughter's mockery of her portentousness, the more because the latter was sincerely intended. 'God knows I thought you'd maybe slipped his leash yestreen. Ay, and looking at you now I'm tempted to suspect you did—but I doubt it.'

Having dismissed from her reckoning Alec, who had dismissed himself, she was looking from Candida to Gavin, inordinately vexed by her inability—and Candida's awareness of it—to detect what was passing between them, recalling her suspicions, hopes, confused reflections in the bothy and more recently at the bar. And her lapse of percipience or intuition, or possibly her nebulous, quite ridiculous, consciousness of jealousy provoked her into saying recklessly,

'Ach well, if you don't get your belt unbuckled soon, there'll be never a man wagging his tongue at you, my girl—either upper or nether.'

'My predictable mare runs to form,' said Macandrew, 'and carries me back up the course I have been unfairly diverted from by our young savant's facetious digression on the secondary senses of words originally designating parts and functions of the body—a digression, be it noted, intended to obscure, a mist of bromides suspired to hide, a wreath of fig-leaves woven to swathe prudishly the very corporal organ at issue, so to speak. All that he says is common knowledge, indeed; and therefore of minimal consequence. Our little scholar has forgotten the seer's apophthegm: To generalise is to be an idiot. And he exemplifies its truth. Pray remark, the usages he cites—as brow of a hill, bosom of the family, belly of a sail—imply imperfect or non-existent resemblances between what they pretend to describe and the bodily features originally denoted by the words employed. No-one would mistake one for the other, any more than he would the groin of a vaulted roof, an artery of commerce, a skeleton at the feast or in the cupboard for the anatomical elements so designated *ab initio.* Undoubtedly, the derivative or associative senses of such words have but tenuous links with the original. But consider, gentlemen, I beg you: we find a horse of an altogether different semantic shade when we examine the Apostle's specific application of the word, or thing, that so excites us. Or some of us,' he added ambivalently, as his dull eyes swivelled round the table.

He had lost his audience; only Alec was in fact asleep, but the others were patently indifferent to his exposition. Turnbull was sombrely pondering the *trahison des clercs* in general and particularly the Jesuitical vitiation of language and life spewed like bile by Macandrew. Gavin had escaped into pleasurable comparison of mother and daughter and the promise and mispromise thereof. Candida was happily resisting sleep by dreaming awake. And Elspeth was again incredulously submerged in foreboding, which she could not explain but which suddenly seemed chronic. Macandrew, however, used to travelling hopelessly to no destination, proceeded unperturbed by their inattention.

'Who can fail to acknowledge the unmistakable similarities between the members identified, whatever name we give them? I refer to likenesses of shape, disposition, location, and—to a lesser extent, admittedly—function. Envisage easily enough their form and adjustment, elongated and pendulous from the root but by no means invariably inert. On the contrary, hypersensitive and reacting to stimulus or circumstance; in the one case, exclusively physically; in the other, figuratively, as may be observed in the familiar locutions: sharp-tongued, smooth-tongued, a tongue like a whip-lash, and—however inapposite—a tongue dripping honey.'

'And a tongue oozing ordure,' interposed Gavin sourly, faintly and unhappily astonished that his ears were still attuned to the discord emanating from Macandrew, who, choosing to ignore the interruption despite its pertinence to the objective of his argument, continued, his habitually level intonation becoming progressively more strident as if contemplation of the activities he depicted and their outcome incensed him beyond restraint.

'Consider next the location and functions of the organs, each placidly ensconced in its vault or alcove but when aroused seeking otherwhere comparable lodgment for its restricted but potent mobility. Are all these various and punctilious similarities of the same contrived order as the fanciful resemblances instanced by you, my infant pedagogue?'

His face contorted by the vehemence of his utterance and the frenzy of titillation that excited it, he bent menacingly over the table towards Turnbull for his triumphant conclusion.

'Further evidence aplenty I could adduce to outface your insolent confrontation. There is no need. For even your obtuse ignorance cannot persist in misinterpreting what the Apostle intended by his denunciation of the little member, the unruly evil, which he further says "defileth the whole body and setteth on fire the course of nature", and the identity of which in his eyes and mouth and loins and in mine and yours and every man's is indisputable, execrable, and deserving of his objurgation—and mine.'

He had risen with his voice unsteadily from his chair, louring down on them and wagging his finger ludicrously so that silence shuttered the room.

At length, little Turnbull, intimidated by Macandrew's frantic address and demeanour but impelled by vexation at his flagrantly indecent discomposure of language and Scripture, bravely spoke into the scandalised hush:

'Minister, minister, your title ill becomes you, for you serve us like a treacherous steward, extravagantly purveying spicy gobbets of error to us simple ones, whose appetite is for the bland diet of truth. Your sinister semantic legerdemain is the more reprehensible because you speak, as you well know, tongue in cheek—or tongue in caressing fingers, if one understands the operative word as you pretend it. This is mere abuse, not merely of self but of all of us, who listen expecting verity to nourish and fortify us but hear only prevarication inanely shuffling to a sterile end.'

'You stumble into sense, little schoolmaster,' said Macandrew with restored complacency as he resumed his seat, secretly pleased to exchange the philological cesspool of his own excreting for firmer footing on familiar ground. Definitively he affirmed, 'A sterile end is the only end worth the fertility of man's invention.'

Gavin frowned but disdained reply. Turnbull turned his bottled gaze uncertainly on Macandrew and said, almost conciliatorily, 'That's an amusing paradox, Mr Macandrew. But I jalouse it's not meant to be amusing.'

'It is not, jackanapes,' replied Macandrew with renewed asperity. 'It is no secret that I do not find the human condition, as they call it, or the entire planetary circumstance, conducive to frivolity. Rather I find them monumentally absurd and susceptible of remedy only by radical and irreversible treatment. Nor do I consider my assertion a paradox, but an axiom, Mr Turnbull.'

'If axiom it be, or claim to be,' said Turnbull, 'it is even more unsound than Descartes' notorious syllogism. You say in effect, Mr Macandrew: I think; therefore I must think how I can cease to be. Man is richly inventive; therefore he must devise the means of his demise.'

Macandrew, whose irascibility, he himself recognised, was mounting again in line with Turnbull's insufferable patience in altercation, protested almost querulously: 'I did not say *therefore* he must, as a logical inference from the single premise. I have no concern with abstract ratiocination. I aver simply and without reservation that because man, uniquely in the animate creation, has the gift of invention, it behoves him to employ it to contrive the annihilation of that despicable creation. The grass, the shrub, the tree, insect, fish and fowl, reptilian and lower mammalian scions of unnatural selection—all of those categories are powerless to perceive and therefore terminate the purposeless and repulsive sequence of generation that engages them. Merely they exist to persist remorselessly. But man, alone endowed with intelligence, that dubious attribute, aware of the macabre dance of death in life he crazily cancans in and out of, must surely, ultimately, sardonically but gladly, effect its end.'

Slowly shaking his head as if bearing with a clever but obstinate pupil, Turnbull replied: 'You seem, minister, impregnable to argument or resolved to disregard its rules as inapplicable to the extraordinary extra-canonical dogma you propound. There is no compulsion on man, logical or moral or spiritual or physical, to seek as a desirable end his own extinction and that of all animate existence. There is, you maintain, because man cannot fail to apprehend and therefore covet the fruition of extinction. But in fact man has failed, from the beginning and onwards, to apprehend any such preposterous prospect—except in times of personal tribulation or despair. Such as yours, I fancy,' he added barely audibly.

But he was heard. And both Gavin and Elspeth looked from him to Macandrew; Gavin covertly, in some trepidation for the little fellow's safety, Elspeth with frank curiosity and expectation. But Macandrew made no response, though he lidded his blank eyes and his tongue slithered out momentarily and along his lips. Turnbull continued, intent on the line he was selflessly following, seemingly oblivious of the danger into which it might lead him.

'And even then, when overborne by calamity, he has yearned for—and sometimes achieved—his own end only, not that of the entire hypothec. You would, therefore, minister, appear to be singular in the depth and range of your pessimism—a mental state with which I am, in my more commonplace and trivial fashion, not unfamiliar. And it is well established and incontrovertible—I speak from humble experience—that such conditions are more susceptible of understanding through investigation of their source than of the clinical condition itself or its symptoms. But of course, my dear Mr Macandrew, in your case I would never presume to essay, in my amateurish way, such an analysis. Though there are those here whose testimony would doubtless advance it,' he concluded, his lenses swinging from Candida to rest on Elspeth.

Turnbull's tone was not sarcastic or wilfully offensive. Knowing little of Macandrew or his history he was preoccupied with his argument. But this time he had poked too far into the wasps' byke murmuring within his adversary.

Macandrew, mortified by his recent displays of ill-temper so at odds with his habitual outward equanimity and more by his failure to isolate the cause of them, was moling awkwardly through the warren of possibilities anxious to regain his lost assurance of direction, bypassing the extreme despondency he had carried with him like a clinging odour from the wynd, dismissing with more haste than conviction the teasing barely clad torsos that flaunted back and front about him and embodied the aphrodisiac conceits he had fathered on the innocent apostle. James he had shamelessly impressed to squire him in his forlorn polemical sally, which he had made like so many beforetime from his beleaguered fortress, to relieve the tedious darkness that invested him, only to be repulsed by this stunted tumshie of a dominie and his mounted infancy of schoolroom lore that now propelled its vanguard of effrontery to encircle and subjugate his dismal but unassailable doctrine, its steady sulphurous volcanic glow piddled on by the drivelling tongue of a nincompoop. He could endure no more and would not.

Struggling from his chair and with difficulty sustaining a semi-erect position, his lean body seeming all a-tremble, brows down over almost invisible eyes, Macandrew excoriated his tormentor, his drink-shrivelled tongue articulating with exaggerated distinctness.

'Pretentious, smatter-prating ignoramus, what can the likes of you know of the condition, as you insolently call it, of your intellectual emperors—and the source of that? You are nothing but a tom-fool, sir, a petty primer-read sciolistic dibble-dabbler in waters far beyond your depth. You are even more ridiculous than your coadjutor here, this quasi medical'—and he pointed a shaking finger inaccurately at Gavin. 'He at least, until yon peacock-pouting tail-trailing gamy game-fowl Elspeth decoyed him awry again—he at least was beginning to see the point of the pointlessness I am at pains to point out. I can no more. Let the pair of you wriggle back into the rotting cabbage of life and worm your way through it blindly in wilful incomprehension.'

And he staggered from the table towards the street door and out, his exit fanfared by the unmistakable sound of vomit splashing the flagstones. They were silent, the women in indifference, the men—including Alec, whom Macandrew's tirade had awakened—in uncertainty and a reluctant solicitude.

'He's not well,' said Gavin presently. 'Mrs Macandrew, shall I—?'

'Let him be,' she replied quietly. 'The de'il takes care of his own.'

'I've never believed that,' said Gavin. 'The devil must surely be selective. Or none of us would take harm.'

'Havers boy,' said she laughing. 'We're mostly God's children—and our abundance makes our Father neglectful. But Satan watches over a comparatively small family, and so they endure against the odds. As Macandrew will to spite us all—especially me.'

'I'm not so sure,' Gavin remarked and said no more. He was contrasting Macandrew's irritability culminating in ungovernable rage with his equability of temper in the back parlour and in the gutter. The man's behaviour was abnormal surely, even for one so drunk and so unbalanced.

Despite her nonchalant dismissal of Gavin's concern and her

habitual heedlessness towards Macandrew's ill-being, Elspeth was frowning in some perplexity over his unparalleled loss of control. Misunderstanding her expression, Turnbull said hesitantly, 'Mrs Macandrew, I hope you're not annoyed with me. I'd never have thought the minister would take umbrage like that.'

'Don't you be fretting yourself, Mr Turnbull,' she replied. 'It's a strange man is that one—as if you needed telling.'

'Strange he is, right enough,' said Turnbull reflectively. 'If I'd known how strange, I'd never have wagged my tongue at him the way I did. And when I think of it, my feeble joke it was that set him off.'

'Whisht, will you now,' said she, patting his cheek. 'It's no secret hereabouts Macandrew needs no starting-gun to set him off.'

'Does he always run the same track?' asked Gavin.

'Always,' she replied. 'With the same end in sight.'

'You mean,' Turnbull enquired with more than a hint of disbelief, 'you mean—the end of everything? He's really serious then about—how did he put it?—the only end worthy of man's invention being annihilation?'

'Do you doubt it?' asked Elspeth.

'Can you blame him for doubting it?' said Gavin a shade crossly. 'It's an incredible enough stance, surely, for a man of his cloth. For any sane man if it comes to that.'

Turnbull was fidgeting again with his torics, squinting through them from Elspeth to Gavin, obviously trying to weigh the apparent seriousness of their tone against the bizzareness of their topic. Alec was gazing at the sleeping beautifully Candida, enchanted by the hyperbolic curve of her lashes, the rhythm of her breathing, the Leonardine enigma of her smile. Turnbull, his bent for research now inclined towards the problem of the minister's aberrancy, having decided he must ascertain beyond question whether or not his companions were in earnest, finally enquired: 'But Mrs Macandrew, you're not really suggesting the minister meant what he said?Likely he'd just be having me on, making fun of me. People often do, you know,' he added ruefully.

'There wasn't much fun in his curtain speech, was there?' said Gavin. 'Pretentious smatterer, he consigned you, crawling worm—ay, and me—to the decayed cabbage of human futility.'

'Maybe I belong there,' said Turnbull sadly.

'Come, my dear fellow,' remonstrated Gavin, 'don't be mock-modest. Surely your rebuttal of his filthy verbal fiddledeedee was hardly cabbage-headed—or futile?'

'Ach,' said Turnbull, 'that was only useless word-play.'

'Ay maybe it was,' admitted Gavin, 'but dexterous enough to parry your opponent's. For what were Macandrew's flourishes but simply arabesques squirted against an immaculate wall?'

Gavin knew differently, but he was intent on giving the schoolmaster an opportunity of taking his congé with the dignity his efforts merited and so leaving the rest of the night less obscured by the mirk of disputation. But Turnbull was not of a mind to leave it there.

'I doubt it,' said he. 'I'm thinking his words spill from a deeper well than mine.'

'That they do, Mr Turnbull,' intervened Elspeth. 'A deeper well—a well well beyond your soundings, I hope. A muddied poisoned well, one that appeases no thirst but parches and dessicates the drinker. Does it not, little dry-as-dust daughter? God, what did I tell you? The hussy's asleep—asleep with all you magical men about her. You'd never believe it—unless you knew, as some of you may know, she's no more than an empty ornamental dish on her welsh-dresser of a guardian. Look, puppy, look, but don't dip your muzzle in.'

And all three men were looking, drooling more or less discreetly—even little Turnbull, who had never seen the like so close. But almost visibly withdrawing from the dish unprepared for others, he addressed himself to the matter out of hand.

'Surely only some profoundly wounding experience,' said he, 'could cause such disequilibrium, such disorientation from normality.'

'Ay, that'll be right,' murmured Elspeth absently.

'And from his apparent preoccupation with the little member, the unruly evil,' continued Turnbull, 'it's fairly obvious what kind of experience that must've been, isnt' it?'

'Blethers, man, blethers,' interjected Gavin. 'With a woman like that in his bed every night, how could that have been?'

'Really,' exclaimed Turnbull, 'that's an outrageous thing to say.'

Elspeth laughed and rearranged herself involuntarily, saying, 'Not at all, Mr Turnbull, on the contrary. It's a flattering thing to say. But it's no way between the sheets of probability. For I've never been in Macandrew's bed, or he in mine.'

'A strange one he is surely', almost whispered Gavin, eyeing the plenitude exposed and guessing the rest. 'If we believe you, Mrs Macandrew, as we must, then presumably we need look no further for the dry root of the minister's psychosis.'

'Ay, but you would then,' said Elspeth. 'But I'll not be making myself your spy-glass—not tonight anyhow.'

'We'll not be asking you, ma'am,' said Gavin soberly. 'We've presumed too far as it is, I'm inclined to think.'

'For sure we have,' emphasised Turnbull. 'But, do you see,' he continued, pricked on by his recent success to overcome his habitual compulsion to side-step the encounter, 'it's just that, if you understand me, the minister's uncompromising posture interests me. I've got a modicum of sympathy with him.'

'Have you now? asked Elspeth mockingly. 'I'd never have thought so a while back.'

'But that was just rhetoric, as I've said,' replied Turnbull, willing as always to depreciate himself.

'Nothing of the kind,' interposed Gavin. 'It was a normal right-thinking man's rejoinder to eccentricity of a peculiarly unsavoury kind.'

'Well, yes, maybe,' said Turnbull, his glazed embarrassment downcast on the table-top. 'I suppose, like Margaret Fuller, a sensible man's bound to accept the universe. But he needn't approve or admire it, you know. You're saying Mr Macandrew's eccentricity's unsavoury. You're likely enough right. But is the cycle of nature he'd be glad to escape from any less so?'

Gavin stared at the frowning little wiseacre and for a moment he was tempted back to the gutter of dejection and stayed silent. Elspeth exclaimed, 'God, man, you're not telling me that devil's clawed you in now?'

Turnbull snickered and moved uneasily in his chair. Although his quite unexampled evening's tippling with Elspeth and her provocativeness of one kind and another had fairly loosened his tongue and made him a foot taller, his innate inbred shyness now threatened to envelop him again. But he felt an irresistible urge to sustain the esteem he seemed to have earned by his rout of the minister, rejecting the suspicion that he might not be going the right way about it.

'No, he hasn't', said he. 'The minister goes too far for me, or sanity. But I have a glimmer of understanding of his despair, as I'm sure it is.'

'For God's sake then—and your own,' said Elspeth, 'don't fan it. Snuff it out. Or it'll flare and incinerate you, as it has him—and others.'

'I'm sure you're right, Mrs Macandrew,' said Turnbull, 'and

I appreciate your solicitude. But I have misgivings sometimes, when I look about me. And I can't help wondering, you know, if all that aeons-long travail of evolution has produced anything but a vicious stupid mouse better still-born.'

Elspeth was looking at him in dismay; Gavin's eyes were looking inward; Alec's were drooping again; and Candida's were closed. Turnbull was virtually certain he was making a fool of himself; but he could not help thinking of his dullards in class rolling pencils up and down their desks or projecting inky paper pellets or gaping vacuously here and there while he strove to kindle interest in simultaneous equations or Greek mythology or batrachian anatomy or even crop rotation or the Highland clearances.

'Ach,' he concluded resignedly, sensing their unspoken hostility to his slipping back on Macandrew's slime, 'maybe it's just that I'm ill-equipped for the business of living.'

'Aren't we all?' asked Gavin lugubriously.

'But it's surely different for folk like the lot of you here,' protested Turnbull. 'Good-looking, full of sand and self-confidence, socially adroit—ay, sexually too if it comes to that.'

'Oh, it comes to that, Mr Turnbull, sooner or later,' said Elspeth neutrally, adding with mock condolence, 'But we're maybe not all so accomplished in that connection as you seem to think.'

Although he knew she could not be apprised of his recent misconnection in the heather, Gavin was nettled by her arrogant diminution of others less gifted than herself. He glanced at the apparently dormant Candida, whose expression revealed that she had heard her mother's gibe, and at Alec, who obviously had, scowling as he was in intent silence. And so, initially and unaccountably concerned to restore little Turnbull's dwindling assurance, he now felt constrained to restore his own and possibly establish the fastidious bumpkin Alec's, and less altruistically thaw the frigid Candida out of her snow-hole—and all this, let him admit it, in a frustrate effort to best the imperious whore of an Elspeth.

'Come now,' said he, 'for Saint Paul's sake—and our own—don't be letting us elevate the commonplace business into an art form or even a virtuosity. It may be susceptible of elegant variations by addicts or compulsive practitioners' (and he stared along the line of his sketchily pencilled antagonism at Elspeth). 'But biologically it's no more than an instinctive act of generative conjunction of a rather awkward, and some would suggest, ludicrous character.'

'God,' said Elspeth with affected incredulity. 'have I been wrong all those years—and times? Knowledge seems to reduce everything to nothing.'

'I'd not say that exactly, Mrs Macandrew,' said Gavin, recalling despite his intention this encounter and that. 'I'm speaking as a theorist, not a participant.'

'I'm relieved to hear it,' said she with no remarkable implication. And Turnbull, resurgent, announced with animation: 'How gratifying to have one's secret opinion endorsed from an unexpected source.'

Gavin looked at him with amusement but uncertainty.

'And yet it's not just my opnion,' continued Turnbull. 'Others with infinitely more experience than I to justify its formulation have considered it a most inept form of bio-engineering, so to speak. You may know, for example, what Sir Thomas Browne says. Or perhaps not, for doubtless it stuck in my adhesive memory because it fortified me in my inhibitions. Browne says (in *Religio Medici*): I could be content that we might procreate like trees, without conjunction; or that there was any way to perpetuate the world without this trivial . . . this trivial and vulgar way of coition. It is the foolishest act a wise man commits in all his life.'

'Would you credit that now?' exclaimed Elspeth. 'The foolishest act a wise man commits! Ach well, he'd likely be a scholarly, monkish kind of a man, like you, Mr Turnbull, more fluent with his pen than his—if you see what I mean.'

'I see what you mean, Mrs Macandrew,' said Turnbull. 'But his biographers tell another story. Nearing middle-age, he married a lass sixteen years his junior, who bore him seven bairns in the first nine years of wedlock.'

'A fair reward you might say,' remarked Elspeth, 'for diligent husbandry. But a wee thing at odds with his opinion.'

'And five more in the next twelve years,' added Turnbull.

'A diminishing return,' said Gavin. 'The tilth was getting exhausted, I guess.'

'Ay, or the tiller more likely,' said Elspeth. 'Or it could be with advancing years he grew wiser and found the act more foolish. A daft-like story yon, if ever I heard one. Man, Mr Turnbull, I'm thinking your Sir Thomas was a hungry old humbug, with one tongue telling a different tale from the other.'

'So it would seem, right enough,' said Gavin reflectively. 'But mind you, his is probably a valid enough sentiment. And it may well be that, in time, present painstaking and often frustrating methods will become outmoded as primitive and inefficient.'

'Balderdash, Mr Ewart,' said Elspeth without pronounced feeling, rather as if it scarcely needed saying.

'But you'll observe, Mr Turnbull,' proceeded Gavin on that assumption, 'your philosopher is contemptuous of the means, not, like the minister, the end. You don't really go along with Macandrew there?'

'No sir,' replied Turnbull gravely. 'Not when I contemplate life rationally, unaffected by a recurring revulsion from the dreary repeating decimal of human error and squalor and stupidity. That repugnance may be due, of course, to a conviction of my own ineptitude. And perhaps to a silly unfocussed belligerence generated in me, I'm sure, by disgust at my illicit begetting.'

Gavin had no immediate response to these melancholy revelations. But Elspeth was not so blate, unhesitatingly through laughter exclaiming, 'What a charming way of saying you're a bastard, Mr Turnbull. We'd never have guessed, you know. And why, in the devil's name, should it disgust you? It doesn't us, I'm sure. And I'll wager there was as much sport at your making as there is at any bespoke-tailored brat's.'

'Maybe,' said Turnbull, 'but I wasn't there to enjoy it. And I still don't.'

'Ach, you're daft, laddie,' said she more seriously. 'Surely a man of your intellectual pretensions should take a more sensible approach to a trifling accident of that kind.'

Turnbull stayed silent, seeming smaller and quite deflated in his chair, so that even Elspeth's raillery was stilled momentarily. Gavin, controlling his anger, said, 'Mrs Macandrew has reason on her side, Mr Turnbull. But she's looking from a viewpoint far away from yours. She's familiar with the sport, but her bastards aren't—any more than you are, Mr Turnbull.'

Candida opened her eyes and looked at Gavin, who ignored her, his own locked with Elspeth's. She held her tongue and his cold gaze with amused disdain, staring him down effortlessly so that he was obliged to save face by spending more words in consolation of Turnbull, with whom he felt himself nourishing an improbable sympathy. Normally he would not have seen the little kail-runt in his company, but he was nettled, or thought he was, by Elspeth's playful manipulation of her comical puppet, whose bashfulness almost certainly only drink or verbal contention could dispel and who, with the dilution of the effects of one and the decline of the other to the personal plane he seemed least at ease on, was visibly returning to the shell that Gavin suspected he seldom emerged from. It just was not good enough. He must break a spear for little Turnbull. And so he propounded pompously (like little Turnbull, come to think of it):

'Any disquiet and sense of insecurity you may feel, Mr Turnbull, are readily comprehensible and by no means peculiar to you. It's universally recognised by sociologists and such-like interested parties that knowledge of his illegitimacy can maim a person psychologically. Everyone maintains that it shouldn't; but many a bastard knows that it does. And from my limited acquaintance with yours, Mrs Macandrew, I should think that you're not unaware of the fact.'

He concluded much more trenchantly than he had intended and buckled himself to sustain her counter. Elspeth relinquished her negligent revealing posture, which Gavin dimly acknowledged was possibly partly responsible for his arousal, and withdrawing from the table she sat upright and arrowed venomous eyes and voice at him.

'Mr Ewart,' said she, 'you're a greater fool than I took you for. From your encounter with him here—and elsewhere—even your lubberly wits should inform you that it's Macandrew's influence, not their origin, that afflicts my wretched beautiful daughters. Look at that one—and you see both. Are you suggesting she's maimed, as you dramatically call it, by knowledge of her ecstatic conception? God, even a decrepit medical student of your feeble capcity should be aware she's aching for the like experience. But she'll never have it, poor virgin bitch, with the shilpit droopit likes of you shauchlin' about her.'

Although rigorously controlled, her tone was so incisive that the bar-perched and the table-tipplers were all again agog with varying degrees of amazement and incomprehension. Inclining his head in salute to his vanquisher, Gavin subsided, mildly astonished by the temerity of his challenge. Alec, sobered by sleep and renewed anguish, sat pondering Elspeth's words and their relevance to his frustration in the coppice. Candida, still decoratively disposed as usually in public, was inwardly disordered by uncertainty whether to admire her mother's insolent aggression or resent her directing it at Gavin, whose downfall she deplored, whose upstanding she coveted. Turnbull, retreating from the turbulence, dipped a valedictory oar in courageously.

'Please, Mrs Macandrew, I'm sorry,' said he, 'if I've caused dissension among you. It was never intended, believe me. There's small doubt it's just the unruly evil wagging indiscreetly, like the clapper of a bell shaken at the wrong time, alarming folks and causing camsteerie through-other. What should such a bookish monster as I do crawling from between the pages to sound off about copulation and birth and the gift of tongues upper or nether. I'll just be away home to my digs, where I can hold the one and sometimes the other at pleasure, and try to forget my intrusion.'

He sounded and looked so disconsolate that all four regarded him sympathetically, even Candida, whose compassion had long been cornered for her own consumption. Laying a hand on his that rested limply on the table, Elspeth said gently, 'That you'll not then, Mr Turnbull. You'll be squiring me to the dance now, where you'll see the Ferlie randies, whose tongues are recklessly in service on and off the floor, intruding wherever an opening presents itself.'

God, thought Gavin, does she never let up? But his inclination to remonstrate was forestalled when the door to the street was flung violently open and in stumbled Niven oxtered by a young fellow, stalwart enought but still inexpert in the office and clownishly uneasy in the surroundings the door had opened to him. Feet planted wide and shoulders hunched, Niven glowered round the room until he found what he was seeking. He moved carefully across to stand threateningly over Alec, who grew visibly tense where he sat, recognising trouble and guessing its cause.

His words slurred by liquor and rage but audible to all, 'So it's here you are then, you great dozent gomeril,' he growled. 'Sippling and daffing wi' the likes o' yon' (and his head moved in the direction of Elspeth) 'when I laid strict charge on you to hie off home wi' Queen. Did I not then, you muckle great sumphish shame to your father?'

Alec nodded, knowing the worst now but saying nothing.

'Did I not tell you to lead the mare home to Braelochy and stable her yourself? You'll maybe have mind o' me saying she was a wee thing flighty—pedigree flesh that she was—and needed careful handling? Ay, you'll have mind o' that, eh? And you'll not forget me saying—fool that I was—that though you're less o' a farmer than a dominie—God save us! is that wee wally-draigle here forbye? It's gey orra company you're in tonight, Mr

Turnbull. Losh man, I ne'er thought to have seen our scholarly wee schoolie hob-nobbing an' boozing like the lave—ay, wi' the manse light-skirts no less. Aiblins God kens what the world's coming to, for I dinna.'

Turnbull had no answer to this, nor did Niven expect one, swaying back to Alec and pausing momentarily to recover the line of his invective before resuming: 'Ay, that's what I said surely. Though you'll never—more's the pity—make a farmer, you've an unco skilly hand wi' a horse. That's what I said, was it not? But where was that skilly hand when it was needed, tell me? It was here or otherwhere in Ferlie, fondling a glass or a wench, or idle as your slurry-filled noddle, you great dollop o' pig-shit an' piddle.'

He leant over Alec, spattering him with the spittle of his fury where he sat grasping the arms of his chair, his knuckles white as his face, making no defence. Elspeth and Candida were looking at the pair of them with unconcealed amusement. Gavin and Turnbull with patent discomfort. Niven drew breath gustily for renewed onslaught.

'I told you, I told you well. But you men o' education aye ken better than your betters. So what did you do, eh? What did you do? I'll tell you, since you're mute wi' shame an' stickit for an answer. You gave charge o' the mare to the hafflin here, new out o' school an' handier wi' tractors than bestial. Were you thinking he could handle her—a swank lass the like o' Queenie?'

'But I could, Mr Niven, I could, Alec, had it not been for the car,' said the lad, fearful but eager to justify himself to Alec.

'And what car would that be?' asked Elspeth, not for information.

'Why, it was Braelochy's here, ma'am,' he replied a shade hesitantly. 'We were making along cannily, Queenie an' me, till I heard the car ahint. So I hauled the mare in till she was slap against the dyke at the brig end. But round the bend it came, its lamps beaming a sudden bright light that near blinded me. An' what wi' that an' the noise, she gave a terrible eldritch nicker an' upped her head an' her fores an' flang clean owre the dyke an' into the burn ablow, near taking me wi' her gin I'd held on.'

'You should aye hold on, laddie, you should aye hold on,' said Niven wearily and without rancour.

'Ay, maybe, Mr Niven,' retorted the lad, gaining confidence from the other's loss of mettle. 'An' did you want my brains splashed on the rocks to feed the trooties? I tell you, there was no holding her. Alec could ne'er have held her—nor the two o' us together. An unco powerful beast was yon Queenie.'

'For why do you think, boy, I bought an' paid for her such a hantle o' siller?' said Niven testily. 'For her chest like Mary Taggart's to lip an' paddle an' paw?'

Among his listeners only Gavin saw the pertinence of this exotic allusion, and while the others were preeing it with relish or distaste he, feeling compelled to show interest in Niven's grievous misfortune, enquired soberly: 'Are we to assume, Mr Niven, the mare's still in the burn, then?'

Given another butt for his guttering anger, Niven turned his scowl on Gavin and said with scorn, 'An' where the hell else would she be, d'you think? Was I to lift her out by the lugs like a rabbit—the great glebe-battering noble beast that she is? Or was, for she's done for, my bonnie Queenie. She is for sure—under the brig wi' a broken leg an' God kens what hurt besides.'

And knuckling wet eyes, he drew from a pocket an all-purpose handkerchief and blew a last post on his purple-veined bugle of a nose.

'Man, Donald,' said Elspeth, trying not to laugh, 'you'd think you'd lost your wife, the way you're taking on—instead of a working mare.'

Niven, still on his feet and rocking precariously for no-one had dared invite him to sit, thrust his head towards her and like a snake ejecting poison spat out his rejoinder: 'Elspeth Cameron, Mrs Macandrew, an' how would you be knowing what a man might think o' a wife an' a working mare—you being both at the same time for long years syne.'

It was not Elspeth's way to defend herself and she made no attempt to refute his slander but merely turned his own weapon against him, saying contemptuously: 'And if that's so, Donald Niven, you'll not be forgetting I've never worked for you, though more than once you'd have yoked me—aye too stoven in drink, as you are now, to come at it.'

Niven, too bemused to meet this effrontery, keeked at her from under bristling brows and said submissively, with a hint of admiration even: 'You're a brazen bitch, if e'er I met one. And there's no coping wi' you, so I'll not be trying. An' forbye that, it's not for you I've come. I'm here for him.'

And he raised a fist at Alec, who had not stirred since his father's invasion, and, his vituperation renewed by Elspeth's repulse, he assailed him again: 'You fusionless, mother-pettit gowk, have you naught to say about the mischief you've caused? Are you for sitting there forever like a gravestone in memory o' the sonsie mare you've done for?'

Alec rose from his chair and, grasping his father by the shoulders, turned him round and pushed him forcibly into it, where he sat like a chidden child, looking up with dismay and apprehension at his son, who eyed him scornfully for a seemingly long time before squelching him like a peeled mollusc with as much contumely as he could find words to convey.

'This I have to say, you druckensome old devil,' said Alec deliberately. 'I'm real sorry about the mare. She was a braw beast, an' it's a black burning shame to you she's had a down-putting the like o' yon. For if it's a' by wi' her, the blame's no' at my door—nor at young Pate's here. It's at yours, you doitit maggot fodder, careering about the roads wi' your belly a-swill wi' whisky an' your een a-droop wi' sleep. You daunert liquor-sodden auld has-been, 'twas you that cowpit Queen into the burn, an' fine you ken it. So get you away back to the brig-end an' make your peace wi' her. Or lift her up on the three legs she's left wi' an' ride her to hell an' bide there.'

And out stalked Alec. Elspeth beckoned Nigel, who had been observing their ongoings throughout with increasing foreboding and now came smartly, hopeful of a temperate conclusion.

'Nigel,' said Elspeth, 'bring a dram for Mr Niven. He's in gey sore need o't.'

CHAPTER THIRTEEN

Congregation at the Choir Dance

What revels are in hand? Is there no play
To ease the anguish of a tortured hour?
William Shakespeare

What we call the beginning is often the end
And to make an end is to make a beginning.
The end is where we start from.
T. S. Eliot

For the lips of a strange woman drop as an honeycomb, and her mouth is smoother than oil:
But her end is bitter as wormwood, sharp as a two-edged sword.
The Book of Proverbs

THEY WERE all there, or nearly all, submerged under the din or floating obliviously upon it or swimming arduously against it, as the Bothy Badlads drummed and squeezed and scraped it out relentlessly. The cronies were there, disguising asserting unheeding their week-end bar gloss, according to its degree of brilliance and their temperamental inclination, but all as one appraising the herd, with leering anticipation stripping the willing and dashing their white sergeants into the breach of this one or that or all seriatim like pedigree sires—which they were not—among the expectant cattle. And they the while danced with abandon or postured on the edge of the floor, easing elastic, adjusting straying straps, or sat deprived or relieved, conning the chosen ones and their hopeful partners. And there was continual traffic between the hall and the night outside for the purposes inseparable from such an occasion, and the kirk walls and the gravestones endured charge and discharge of one kind and another, and cans and bottles were drained and discarded, and oaths and giggles and screams and grunts and unholy drunken laughter made medley rivalling the clamour inside.

Young Alec sat hunched against a gravestone, almost as devoid of impulse as the long gone one it commemorated, pale and morose in the mirk. Deaf to the noises about him he heard only, like the frightened mare's in the full beam, his own womanish scream rising as the shrouded McNish came falling to cover him as he had beforetime risen coming to cover many another to a like vocal response. What an asinine anticlimax to his bar-room swagger—and all through that drunken interfering crazy Ewart and his daft stair-climbing corpse-peeping sacrilegious word-spilling coffin-spilling ceremonial. Christ! what a ranting lunatic that was for a cousin. And Ewart's nicely fluently enunciated extravagances echoed in his ears, their expression so at odds with their enormity, approving applauding lauding the beast McNish, who rotted in the dark room under the decent shroud as previously under the sleazy easy fly-opened breeches, rotted like the Ferlie folk beneath and about him, dead or quick or quickening as he was ridiculously with Macandrew's erogenous imagery stencilled still on his eyeballs and as aimlessly as against her haunches by the lochan as smooth and warm, though he'd never palmed them, as Queenie the mare's or the oaken hand-rail he caressed on the ascent to the corpse that had fingered and prodded every buttock and cleft available. And poor Queenie lay deposed under the brig wantonly undone while he foraged about the village as ineffetually as ever.

Alec swallowed the nausea rising in his throat, and his fists clenched straining for the violence that Ewart had thwarted, that might have appeased him as makeshift for the other; and he shuddered as he recalled the temptation to wreak it on his drunken Queen-keening father. Damn Ewart, glib as a pedlar, misguided as a gull. But Ewart was guiltless of his too familiar discomfiture. Only envy blamed Ewart, who was assured and adroit as himself was the reverse. That one, as appetising dressed for the table as she had been birth-raw on the shore, would never have slipped from Ewart's fly, unhooked and deftly glutted before she knew it. And he savoured the doing of it, more lubricious in fancy than the rest of them in fact. And he reviled again the milk-soppish mother-nurture unwittingly abetted by old Deuchar's classroom poetasting porridge that had starved and bereft him so that he lowed over the pasture like a percipient bullock aware of his lack and lamenting. Lamenting what? The deed and the doing could never rival the expectation, any more than the sight of the gaffed salmon could the strike and the playing. Not for him at least; though others felt otherwise, he knew, recalling the florid triumph of the stock-broking anglers on his father's beat over a camera-caught tail-held fish alive still for smoke-room bragging, whereas he, with more skill at the game than the whole Exchange, looked askance at the gap-mouthed victim as he frowned at the gralloched humbled stag he had cannily stalked and precisely picked off. It seemed then there was no appeasement in achievement for him, whose winning try putt punch or whatever coup de grâce evoked from him not exultation but shamefaced compassion for the vanquished. What kind of a namby-pamby was he then, maudlin for the defeated, himself defeated when it came to the bit, on whose forbidden ear the sounds nearby of triumph broke agonised and clear? Surely if to comprehend a nectar required sorest need, he had the requisite—but never the nectar, which stayed beyond his quaffing and which, should he sloppily mouth it, would certainly prove brackish on his tongue; for every experience vexed him by its failure to allay his childish discontent.

All those poets and artists and musicians old Deuchar had introduced to him and whose fellowship he had since cultivated assiduously, what had they done for him but done for him, their exaltation of one kind or another degrading him to commonplace so that everything he did or felt or thought or imagined was immeasurably too base or trivial to gratify him or abide his insistent questioning, his insatiable dumb infantile pulling at the nipple of life for more, more, more assuagement than it could ever yield? Not madder music he called for but more sublime than the most, not stronger wine but more remedial, desolate as he was and sick of an adolescent passion for the unattainable. He could not absorb and make his own the sunset or the pines in silhouette or the scintillant constellations above Ben Cromach. The music's majesty abdicated with the needle-arm's return to its rest, and not only could he not recapture it, he could not possess it even when it resounded in his ears.

But, recoiling from self-depreciation, he sombrely descried and decided that, estranged from the contemptible bull-pizzle flogged and flogging cronies and their multiple like, others facing forward saw the same blind-alley as he blankly stared at. All those words upon words upon all those pages of mighty poets gone and still living in his clogged memory, what were they but fumbling two-finger exercises on a theme far beyond their compass, because no better than baffled he could they realise the false-promising potential, producing only miscarried things for the waste-pipe of doomed endeavour and casting about variously for palliatives to ease the pain of frustration; like the Irish giant gyrating in his void of factitious occultism; or the English virtuoso parchment-wrinkled slippering nightly from his provincial kitchen to his deviant sheets; or the ascetic classicist swopping his cynical recognition of dislocation for the consolations of orthodoxy; or the anguished Jesuit going gladly but far from gently into his early goodnight, preceding the delirious trembling Cymric, his polar opposite in all but their common torturing of language on the rack of rhythm that it might confess the ineffable and ferry them across the straits between their apprehension and its utterance. And all those pallid eminences were no more than specimens of the prototype made long beforetime, all alike crucified on the rood of the imperative, its cross-beam of denial balking its vertical of aspiration as cow-smelling Meg mated his.

But Alec sucked little solace from his confected conclusion that his deprivation was only a crude allegory of every man's whose inward eye discerned no bliss but rather heartache and the numbness attendant on the certainty of non-fulfilment inherent in the circumstance. *Hinc illae lacrimae* washing down the course of history; and hence *Alexander ille minimus* disjaskit and dejected, meditating perplexedly on mighty makars in their misery dead and escaped with relief from hope forlorn, young Alec, brooding like some precocious owlet on the predicament of animate being, decoyed as so often before into Macandrew's net of negation.

But Macandrew was sitting by the dance-floor cradling a spiked mug of milky tea, outwardly impassive but inwardly afire with whisky and itch as the revellers cavorted before him and he surveyed nylon thighs revealed in the birl and loose bosoms jiggling in time to the measure. And Nanga Parbat hung in the snow and the sheet lightning came and went to and from non-entity and the stars glittered in unpeopled space, but Macandrew their devotee denied them, backsliding again as the Ewart body had lapsed, aware in the gutter, besotted in the lounge. And he sneered at the oaf's apologia for the beauty and majesty of life, stammered out in the sordor and degradation they both loitered in. And still loitered in, despite the pseudo-Dyonisiac fever pulsing about them. And would loiter in till death with their misbegotten fellow creatures. Ach, but he was weary of it, near past tholing weary of it, waukin aye and weary. Thinking on his dearie, was he? And reluctantly but irresistibly he turned his gaze on Elspeth, where she sat embowered again by admirers and aspirants—supplanters of him who had too long disdained his office, absentee landlord of so fair a property abandoned by him to tenants and squatters and travelling people, who moved in moved out rent free. And into his befogged and libidinous senses there pressed again the urge to oust them all, these here and all others before them, and take up belated residence, to enter and occupy at pleasure. But he winced almost visibly—though no-one was looking—at the prospect of such invasion, which she would convert to her own triumph. Strangely torpid in spirit he might be—could he be drunk beyond even his notorious tolerance?—but that surrender he cowered from, peering instead uncertainly through his clouded consciousness at the combustion of lust spontaneously ignited seemingly in his sodden haystack of flesh, and ruefully suspicious that such tongues of flame as might emerge would flicker and go out not in. And who had spoken of tongues of flame with tongues of men and of angels of death wing-flapping over Ferlie and fanning the conflagration of Gehenna fed with malt and must and stoked by him and his ministry. Eaves-dropping at what door at what window had he heard himself dubbed Satan himself auld Hornie Nickie-ben what parlour had he intruded unasked as he ached now to do?

Macandrew was fumbling stumbling in his reeling wits to regain the balance he had lost somehow somewhere. And his nostrils twitched in the cloacal stink of McNish's gutter, where prostrate he had digested despair too constipated for easy voiding by his crushing of the good Samaritan the gravelled Ewart and clotted further how and when he strove to remember. And through the spirituous miasma that wreathed about him appeared like the bloody child the obnoxious pedant manoeuvring his horn-rimmed text-book metaphors and elementary snippets of psychology like the weird twin sisters' riddling prophecies emerging from the fog and filthy lochan waters to confound him like his dubiously parthenic Candida black as a boot and presumed drowned but resurrected to sit cheek by enamelled jowl with her meretricious in its original sin sense mother who had implanted horns upon horns upon him and he nothing in her but elsewhere tonight for sure.

For there were others on offer who might slake the malignancy parching his mouth, swab or swallow the gall oozing from his armpits, distending his pupils, stirring his sluggard. And his eyes turned on Mary Taggart, who was jiving vigorously but aloofly with some nondescript her eyes avoided; and on Marion distantly revolving with the sedate bachelor organist organless like her seemingly; and on the bastard Candida not drowned in the lochan but castaway on the shore of the dance-floor like the half-bred maroon from life he had made her—to spite her mother, to vindicate himself, it mattered little which. How poetically just, how gruesomely appropriate, if like some privateer landing to water and finding a treasure, he should rescue her from the dereliction he had stranded her on. And his fingers slid up and down the cup's smooth surface as he recalled what he had pilfered of her and the other as they lay in sandwich in the moist darkness under the net of self-abnegation.

He closed his eyes as the distinctness of the recollection directed his errant musings. What satisfaction he might give through her daughters to Elspeth, who had so long vilified him for securing forever their chastity. Often conceived and as often dismissed, the hideous aspiration rose inside him like sickness while he stared down at the curdled skin on the mug he held now like some vessel of revenge, some unholy grail of retribution at length found after barren years of searching. Surely it was time to assert in deed the lifelong malevolence towards life he had passively cherished and prated of. Hitherto he had cared not at all that his discourse and diatribe had made no impact, his doctrine no disciples; because there was virtue only in sterility, there could be none in proselytising—except perhaps a transient analgesic, like the release he coveted now and had found beforetime in short-time embraces east and west. But possibly he had mistaken his destiny, or refused it. If in truth he was the devil himself, let him extend his hell beyond him. Instead of excruciating his flesh and spirit in solitude, perhaps he should have spread the word, disseminated his malady and the recognition of its source, founded a school, toured the cities and the plains like some contra-evangelist, some revivalist in reverse, preaching not, Arise, ye more than dead, but, Go down Moses and set the people free—from the curse inflicted on them.

And the absurdity of his fancy betrayed his mouth and his eyes to a smile so incongruous that Candida, flower on the wall, by chance glimpsing it, found her eyes fixed and fixed more securely as his smile changed to a cockatrice glare so baleful that she flinched and astonished the sudden inviter to the dance, who had come diffidently on a challenge and found himself, unknown to him, a welcome way of escape from the fascination that revolted her. And should have done, for Macandrew, discarding the ridiculous project he had conjured up, felt his inclination steepening with his lust, the cause of which he was at a loss to identify—unless it were a physical counter to his inordinate gutter-bred sickness of heart. The licence aloud about him and beyond in the graveyard, where Alec lingered similarly immobile in rampant frustration, did nothing to quell it.

Sure there was solace abounding here and in the kirk precincts, but although both were aching, neither was taking noticeable action or advantage. Young Alec reclined still like an uncoffined corpse, while Macandrew sat regarding the manikin Turnbull, who was hopping around the floor like an animated tawtie-bogle frightened by the birds he was meant to scare.

Taunted by his pagan divinity, Elspeth, Turnbull had asked Candida to dance, though he had no notion how to and was not learning fast. As he hirpled about in inept conjunction with his improbable partner, his expression was one of childlike delighted absorption; for Turnbull had never made physical contact with a woman since he left nursery school, and the bodily closeness of Candida bewildered and enchanted him like a baby's first encounter with snow. He was immersed in a novel element, enthralled by the astonishing warmth and smoothness of her back under the fabric beneath his hand, by impact with her breasts and belly as frequent collision with other dancers thrust him against her. He snuffed her perfume that only just or did not quite mask the more intimate exhalation of her perspiration no less musky in his novice nostrils. The olive gloss of her skin, the barely visible fissure that parted her bosom, the little knobs her nipples raised in the stretched texture of her blouse—every feature of this exotic aroused in him not so much sensual pleasure or expectation as wonder at the novelty of his experience.

But young Turnbull, though virgin in this realm as in many others, was not so intoxicated by one thing and another on this unparalleled occasion that he failed to glimpse the unlikely possibilities inherent in it. Despite his inhibitions, he was male. And the longer their clumsy antics on the floor continued, the more aware he became of an excrescene at his middle, which became progressively more difficult to ignore or dispose of. No words passed between them, because neither had anything even remotely appropriate to say, and if they had had, it would have been inaudible under the din. But presently Candida, not unaware of his untidiness and weary of his speechless ineptitude, was constrained to say: 'Mr Turnbull, don't you think we might collide more enjoyably elsewhere?' And crooking her fingers in his, she teased him like a ravelled thread through the dancers on the floor and the throng in the vestibule into the kirkyard heavy with darkness, alight with levity.

As they stood in an angle of the church wall unexpectedly not preempted, their hands still linked, they wondered at themselves and about each other. Candida, who would have welcomed the devil's invitation to the dance that she might turn her back on the menace of Macandrew's stare, was glad it had been little Turnbull who had unwittingly rescued her, rather than Alec or Ewart or some other. Although a mite put out to be left out, she had been not unwilling to accept her apparent rejection not only by the lads of the village, usually queuing to snuggle and finger as suggestively as they dared, but by Alec, who had forsaken the field, and Ewart, whose attitude towards her she could not fathom and no wonder. He was fishing probably and successfully for Elspeth—and who could blame him? But she had been aware in the Crown and later of his gaze dwelling upon her, his eyes puzzled and compassionate like a mother's contemplating an ailing or uncooperative child—like Elspeth's often. Damn their solicitude! She'd have none of it.

And almost involuntarily she gently drew their clasped hands round to rest on her buttocky unconfinement and slid them up and down, savouring the sensation as so often alone or with Nig, and wondering about him, who was wandering about her with his other inexperienced reconnoitring hand, poor seduced little scholar, accustomed to jerk on other strings and astray when released—astray but seeking however tentatively, uncertain what he would find and what he would do when he found it if he did find it and though he didn't know it he probably would if Candida should play to form but would have little chance of doing anything with it if she did as she would though he didn't know that either poor little Turnbull, half wishing he was playing the burn with old Deuchar and a worm as clumsily fumbled as Candida to her perverse pleasure and his; and yet so wishing not because he was not enjoying his unfamiliar assay, and not because he apprehended the humiliating anticlimax of his inevitable failure to consummate it, but because in his indefatigably busy self-analysis he was ruminating on the plight he found himself in and its implications.

Enticed, indeed coerced, by Elspeth at the bar into the maze through which he had been noctambulating since, at times confidently at times warily, he was now confronting the Minotaur, abnormal progeny of Els-Pasiphaë contrived for his undoing. But surely not, for she was no Minotaur, this self-sacrificial heifer hornless and hideless almost as he grew to his astonishment more venturesome. And yet he knew she was in fact and would devour him, as his mother had warned him repeatedly rehearsing the perils of the blandishments of women, who would divert his advance insidiously into their ambush and swaddle his ambition in nappies. And what would then become of his post-graduate thesis on manic-depressive instability as a begetter of art by a comparison of Swift the epistolary eunuch and Burns the compulsive performer, alike in their conviction that odious little verminous man was made to mourn; and, dearer to his heart and temper, his grand psycho-philosophical-historical-critical treatise on the creative potency of celibacy down the centuries from Jesus of Nazareth to Angus Moudiewart Turnbull? And he reproached himself for his self-betrayal, suspecting that this was an addictive tonic he would find it difficult to wean himself from. Ach, but it was only a chance aberration this with return to the known security for its only end, he reassured himself, clutching at straws and what else presented itself. It would never come off—but it did despite his fingers all thumbs to spill out more for his ambivalent rapture and disquietude.

What a pathetic puddock he is, Candida was thinking, submissive under his gig-lamps, which reflected the light from the windows, and his little damp paws slithering here and there about her so innocuously. Even with her vigilant connivance how could such a driblet of a man percolate where others more stalworthy had jetted in vain? So childlike, so innocent was his doodling manipulation, like an infant caressing his mother, that it was lulling her into oblivion like the warmth of the foal in her arms. Perhaps, half asleep on her feet, she might envelop him like the weary pro against the wall eating fish and chips while the little sailor sailed into port and out again without her noticing. And at that preposterous possibility she shook with repressed laughter, whereupon he drew away from her but without relinquishing contact and said, 'Don't be laughing at me, Miss Macandrew. I know I'm not very good at this.'

'Ach, you're not to be fretting yourself, Mr Turnbull,' she whispered. 'You'll be better next time.'

'Next time?' he wondered audibly.

'It's just like the dancing,' said she. 'You improve with

practice. And you can practise almost anywhere almost any time.'

'With you?' he asked after a pause.

'You flatter me, Mr Turnbull,' she said. 'You'll not be needing me for that. My scatter cushions are no more pneumatic than others'.'

'I dare say you're right, Miss Macandrew,' replied he, comically coy. 'But I've got to like them, you know.'

'I can tell that,' said she. 'You'll be deflating them, if you're not careful.'

'I hope . . . I hope, Miss Macandrew,' he stammered, 'I've not gone too far?'

'God, no, there's a bit farther to go, Mr Turnbull,' she said and, at once amused and exasperated by his pusillanimity, she adjusted herself to facilitate his farther going. But he demurred, not to her astonishment.

'Perhaps I've progressed far enough in my first lesson, Miss Macandrew. One mustn't push pupils too hard,' said he with an affected little laugh.

'I bow to your professional expertise, Mr Turnbull,' said she, adding maliciously, 'But hard is hardly the *mot juste.*'

She could almost feel—or thought she could—the radiation of his embarrassment and outrage, before he mumbled, 'But I told you, didn't I, I wasn't very good at it?'

'Of course,' she replied soothingly. 'But still, it's a lot more fun than the trees have, don't you think, Mr Turnbull?'

'Fun is not the object of the process of procreation, Miss Macandrew,' he pontificated, on surer ground again. 'Either in the vegetable kingdom or the human.'

'No, perhaps not,' she said. 'But it makes the silly business a damned sight more tolerable. Fancy doing it at arm's length or by banker's order or something,' she suggested. And she frowned in the darkness, half hoping it might be so, half hoping it might be otherwise sometime but assuredly not now.

'If it were less sensually pleasurable, it might be less casually engaged in,' replied he with gravity unassumed, thinking of his mother bairned at sixteen and condemned to rear and educate him on her own through years of drudging poverty and rejection. Maybe he'd been got in some such corner as this by someone bolder and better at it than he, poor misbegotten misfit misguided by his betrayed mother to cleave to her forsaking all others so that always and everywhere he was apart, suspecting evading all contact, a doomed solitary aborted not inside but outside his mother to his incorrigible self-miscarrying. The pair of them had made him in a hurry—and he looked it—but she had spent his lifetime and most of hers stiffening his stance not as a man of the world of men and women but rather as an anchorite steadfast against that and its encroachments, ostensibly for his own good but unconsciously, he sometimes suspected, to deny him his detested father's opportunity. Her son would never ship cargo in some random hold as his father had shipped his before passing in the night. And yet, maybe that was fanciful. Maybe she had caged and cosseted and trained him for a credit to herself to offset the discredit left by his transitory begetter. And train him she did, to emerge unassumingly from his hole in corner and jump through the hoops of education with mounting success until his tutors were glad to see the back of him when he retired to Ferlie to till his allotment of talent inherited whence, he wondered, for his lumpen exterior did not come from his mother, who was still so fair and alluring that close as they normally were he sometimes contemplated her with unexamined longing, but in no sense intellectually burnished. But his father might have been an ugly genius as he was or would be, or perhaps some recessive gene from God knew what anonymous forebear had brought forth his scholarly abilities, or perhaps it was only head-down plodding in the only plot allowed him. Wherever his talents came from, he would polish them; and no Circe like this hybrid slut would make a domesticated monkey out of him. And when in time his fame was abroad, none could sneer and say, Ach, wee Turnbull! I kent his feyther; for no-one did—not even his mother.

Ach, but she must have been by-ord'nar' bonnie, his mother, bonnie as this one and maybe just as eager and asking for it. And he was in his father's hands caressing her but his father was not in his, which still idly lingered over the contours of Candida going nowhere. But now he had a fair idea where to go and felt like going, having browsed in fresh pastures tonight at the Crown and since and getting the taste of it and the feel of it forbye. But she, who was fondling him intimately as her whorish mother had verbally at the bar, crooning the while: Let God stand up for bastards since they can't stand up for themselves, suddenly withdrew. For she was in fancy Elspeth conceiving herself and Nigretta among the Nabob's cushions with the silken girls bringing gin and lime before and after and possibly during the fact for that great white cat was as uninhibited as a lioness in season and for him making love was as normal a use of his equipment as making water. And the erotic luxury she projected was so at odds with the lamentable indignity self-imposed in the country churchyard, where this retarded child-minder meandered groping about her like innocent Adam investigating his metamorphosed rib, that she leant against the wall shaking with laughter.

'Ay, laugh in your lewdness, woman of Gomorrah that you are,' uttered from the darkness the back-parlour prophet, and a beam of light immobilised her on the wall like a detail from some oriental mural in high relief.

'God, Hector,' came Deuchar's chuckling voice, 'but you've pinned a rare specimen this time.'

'Devil the rarity o't,' exclaimed Hector. 'As common as tea—as common as coupling.'

'Well now, she's maybe got a wheen components in common wi' the lave,' said Deuchar with a comical affectation of deliberation. 'But they're uncommonly braw specimens, you'll not deny now.'

'I've come here to chide sinners,' protested Hector. 'Not to leer at them covetously like the elders at Susannah.'

'Maybe so, maybe so,' replied Deuchar placidly. 'What need then of the illumination? Though I'm not complaining mind.'

'This light shines,' bellowed Hector, 'like a shaft from the eye of God to blast the recreants, even in their very fornication. Ay, to lay bare their furtive carnal grappling and coiling and covering—belike to bring shame on their unregenerate heads and other parts. Though I have my doubts yon Jezebel daughter o' the manse would ken shame gin the Lord Himself came down to chastise her.'

'Ach, be easy,' said Deuchar. 'You're not doing so badly yourself.'

'Man, ' continued Hector with unabated fervour, 'were I not seeing what I am seeing—'

'But you are, Hector, you are,' interposed Deuchar.

'Were it just hearsay or foul-mouthing,' said Hector with pretended patience, 'I'd ne'er credit the like o' yon.'

'Did I not tell you?' said Deuchar. 'It's a rare lass you've got there—uncommon comely.'

'Comely, says you!' retorted Hector. 'That's not the word I'd choose. Indecency the like o' yon I've ne'er heard tell o', leave alone clapped een on, and me wi' my feet shauchlin' into the grave. Standing there in the light, near mother-naked, wi' ne'er a thought o' the privacy o' what she's exposing the impudent unabashed besom.'

'Come now, fair's fair, man,' remonstrated Deuchar without heat. 'It's not the lass that's exposing her bonnie bits o' things. It's that eye of God you're clutching there. And I think it's time you dowsed it. I'm not tired o' looking, for I'm past doing aught else. But it's a gey unseemly thing you're at—a sight worse than what she's been at. And when I think o't, how comes it God's eye—and your own two forbye—cleaves only to the quean? Houghmagandie's not played solo. You'll not tell me yon lassie's been groping by herself. Does God's wrath—and yours—not take tent o' the male correspondent?'

'Eh now, that went clean out o' my mind,' said Hector with apparent astonishment but no move to release his captive from his prurient surveillance.

'Ay, we can see why,' said Deuchar, 'but you've surely seen enough. Let the wench get her clouts about her, while you rain shame on the lout who's been enjoying what you've been coveting.'

'You've no call to be saying the like o' that, Deuchar,' roared Hector in a rage. 'Me, an elder o' the kirk and a scourge o' the ungodly, to be lusting after womankind. Yon's a gey scandalous thing to say.'

'I hear you, I hear you,' said Deuchar sardonically.

'At my time o' life, wi' the coffin open for me,' whined Hector, relapsing into self-pity, 'it's a' by for me wi' sic louping an' ryping.'

'Ay, ay,' said Deuchar, 'I ken fine what you mean. But it's a gey auld horse doesna nicker when it sees the corn. But yon corn's not for your lipping. So give owre tantalising yourself. Have done wi't man.'

And he drew Hector's hand that held the torch towards him so that its cone of light slid beyond Candida to settle on Turnbull crouched in the corner, his face in his hands, pretending invisibility. Candida, who had not deigned to stoop to gather up the garments round her ankles, preferring to hold her provocative pose against the wall, savouring the old men's impotent salaciousness —not, she ruefully acknowledged, very different from her own— now stepped out of them, unhurriedly picked them up, and vanished into the darkness, abandoning young Turnbull to the wrath of the righteous as he had cravenly abandoned her.

'God bless my soul,' exclaimed Deuchar, genuinely taken aback. 'Surely that's not my perjink wee high-minded celibate assistant. Eh, Mr Turnbull, congratulations. I ne'er thought you had the smeddum for a joust the like o' yon.'

But Turnbull made no reply. He was consumed not only with mortification at his discomfiture but with rage at the old men's shameless voyeurism. And yet, that trollop had enjoyed it, he was certain; he had observed from beyond the perimeter of light her placid breathing and the little smile unseen by the others, whose eyes were elsewhere. Assuredly she had relished their lickerish scrutiny of her, as she had his inexpert exploration; as indeed her mother had his accidentally finding her in flagrant delight with that counter-mopping smooth-talking vulgarian barman. And he wondered afresh at the insolence of women; not only the manse loose fish, too wily for his unpractised hook that was not sharpened for the strike even by her brimstone whetting; but his mother agape for his fortuitous father whoever he was or might have been, for he had little doubt she was habituée in the gynaecian catacombs so starkly lit for him by tonight's revelations.

He was only vaguely aware of Hector's vituperation and Deuchar's occasional gibes; for little Turnbull, having found and lost his docile Minotaur, was still grievously astray in the labyrinth he had entered unwittingly through the door of the Crown lounge, where Elspeth-Ariadne had snipped his mother's apron-strings and replaced them with the clew that had treacherously misled him on but was not spun to lead him back to his one-time one-track progress towards achievement of his own design. So at odds with his habitual assurance of purpose, his perplexity appalled him. The unfamiliar hankering smouldered in him still, and he shrank in humiliation at his limp failure to control its flame, and he felt himself at once captivated and repelled by her who had so contemptuously kindled it and those others who would kindle it in future; for he reluctantly acknowledged that his feet were hobbling now towards a goal he had turned his back on. Regretfully he enrolled himself, one more, in the endless cortege of the life-participants, the procreants begetting themselves amid a myriad distractions from the high-minded objectives that homo sapiens should exclusively pursue. And he saw himself among his contemporaries, all entangled in futile liaisons or affiliation orders or king-sized couches and princeling carry-cots and imperial mortgages; and worst of all, chafed by the spouse spur pricking them on in the beaver careerism that gnawed at the tree of self-knowledge and magnanimous commitment to disinterested endeavour, the only valid raison d'être. And he grieved for the loss of the harmless upper and nether chubby cheek-patting of the little boys in the back seats, confessing it would no longer suffice after this baptism in the waters of Aphrodite tepid enough tonight perhaps but destined, he knew, to boil and boil over. His lenses misted as he viewed in prospect through them his newly charted voyage and in retrospect the placid anchorage he had forsaken. And suddenly in his dejection he wanted his mother, though he was uncertain why or how. The flick of a woman's hem-line blows away all your conviction, Macandrew had said to that lout Ewart. And as he stumbled past the unheeding elders, whose fire was out, he wondered if Macandrew was right, not only in his misogyny but in his total rejection of all created being as pernicious and purposeless. Perhaps he should abandon his aspirations and sit at that Apollyon's feet, meditating on the desirability of life extermination.

As little Turnbull vanished in the darkness, disconsolate in his self-betrayal, the guru whose wisdom he thought of enlisting was sitting still ensconced in his apostasy pondering rape and its contriving. Of all the revellers who rollicked about him, none addressed or even approached him, where he stayed motionless in his *cordon sanitaire* like some powerful totem which his tribe dared not partake of or come near to. Were he to make the remotest advance to one of these impossible victims, she would scuttle from cover like a lady crab in a rock pool. The granite effigy he presented, the inaccessible fastness he inhabited alone precluded encounter of the kind he now whimsically craved.

He fingered in his pocket the key to the vestry, knowing it would open no door to his satisfaction unless with his fosterlings or their mother to pleasure him. But the twins were out of reach, one at home in bed busy with herself or sleeping, the other outside in a corner tormenting the skelf of a schoolmaster. Doubtless he could come at them later, but by then his rapacity would have abated unsatisfied and he would have reverted to his wonted neutrality. And he rebelled at that, frothing at the snaffle that had fretted him lifelong, forged and polished and inserted by his insatiable holy father, whose tireless generation of miscarried things and infant ephemerids had harassed his childhood and implanted the seed of disgust that he had nourished to perennial fruition, feeding on the crop and chewing its bitter cud with teeth set on edge forever. And he reviewed again, with a novel captiousness he did not pause to examine, his long alienation from so-called normality, a permanent exile interrupted now and then by compulsive jaunts of repatriation brief as the need that occasioned them and none briefer than his foredoomed marital experiment with Elspeth, whose inordinate vitality he had fondly hoped might by some benign symbiosis transform him. In fact, that vigour of hers, almost obsessively sexual, had had the reverse effect, reminding him of his father's secretive dour and joyless perseverance in venery that had initiated his traumatism, so that he had insulated himself even more securely and fortified his position against intrusion.

But now in the church hall, which drummed and trembled with barbaric rhythms and appetites, and in his unaccountably mutinous vindictive mood, Macandrew felt himself infected beyond immunity. As the hand in his pocket traced the pattern of the web of the vestry key, it fingered in fancy other interstices, and he wondered if the key would fit and at length release the bolt that, rusted in immobility, had so long barred their encounter.

His eyes turned outward again to find Elspeth, who had not moved since she took regal station on entering but who was no longer fenced by her entourage of pretenders. The lady was not for dancing or even for daffing, grown tired of their uncouth ministrations. They had drifted away in search of less racy but probably more manageable mares. Even Nigel, shrewdly recognising he could not hope to stay the course on going like that, was looking for another mount from the local string of selling-platers, such as remained unclaimed as the hour grew later. Only Ewart stayed faithful, wolfing the residue of the bridge-rolls and fruitcake purveyed by the ladies of the choir without benefit of clerical assistance, in a foolish effort to soak up some of the liquor he had swilled during his reckless reel through Ferlie.

God, he was gloomily thinking, what a way to prepare for his father's gift of a last chance to his ne'er-do-well son. Far better to have stayed in his known resorts than brave this rural bedlam inhabited by boorish men and nymphomaniac women and dominated by that doom-breathing dragon Macandrew, who seemed to shrivel anything that promised fair. Prone as he was to the lotus and the gutter, he had better withdraw from this intended retreat before it swallowed like a moor bog his father's hopes of his rehabilitation. My father, methinks I see my father nervously stroking his baldness, frowning through his half-moons or twinkling ingratiatingly over them in an effort to achieve some rapport with his wayward incomprehensible Gavin. My loving unbeloved father, who thought to offset vicariously his own nondescript career through his one-time brilliant schoolboy son turned drop-out student diligent only in dissipation, stumbling over easy hurdles, balked time and again by the final one, not by its height but by his refusal to measure up to it, crawling as he was on his belly in the mire of debauchery and dilettantism.

His conduct, he was obliged to acknowledge, endorsed the quasi-philosophy of that nevermore ever croaking raven Macandrew, despite his attempts to refute it. Better have done with such folly, leave that egregious clergyman in the crypt he rotted in, return to his sorrowing father and the lean calf of endeavour. Gavin sensed the halo encircling his penitent head. Let it shine there awhile and it might become part of him, like his once discriminating intelligence, his absorbent memory, his earnestness of purpose, his deft dissecting hands, his promising diagnostic skill. He would not believe all his gifts and acquisitions were beyond recapture or, as Macandrew would have him and all others believe, not worth the exploiting. What sinister emanation dribbled from yon gargoyle that tempted one to heed him rather than ignore or deride him? What saliva-like secretion did he exude that emulsified one's resistance as the anaconda beslavered and softened its prey for engorgement?

But recalling Hector's indomitable defence and counter-attack in the back parlour, he owned that Macandrew could prevail only over someone predisposed for some reason to permit him, as he was despite himself and his newly donned angelic armour of righteousness; though this lovely Thais by his side surely provided ample denial of the joyless nullity of life. Ay, but would she not also seduce him from his celibate cell of high resolve so recently entered? he asked himself, adjusting his nimbus hopefully. Perhaps not, it occurred to him half wishing half fearing. Perhaps he presumed too far. Maybe that other, her heather-happed half-baked Alaskan bastard had inherited her contrary inclinations from her mother, who would tease him on and toss him off as she had done. But he didn't think so, glancing at Elspeth and obtusely wondering where Candida had got to; probably being sick somewhere down her party blouse or coiled in some innocent bestial embrace with a weanling calf or lambkin or cherishing in her coverts mice or snails or puppy-dogs' tails that little boys were made of as makeshift misfit for the awful lot of Ewart she had spat out, the pathetic little frigid lass forlorn. He felt only compassion for Candida all hot and abloom under her mother's tropical example and tutelage but frozen inside by her arctic fossilising foster-father. What could a girl like that do with her enforced integrity? And to his astonishment tears welled in his eyes and through them he glared malevolently at the blight on the crop, the murrain on the cattle, the poisoner of wells, the neuter thing, who unknown to him was immersed in libidinous intent that threatened to drown him, its outlet silted with uncertainty.

Macandrew, observing Ewart's aggressive stare, ignored it. He was not unaccustomed to hostile or incredulous regard, and moreover he was preoccupied with Elspeth, not only her repulsive physical promise but her reversion to the brooding silence he had witnessed in the bothy. The source of that he had divined, having overheard her conversation with Ewart concerning the false suspicion of Candida's off-shore farewell; but now his participation in her crude mental processes was diverted partly by the mindless animal noise and activity pounding about him and more perhaps by his obsession with her odious hitherto rejected flesh, so that he could not make telepathic contact with her and was at once chagrined by his failure to achieve so simple an objective and dismissive of it as irrelevant to his immediate purpose, the accomplishment of which he was becoming aware was postponing itself beyond his capacity. This indescribable malaise afflicting him all evening, it was more, he was intuitively aware, than merely physical liquor-induced revulsion, to which he was habituated. It was a sickness at the very heart of his darkness, for which he was seeking, he obscurely suspected, some mitigation some orgastic relief, in this sudden eruption of lust. But he misdoubted the efficacy of his intended remedy, even should he succeed in administering it. Had he but known it, the likelihood of his doing so was diminishing out of sight; for the Elspeth he in his derangement coveted waywardly was closer to sympathy with his abhorrence of her, further from the marriage-old antipathy that had its only end in their coition, than he could have believed.

What ails you, Eppie? she wondered as she inserted a restless hand and cradled a breast that so many had. Why weep you on the side, lady, like your sooty brat Candida back to the wall fending of the calloused hands of the village for the ink-stained page-pawing fingers of the academic whom she had flung down like a shabby tooth-chewed glove for her daughter's scorn not her immediate amazing acceptance? And where now the girl and the glove? By some coign in the kirk wall or flat on a yielding gravestone out there in the dark? Ridiculous to think of such an event when who knew how many more likely had failed to come to conclusion with her gelid unthawable daughter. But who could guess what a girl like yon would be doing—unlike her mother, known to be doing always the same thing? But tonight she wasn't inclined to, and why not, after such a promising start with the Nigel self-tendering barman gone away now to other opener earths than hers suddenly stopped like her twins'? Whence this depression before the impending act and not after as the wise men said, though it had never been like that with her? This was a renewal of her anguished introspection that had assailed her earlier in the Crown and yonder in the bothy. Prompted by her anxiety about Candida it should have gone with that, but it had not, and threatened to dominate her. Dismayed she was to find herself receptive of the possibility and concerned to discover why. Macandrew unaware beheld his Elspeth beset by some of his familiar demons and giving way to them.

She was again scrutinising Elspeth as lately in the gantry mirror, not now for minnows of maternal misprision, but for the leviathan of self-disgust into whose belly she felt herself being sucked with little resistance. Although not deceived into sharing Macandrew's lunacy, she not for the first time but never before so sharply discerned, if not its justification, its provenance. Through eyes downcast on her hands now laced motionless in her lap she regarded the soilure and futility of her past present and probable remainder. She felt that upstart homunculus Nigel the swizzle-sticking cockalorum intruding in his insolence on her open privacy hoping to insert some noxious something of his own. God, Elspeth, what a level have you fallen to? And reluctantly she remembered her mischievous sport with the eye-popping toad-faced Turnbull one minute inflated the next punctured flat, although she had admired his confutation of Macandrew despite her tipsy-tight loose-tongued contributions that so offended the gallant Ewart there, whose masculine parts under the covers of the bothy bed she still had a hankering to try out although she still half-suspected her daughter had forestalled her. Ach, anything Candy had or hadn't provided, assuredly she could improve on. But it was unlikely she would.

She glanced at him, where he sat scowling at the ring-stained table-cloth, pushing escaped currants about aimlessly. Where was Mr Valiant-for-Truth, whose philippic against Macandrew in the Crown had so exalted him in her esteem—and given her promise of a stand-in for the white-jacketed *cavaliere servente* whose bartended services she now shuddered to think of. But why? for Nigel was a man in the dark when all was said and to do. Why so suddenly squeamish, Elspeth? But it was not mere niceness of choice or this one opposite would have pleased and pleasured her bonnily. The salt was incredibly out of her, and the savour out of living. The absurdity of such a conclusion failed to impress her, subdued as she was by the burden of her avowal of her thistle-down folly in chasing the wild goose pleasure or passion or appeasement or something in this or that bed or barn, indoors or outdoors or wherever the fancy found her or she it, although she knew it would always elude her; ay, and in cherishing to her undoing her aspiration to exorcise her familiar demon of a non-husband.

It was no sense of guilt that afflicted her, but the belated recognition of feckless self-prodigality, of squalor and frustration. In the cracked and misted glass of memory appeared and vanished, rose and fell, all those sleeping and wakeful partners, for the most part concealing the malfunctioning of their equipment with verbal lingual digital palmar engineering indescribably tedious. The game was not worth the guttering candle of infrequent rapture—all that boring copy-book build-up for so few goals scored. And the letters and telephone anger and recrimination, the accusations and denials, the breaking-up and making-up, and the invariable relief at parting from them, pin-headed pin-pricking amateur jockeys, gentlemen riders so fidgety and slithery and struggling for control when up, so whip-flourishing boot-smacking self-satisfied when down. God, what a scrambling mucky pellmell of a point-to-point it more often than not was; and her joyless compulsive galloping pursuit of it nevertheless, what an expense of integrity in a waste of shamelessness, with only the occasional oasis of delight soon smothered under the sand of her shiftlessness, like dust swept under the carpet by a slatternly housewife.

In review it was not an edifying biography, she conceded, even if the mood of the reviewer a little discoloured it. And yet, she wondered, willing to defend herself though with slight conviction, what had the options been? In spite, or by reason, of her expensive education, she had been fitted for little else and for nothing else that was so well designed for what attributes she had. From her precocious girlhood she had been no more than a delectable beast in view for every male eye that spied her, and every other female. And early assurance of the power she could exert without effort had discouraged her from effort directed to other less immediately attainable ends. And oh, it had doubtless been fun, she supposed, whoring around to the delight of her short-loved favourites, the chagrin of her discards, the dismay of her scandalised family and other well-wishers. A fleeting smile lit her eyes as she culled this and that occasion from the disorderly file of recollection. Oh yes, it must have, surely it had, been fun? Whether or not, it was all gone now, and only the tunnel of retrospect remained to her, lighted only by infrequent fading lamps of remembered ecstasy, musty and redolent of addled excretions. An uncontrollable spasm of abhorrence shook Elspeth, so noticeable that Gavin, still intent on contemplation of the heinousness of the ogre Macandrew, raised his eyes to hers interrogatively.

'How did you come to marry him, Mrs Macandrew?' he asked, thinking his question had more pertinence to her shudder than it had, so consonant was it with his own meditation. Her sad eyes rested on his a long time in silence, a silence more pronounced because the Badlads had retired for their final intermission, and only the pianist kept place and time, before she said:

'That's an uncommonly mannerless thing to be asking a respectable married woman—and her the minister's wife forbye.'

'I suppose it is maybe, when I think of it,' said he, not thinking of it but of her, who looked no more like a minister's wife than he did, smooth and copious as she was, in and out of her décolletage, with her jewels brighter now than her eyes and her face still unfairly fair considering the rigours of the evening and the life behind her. Appraising her rarity in contrast with the male Medusa her husband, the breadth of the floor apart from her physically and in all other conceivable respects God perhaps knew how much further, he thought his question, however offensive it might be, was amply justified. But he had no need to defend it; for at length, with a melancholy smile, she echoed it.

'How did I come to marry him? Mr Ewart, that's a tale that would frighten maids from their play and old men from their reveries.'

'I can readily believe it,' said Gavin sourly. 'But how did it come about? I mean, what in God's name could you possibly see in a creature like yon?'

'A singularly naïve, not to say commonplace question, Mr Ewart,' said Elspeth. 'He didn't always look as he does now. A shade gaunt maybe, and sullen-eyed, but not ill-favoured, as they say.'

'I was not alluding to his physical attractions, Mrs Macandrew,' said Gavin, 'as you well know.'

'I didn't think you were,' replied she demurely enough. 'Well, it's not an uplifting story, and little credit to me. And it's none of your damned business. But ach, what's the difference? You may have heard,' she continued after a reflective pause, 'what's sometimes said of a child that's tempted to eat more than his digestion can cope with? His eyes are bigger than his belly.'

'It was said more than once of me,' said Gavin grinning.

'No doubt it was,' said she. 'And it might fairly enough be said of you tonight.'

'I'll not dispute it,' he conceded glumly. 'But what's the connection—I mean between the gluttonous bairn and your relationship with Macandrew?'

'You're not very sharp, are you?' said she a trifle crossly. 'It's merely another kind of appetite, isn't it?'

His head and his eyebrows came up as he looked at her with almost childish wonder. Eventually he said, 'I'll just not believe it. Surely you're not telling me you . . . you lusted for that one when you set eye on him?'

'You've an Old Testament turn of phrase, Mr Ewart,' Elspeth remarked with amusement. 'Was your father in the Church maybe?'

'Ay, from time to time,' he replied. 'But not professionally.'

'Mr Ewart,' said she in mock reproof, 'this is not an occasion for undergraduate facetiousness. We are discussing—though God knows why—a matter of notable delicacy.'

'Do forgive me, Mrs Macandrew,' begged Gavin more contritely than he meant. 'I do appreciate that, believe me. To tell the truth, I'm a wee bit fuddled—and it's not only the liquor, mind you.'

'Of course not, dear boy. You're bemused by my notorious allure,' suggested she as she leant towards him, wondering the while why the hell she was bothering, because she was no longer interested and neither, she was virtually certain, was he. And he wasn't, barely glancing at what was proferred, concentrating on finding some form of words that might evade the merely routine invitation without overtly declining it and at the same time might redirect her attention to the problem preoccupying him. At length he risked saying, with no remarkable conviction:

'These must be the most mouth-watering loving cups I've never had the privilege of lipping. But,' he added more forcefully, 'you didn't imagine, did you, they would quench the thirst that parches Ozymandias yonder?'

He had chosen wrongly: and he sensed her withdrawing from him, though not physically. Her lids drooped over her eyes and her breathing deepened visibly as she recalled how her mad-brained Hari would bedeck her nipples with the emeralds that now hung from her pierced earlobes and embed in her navel the multi-carat diamond that she never dared wear and girdle her loins with pearls and devise innumerable other amorous pleasantries from his Aladdin's treasury. God, why hadn't she stayed with him and his other toys in eastern luxury instead of reverting to her magnetic north frozen opposite in his austerity?

'Surely,' said Gavin insistently, interrupting unwittingly her dream of the faraway and her prospect of chilling reality, 'surely you didn't delude yourself you could bring milk and honey to the desert he inhabits?'

'And why not?' she retorted, nettled by his prodding at the tooth that ached and ached beyond remedy. 'I've appeased many others in my time.'

'Ay, no doubt you have,' he replied dourly. 'But they came from a fish-kettle different from that one's.'

'From various fish-kettles,' said she absurdly defensively for her heart wasn't in it.

'I believe you,' he replied. 'But nobody else from his. For there's never been anyone else in it.'

'Ach, I know what you mean,' she admitted with more than a hint of dejection. 'But you could be wrong, clever boy. For I'm nearly in it myself.'

'You see,' said Gavin, seizing her admission, but soberly, 'it's as I thought. Instead of your succouring him, he's syphoned off the zest that was in you.'

Now that each had ceased considering the other physically, Elspeth could not quite decide how to deal with this scowling young one-time hopeful; whether to acknowledge his obviously sincere solicitude or confound, as she so caustically could, his interference. But she could not accept this.

'Havers, laddie,' she said dismissively. 'Syphoned off my zest, indeed. You're way adrift. It's only of late I've felt a bit dowy and downcast. It's all of twenty years since I married Macandrew.'

'And why the hell did you? Marry him I mean?' asked Gavin, only too willing to jettison his ill-considered diagnosis. 'Surely there was no need.'

'You're an insolent young bastard, Mr Ewart,' said she evenly. 'How would you know? There were reasons—practical reasons, family reasons if you like.'

And she heard her father, not outraged, the old still active reprobate that he was, but vexed by her imprudence: There have been whores in this family before you—I'm maybe the by-blow of one myself—but they always let the blanket, wrong side or right, conceal their bedding. In the devil's name, why must you flaunt your readiness all over the countryside? There's never a guest or a groom doesn't covet or cover you. It's past tholing, the way you frolic. I should've—God knows I could've—taught you better. But since it seems I didn't, hear this, my hot-bottomed daughter: Unless you cool your ardour down and keep your drawers up, you'll get to hell out of here. I'll no longer be made a laughing-stock—or an object of compassion—in my own place. Ay, and far furth o't, if rumour's true. If you're for staying here and keeping the place going after me, now your brother's gone—more's the pity—you'd best find yourself a husband. Ay, somebody that'll maybe curb you—or put a gloss of respectability on your caracoling. Though what sensible man hereabouts would have a piece of used baggage like you I'll not be knowing.

Of course, she could have taken off and left him to it. She had earning potential, so to say, far in excess of the estate's, sore run down as it was by his and his forebear's extravagance. But she had stayed had young Elspeth, consistent in her frowardness; absurdly loyal to the family and its worn-out acres, fond of the country life—and country manners—she had been bred to, affectionately bound to her handsome reckless womanising father; and perhaps just a mite afraid of the glittering circles in which she might have, and since had, whirled with such admired agility. Yes, she had stayed. And partly for her father's reasons and partly for her own—if one could call them reasons—angled for and hooked Macandrew, the minister at Ferlie.

God, what a folly that had been—a catch far too fishy for her netting, or any woman's however naïvely assured of her capacity. She had married him because he hadn't wanted her, eccentrically and provokingly refusing to rise to the poacher's lure she had floated for him (and why he had ultimately swallowed the marital hook she had never understood); because she had wished to astonish amuse mollify her incredulous father; because she had thought to *épater le voisinage* by flitting from the manor to the manse like a butterfly evolving in reverse. What infirm grounds from which to leap into the darkness that had immediately enveloped her. Look at Elspeth on her bridal night rejected by that crabbed hermit from normality and rejected ever since to humble her. And recall your father, Elspeth, not cynically smiling but enraged to think of his mettlesome mare saddled with or by her black-coated black-hearted self-stickit minister. And remember everyone else, gentle or common, only nine-days-wondering at the latest indecency of that blatant bitch Elspeth Cameron. No, it had been an event of minimal consequence except for her, its instigator. And yet how could she, young and brash and irresistible, have foreseen what was to come? Surely there was no need to marry him, young Ewart was saying, unaware that there had been a mistaken need to marry someone. But there had been no need, no reason, to marry him, Macandrew, except to parade her bravado, to take what she fancied just for the hell of it. And the hell of it she'd got.

There had been temporary deliverance aplenty, sure enough, but never the consolation of triumph. He had won all the campaigns in the war between them, withstanding easily her every advance; he had captured and subjugated her children; and, most bewildering of all, he had breached her redoubtable self-sufficiency so that his bleak life-corroding creed had infiltrated and taken possession of her. A dismal conclusion to a mischievous girlish frolic, she was thinking, as she sat slumped in her chair, careless of the shapeless figure she was publicly presenting. But enough was enough. Let you be off home, Elspeth, to the sleeping pill or the sleepless pillow.

'Shall we dance the last dance, Mrs Macandrew?' said Gavin, who had been observing her melancholy self-communion without presuming to intrude. And she became aware that the Badlads were back, powerfully refreshed and flooding the almost empty hall with an ebbing tide of slow-tempo syrup. She rose to wade in it with him—what else could she do?—and found them moving with fluency and precision round the floor, which was by then deserted by the majority with other things in hand under hand out of hand. But there was Marion still distantly tittupping with her current stagnant swain. Poor Marion, ever hoping never coping, would she ever doff them? Probably not, girdled tightly like her brother Alec. And what was he up to? she wondered.

But Alec was up to nothing, snoring in troubled sleep, dreaming of his frightening destiny. Naked and trussed like a plucked capon, he wilted before the tribunal that was condemning him on unspecified charges. The shrouded McNish sat there, bewigged and black-capped, peering through his pouched eyes while his assessors, identical marble madonnas, bent sorrowing gaze on the docked lackey's feeble gentleman. And the sentence came incomprehensibly in the monotone of Macandrew, who nevertheless arrived behind him on a nightmarish stallion, wielding the hungry Excalibur for his decapitation not death, however strange. But as Macandrew dismounted and brandished his weapon preparatorily, gentle voices murmured—Marion's Mary's whose?—in remonstration against mangling truncation, insisting on bloodless castigation so that this plastic disc would seal the severance precisely, its dimension calculated by the number of tiny ball-bearings that would cover it, and so his stalwart body might endure and journey on despite its foredoomed lack of destination. The headsman reluctantly assented and after a few practice swings poised for the strike.

And Macandrew, inserting the key in the vestry door, heard Alec's awakening scream, mistook it for something else and proceeded. Donning his vestments, he entered the church and mounted the pulpit stair.

CHAPTER FOURTEEN

Macandrew into Water

In fifty or a hundred years hence the descendants of these two will act and feel worse than we. They will see weltering humanity still more vividly as we do now as
Shapes like our own selves hideously multiplied and will be afraid to reproduce them.

Thomas Hardy

We cannot think of a time that is oceanless
Or of an ocean not littered with wastage.

T. S. Eliot

There is very peace and false peace, and they be full diverse. Very peace is grounded in God; false peace in rest with our enemies.

John Wycliffe

HE FOUND himself awake and on his feet, stooped over the lectern, his forearms laid along the randomly open Bible, beholding stonily the congregation that filled to capacity and beyond the pews beneath him. They were all there, and many more besides; all the parishioners with whom he had ever had dealings, pastoral or other; and all who, to his relief, had shunned dealings with him of any kind. And the repugnance he had always experienced as he looked from his vantage point was stronger than ever, in proportion to their numbers; so strong that it threatened to emerge and bespatter the communion table below. But he swallowed and boked and belched and at length achieved deliverance.

'You will find my initial text, my besotted brethren, in the Book of Job, Chapter Thirteen, Verse Thirteen, appropriately enough: Hold your peace, let me alone, that I may speak, and let come on me what will.'

He paused before repeating ruminatively, as to himself:

'That I may speak, and let come on me what will.' And then, recalling himself, he proceeded.

'But let you not be thinking that I speak like Job, to contend with my God or my comforters. For I long ago cast off the one and have never encountered the others. Nor do I speak to contend with you or the like of you. For none of your ilk—or any other—is worth my strife. It must be said, nevertheless, that there are among you a handful who have ventured to wag their slack tongues against me.'

And he searched for and found old Hector, who lifted his beard but not his voice; and the chalk-dusty verbalist, Turnbull, goggling up at him, eager for enlightenment; and Ewart, that recreant changeling, who momentarily cast a known malevolent glare on him before reverting to his brows-down sullenness. Dismissing them, he continued.

'Why then, you might wonder, had you the wit to wonder, do I utter at all to so uncomprehending an audience? And I say unto you, For relief, dearly detested. For the same reason, merely, as a man evacuates from his bowels the putrescence that clogs them. I would void this on you—for the last time, I jalouse—in the doomed hope that its rank, sterilising effluvium might asphyxiate and destroy you, and through you contaminate in ever widening areas of annihilation your neighbours and their oxen and their asses and every animate thing that is theirs, until in overdue course, on the whole earth and in the waters under the earth, there might persist nothing that breathed and lived to multiply.'

His words washed over their heads bent in bovine submission beneath him. Their lack of response in no way affected him, accustomed as he was professionally to a captive somnolent convocation. He resumed with mock lugubriousness.

'Yes, in my weakness, I must seek transient solace for the torment that racks me, if only by affirming once more the conviction I have cherished within me all the days of my life—to my undoing, the world will say. But how can an honest man avert his attention from truth? or lapse into acquiescence with folly, simply for companionship with the foolish? For it is all folly, and there is no point or merit in it anywhere. In trivial local illustration, do but consider this night's on-goings within these supposedly hallowed precincts. Recall the mind-blunting din of barbaric strings and pipes and timbrels, the drunken ribaldry and licence, the goatish capering in the hall, and the lewd coupling in the curtilage. And all yon execrable, orgiastic carousal, be it noted, sponsored by the church choir and the douce matrons and pillars of the parish. But do not blush,' he added immediately, his voice ponderous with pretended consolation. 'Nay, do not blush, I beseech you, or bite the lip of mortification. For I do not go about to chide you. You are, inescapably, what you are: the offspring of your forebears, like them egging yourselves relentlessly along the Fallopian tunnels of time, ignorant why or wherefore. In the words of Jeremiah, you are but "A wild ass used to the wilderness that snuffeth up the wind at her pleasure. In her occasion who can turn her away?" Assuredly I cannot. Nor have I ever endeavoured to. Simply, I have been aware, and cried out from the wilderness of my cognisance against the asinine snuffers of the wind in the wilderness without. Few, indeed, have heard me; and none has hearkened. But I have been, if not a bonnie fechter, an indomitable one; more intent, be it admitted, on the virtue of the conflict than on the victory unattainable. I have been a Saint George who knew he could never slay his dragon but revelled like a salamander in its fiery breath. Yea verily, implacable opposition have I ever presented to the lethally omnipotent life-force so admired and revered by the gravel-blind pseudo-sages, and so beloved by the hearts and loins of the ignorant lumpen-mass.'

He blearily scrutinised the congregation and with pointing finger directed their heedless attention before enunciating with scornful clarity: 'Regard yonder the shrouded lecher McNish, propped between his cast-off carlin doxies. And applaud the life-force. Or observe around him his acolytes and emulators, Rab and Tam and Wull and the lave, helots of the glebe, who labour among the clods and the bestial to scrape and rake the wherewithal for their debauches. Those are Lilliputian but representative jackstraws, borne along on the ceaseless wind of creation. Think of them, if you dare, multiplied infinitely not only in number but in species animal and vegetable, each and every unit exclusively bent on reproducing its meagre, worthless self, and capable of little or nothing else. And applaud the life-force. Are not those ever tumescent bumpkin sons of Belial notable exemplars?'

For a moment he regarded them almost wistfully, or so it seemed to his wondering self, and continued. 'Certainly, brethren, in your moronic hebetude you do not applaud. You merely submit yourselves uncomprehendingly. But have I not frequently drawn to your notice the patent absurdity of it all? Have I not cited, as I cite again, the words of the preacher Ecclesiastes? He says, you cannot have forgotten: Therefore I hated life; because the work that is wrought under the sun is grievous unto me; for all is vanity and vexation of spirit. Indeed, there have been others like your own disregarded shepherd, whose eyes were not put out. But, with few intrepid exceptions, the allegedly wise ones prefer to praise, laud, and bless in the face of all the evidence. There are, in silly fact, at least two among you who would exalt and promote all those apostles of quasi-enlightenment. They, being young men of education, are, to their discredit, rigidly conditioned by their counsellors and move in their minds like sheep before a collie, lacking direction of their own choosing. They decline to avow the truth: that all yon glamour of art in its many guises; philosophy, skein on skein of mind-entangling verbiage; theology, the apogee of man's doomed endeavour to vindicate his *raison d'être*; and all the other toys and tricks of ingenious invention—what are they but the rattle given to an awakened, whimpering infant to distract it from the misery attendant on its intuitive awareness of its destiny? And furthermore consider: all such diverting baubles aesthetic and intellectual, devised down the ages by the race's pundits and artificers for the self-beguiled intelligentsia, what have they to do with the myriads of mankind intent merely on survival and struggling brutishly towards that end like their ostensibly baser siblings? Specious relevance, or none at all, have they to that futile effusion of animate being that edges hourly from birth to early demise and decay.

'And dare I ask you, dear simpletons, to advert your inattention to the millions of years it has taken, years of inexorably passing time, for the primitive, obscene forms of life that propelled themselves avidly from the waters to evolve laboriously, this way and that, into you—the beauty of the world, the paragon of animals, still as odious, still as obdurately obsessed as your earliest progenitors? Is not this, my obstinate brethren, a pretty sequence of selection? And did it not daunt the men of Scripture beforetime? Hear you the voice of Noah's phantasmal deity in Genesis, Chapter Six: And the Lord said, I will destroy man whom I have created from the face of the earth; both man and beast, and the creeping thing, and the fowls of the air; for it repenteth me that I have made them.'

He surveyed the congregation once more, the contempt displayed in his eyes and lips converting itself despite him to compassion. Or was it self-pity? he asked himself in some dismay, but did not stay for an answer, instead resuming the onset.

'It repenteth me that I have made them, said the Lord. And justly might he have regretted his creation, and with reason sought to contrive its destruction. But alas, it was not to be. For his fabled deluge came and went, but the Ark prevailed, and with it the cargo of generation and its concomitants, accelerating in turpitude. Have I not taken you by the hand, time and again, guiding your shuffling footsteps through that Old Testamentary chronicle of vice and fecklessness from hungry Eve ever onwards, a chronicle that can be paralleled in the history of all peoples of the earth?

'And lest you should think me, if think you can, an inverted nonesuch, a unique, demented misanthrope, recall the objurgations of the prophets relaying like satellites the voice of their jealous God, who so often sounded forth in exasperation with his incorrigible chosen people, incorrigible necessarily by reason of their essential mode of being. Does not Jeremiah tell us, quoting his God, provoked beyond patience by his sottish children: I beheld the earth, and, lo, it was without form and void, and the heavens, and they had no light. I beheld, and, lo, there was no man, and all the birds of the heavens were fled. . . . For thus hath the Lord said, The whole land shall be desolate; yet will I not make a full end.

'Mark, my brethren in affliction, how this percipient preacher, like his fellow faint-hearts, flinches from the ultimate arbitrament, as your Ferlie pastor scorns to do. Like time-serving physicians they concentrate on the virulent symptoms, but choose not to identify the root of the disease or prescribe the only remedy; videlicet, eradication and a full end. A full end, I repeat; not some poltroonish, punitive measure like the piddling deluge. For, be it understood, even had the Ark foundered with its copulating complement, yet would the rain-maker's life-saving compromise have achieved its purpose. Our cunning men of science assure us that, in the beginning, life emerged from the waters. And so, even without Noah and his menagerie, the heinous evolutionary process would doubtless have proceeded. You must know that water is the female principle; cupful, pool and puddle; lochan, lake and ocean; all harbouring in their ovarian shallows or their womb-like brooding depths the germs of generation. Hence has the Gaelic *uisge beatha*, water of life, a significance alternative to that more commonly and acceptably applied. Which reminds me.'

Fumbling through the folds of his gown, he drew from a

pocket a flask and, tilting his chin, imbibed a long draught. He swallowed the upsurge in his gullet and clung to the lectern to support his swaying body. It seemed he could not continue, but he did; though the congregation beneath him had almost vanished from his vision and had quite from his concern.

'Verily, the water of life: feminal fluid, inexhaustible reservoir, conceiving, gestating and bringing forth incessantly, insanely, in abominable plenitude. Even the ancient Moses, exhorting his hapless tribes to multiply and people the earth, would seem to betray a compulsive aversion from the means and the matrix. Have I not often recited to you the divers laws and ordinances in his Fourth Book pertaining to birth and carnality, especially with relation to woman? Indubitably, the venerable one was repelled by the uncleanness of the act and the egg-bearing hostess that cherishes the parasites it spawns; and that, significantly surely, although his weight of years must have borne down often on willing or reluctant recipients—as did my reverend father's on my miscarrying mother.'

He closed his eyes and clasped the lectern even more tightly in an effort to control the tremor that shook him. His lids still lowered, he eventually continued in a whisper that betrayed his horror of that long past but ever present revelation: 'How often, through still innocent but appalled eyes, did I behold them at it, gasping in preposterous conjunction. But let me not dwell on that clandestine espial, that furtive nibbling at the apple of knowledge, which soured my palate for life thereafter. Verily, saith the patriarch: The nakedness of thy father or the nakedness of thy mother shalt thou not uncover. For whosoever shall commit any of these abominations, even the souls that commit them shall be cut off from among thy people. Thus have I been cut off and spewed out from cohabitation and fellowship with all that live and fulfil their only destiny. Thus have I, condemned, drawn out my lonely exile, a monstrous sport.'

To his chagrin, tears were escaping to ooze down the deeply graved lines on his face, and his voice was faltering, betraying self-commiseration and even recantation, which he could not, would not countenance. He was beset not only by the nausea that had afflicted him—for how long he wondered—but by a premonitory sadness of heart the proximate source of which eluded him. Never acquainted since childhood with happiness or contentment, he had nevertheless learned to live with himself and even relish his isolation. He must dispel this cloud of self-doubt that darkened counsel and confidence and reassert his dominance. Shaking his head painfully in a vain effort to clear his muddied thoughts and eyes, he slowly brought into uncertain focus the lean-brained, swollen-bellied, fusionless flock beneath him, and more distinctly her, nudely expectant like a sin-offering on the communion table. Aroused from his gathering stupor by her posture of insolent surrender, he lifted up his voice once more.

'But let none among you in your foolishness fancy that I repine or regret my self-banishment. Nay, jetsam drifted to a distant shore would I rather be than alive and afloat with the sewage in the polluted sea of life. Nor, like the Pharisee do I proclaim my otherness, for none that lives can escape defilement. Who can bring a clean thing out of an unclean? not one, says Job. Therefore, I acknowledge that I too am bedaubed with the ordure of vitality. But I have not like the swine wallowed in it, grouting about hungrily for beastly satisfactions. Rather have I since my misbegotten childhood abjured it, aspiring, albeit forlornly, to inorganic essence—like this brass spread-eagle on the lectern, more to be admired than its living prototype a-wing above the corrie or the grotesque egg-broken offspring gorging in their eyrie. Or like the petrification of the jewels bedecking that giglot there, more to be desired than her sprawling tainted flesh. Or like the light sparkling from their facets, more alluring than the lustre in her eyes. An end I yearn for, an end to the begetting, the seeding and the bringing forth for loathsome corruption in inevitable, infinite series. Verily, I reiterate: if existence there must be, let it be unborn and barren. Hath the rain a father? or who hath begotten the drops of dew? Out of whose womb came the ice? and the hoary frost of heaven, who hath gendered it?'

He was naggingly suspicious that this superficially apt interrogation was at variance with his previous argument; but weary to the point of utter depletion, he cared little for that. He cared little indeed for anything. The congregation was barely visible through the seemingly red mist suffusing his eyes. But she in her splendour remained boldly embossed on the altar, attendant on the priest's design. And the realisation of his impotence against her, of the futility of his lifelong self-flagellation, of the vanity of his conviction illumined luridly his stupefaction like a lightning-shaft piercing a cloud, and he cried aloud in his desolation and trembled like a withered branch in the wind.

'There is no hope, there is no purpose. Can I draw out Leviathan with the hook of my tongue? All my protestations are like the crackling of twigs under a pot, a pot a-boil with folly, folly. But I shall put out the fire. With water, the heinous element, I shall extinguish it.'

He cackled dementedly as he felt his own water, released in the paroxysm of his distress, run down his leg to saturate the pulpit carpet. The congregation appeared and vanished beneath him, but she remained always unobscured, rounded and radiant, and through flickering eyelids he gloated over her.

'Yea verily, with water, the life-spawner and nourisher. Not, be it insisted, with wine, the pale Galilean's symbol of immortality, pressed from the grape pregnant with succulence as a woman with child. And yet his intrusion into my valedictory maybe prompts a last supping.'

Chuckling ridiculously, he swallowed another draught from his flask, inexhaustible, he dimly reflected, as the widow's cruse, and intoned solemnly: 'Ay, forsooth, my brethren in abysmal tribulation, as we are assembled in this holy place consecrated to the perfectibility of man, here or hereafter, it seems good to me, your lang-syne solicitous pastor, that we celebrate my last rite of communion. Nor will you, I jalouse, take it amiss or indict me for heresy if on this ultimate occasion, I diverge from the ritual to which you are blankly conformist. I shall not bless and offer you the body and blood of your putative saviour. It is no secret from you, my plaintively bleating mutton-heads, that such cannibalistic whigmaleeries, variously interpreted by the erudite shamans down the anno-dominical centuries, I have never endorsed or given credence to—any more than I have the gospel of him to whom they appertain. For that, like all other such delusory tidings, is mere tinsel embroidery on the huckaback of reality. Have I not told you? And will you not listen?'

He ceased abruptly, astonished to find himself pontificating in his habitual strain, forgetful of his recent acknowledgement and intended conclusion. And epiphanously it shone on him that it was all words. All his creed or philosophy or attitudinising was merely words, as it was in the beginning and always. Call it what you would, that was what it was, like that of all the others down the ages, no different as he pretended, or had pretended, to himself but just the same. He had with saturnine arrogance maintained its truth. But what was truth but multifarious mutations of words, words, words, as he had discerned in his student youth? *Fatua est veritas et numquam praevalebit.* Not even his version. Certainly not his version. For what was truth but what people chose to believe? And who but himself would choose to believe that the best thing in life was never to have been born? And yet someone had so chosen, someone else. For someone had said that. He couldn't remember who it was. Had it been perhaps himself? It well might have been, for it was absurd paradox, and he was compact of paradox, gulping the breath of death to sustain him in being because cravenly, in his loathing of physical corruption, he had stupidly refused to accept that the only way of coming to terms with life was by dying. Let him accept it now, and make an end.

With ebbing resolution he drew himself almost erect and found it difficult to remain so. His head felt strangely light. He passed a hand over it to check its whereabouts, but its contents were beyond his sounding. He knew that all his granite certainty was gone. Let him go with it—and soon. My face is foul with weeping, he moaned, and on my eyelids is the shadow of death. But a last, definitive avowal he demanded.

'*Ecce femina*!' he proclaimed in a voice that astonished him with its vibrancy and prodded a finger at her beneath him. '*Ecce vetula*, the ageless harridan, the uterine sink of conception! Behold her, the fork-legged, belly-up, reptilian wife of my confusion, and yours, and everyman's. See in her the eternal emblem of the mindless insistence on fertility. Her I give unto you, brethren; a symbol more fitting your need and inclination than that other; a cup, a goblet brimming with intoxicant more potent, more appropriate than wine. Drink, partake of her, not consecrated but accursed. And while you celebrate your communion, I, like the scapegoat of old, shall depart from among you, bearing the burden of the sin of creation into my wasteland.'

He bared his teeth and brayed like an ass, as he lingered to watch them sidle from the pews and come forward to the table in procession, groping at their middles, mount, join, and vanish within her, engulfed totally like the Gadarene beasts that they were, or the lemmings by their self-destruction preserving their kind.

With a last brooding stare at Elspeth, who lay still as a placid sea beneath him, he descended the steps and entered the vestry, leaving the dark church as empty as he had found it. Without doffing his robes, he made his unsteady but purposeful way through the graveyard, once more possessed by its hushed occupants, along the vacant streets and on to the road that led home. But his destination was not the manse. Climbing awkwardly over a gate, he traversed the pasture, where the cattle snuffled and stamped and browsed or gazed with sad eyes into the darkness, and came presently to the lochan, which lay unruffled reflecting the stars. He sat himself on a boulder that his clerical buttocks had smoothed over the years, as the water and the ice, the frosts and the winds had over the millennia beforetime. He gathered a handful of pebbles, caressing their hard objectivity, hearing them grate one against another. Discarding them, he stumbled to the water's edge, his eyes on the stars; and then searched about until he came on what he sought—two rocks almost the size and weight of curling-stones. He hefted them up to rest one on each thigh and trudged into the lochan until he could go no farther. He sank to his knees and then prone beneath the surface, anchored by his stones among the weeds and the fishes and the water creatures and all the infusorial denizens of the element he abhorred but could not escape.

The lochan, briefly disturbed by his incursion, resumed its calm.

FINIS